Widows and Orphans

Widows and Orphans

a novel by

MICHAEL ARDITTI

Arcadia Books Ltd
139 Highlever Road
London W10 6PH

www.arcadiabooks.co.uk

First published by Arcadia Books 2015

ISBN 978-1-910050-23-1

Typeset in Minion by MacGuru Ltd
Printed and bound by CPI Group (UK) Ltd., Croydon CR0 4YY

Arcadia Books supports English PEN *www.englishpen.org* and
The Book Trade Charity *www.btbs.org*

Arcadia Books distributors are as follows:

in the UK and elsewhere in Europe:
Macmillan Distribution Ltd
Brunel Road
Houndmills
Basingstoke
Hants RG21 6XS

in the USA and Canada:
Dufour Editions
PO Box 7
Chester Springs
PA 19425

in Australia/New Zealand:
NewSouth Books
University of New South Wales
Sydney NSW 2052

For three friends and colleagues:
Clare Colvin, Jane Mays and Ruth Leon

'Be kind, for everyone you meet is fighting a hard battle'

Philo of Alexandria (Attrib.)

One

Francombe Pier Inferno

by Ken Newbold

Thursday, 19 September 2013

Francombe watched in horror on Monday night as a sea of flames swept through its historic pier, reducing much of the 980 foot structure to ashes and rubble.

For ten hours, seventy firemen and eight fire engines battled the blaze, their rescue efforts hampered by high winds and poor visibility. Roads were closed and nearby residents advised to keep their windows shut.

Sam Vernham, chief fire officer of Sussex Fire and Rescue Service, confirmed that the cause of the fire had yet to be established. 'Full investigation must wait until structural engineers give us the go-ahead. Meanwhile, I urge people not to speculate, which will only cause more distress to those affected.'

This is the latest in a string of disasters to hit the 144-year-old pier. An earlier fire in June 2000 destroyed the Moorish pavilion. The pier itself was closed to the general public in June 2008, after two of its support columns were found to be in imminent danger of collapse.

In March 2009, a Save Our Pier petition, organised by the *Mercury*, attracted over 15,000 signatures and, in May 2011, Francombe Borough Council finally approved the compulsory purchase of the Grade II listed building from its Panamanian-based owners, Rockingham Securities. Last May, the Council narrowly voted to sell the pier to Weedon Investments, owned by controversial local entrepreneur, Geoffrey Weedon, whose plans for it have yet to be disclosed.

After surveying the devastation, Glynis Kingswood, Chair of the Francombe Pier Trust, declared: 'This is a tragedy. The pier is Francombe and Francombe is the pier. We must all work together to rebuild this unique piece of our heritage.'

Of all the campaigns Duncan had launched in nearly thirty years at the helm of the *Mercury*, the one to secure the future of the pier remained closest to his heart. After three years during which the structure had been left to rot, the paper had set up the Save Our Pier petition, attracting the signatures of almost a fifth of Francombe's residents; given away 10,000 stickers that had been plastered on windows, windscreens, walls and the Diamond Jubilee statue of Queen Victoria; and organised a Day of Protest in September 2009, which saw more than 2,000 people march on the Town Hall to demand that the Council take immediate action to purchase the pier from its absentee owners.

The march, extensively reported in the national media, achieved its objective. After a further two years of legal wrangling and a costly programme of emergency repairs, the Council assumed control of the pier. Meanwhile, the Francombe Pier Trust was established with the aim of restoring and running the pier as a viable local concern; but, although the Trust was awarded an £85,000 feasibility grant by English Heritage to conduct a structural survey and draw up architectural plans, it failed to obtain capital funding from either the Heritage Lottery or the EU. This bitter blow was compounded in May 2013 when the Council announced that, in view of both the Trust's inability to raise finance and the assessors' estimate that a sum in excess of £25,000,000 would be needed to repair the fabric, plus a similar amount to resume operation, it had agreed to sell the pier to Weedon Investments. Duncan, who attacked the decision in a series of hard-hitting editorials, had never given up hope that the sale might be revoked – until the fire.

For Duncan, the pier had always been the best of Francombe. At school, his home town had been derided by boys who, if they holidayed in England at all, headed for the more refined reaches of Cornwall and Suffolk. Even in its Victorian heyday, it had never enjoyed the prestige of its neighbouring resorts. While Brighton, Eastbourne and Worthing attracted the affluent middle classes, Francombe catered to 'clerks and other working people' from London's East End. By the 1960s, any lingering claims to gentility had been abandoned in a welter of binge drinking and gang warfare. But amid the bug-infested guesthouses, grimy pubs, litter-strewn beaches and vomit-splattered pavements, one monument remained unsullied. From the octagonal tollbooths and glass-covered Winter Garden to the multi-domed pavilion and horseshoe arcade, the pier stood comparison with any in the country.

The midget photographer with the monkey that never blinked; the gypsy fortune teller with the aniseed-scented booth; the sad-faced silhouettist with scissors as adept as a brush; the flea circus boasting 'the smallest big top in the world': these formed the pattern of Duncan's childhood memories, as they did for so many in Francombe. Then in 1969 when he was five years old, there was the unforgettable celebration of the *Mercury*'s centenary. His father hired the pavilion for a banquet attended by his entire staff, past and present, and a host of local luminaries. Duncan, pledged to be on his best behaviour, sat rigidly through the profusion of speeches, disgracing himself only once when he asked in a piercing whisper why the Mayor was wearing a necklace. He danced with his mother, his sister Alison and, as she had never ceased to remind him, his father's young secretary, Sheila. He watched the fireworks, which magically spelt out *Mercury* and *100 Years* across the night sky. Then, lulled by the swash of the waves against the columns, he fell fast asleep.

Emerging from his reverie with an acute sense of loss, Duncan was tempted to approve the dummy front page with its one-word headline, 'Gutted', above a photograph of the pier head smothered in smoke and looking eerily like St Paul's at the height of the Blitz, but he shied away from the twin offences of sensationalism and sentimentality. Now, more than ever, he was determined to stick to the standards for which the paper was known – and, in some quarters, ridiculed. So, having settled on the more sober 'Francombe Pier Inferno', he signed off the page and put the paper to bed.

He walked into the reporters' room, which as ever contrived to look both cluttered and depleted. Despite the eight empty desks, Ken, the news editor, sat facing his two reporters, Rowena and Brian, at a single desk in the centre, with Stewart, the sub, and Jake, the sports editor, at desks on either side. While Stewart's was obsessively neat, with even the pens in his tray graded according to size, the others were in varying states of chaos. Files, books and papers were scattered across every surface, along with a hairbrush, make-up bag and headache pills (Rowena), an electric-blue T-shirt and large tub of protein powder (Brian) and, ominously, a spike full of invoices (Ken). Although Mary, the cleaner, made sporadic raids on the news desk, Jake had berated her so often for disturbing his filing system that she had given up on sport, with the result that two half-eaten pizzas rested on a pile of football programmes as if he were preparing a feature on botulism at the ground rather than analysing Francombe FC's prospects for the new season. Four ancient computer monitors gathered dust beside the packed bookshelves. Slumped over one was Humphrey, a giant teddy bear who had been left unclaimed after a competition and adopted as the office mascot. Much prized for his soothing presence, he was regularly called on to mediate in staff disputes. Whatever layers of irony had once informed Rowena's *You don't have to be mad to work here but it helps* poster had long been worn away.

Although he lacked his father's easy conviviality, Duncan prided himself on running a close-knit team. Foremost among them was Ken, not only the paper's news editor but his deputy, a role that had been nominal for the past three years during which he had not taken a single day's holiday or sick leave. Having, in his own words, 'fallen in love with journalism' on his paper round, Ken had been hired as a junior reporter straight from school in 1970. His starting salary was £6 a week, of which he paid £2 to his mother for his keep, £1 on travel, and 30 shillings to the retired secretary who taught him shorthand and typing; sums that seemed as comical to the generations of juniors to whom he described them as did his lifelong dedication to the paper itself. Unlike them, he had never seen the *Mercury* as a stepping stone to Fleet Street but remained passionately committed to a strong and crusading local press. He had kept the faith for more than four decades, but in recent years it had been severely tested, first by the paper's relentless struggle to survive and then by his only daughter's death. In the one human-interest story he chose not to write, he had donated a kidney to her, which her body rejected. 'It's a good thing it wasn't his liver,' Rowena had said when she found him drunk at his desk.

Rowena herself had been with the paper on and off for almost twenty years, the 'off' being the three years she spent at home after her daughter was born: the daughter who, on her parents' acrimonious divorce, had elected to live with her father, a move that Rowena imputed solely to his greater spending power. This in turn fuelled her resentment of the editor-proprietor who consistently undervalued her. She was forty-five years old, a fact that Duncan acknowledged guiltily, given her objections to the frequency with which women's ages were printed in the paper compared to men's. Since her divorce, she had been reluctant to cover anything that might be considered women's issues, be they jumble sales, zumba classes or multiple births. Meanwhile, she relished every chance, however inopportune, to highlight male hypocrisy, as in a recent piece on a golden wedding when she caustically pointed out that the husband's claim of not having looked at another woman for fifty years had been 'flatly contradicted when he fondled my bottom as he showed me out'. She then turned her fire on her male subeditor when the line was cut.

Stewart, the subeditor in question, had been at the paper

almost as long as Rowena, although he could not blame his lack of advancement on the demands of childcare when it was the absence of children that had blighted his life. Having struggled for years, first with the stresses of IVF and then with the hormonal changes that the treatment produced in his wife, Gillian, he had finally left her for Laura who, as fate would have it, also failed to conceive. Their hopes of adoption were dashed by Gillian's damning testimonial. In company he made light of it, citing their greater disposable income, but in private he dropped his guard; Duncan had found him in tears over the story of a woman and her three young children burnt to death by a fallen candle after their electricity was cut off. His emotions were heightened by having to check copy, devise headlines and input pictures for the entire paper. The increased pressure led to errors, such as the once exemplary *Mercury* printing a photograph of the new Lady Mayoress under the caption 'Mystery Beast Spotted in the Woods', eliciting furious protests from the Town Hall.

Like Stewart, Jake had joined the paper as one of a department of three but, unlike Stewart, he relished the chance to run it single-handed. Duncan, whose involvement in sport had ended when he left school and whose interest in it waned after Alison retired from professional tennis, was happy to cede responsibility for the four back pages to a man who was a passionate enthusiast for every kind of game except cricket, for which he displayed such aversion that he insisted on covering it under a pseudonym. A classic armchair enthusiast, Jake was large and lumbering, the balls of paper around the bin a token of his ineptitude. During his first years at the *Mercury* he lived with his mother, who sent him to work every day with a packet of fish-paste sandwiches. When she died following a massive stroke, he discovered that she had changed her will, leaving her house to the long-estranged sister who had come to nurse her three months before. Duncan was one of many who urged him to contest the will but he refused, preferring to rent a room from an elderly widow, who cooked and cleaned for him, and even made him fish-paste sandwiches. On evenings when he wasn't at work and she at bingo, they watched television together. Duncan, who had dinner with his mother twice a week, found their domesticity a threat. Brian, on the other hand, claimed that they were conducting a torrid affair. 'You're a gerontophile,' he said, with all the relish of one who had just learnt the word.

Jake's pained expression made it clear that the idea of such an affair (or, indeed, of any affair) had never occurred to him. 'What do they teach you at school these days?' he asked.

This was a question that had long exercised Duncan in respect of his youngest member of staff. Like Ken, Brian had joined the *Mercury* straight from school, but the intervening four decades had given him a very different outlook. In his three years at the paper he had shown both a genuine desire to learn and a tacit contempt for his teachers. It was impossible to fault either his commitment or his work. Despite the lurid tales of his nightly exploits, which Duncan suspected revealed a talent for fiction as much as for reportage, he was at his desk by 8.30 each morning. He embarked on every assignment that Ken gave him, from Council meetings to 'death knocks', with the same enthusiasm that he did his various dates, insisting on the need for experience before he respectively specialised and settled down. He was the one writer who never complained of the extra work involved in maintaining the website (while regularly complaining of the flaws in the site itself). His confusion of brashness with charm would land him in trouble should he ever secure the Fleet Street job he so desperately craved.

While the rest of the staff laughed off Brian's posturing, Sheila took it seriously. Too shrewd not to realise that his deference was a form of mockery, she nonetheless succumbed to it, responding with a skittishness that only incited him further. Her repeated claim that 'I'm old enough to be your mother' was particularly unfortunate, given his calculation that she was old enough to be his grandmother, or even his great-grandmother had she followed the Francombe trend for underage pregnancy. Sheila had joined the staff in 1967 as Duncan's father's secretary. Even Duncan, who had known her all his life, found it hard to credit that, along with her shorthand and typing speeds, her chief assets had been her breezy manner and infectious laugh. He could not help equating Sheila's faded appeal with that of the paper itself. When he restructured the company on his father's death, Duncan had promoted her to office manager, which, as she wryly remarked, combined her former responsibilities with those of receptionist, administrator and general dogsbody.

In this last capacity she entered the room, bringing the two bottles of wine that Duncan had requested to thank the staff for their efforts in covering the fire. 'Three for two,' she whispered to him. 'I've hidden the other one in your desk.'

'I think we can rise to a third on this occasion,' he replied, ignoring her frown. 'Does anyone have a corkscrew? Oh, it's a screw-top,' he said, abashed. He poured the South African Shiraz into seven plastic cups, dismissing Jake's protests that sport had been unaffected by the last-minute page changes. 'Cheers, one and all! You've done the paper proud. For once we're about more than offloading someone's old car.'

'Should shift a few copies,' Ken said. 'Your father used to say that readers loved big disasters; it was small ones that bored them.'

'Cheery chap, your old man!' Brian said.

'He was,' Ken said sharply. 'A real gent!'

'Just be grateful that it happened last night,' Stewart said. 'Think if it was tonight or tomorrow and we couldn't cover it till next week!'

'We'd look more out of touch than ever,' Rowena said, swilling her wine so rapidly that Duncan felt aggrieved.

'Don't forget the website,' Brian said. 'I'm updating it every couple of hours. Not that there's much new. Just a load of hot air from the usual suspects. "This is a sad day for Francombe" and all that!'

'Well, isn't it?' Duncan asked mildly.

'Yeah, but you know as well as me that none of them have set foot on the pier for years.'

'No one has,' Ken said. 'In case it's escaped your notice, it's been closed for the past five.'

'Any word yet on a possible cause?' Sheila asked.

'At last time of asking, the firemen still hadn't been given the green light to go in,' Ken said.

'It's obviously arson,' Rowena said.

'Why *obviously*?' Sheila asked.

'Who stands to benefit? Weedon, of course.'

Duncan was glad to hear Rowena voice suspicions that, given his personal connections, he was wary of voicing himself.

'I don't see why,' Jake said, as ever favouring natural causes. 'It only means they'll have to rebuild – or at any rate underpin – the structure.'

'They were doing that anyway. That is, if the sale went ahead. Who's going to fight it now? Who else has the cash? Not you and your Trust, Duncan?'

'Empty pockets, I'm afraid. We've come to the end of the road.'

'No offence,' Brian said. 'But why all this fuss about a pile of crumbling masonry? No one I know would be seen dead on it, except to laugh at the grockles.'

'It's those grockles, as you so graciously put it, who keep Francombe afloat,' Duncan said. 'Our business plan showed that since the pier's been out of action the town's lost 600,000 visitors a year and millions of pounds of income.'

'All the more reason to support the Weedon bid!'

'Maybe, if it were anyone but Weedon. It'll be the Olympic

pool saga all over again; the pier turned into another wheel park or extreme sports arena.'

'Motorcycle jumping over the parapet?' Brian asked.

'Piers are about families,' Duncan said. 'They're the ultimate seaside entertainment. All the excitement of being above water combined with the security of being on land.' He broke off at the realisation that none of his six colleagues fitted the standard family mould any more than he did himself. Was it the result of their particular working environment or of a broader social collapse?

'I hear that he plans to turn it into a gated community full of luxury flats,' Ken said.

'Why?' Brian asked. 'Would it count as an offshore tax haven?'

'How could it support the weight?' Jake asked. 'The structure's wobbly enough already.'

'By shoring it up,' Brian said. 'They have this remarkable new invention called concrete.'

'He'll never get permission,' Jake said, ignoring Brian's tone.

'Says who?' Rowena asked. 'Geoffrey Weedon has the Planning Committee in his pocket.'

'That's libel! Wouldn't you agree, Ken?' Brian asked, switching targets. 'You being such an expert and all that?'

Ken drained his cup, as if to drown the memory of the most humiliating episode of his career, and wordlessly held it out to Duncan to refill.

'Surely it's better that he takes it off our hands,' Brian added, his slurred 's's suggesting that his bumptiousness might be fuelled by alcohol. 'Does no one here read the *Mercury*? Thought not. But there was a piece last summer – I think it was one of Ken's – about the Council spending hundreds of thousands of pounds on insurance and scaffolding for the boarded-up pier. Meanwhile, it's cutting back on facilities for kids.'

'Not just kids,' Sheila said. 'Old people's homes too, as I've found to my cost.'

'Aren't you still a year or two away from that?' Jake asked innocently.

'Not me, my mother!' Sheila replied with such vehemence that Jake crushed his cup, splashing wine on his shirt.

'What about tonight's exhibition, Duncan?' Rowena interpolated quickly. 'Is it still going ahead?'

'Most definitely. I've spoken to Glynis and the Chief Librarian. The children have been working their socks off over the summer. It would be monstrous to disappoint them.'

'Is it true that there used to be two piers in the town?' Brian asked Duncan. 'That's what your Battle of Britain pilot told me, but I didn't want to press him in case he'd lost it.'

'No, perfectly lucid. Just old,' Duncan said.

'And a hero,' Jake added.

'The second pier was at Salter,' Duncan said, 'but it was torn down in 1940 in case the Germans used it as a landing stage.'

'But they left Francombe's?'

'Yes. I think the seabed had silted up so that boats wouldn't have been able to reach it.'

'There's an old joke,' said Jake, who was notorious for his lack of humour, 'that Churchill believed if the Nazis landed at Francombe, they'd lose heart and turn back.'

'Right!' Stewart stood up abruptly. 'If that's all, chief, I'm off. Some of us have homes to go to.' His departure provoked a general exodus, leaving Duncan alone with Sheila, who gathered up the cups.

'Don't worry about those,' Duncan said, 'you go. Mary'll be here any minute.'

'Are you sure? As long as I'm not leaving them for you. I promised Mother I'd look in on her.'

Duncan bit back the automatic enquiry, anxious to avoid another tortuous conversation in which he struggled to assuage Sheila's guilt at having put her severely demented mother in a home. A succession of painful incidents, culminating in her burying Sheila's collection of porcelain dolls in the back garden, had brought about the rupture that a lifetime of bullying and put-downs rendered long overdue. Yet every night after work Sheila visited her mother who, on the rare occasions that she recognised her, either sat in steely silence or vented a stream of abuse.

'I'll be off then,' Sheila said, taking out one of the extra strong mints to which she had become addicted after reading a magazine article claiming that bitterness caused bad breath.

Inspired by his secretary, Duncan returned to his office and rang his mother. As always, she answered on the fifth ring, which she judged to be the proper balance between eagerness and indifference.

'Darling, how lovely to hear your voice!' she said, launching straight into an account of how the smoke from the blaze had triggered her asthma.

'But, Mother, that's impossible,' Duncan interjected. 'The wind was in the opposite direction. It's in our report.'

'You of all people should know better than to believe what you read in the papers,' she replied coldly. 'I don't see why you bother to ring when you just want to quarrel.'

Scorning his spinelessness, he conceded that there might have been a crosswind. 'Exactly,' she said, mollified. 'I knew that the pier was heading for trouble when the Winter Garden tea room started serving ketchup in plastic tomatoes.'

Mention of the tea room made him long to speak to Jamie. He wondered how many of his son's memories of the pier chimed with his own. Did he, for instance, recall how he posed for a photograph with his parents, their heads poking through the holes in a seabed tableau, a photograph that Duncan still treasured even if the split between the octopus and the crab prevented his keeping it on display, or how he wet himself laughing when the stone god in the Jungle Playground spat water in his father's face? And if he did, would he give him the satisfaction of admitting it or retreat into his usual silence, as though both question and questioner bored him? In the event, Duncan had no way of knowing since, when he finally steeled himself to ring, he was sent straight to voicemail, leaving him with the vision of Jamie out with friends, having dinner with Linda and Derek, or, worse, checking his caller ID.

Preferring to sit alone in his office, which passed for dedication, than in his flat, which felt like failure, Duncan switched the television on to *South East Today*. The lead story concerned a young man who had thrown himself off the ruins of Francombe Castle. The police efforts to talk him down had been thwarted by bystanders egging him on and taking pictures on their phones. 'What's the world coming to? Are we just items for each other's Facebook pages?' a stunned sergeant asked the reporter, before warning that the CCTV footage would be carefully studied and charges of aiding and abetting a suicide could not be ruled out. Duncan, spotting a possible splash for next week's issue, emailed Ken to look into it. The second item concerned the pier, with the Mayor, the Chairman of the Francombe Chamber of Commerce, and a spokesman for the Hoteliers Association all making sombre comments in front of the smouldering structure. They were followed by a dauntingly bullish Geoffrey Weedon, who promised that the *tragedy* (a word that made the purist in Duncan bristle) would cause only a slight delay to the refurbishment plans. Then, in a startling non sequitur, he turned his practised smile to the camera. 'Given the rumours sweeping through town,' he said, 'I'd like to state quite categorically that I played no part in starting the fire.'

The reporter's response was drowned out by a Hoover, as Mary peered round the door and asked if Duncan wanted her to 'do' the room. 'Thank you,' he said, welcoming the intrusion, since Mary's stoicism was an inspiration should he ever feel prone to despair. She lived in a cramped fisherman's cottage with her husband Bob, twin daughters Jilly and

Janine, son Nick, his wife and their two children. Bob had lost his boat after being fined £25,000 for exceeding his EU cod quota. Nick, who worked with his father, fell behind with his rent and moved his family in with his parents. Both Jilly and Janine had been unemployed since leaving school three years before but scorned to become 'skivvies' like their mother. The domestic tensions were exacerbated by what Mary euphemistically called Bob's temper. 'He lashes out when he's had a drop – but only at the furniture. Last week he broke the settee. It's a good thing our Norman's still banged up in Ford. With Nick and Tess and the kiddies squeezing in, he'd have nowhere to sleep.'

Duncan had protested in print against the injustice of Bob's sentence. Even a non-fisherman knew that the autumn seas teemed with cod and that it was impossible to lay down nets without bringing up a bumper haul: in Bob's case, nearly two tons. His defence was that he had been planning to adjust his future catches to comply with the quota, but the judge upheld the DEFRA inspector's ruling that the quota should be divided into twelve equal shares. Even the *Mercury*'s front-page story that this was the same boat in which Bob's grandfather had made three trips across the Channel to rescue soldiers stranded at Dunkirk failed to influence the court. Faced with a fine of more than half his annual turnover, together with legal costs that tripled after an ill-advised appeal, Bob sold his boat. Over the following months he took to drink; Nick to antidepressants; and Norman, his younger son, to crime, selling a mixture of cocaine and baking powder to holidaymakers, students and two undercover policemen. 'It's right that our Norman was charged. He's a bad lad,' Mary had said. 'But not our Bob. What good would it have done anyone if he'd thrown the fish back in the sea? It's just spite!'

The strain of her various cleaning jobs, plus a regular weekend shift on her brother-in-law's fish stall, had taken its toll on Mary. It was hard to believe that at forty-four she was only two years older than Linda. Despite his contempt for television makeover shows, Duncan secretly hoped for one to visit Francombe and work its restorative magic on Mary. Meanwhile, he helped her as much as he could, recommending her to Henry Grainger at St Edward's after he was forced to cut her hours, and giving her both an office computer when Nick's was repossessed and a set of his mother's old china when hers was mysteriously smashed.

'Would you like a glass – that is, a cup – of wine?' he asked Mary, who looked alarmed. 'It's been a tough day. I think we deserve it.'

'Best not. It goes straight to my head and I have to make them their tea when I finish here.' With five able-bodied adults living at home, Duncan failed to see why none of them could cook dinner, but Mary insisted that that would be 'rubbing their noses in it'.

'Then why not take the bottle? Three for two, so it cost me nothing,' he added tactfully.

'Best not,' she replied after a pause. 'Too much temptation. Bless you.' Then she switched on the Hoover, as if afraid of what else she might say.

Duncan went up to his flat. When he built Mercury House in 1922, his great-grandfather had reserved the top floor for his private use. Although he and Duncan's grandfather had slept there in emergencies, Duncan's father did so regularly, citing 'late night meetings', the true nature of which Duncan only discovered after his death. He himself had moved in on his divorce seven years earlier, a temporary expedient that convenience and thrift had made permanent. Small but serviceable, it comprised a galley kitchen where he ate his meals, having sworn off TV dinners after a shot of a shit-filled bath in a documentary on child neglect; an airy sitting room with a carved oak frieze; and two bedrooms, one of which, as the door plaque announced, was Jamie's. Shortly after the divorce, they had spent a Saturday morning at Debenhams where Jamie, exploiting his new licence, chose a red racing-car bed, tiger-print beanbag and *Jungle Book* wallpaper, which was replaced when it gave him nightmares. In recent years he had stayed so seldom that Duncan had appropriated the room for his exercise bike.

Thoughts of Jamie filled him with an eviscerating loneliness. When Linda left him, his one consolation had been that she was remaining in Francombe, enabling him to see his son twice a week and to be close at hand in a crisis. But as the years passed, his so-near-yet-so-far status had grown ever more painful. Rather than restricting his access to Jamie, Linda had included him in so many family events that Derek would surely have objected, were it not for his even more convoluted relationship with his own ex-wife. Nevertheless, he was the perennial outsider, grateful for their indulgence of what should have been a right. Jamie's edginess when they ran into each other in the street made him feel like a stranger. It was as though 'Dad' were a subject with a set place on the timetable, which he refused to study out of hours. In his bleaker moments, he wondered whether he had been rash to rule out sending Jamie to boarding school. At least then he and Linda would have been on an equal footing, sharing both the holidays and the emotional reserve. But even if he had broken the solemn vow he made on leaving Lancing, he could never have afforded the fees.

The next morning he went down to the office at 8.30 to find Ken busy at his desk. As expected, he was fully informed about the castle suicide and had sent Brian to visit the bereaved parents. 'Is that wise?' Duncan asked, dubious of Brian's discretion.

'Still waters, young Brian!' Ken said. 'Besides, he's the same age as the victim – or should that be perpetrator? It might help them open up.'

Rowena had gone to the Town Hall on a tip-off from an anonymous guest that at a wedding on Tuesday the bride's two teenage daughters had taken the 'no confetti on the steps' rule to heart and, instead, thrown their late father's ashes over the newly-weds. Ken himself planned to monitor developments on the pier where, according to his source in the fire brigade, charred bedding had been retrieved from the rubble of the Winter Garden, fanning conjecture that the blaze had been started by one or more vagrants.

'Surprise surprise!' Duncan replied. 'Any bets as to how soon it becomes a gang of the Albanian/Iranian/Kurdish asylum seekers who are overrunning the town?'

As usual on a Thursday, Duncan spent the first part of the morning reading the paper from cover to cover. Echoing his father, he found that no matter how closely he had examined the dummy, the stories 'smelt' different on the printed page – which had, of course, been literally true in the days of hot metal. He was pleased with both the reporting of the fire and the leader in which he called on the town to reassess its values as it rebuilt its pier. His one regret was the use of agency photographs, identical ones having appeared in both the *Telegraph* and the *Mail*, and he tormented himself with the thought of the unique perspective that Bert Ponsonby would have brought. His reading was interrupted by three calls of complaint. The first was from a Mrs Greene, furious that her name had been rendered 'commonplace' by the omission of the final 'e' in a list of volunteer tree wardens. The second was from Luca Salvatore, owner of Pizza on the Prom, warning him to keep away from his restaurant after the story on mouse droppings in his kitchen. The third was from Heather Bayley, a local Brown Owl, accusing him of 'blatant prejudice' against the Brownies for his failure to feature the 1st Switherton Pack's Annual Fun Day. 'We had face painting, knife carving and an inspirational demonstration of balloon twisting from Tawny Owl.'

At four o'clock Duncan left the office for the Central Library to attend to the final arrangements for the Pier Project exhibition, which the *Mercury* was sponsoring. In an emergency meeting the previous day, the Francombe Pier Trust had decided that, despite the wretched timing, the exhibition should go ahead, both to avoid disappointing the many children who had taken part and in the hope that images of the pier's illustrious past might influence plans for its future.

Struck by a bitter wind as soon as he stepped into the street, Duncan cast a solicitous glance at the four thinly dressed middle-aged men in the graffiti-sprayed bus shelter, members of Francombe's army of homeless huddled together for warmth until their hostel reopened at six. One had a bandaged wrist and another a black eye and split lip, injuries sustained either in bouts of insobriety or in fights with visiting youths for whom attacking the locals held more appeal than legitimate entertainments. Duncan's cheery 'Good afternoon' was met by three vacant stares and one 'You don't say so, old bean', which at least showed spirit. He turned away down the shabby side street, which in his childhood had housed a row of specialist shops dealing in coins, maps, cameras and fishing tackle. Now only the coin shop remained, although its heavy grille, stamped with an advert for its website, was generally down. Elsewhere, a café offered all-day breakfasts with OAP discounts; a tattoo parlour blazoned its designs on assorted body parts; three charity shops ran the gamut of Francombe concern, from Age UK through Cats Protection to the Fishermen's Mission; and a 24 hour mini-mart sold Iraqi, Kurdish and Afghani produce to the refugees and asylum seekers who, with an irony to which only immigration officers could be blind, were housed in the same hostels as the drunks.

He walked up the Parade, the town's main thoroughfare, where a string of chain stores competed for what remained of its custom. He was accosted by Enid Marshall, his mother's bridge partner, who had lost her husband to their GP, her divorce settlement in a failed Lloyd's syndicate, and her only son in a Texan cult suicide, but who refused to dwell on the past, brushing off every expression of sympathy with a brusque 'Worse things happen at sea'. Dropping a pound into her RNLI collecting tin, he continued on his way, past the statue of Queen Victoria, her glower finally justified after cuts to the Council's cleaning budget had left her permanently daubed with seagull droppings, and entered the library. He crossed the vaulted marble hall with its bas-reliefs of Aristotle, Shakespeare, Dryden, Scott, Dickens and Carlyle, the last of whose books had long since been dispatched to storage, and climbed the well-worn stairs to the Reference Section, its usual sober display replaced by the vibrancy of the Pier Project entries.

Back in March, with hopes high for its own bid, the Francombe Pier Trust had sought to stimulate interest in the restoration by holding a children's art competition. The *Mercury* agreed to sponsor it, provided that the three prizes of £1,000, £500 and £250 consisted of books for the winners' school libraries. The sheer weight of entries confounded the Jeremiahs, who had claimed that without a personal incentive nobody would take part, and although the Project had been overtaken by events, Duncan found cause for celebration in the vision and accomplishment of the various paintings, models, collages and lone digital projection on show.

This projection depicting the Moorish pavilion in five of its incarnations – concert hall, palais de dance, variety theatre, roller-skating rink and disco – had been awarded first prize, a decision Duncan suspected had been shaped, at least in part, by its use of technology that neither he nor his fellow judges understood. The runner-up was a small camera obscura, through which could be seen an image of the large camera obscura that had stood on the pier head until replaced by a helter-skelter in the 1920s. Third prize went to a painting of a mob of teenagers storming the pavilion during the infamous 1974 concert by The Who. For the rest, he was struck by two scale models of the pier, one made of Francombe rock with a gingerbread pavilion and kiosks, the other, with what seemed like uncanny prescience, made of matches; a painting of the 1932 disaster in which twin sisters drowned during a display of synchronised diving; and a collage of photographs of the Black and White Minstrels, star attractions at the pavilion throughout the 1960s, interspersed with newspaper cuttings of race riots.

After running through the order of ceremony with Glynis Kingswood and the Mayor's PR, he paid a precautionary visit to the lavatory, crossing the tessellated floor to the stately urinals where the library's Victorian benefactors had been able to pee with pride. He had scarcely unbuttoned his flies when the outer door was flung open and a jovial voice called his name. Twisting so abruptly that he risked exposing himself, he spotted Geoffrey Weedon advancing on him with a smile as gleaming as the tiles. He turned back to the wall as Geoffrey, confident both of his own propriety and Duncan's discomfort, stepped up next to him and unleashed a loud stream of piss. He stood motionless while Geoffrey seized his advantage and started to chat.

'Fancy seeing you here.'

'We're sponsoring the project,' Duncan said, vainly coaxing his penis. 'And you? Weighing up the opposition?'

'Many a true word ... The past *is* the opposition in this town. The myth of a Francombe Golden Age, which blokes like you – no offence, Duncan – do all you can to promote.'

'And why should we want to do that?'

'Nostalgia? Security? I'm no trick cyclist. A world where the *Mercury* meant something?'

'Whereas for you, the past is disposable,' Duncan said, pondering the effect on both bladder and morale of admitting defeat by buttoning his flies. 'I saw you on the news insisting that you weren't responsible for the fire.'

'Best to clear the air.'

'Some people might think it a smokescreen.' Geoffrey guffawed. 'No pun intended.'

'Why would I burn down the pier? I've already got what I want. This just complicates things. Insurance claims. Emergency repairs.'

'So it was fate?'

'I don't believe in fate, Duncan. Fate is the name that losers give to chance. And on Tuesday night chance took the form of Afghan asylum seekers.'

'Oh, they're Afghans now, are they? How's that? Did they have Kabul stamped on their bedding?'

'Is it my fault if my sources are more clued in than the *Mercury*'s?'

A young librarian entered the room, stopping short at the sight of the men cheek by jowl beside four empty urinals. 'Come on up,' Geoffrey said, as if it were his private preserve. 'No need to be shy. Just two old friends measuring their dicks – metaphorically.' The librarian gave him an uneasy smile and made for the furthest urinal, where the steady patter showed that he shared none of Duncan's reticence.

'You and your lot should be grateful to me,' Geoffrey said.

'For what precisely?' Duncan asked.

'The Council survey found that, if they couldn't come up with a buyer, the only option was to demolish the pier at a cost of four million quid. In other words, a lot more cuts to the day centres, youth clubs and, dare I say it, the libraries that the *Mercury* is always banging on about.'

The librarian washed his hands and hurried out without drying them. Geoffrey followed him to the basins, where Duncan was surprised by how meticulously he soaped his hands.

'I've been thinking about the difference between us,' Geoffrey said.

'I'm flattered.'

'Why? You're practically family.' Duncan shuddered. 'The distinction may be a little crude – a little binary – but I try to make people happy, whereas you try to improve them.'

'Is that so?'

'Take the motto on your masthead: you know, the one that sounds like the Pope.'

'*Celeritas et veritas*,' Duncan said, concentrating on the water gushing from the tap.

'What does it mean?'

'You know what it means.'

'Yes. But we'd both like it so much if you told me.'

'Promptness and truth.'

'Then why not say so? Do you never ask yourself why you've chosen a phrase that ninety-nine point nine per cent of readers don't understand, that makes them think the paper's not for them?'

'We've used it since the very first issue. It's tradition.'

'Is that your answer to everything? You're speaking a different language. Literally.'

'It's only three words.'

'Is it?' Geoffrey laughed as he tugged the recalcitrant roller towel. 'One last piece of advice and then I'm off: book an appointment with your doctor.'

'What?'

'I can't help noticing you're having problems with Percy there. Sure sign of an enlarged prostate. Best get it checked out.'

Geoffrey's diagnosis was disproved the moment he walked out. Duncan felt a surge of relief, followed by anger at having allowed his old adversary to gain the upper hand. He returned to the Reference Section, which was busier than he expected, as if the exhibition had become the focus of communal grief at the destruction of the pier. He caught sight of Jamie in a huddle of larger boys, among them his stepbrother, Craig. Flouting the veto on public displays of affection, he walked over and ruffled his hair, causing Craig, whose own hair was spiky, to smirk.

'Good to see you here, boys,' Duncan said. 'Do any of you have entries in the competition?'

'For fuck's sake, Dad!' Jamie said, as Craig and his three companions sniggered.

'Is the idea so inconceivable?' Duncan asked.

'What's that mean then?' one of the boys asked, playing dumb.

'It's like wearing a condom on your brain so that nothing can get through. Isn't that so, Mr N?' Craig asked, as usual spurning Duncan's Christian name.

'I expect that there's an etymological link, Craig,' Duncan replied, 'but there are simpler definitions. If you have so little interest in the artworks, why have you come?'

'Three line whip,' Craig said. 'My mum, my dad and my stepdad. All the Weedons have to be here, what with the development plans for the pier.'

'Plus, of course, there's the totty,' one of his friends said.

'Totty?' Duncan asked.

'That's right,' Craig said, assuming a donnish air. 'I expect there's an etymological link with "tot" meaning "little child", though I trust that there are no paedo undertones in this common – or street – usage for what, in your day, were known as "chicks" or "floozies".'

'Thank you, Craig, that was most illuminating.'

'Any time, Mr N.'

'We need to talk, Dad.' Jamie grabbed his arm.

'Catch you later, Squirt,' Craig said.

Duncan winced on behalf of Jamie, who was hypersensitive about his height. 'Goodbye, Craig,' he said. 'See you again.'

'Yeah, whatever.' Craig turned back to his friends.

'Why must you always do that, Dad?' Jamie said, dragging him away. 'Do you enjoy showing me up?'

'What did I do? He's your stepbrother. I can't very well ignore him.'

'Why not? Do you think he wants to talk to you? Do you think anyone wants to talk to you?'

'Now you're showing yourself up,' Duncan said, as heads

turned in their direction. 'I'm pleased that you get on so well with Craig, but I'm not sure that he's a good influence.'

'Like I care!'

'And I'm none too keen on the way he talks to you.'

'For fuck's sake, Dad, you just don't get it! He's sixteen; he lets me hang out with him. Isn't that enough?'

'No, it's not. You're worth more than that. And what's with all the swearing? Is it part of earning his respect?'

'Why are you always picking on me?'

'Perhaps because you never let me close enough to do anything else?' Duncan replied. 'Because you'll discover as you grow older that self-respect is worth more than any other kind,' he added quickly, trusting that Jamie had failed to detect the pain in his voice.

'Maybe in the Middle Ages. Not now.'

'Look, there's your mother!' Duncan said, seeing Linda talking to an attractive, smartly dressed brunette. As he admired the woman's cream silk blouse, grey tailored jacket and lemon pleated skirt, Linda's former complaint that he never noticed anything she was wearing flashed across his mind. Chastened, he attempted to rectify the omission, but she kissed his cheek before he had the chance.

From the corner of his eye he glimpsed Jamie shuffling his feet, betraying his usual unease at seeing his parents together. It was as if, having braced himself for the bitterness of their divorce, he felt threatened by – even resentful of – their residual affection.

'Duncan, meet Ellen Nugent, Rose's new speech and language therapist. Ellen, this is Duncan Neville, Jamie's father.'

'Really? Isn't Derek his father?'

'Stepfather,' Linda said quickly. Duncan felt sick.

'Of course, I'm sorry. I thought I heard Jamie call him Dad but it must have been Stepdad.' Ellen laughed nervously. 'Honestly, you'd think that in my job I'd pay closer attention to what people say!'

'Have you been a speech therapist long?' Duncan asked, coming to her rescue.

'I graduated in 1995, but I haven't practised for years. I wanted to go back part-time when my children started school, but my husband wouldn't let me.'

'Really?' Duncan said, surprised by her acquiescence. 'Is he very old-fashioned?'

'No, just controlling. But the operative word is *was*. We split up last year and I wanted – I needed – to work. But with all the cuts, SLT jobs are thin on the ground. Martin Casey, one of Matthew's – my ex's – old colleagues, runs the Child Development Centre here. He pulled a few strings and after a two-week induction course – which was a wake-up call in itself – and a commitment to regular supervision I took the plunge.'

'I'm guessing you're not from around here,' Duncan said, confident that he would have remembered her had they met before.

'No, we moved down in the summer from Radlett, a village – well, more of a commuter town now – in Hertfordshire. The job was the main incentive, of course, but I liked the prospect of living by the sea. It seemed the perfect place to make a fresh start and bring up the kids.'

'How many do you have?' Duncan asked, ignoring Jamie's snort.

'Two. Sue's sixteen and Neil's thirteen.'

'Really?' Duncan replied, grateful that Linda's and Jamie's presence prevented his blurting out 'But you don't look old enough!' or some similar inanity to which he suddenly felt prone. 'The same age as you,' he said, turning to his son.

'So?'

'I'd hoped to start work straight away, but my CRB check was delayed.'

'It's madness,' Linda said. 'Heaven knows, children like Rose need protecting –'

'She has me,' Jamie said.

'Of course she does, darling,' Linda said, kissing the crown of his head. 'But there's far too much red tape. Duncan has campaigned tirelessly against it. What was that case … the bell ringer?'

'Ellen won't be interested.'

'Why not?' Linda frowned at him. 'The one where the boy complained because the man said something that could be taken two ways.'

'"Do you want a tug?"'

'That's right. "Do you want a tug?" You have a dirty mind, my son,' Linda said, as Jamie grinned for the first time that evening. 'I don't know where you get it from. Not from me and certainly not from your father.'

Maybe from his stepfather, Duncan thought.

'"Do you want a tug?" He's a bell ringer, for heaven's sake! The *Mercury* went to town on it.'

'True,' Duncan said, still wondering if the publisher's disclaimer that the models were over eighteen (a mere fig leaf, given their smooth skin and boyish faces) had justified his decision not to report the police discovery of the bell ringer's stash of *Fresh Meat* magazines.

He was saved from further soul-searching by the Mayor's PR, who informed him that 'battle is due to commence'.

'Oh no, Dad,' Jamie said, 'do you have to?'

'Fraid so. The *Mercury*'s sponsoring this jamboree. As well as an excellent cause, it's good publicity.'

'But how can you afford it? The paper's going bust.'

'What? Who told you that?'

'Mum.'

'No, I didn't.'

'Yes, you did. Why can't any of you ever be honest?'

'I may have said it was having difficulties…' Linda floundered. 'But who isn't these days?'

'Derek and Uncle Geoffrey.'

'That's not clever, Jamie,' Linda said, with a spark of genuine anger.

'Don't worry,' Duncan interjected. 'I won't have to cut your pocket money. Your old man's not quite on his uppers.' Jamie looked pained. 'That was a joke.'

'I'm not thick! But jokes are supposed to be funny.' He gazed around the room. 'Please, Dad, there are people here who know me. Promise you won't tell any more.'

'Thanks for the vote of confidence!' Duncan said, forcing a laugh. 'Are your kids like this with you?' he asked Ellen.

'You should have heard my daughter on this skirt.'

'She must be mad. It's perfect on you ... I mean it suits you perfectly.' Flustered, he looked at Linda, whose studied vacancy spoke volumes.

He made his way up to the podium, stopping to chat to Ken, who stood with camera and notebook in hand. Duncan, for whom the caption 'Editor of the *Mercury*' appeared in the paper far too often for his own liking, was as reluctant to pose for pictures as Ken, who had grown up with a team of specialist photographers, was to take them. Nevertheless, every time he stood among a group of smiling dignitaries, just as every time he held one of his monthly editor's surgeries in the market square, Duncan weighed his embarrassment against the raising of the paper's profile, reminding himself that he was not merely affirming its place at the heart of the community but giving it an identifiable face.

He took his seat alongside the Mayor in full regalia and Glynis Kingswood, whose trademark black now served as mourning. As he listened to their heartfelt eulogies to the pier, he found his mind drifting back to Ellen's remark. Had she genuinely misheard Jamie – after all, her attention would have been focused on Rose – or had he called Derek 'Dad'? And if so, why? Did he long for the security of a conventional family, although the divorces on every side must have shown him that it was an illusion, or did he simply favour Derek? Did the qualities that made him a more attractive husband also make him a more attractive father? Even so, no matter how much

Jamie's preference flattered him, Derek should have corrected it. He too had surrendered his son's day-to-day upbringing to another man. How would he feel if he heard Craig describing Geoffrey as his father? Or maybe he already had? Maybe he was using Jamie to relieve his own sense of exclusion? *What's in a name?* Everything, when that name was Dad.

A mayoral nudge alerted him that it was his turn to speak. He prided himself on never preparing for such occasions, relying instead on a mixture of inspiration and panic. The latter predominated as he looked out at the sea of expectant faces. 'Mercury, as I'm sure I've no need to remind you, was the messenger of the gods,' he said. 'He was also the god of fraud and intrigue, although I trust that his subsidiary attributes did not figure in my great-great-grandfather's calculations when he named his newspaper in 1869.' He dared not look at Jamie, as the few strained chuckles bore out his warning. 'Francombe Pier was built just a few years later in 1883. These two venerable institutions have remained at the heart of our civic life ever since. So it's fitting that tonight the *Mercury* should be sponsoring a competition that celebrates the pier's history.' Warming to his theme, he fixed his gaze on Geoffrey, who stood at the front of the crowd. 'And equally fitting that the presentation should take place in this great library, another vestige of Francombe's golden age.'

He congratulated all the children who had taken part and summoned the three winners in reverse order to receive their cheques. As Ken snapped him shaking their hands (the runner-up's dismayingly sticky), he struggled to silence the inner voice that was treacherously totting up how many extra copies might be sold to adoring parents, grandparents, uncles and aunts. No sooner had the first prize-winner moved away than the Mayor stood up to announce a surprise presentation by Geoffrey Weedon, the new owner of the pier. Duncan turned to Glynis, whose puckered brow showed that she too had been caught unawares, fuelling his suspicions of complicity between Weedon's and the Town Hall. He watched coldly as Geoffrey sauntered up to the podium.

'I promise I'll be brief. I don't want to keep you from the booze ... that is those of you not under doctor's orders.' He raised a glass of orange juice in mock anguish. 'It makes sense that, as the editor of such a hoary organ – that's h-o-a-r-y,' he said in response to a juvenile giggle – 'Mr Neville should concentrate on the pier's past. But at Weedon's we're looking to its future. There are exciting changes in the air. Watch this space! And the key, like everything else in our entertainment division, is fun. So in a spirit of fun, I'd like to offer all our entrants free one-day passes for themselves and their families to the Excelsior Wheel Park, with additional £100 tokens for each of the three winners to spend at any of our amusement arcades.'

The appreciative whoops for the passes after the polite applause for the cheques left Duncan in no doubt as to where the children's enthusiasm lay. For all his resentment of Geoffrey, he blamed himself for failing to realise that the evening would be hijacked by a man who, according to local legend – nurtured no doubt by himself – had founded his property empire on the sale of a building that he didn't yet own. He stepped off the podium just as Ken prepared to photograph the children swarming around their benefactor. Eager to clear his head of all the flimflam, he searched the room for Jamie, who was nowhere to be seen. So he made his way back to Linda and Ellen, who had been joined by Derek.

'Lovely speech,' Linda said.

'Yes, mate,' Derek said. 'Just the right tone.'

'Judging by the response, your brother caught it better.'

'You know Geoff. Always something up his sleeve.'

'Usually a dagger,' Duncan said, forcing a smile.

'Is he your brother?' Ellen asked, gazing at Geoffrey, who was posing with the children like an out-of-season Santa Claus.

'I got the looks; he got the brains.' Derek gave a strangled laugh. 'No but seriously, he's a brilliant man, my brother.'

'Derek's Geoffrey's business partner,' Linda said, stroking his arm.

'Well, I manage the wheel park and oversee the arcades.'

'You're better at dealing with people,' Linda said.

'But that's not the half of it,' Duncan said, still brooding on the misattributed Dad. 'Derek's first wife, Frances, is married to Geoffrey. His son Craig lives with them.'

'That must make life complicated,' Ellen said.

'Not really,' Linda said. 'We're all grown-ups.'

'It raised a few eyebrows at first,' Derek said, 'especially my parents'. But then I met Linda and things fell into place. A bit like a Sixties swingers party where the music stopped and everyone grabbed a partner. Except Duncan, of course. He's the only one left spare.'

'Darling,' Linda said quietly, 'will you go and fetch Jamie? Craig too, if he's still planning on coming back with us.'

'Aye aye, Captain.' Derek saluted and left the room.

'Derek's always a little touchy when it comes to his brother,' Linda said to Ellen.

'It can't be easy, what with his wife – I mean his first wife.'

'Oh, not that! As I said, we're all good friends. But he's spent his life in Geoffrey's shadow.'

'Fair's fair, Linda. Geoffrey's always been there for him, bailed him out each time he's tried to set up on his own. The one thing no one can fault him for is fraternal loyalty.'

'I know you're not Geoffrey's greatest fan,' Linda said.

'No indeed,' Duncan replied, resenting him all the more for encroaching on the conversation.

'Where's Derek got to with that son of ours? That's yours and mine, Duncan,' Linda said quickly. 'We need to pick Rose up from my mother's.'

'And I must go home,' Ellen said. 'You'd think my two had never seen a microwave. I'll be with you on Monday at three, Linda.'

'Enjoy the weekend!'

'Good to meet you, Mr Neville.'

'Duncan, please.'

'Thank you.'

'Likewise … Ellen. I'm very glad you came.'

'Linda twisted my arm. She said it was time I saw more of my new town than the inside of my clients' houses.'

'I hope that this will be just the start.'

'Me too.'

Duncan allowed his eyes to linger on her as she walked away, before turning guiltily to Linda, forgetting for a moment that they were no longer married.

'I think someone's a little smitten.'

'Rubbish!'

'You could do a lot worse. She's attractive and smart and excellent at her job. Rose adores her.'

'I'm delighted to hear it. But she's only just moved here; she's still settling down. She has two teenage children and, Lord knows, I find it hard enough to communicate with my own son. And … why are we even having this conversation?'

'Because I worry about you. You've been on your own too long. Which isn't surprising, given what's available in this town. Ellen's a breath of fresh air … I shall have to get the two of you together.'

'I'm not sure that it sends the right signals to have your ex-wife playing Cupid.'

'Who else knows you as well? You're a good man, Duncan. You deserve someone in your life.'

'I deserve you.'

'I wish you wouldn't say that.'

'I'm sorry,' Duncan said. 'Was I thinking out loud?'

'No worries. But I really should go.' Duncan scanned the room, which was rapidly emptying. 'I'm afraid Derek may be sneaking a crafty fag on the steps.'

'Just as long as he's not giving one to Jamie.'

'He'd never do that,' Linda said. 'Whatever you may think, he's highly responsible.'

'Of course. It's just … I suppose it's inevitable that Jamie should play us off against each other. Good dad, bad dad. Laid-back dad, uptight dad.'

'Derek's not his father.'

'But Ellen wasn't mistaken about what he called him, was she?' Duncan asked, achingly aware that, as of last July, Jamie had lived longer under Derek's roof than his. 'I know a genuine blush when I see one.'

'It's about Craig, not Derek. Jamie idolises him. Getting close to Derek is a way of getting close to Craig. It's like saying he's my real – not just my step – brother.'

'Thank you,' Duncan said, wanting to believe her. 'Though I don't think I'd pick Craig as anyone's role model.'

'Nor me. But it won't last. In two years' time, he'll be off to uni and Jamie will have to move on. That's if he hasn't already.'

'Not that there's much I can do anyway. I try to talk to him but he switches off. He's either hostile or sullen.'

'He's thirteen years old. That's what he's like with everyone. You just get it in concentrated doses … No, thanks very much,' she said, as Carolyn Blunt, the children's librarian, approached them with a bottle of wine. She turned back to Duncan. 'Boys need to distance themselves from their fathers; it's part of growing up.'

'I thought it was from their mothers.'

'Maybe it's different when your parents are divorced. But if you want my advice, cut him some slack. He grumbles that you're always on his case.'

'That's nonsense. I spend half my time biting my tongue.'

'Maybe that's what he means. He said you gave him a really hard time about quitting the clarinet.'

'My mother had just bought it for him. And it meant so much to her to have another musician in the family.'

'Yes, I know all about that,' Linda said. 'But Jamie's his own man. He won't be forced to follow in anyone's footsteps.'

'Especially not mine.'

'Now you're being silly,' Linda said, squeezing his hand with hollow intimacy before walking away.

Duncan made a final circuit of the room, congratulating two of the younger entrants, commiserating with the rock-pier maker's father on his son's failure to be placed, shunning any discussion of the causes of the fire, checking that Ken had all the information he needed for his article, and noting with surprise that Craig had opted to stay with Geoffrey rather than leave with Derek. He finally escaped outside, where the sight of two large families piling into their cars reinforced Derek's odd-man-out gibe. Feeling as neglected as the sour-faced statue in front of him, he shrank from the prospect of another kitchen supper. He decided instead to go to Vivien's, a café where he was assured of a warm welcome ever since his intervention had persuaded the Francombe Hospital Trust to fund an operation to correct the owner's granddaughter's misshapen breasts.

Threatened with a 'Teen's Life Ruined by Heartless Hospital' headline, the Trust had reversed its initial decision not to license the surgery, and Sharon, who for years had refused either to go swimming or do PE and been convinced that she would never find a boyfriend, let alone a husband, was now a happily married mother of three.

'How's the family?' Duncan asked Vivien, as they chatted in the otherwise deserted café.

'We're in the pink,' she replied. 'My blood pressure's too high and I could do with more customers, but Sharon's expecting again. And it's all thanks to you.'

Two

Mystery Poisoning

by Rowena Birdseye

Thursday, 3 October 2013

A criminal investigation is under way after Dragon Greenslade, 82, was found poisoned in his hut at the edge of Salter Nature Reserve. He is currently receiving treatment in the Princess Royal Hospital, where a spokeswoman described his condition as 'stable'.

Mr Greenslade was admitted to hospital after countryside rangers raised the alarm. 'I hadn't seen Dragon or Cockeye (his dog) around for three days,' said Ben Feasdale, Assistant Ranger, 20. 'When I knocked on the door of his shack and got no reply, I went inside. The stench was awful. I saw Dragon lying on his mattress. His lips were blue and his chin was speckled with blood, but he was still breathing. Cockeye was on the floor beside him, dead.'

Preliminary tests on dog biscuits found at the scene indicate that they had been adulterated with weedkiller. Mr Greenslade has long been a familiar figure outside supermarkets handing out pamphlets that advocate dog food as the only safe alternative to carcinogenic human food. It has yet to be ascertained whether the target of the attack was Mr Greenslade or his dog.

For years Mr Greenslade has greeted visitors to Salter Cove, dressed only in a necklace of shells, extolling the virtues of naturism. More recently, he has conducted a one-man crusade against lewdness in the neighbouring woods and cliffs. Constable Drew Rogers, Diversity Officer for Sussex Police, confirmed that 'Mr Greenslade has filed numerous complaints, all of which have been investigated and several have resulted in fixed penalty notices of £80 being issued to the offenders'.

Insisting that there was as yet no evidence to link the crime to the victim's campaigns, Constable Rogers commented that 'Mr Greenslade had many enemies: local residents who'd fought unsuccessfully to have him rehoused; fishermen whom he'd accused of selling mercury-contaminated fish; even other nudists, who maintained he was giving them a bad name'.

Detective Inspector Andy Griffiths of Francombe and Salter CID, who is heading the investigation, declared that 'no line of inquiry has been ruled out'.

A bald, middle-aged man, wearing nothing but a rucksack and hiking boots, strode up to Duncan and Henry as they walked along the windswept beach. Duncan watched anxiously as, having introduced himself without inhibition, he leant over to stroke Brandy, Henry's snappish fox terrier, who, either out of respect for another naked creature or a refusal to be distracted from the pungent pleasures underfoot, submitted to being petted before scurrying into the gorse. After delivering a paean to the virtues of sea air, during which Duncan allowed his eyes to stray no lower than the stippling of hair on his scrawny chest, the man strode on. Wordlessly, Duncan drew Henry's attention to the imprint of pebbles on his chafed buttocks.

'Why do they do it? It's barely above freezing,' Henry said.

'It's his religion. Like any true disciple, he's out in all weathers.'

'I could do with him at St Edward's. Most of my congregation wilt at the first sign of drizzle ... Here, Brandy!' Henry picked up a piece of driftwood, flinging it away with unusual vehemence, as if at the thought of the empty pews.

Henry was vicar of St Edward's, Salter, popularly known as the Cliff Top Church. While loath to use the word to describe a clergyman, Duncan regarded him as the closest thing to a soulmate that he had in Francombe. His mother had introduced them when Henry moved to the parish six years ago. They had discovered a mutual passion for chess, at which Henry was the more proficient, and Bach, about whom he was the more knowledgeable. After sounding him out on subjects from Genesis to genetics, Duncan asked him to write the 'Notes from the Pulpit' column in the *Mercury*, which he was keen to revive after a gap of several years. Henry agreed, turning in fortnightly pieces of real substance, which, despite several surveys showing them to be the least popular section of the paper, Duncan continued to commission, arguing that, whatever the truth of its doctrines (about which he himself was agnostic), the Church played a unique role in community life.

'Brandy, come here boy!' Henry shouted, as the dog darted out of the bushes with a slither of rubber clamped in his jaws. 'What have you got there, boy? Oh God,' he said, uttering the casual blasphemy that Duncan took to be a diversionary tactic. 'A condom!'

'Do you have any gloves?' Duncan asked, conscious that Henry was soon to give his mother Communion.

'Don't worry, there's no risk. Drop it, you disgusting animal, it's not a game!' Brandy, who with his white coat and floppy brown ears was the spit of the dog on the old HMV logo, evidently disagreed, emitting a playful snarl as Henry swung him to and fro in an attempt to wrest the condom from him. Despite the resilience of the rubber, he finally succeeded, leaving Brandy, tail wagging furiously, to trot off in search of new adventures.

Duncan, for whom disposing of the condom was the essence of post-coital ennui, watched Henry warily clasping the fetid rubber between forefinger and thumb. There were no litter bins on a beach from which the Council was eager to discourage visitors, yet he could scarcely drop it on the pebbles where another dog or, worse, a child might pick it up. He might take it away, but that risked misconstruction if he were to fall and break his leg or be knocked down by a joy-rider on the cliffs and have his possessions logged in hospital or even the morgue. It was easy to picture the headline in the local paper – at least one that was not edited by a friend.

'I'll chuck this away later,' Henry said, wrapping the condom in his handkerchief and slipping it in his coat pocket.

'It's bad enough when it's sweet papers,' Duncan said, seeking to portray the problem as one of hygiene rather than morality. He was hesitant to discuss the clandestine goings-on in the cove with Henry, not because he was a vicar but because he was gay. While the closest he had come to a public declaration was a 'Notes from the Pulpit' in which he expressed support for a lesbian couple turned away from a seafront B&B by its Christian owners, in private he was more forthcoming, speaking of his lifelong conflict between faith and desire. Rebutting Duncan's contention that the more ful-filled the man, the more effective the priest, he claimed that, in line with Church teaching, his only course was to marry or remain celibate. Duncan even wondered whether, for all the craggy beauty of its setting, the chief attraction of St Edward's to its incumbent was the absence of the carnal temptations rife in metropolitan livings. So he must have found it both a shock and a threat to discover them in his own backyard.

They crossed a patch of scrub to reach the rickety steps that led up to the lane. As he scrambled over the first few cracked stones, Duncan gazed sceptically at warning notices, which, while they might deter the casual visitor, gave the determined adventurer the illusion that he was safe from detection. For as long as he could remember, Salter Cove had been a haven for nudists. As a young boy, walking in the woods with his mother, he had broken free and dashed down to the shore, to be greeted by an array of old and young, male and female, firm and flaccid flesh. He had failed to find the words in his six-year-old vocab-ulary to question his hotly pursuing mother who, clasping her hand over his eyes, placed him on his honour never to go near the beach again. She explained that the people he had seen were too poor to afford bathing suits and it would be wicked of someone more fortunate to make them feel ashamed. For years he had believed her until, stung by the mockery of more knowing friends, he had accompanied them to the cove, first to jeer and then to ogle. Now, the harmless *Health and Efficiency* world of his childhood had been replaced by the sexual free-for-all to which Dragon had taken exception.

Thoughts of Dragon came to the fore when they left the steps for the brambly track that snaked round the cliff. Its mossy handrail was broken in several places where illicit paths had been beaten through the bushes, on one of which a strip of chequered crime-scene tape fluttered in the breeze.

'Any news of Dragon?' Henry asked, as they passed the tape.

'You mean you haven't checked on our website?'

'Should I have?'

'You'll increase our traffic – I think that's the word – by fifty per cent. Brian's posting regular updates. From what I gather, Dragon's out of the woods – sorry! – but it's unlikely he'll ever be able to come back here.'

'Especially now the Council's demolished his home.'

'That fast? I knew it was on the cards. On the bright side, at least they'll have to rehouse him. It can't have been much fun, stuck in that musty shack with no human contact for days on end.'

'Put like that, it holds considerable appeal.'

'Are clergy allowed to be such cynics?'

'It's in the contract … Brandy, come here!' he called, as the dog wandered off into the undergrowth. 'All in all, Dragon and I have a lot in common.'

'How do you make that out?' Duncan asked, struggling to spot the least resemblance between the wild-eyed recluse, hair unkempt, beard matted and skin crusted with grime, and the urbane priest, immaculately turned out even after scrabbling up the rutted path.

'We're both loners, sickened by so much of what goes on in the world. But at least he was brave enough to turn his back on it. Whereas I…? You know what's the most unconscionable of the many unconscionable things I do?' Duncan shook his head. 'Offering marital advice to newly engaged couples. What on earth can they hope to learn about sustaining a relationship from a man whose closest companion is his dog? Brandy!' he yelled in a voice that belied any claim of affection. 'Pay no attention, I'm just an old grouch! There's nothing like being the vicar of a small seaside parish to make you despair of your fellow man.'

'I'd have thought it was quite the opposite,' Duncan said, disturbed by the new edge to Henry's disenchantment. 'Here, people have the space to see the bigger picture. In a city there are too many distractions.'

'Have you taken a look at my congregation lately?' Henry asked, as they traipsed beneath a vault of interlaced branches and out into the empty car park. 'Don't worry, that's not a dig.'

'Not lately, no,' said Duncan who, now that his mother received Communion at home, only accompanied her to the Easter Vigil and Midnight Mass on Christmas Eve.

'A few old ladies currying favour with the Almighty. The odd young man struggling to sublimate his passions. A handful of pushy parents desperate to get their kids into the nursery school. I'm starting to think that the most honest service we provide are the weekend teas for cliff walkers.'

Brandy tumbled back to them as they entered the home stretch.

'What you need is a holiday,' Duncan said, prescribing a remedy that he himself had failed to take. 'When was the last time that you had a complete rest?'

'Where would I go? Who with?' For an anxious moment, Duncan feared that he had laid himself open to an invitation.

'How about a pilgrimage to the Holy Land?'

'You are joking?' Henry said, stopping short.

'Yes of course,' Duncan replied, blushing.

'Maybe what I need is a complete change? Mine's one of the few remaining jobs for life, barring madness or scandal and, come to think of it, not always then. What I admire about you, Duncan, is that you genuinely believe in what you do. You put your heart and soul into that paper. But what about me? Do I believe in the Church or am I simply too old and scared and jaded to move on?'

'I can see why you'd have doubts about the Church, but surely you believe in God?'

'Do I? Or am I spouting the same cosy formulas I learnt

as a child? I moan about my workload but, really, I should be grateful since it keeps me from having to think. Every day we learn more about mankind and our place in the universe. Religious experience itself has been linked to some kind of brain dysfunction. And here am I, clinging to a belief system that hasn't changed in two thousand years!'

'Isn't that the point, if you think its truths are eternal?'

'I have to think they're eternal or how else could I justify them? Yet all I see are people tailoring God to their own needs: I'm lonely, so Christ was an outcast; I'm suffering, so He heals my pain; I'm poor, so I'll reap my reward in heaven. How is that any different from a sun- or rain- or fertility-worshipping pagan?'

Emerging from behind an overgrown hedgerow, they found themselves facing the north wall of St Edward's, a fourteenth-century flint rubble church with a slate roof and a crenellated bell tower that might have been transplanted from the ruins of Francombe Castle. The round-arched porch was the sole vestige of an earlier Saxon structure, although its celebrated gargoyle, reputed to date from the tenth century, was now so weather-worn as to seem almost benign.

'Maybe there's no difference,' Duncan replied. 'But when I gaze up at this glorious church, there seems to be all the difference in the world.'

'Be warned, I have as little time for guidebook Christians as for biblical literalists.'

'No, it's not the building itself that moves me – though I agree it's spectacular – but the tradition. I look at it and see all the people who've worshipped here down the ages, dedicating the best of themselves to God.'

'What I see is a church that's in urgent need of repair: a church built on a rock which, after centuries of subsidence, is at risk of collapse. If I were Matthew Arnold, I could turn it into a metaphor, but I'm not, so I have to live with the inconvenient facts.' Henry opened the lychgate and they entered the churchyard. 'I'll just pop into the vestry. I need to clean myself up and fetch my communion set before we go to your mother's. Are you coming in?'

'I'll wait out here. Muddy shoes.'

Giving him a quizzical look, Henry walked up to the porch where he struggled with the high-security locks, newly installed after a spate of ecclesiastical burglaries. Brandy, showing rare disloyalty, remained with Duncan as he climbed over the gravestones, challenging himself as he had done since childhood to decipher inscriptions so eroded that they might as well have been written on sand.

Brandy's jubilant lap of the churchyard alerted Duncan to Henry's return. After leaving the unsuspecting dog at the vicarage, the two men drove to Ridgemount. As ever on approaching his family home, Duncan felt a pang more suited to one who made less frequent visits. From its fluted chimney stacks and pedimented gables to its mullioned windows and pillared porch, the large red-brick Victorian house exuded solidity. The distinctive fire escape slides on the three top floors had been added after the previous building, a six-teenth-century farmhouse, had been reduced to ashes, along with its occupants, when a lovelorn ploughman took revenge on the dairymaid who had jilted him. Forty years earlier, the mere mention of the man, whose ghost was reputed to haunt the grounds, had been enough to give Duncan nightmares. The ghosts who haunted him now, however, were both more benevolent and more insidious. There was his grandfather who had bought the house in the late 1920s and so skilfully assumed the style of a country gentleman that, shortly before his death, he had declared his greatest disappointment to be his grandson's poor seat on a horse; and his grandmother, who was so cowed by her husband's aspirations that she had withdrawn into herself, reluctant even to visit the nursery for fear of saying the wrong thing. There was his much-loved nanny who had vanished one day with no explanation, until

Alison revealed triumphantly that she had been caught 'going to the toilet with Daddy', leaving Duncan feeling disgusted, betrayed and, for a few months, intensely religious. Above all, there was his father himself, whose lavish bonhomie as he opened the house to friends, neighbours, business associates and vintage car enthusiasts had endeared him to everyone except his son.

His father's presence remained so palpable that Duncan could still smell the citrus tang of his eau de cologne as he stepped out of the car and half-expected to see him standing at the door. Instead, they were greeted by Chris, the chubby, balding thirty-five-year-old, whose diverse roles as his mother's carer, cleaner, cook and confidant led her to describe him as her general factotum, although Chris himself, with a degree of self-mockery that Duncan had yet to penetrate, favoured either 'maid-of-all-work' or 'aide-de-camp'. He ushered them into the overheated drawing room where Adele was sitting with her feet on a beaded gout stool, reading a large-print library book. In Henry's honour, she was wearing a new violet jersey dress and lavender cardigan, set off by an amber brooch and necklace. An ash-blonde plait lay curled on her shoulder like the fraying trim of an old armchair.

The faint whiff of decay emanating from his mother's cheek made Duncan grateful that Henry merely shook her hand. After submitting meekly to her stock rebukes that he was neglecting himself, he sat down in his father's wing chair and listened with amusement as she complimented Henry on his elegance. Although she addressed him with the same mixture of archness and condescension that she did any unattached man, Adele approved of Henry. In contrast to his predecessor, who had insisted on weighing the demands of his parish against those of his growing family, he had both the time and the temperament to minister to her needs. Even the mild high church tendencies that had initially aroused her suspicions turned out to be a blessing, since the clouds of incense that irritated her chest gave her the perfect excuse to request Communion at home.

Adele had suffered from asthma ever since her father's suicide. He was Stafford Lyttleton, whose renown as the composer of *The Sacred Knot* and *Agincourt*, and founder of the Early English Music Society had been eclipsed by his subsequent association with Mosley's Blackshirts, for whom he wrote several marching songs. He had been interned along with other leading party members in 1940 and, although he renounced his fascist views on the revelation of the death camps, his reputation was irrevocably damaged and his music no longer played. In 1948 his wife divorced him, forcing the nine-year-old Adele to testify to his cruelty in court. Three years later, deserted by his friends, disowned by his colleagues and reviled by the public, he shot himself.

Her father's blighted career and violent death imbued him with an air of tragedy in his teenage daughter's eyes, which intensified over time. Confident that posterity would recognise his genius, she had welcomed the approach five years ago of a BBC director who professed to be a devotee of his music. Duncan blamed himself for the ensuing disaster, but he had been as blinded by his mother's enthusiasm as she had by the director's blandishments. Far from offering a reappraisal – let alone, rehabilitation – of his grandfather's work, the programme was a rehash of the anti-Semitic controversy, fuelled by a newly discovered cache of wartime letters. Moreover, by imputing his politics to misplaced patriotism and his downfall to scheming rivals, Adele sounded less like a loving daughter than a fascist apologist. Convinced that she had disgraced both herself and her father's memory, she became a virtual recluse, rarely leaving the house and seeing only those friends who bolstered her belief that she was the victim of a media plot rather than her own ill-founded loyalty.

With Henry ready to administer Communion, Duncan slipped out of the room as discreetly as possible. He wandered into the kitchen, taking the opportunity for a few words with Chris, who he realised with a pang had a more accurate picture of his mother's state of mind than he did himself. Both gentler and more proficient than her long string of female carers, Chris was an effeminate man whose voice and manner suggested that he deplored the disappearance of old stereotypes. At his interview he had allayed Duncan's doubts about his fitness for the job, explaining that he had been brought up by his grandmother and had always preferred the company of older people, whom he found 'restful'. He had worked as a catering manager, most recently at the Princess Royal, but gave it up when his grandmother suffered a stroke, caring for her until her behaviour grew so bizarre that she was admitted to Castlemaine, where she had already crossed swords with Sheila's mother.

'All quiet on the home front?' Duncan asked.

'The food's in the oven. Just waiting for them to finish their hocus-pocus. You're having baked halibut.'

'Sounds delicious.'

'I'd planned on monkfish, but then I thought his reverence might take offence,' Chris said harshly, his customary warmth deserting him when it came to Henry.

'You must admit it's kind of him to come here in the middle of a busy day when my mother is perfectly capable of going to tomorrow's service,' Duncan said, never sure whether Chris's antagonism were directed at Henry personally or at his Church.

'Why? He gets a free lunch.'

Duncan gazed around the room, eager to change the subject. 'I approve of your choice of reading matter,' he said, spotting the *Mercury* spread out on the table.

'Sorry to disappoint you, but I've been polishing the silver before your sister arrives.'

'Ah, well,' Duncan replied, smiling thinly. 'At least it has its uses.' With nothing more to say but reluctant to leave on a negative note, he drifted into the pantry, casually inspecting the shelves until Henry appeared at the door.

'You're safe to come back and join us,' he said. 'Now that she's taken communion, your mother's treating herself to a small sherry. She says whenever you're ready, Chris.'

'Oh, I'm ready. Ever-ready, that's me. Like the battery, on and off in a flash.'

Although he had twice caught Adele sharing a television supper with Chris, thereby breaking two of her strictest rules (always eat at the table and never with the staff), Duncan thought it wiser not to press him to join them with Henry present. Besides, Chris seemed to relish the mixture of deference and control that came from serving. Having tempted Adele to three spoonfuls of lemon cream sauce, he left the room with a fluting 'Bon appétit!'

'My spies tell me that you're making big changes to the church hall,' Adele said to Henry, with a teasing allusion to the gossipy friends who were her eyes and ears in the outside world.

'We're having a mural painted, if that's what they mean.'

'What for?' Adele asked bluntly.

'Mother!'

'No, it's a fair question,' Henry said. 'The hall as it stands is dreadfully dull. This is the perfect opportunity to jazz it up a bit. At the same time we're helping a young offender.'

'Who? How?' Adele asked.

'The painter. He was convicted of spraying graffiti on the promenade shelters. The new ones near the fishermen's memorial.'

'We campaigned against them for months,' Duncan said. 'Not only are they quite out of keeping with the existing architecture, they offer little or no protection against the elements.'

'Don't try to tell me he was objecting to the design,' Adele said severely.

'In essence, yes,' Henry replied. 'The graffiti were highly sophisticated. His defence was that he was an artist.'

'Isn't everyone these days? Some of us have had the privilege of knowing a true artist.'

'Yes, of course,' Henry said smoothly. 'The magistrates showed leniency. Instead of sending him to jail, they ordered him to pay compensation and do a hundred and fifty hours of community service, which turned out to be the redecoration of the church hall. Joel Lincoln, one of our churchwardens, knew Jordan's story. He proposed that, rather than just filling in cracks and painting walls, he design a mural.'

'Making the punishment fit the crime,' Duncan said.

'In effect,' Henry said. 'The PCC saw some of his work.'

'In the shelters?' Adele asked.

'No,' Henry replied, laughing. 'On paper. It showed real talent. He – Jordan – was the best artist in his school. His teachers wanted him to go to college, but there was some family crisis and he left at sixteen to work in a garden centre. This is his chance to express and redeem himself at the same time. Everyone's happy.'

'Are we?' Adele asked. 'I mean *are they*? Does this mural have a subject, or is it modern?'

'The Garden of Eden.'

'That can hide a multitude of sins. How far has he got with it?'

'It's hard to tell. He's put dustsheets up to stop people peeking. It's only fair to respect an artist's privacy.' Adele harrumphed. 'The one person he appears to have taken into his confidence is Mary.'

'Which Mary?' Adele asked.

'My Mary,' Duncan said. 'The cleaner at Mercury House. I had to cut back her hours and knew that Henry was looking for someone for the church.'

'I hope you haven't cut them too much. I've yet to meet a tidy journalist.'

'No matter what I do, I can't seem to persuade my mother of the need to economise,' Duncan said to Henry, his mock exasperation masking genuine concern.

'The truth is that my darling son is ruining himself to provide for a woman who deserted him.'

'You know very well, Mother,' Duncan said sharply, 'I stopped paying Linda alimony when she married Derek. All I give her now is maintenance for Jamie.'

'But why, when Derek is so much better off?'

'Because he's my son.'

'So you'll indulge your son but you're happy to deprive your mother?' She turned to Henry. 'I have nothing except my widow's pension – my widow's mite – and the tiny dividends from the paper.'

'All I've asked is that you keep a close watch on expenditure. This house is a money pit.'

'Which is your excuse for putting me in a home?'

'Who mentioned a home? I simply said that it might be time to look for somewhere more manageable.' At their father's death, Duncan and Alison had agreed that it would be cruel to ask their mother to leave her home of twenty-five years. Now, as he gazed around the large dining room, where an air of neglect confirmed the general impracticality, he feared that the cruelty might be forced upon him. 'Look at me!' he said, in a bid to distract himself as well as Adele. 'I've been reduced to living above the shop.'

'Don't say that!' she said, her face crumpling. 'I've asked you never to say that.' She turned to Henry. 'He only says it to annoy me. It's a charming flat. Your father never complained, even though he sometimes had to sleep there for nights on end.' Duncan blanched, wondering if she were genuinely ignorant of his father's affairs or feigned judicious blindness. 'I used to tell him that he had printer's ink for blood. But he was always a gentleman. He had standards.'

'Yes, Mother, standards that almost bankrupted the company: standards I've been paying for ever since.'

'No, not living standards,' Adele said fiercely. 'Moral standards. There were certain subjects he would never permit to be mentioned in the paper.'

'You mean like "Local Businessmen in Crooked Deal" or "Council Chief Accepts Backhander"? And why? Because they all played golf together or hobnobbed at the races.'

'No, like "Café Owner Fined for Asking Woman to Breast-feed in Toilet".'

'It's the law, Mother. The woman had a perfect right.'

'There were children present. And Muslims. You're the one who's always telling us we should be sensitive to other cultures.'

'Now you're being ridiculous. We simply reported the story; we didn't print a photograph of the breasts.'

'First you embarrass your readers; now you're embarrassing our guest.'

'Hardly,' Duncan said, although a glimpse of Henry staring at his empty glass unsettled him. 'What's the Synod line, Vicar? And has it changed with women priests?'

'I was just wondering,' Henry said, 'whether being banished to the café loo might be the modern equivalent of "No room at the inn".'

'No, it might not,' Adele retorted. 'It takes five minutes to prepare a bottle. But these women are out to shock. They're as bad as the nudists at Salter Cove. No wonder there's all this sexual perversion in the woods – forgive me, Henry,' she said, mistaking the nature of her offence.

'Now you've lost me,' Duncan said.

'It's easy enough to blame the men and it's true that they lack self-control, but are they entirely at fault? Time was when women maintained an air of mystery. Now everywhere you look there's flesh. And not only flesh but bodily functions. Breastfeeding. Childbirth. Of course the men are so put off that they turn to one another.'

Duncan was astounded, as much by the fact of his mother's theories as by their tenor. Further discussion was prevented by the return of Chris, who cleared the plates and brought the dessert. 'Queen of Puddings,' he said, looking straight at Henry.

'My favourite!' Adele beamed. 'Bang goes my diet!'

'You know what they say: a little of what you fancy.'

As he listened to their banter, Duncan marvelled once again at his mother's ability to compartmentalise her life, exempting from her strictures a man whom he presumed to be no stranger to 'sexual perversion', albeit in the comfort of his own home.

After lunch, they returned to the drawing room where Chris had set out Alison's tennis trophies. Duncan wondered if his sister welcomed the reminder of her teenage triumphs or if, were she ever to pay an impromptu visit, she would be relieved to find them locked away. Every burnished cup and shield bore the dent of unfulfilled promise. Even in the cut and thrust of women's tennis, few careers had collapsed as spectacularly as hers. She had always been superstitious, whether lining up her dolls at bedtime or listening to Janis Joplin's 'Try (Just A Little Bit Harder)' when preparing to sit an exam, but what was an innocent quirk elsewhere became a burning obsession before a match. She wore the same skirt for years after a surprise victory at Eastbourne and whistled the first two bars of the *Doctor Who* theme whenever she left the changing room. Most crucial of all was that she tapped her foot every third or fourth step – he forgot which – when coming out on court. In the 1986 Wimbledon semi-finals, a noise in the crowd distracted her and she lost count. Her game fell apart and she was defeated in straight sets. The following year, despite reaching the third round in the French Open, she failed to qualify at home. In 1988 she retired, aged twenty-six.

Privately, Duncan suspected that she had used the distraction as an excuse, either because she knew that she had reached her peak or else to escape the weight of public expectation. She had capitalised on her celebrity by launching a range of women's sportswear, which, more than twenty years on and despite an ill-advised venture into ski accessories, continued to sell. Yet, although aware of the *Mercury*'s parlous state, neither she nor her husband and business partner, Malcolm, had once offered to waive her dividend. Equally galling was to hear his mother explaining why Alison's business commitments prevented her from making the two-hour trip from London more than three or four times a year, while protesting roundly whenever Duncan, who brought out a twenty-four-page newspaper every Thursday, cancelled one of his twice-weekly visits. At forty-eight, he was inured to his mother's favouritism but, as he had made clear in terms that even she could not ignore, the one thing that he would not countenance was that she should extend it to the next generation, belittling Jamie by praising his high-achieving cousins.

Alison arrived on Sunday evening, two hours behind schedule. Duncan met her at Francombe station and drove her to Ridgemount where, knowing that Adele wanted her daughter to herself, he declined the cursory invitation to dinner. The following morning the three reconvened in the *Mercury* boardroom, the annual general meeting being one of the rare occasions on which his mother ventured out. As sole directors and equal shareholders, they constituted the entire gathering. Even Dudley Williams, the company accountant, mindful of the balance sheet he himself had drawn up, had sent a certified copy of the accounts, advising Duncan that there was no point in paying him to attend.

The boardroom itself harked back to happier days, with its ormolu chandelier, oval walnut table, burgundy velvet curtains and portraits of Duncan's four predecessors on the oak-panelled walls. While his mother and sister glanced through their agendas, Duncan studied the men from whom he had received his dual inheritance. In pride of place above a heavy sideboard was his great-great-grandfather, a printer and stationer who had founded the paper to exploit his press's spare capacity and, during its first ten years, had brought out the four-page weekly single-handed, a practice to which his descendant feared that he might soon be forced to revert. By its sixth issue, the *Mercury*'s masthead declared it to be 'Francombe's most influential journal, with a wide readership among the nobility, gentry, clergy and visitors of the borough and its vicinity', a claim that was borne out as its circulation soared, while the various *Observer*s, *Advertiser*s, *Herald*s and *World*s folded.

After forty years at the helm, the founding editor was succeeded by his son, who ran the paper from his father's death in 1909 until his own in 1927. Although the briefest stewardship to date, it was commemorated in the finest portrait – by John Singer Sargent – on which, as he gazed at its delicate palette and subtle brushwork, Duncan struggled not to place a price tag. His great-grandfather was in turn succeeded by his son, Duncan's grandfather, for three decades chairman of the Francombe Conservative Association (and knighted for political and public services in 1958), who used the paper as a platform for his reactionary views, denouncing 'the socialists and rabble rousers who are infecting our town'. Alone of the four editors, he did not die in harness but retired in 1960 in favour of Duncan's father, who took a more conciliatory line both in his editorials and with his staff, less by virtue of broader sympathies than from a longing for an easy life.

Afraid of provoking industrial unrest, he put off investment in new technology and, when he suffered a fatal heart attack in March 1986 while proposing the loyal toast at a Rotary Club lunch, the paper was still produced using hot metal. The inflated wage bill was just one of the drains on the company, which, as Duncan found out, owed almost £800,000 to the bank and the Inland Revenue. He was in his second year at Cambridge when his father died and, although expecting to succeed him in due course, he had never imagined that it would be so soon. It rapidly became clear that the only way to save the *Mercury* and to safeguard his mother's future was for him to come home and take over the paper, the wrench of leaving his friends assuaged at least temporarily by the spate of media interest in 'the youngest editor in the country'. He persuaded his creditors to defer their demands while he streamlined the basic operation. After selling off the bookbinding and design divisions, the staff houses and sports fields, and taking out an additional loan, he invested in a web-offset printing plant, imposed new working practices and prepared to confront the print unions. To his boundless relief, their attention was focused on events in Wapping and he was able to impose the necessary redundancies with minimal conflict.

For the first fifteen years all went well. He had the satisfaction of restoring both the paper's finances and its reputation. He was fortunate in that the *Francombe Citizen*, a free sheet launched in the early Eighties to counter what it saw as the *Mercury*'s subservience to the Chamber of Commerce and the Town Hall, collapsed shortly after his arrival. Its much-vaunted independence was not matched by editorial rigour and, despite a public appeal for funds, it was bankrupted when the Mayor successfully sued it for naming his underage 'carjacker son'. With his rival removed, Duncan established a culture of campaigning journalism at the *Mercury*, which led, among other things, to the rescue of a mobile library, two day centres and an ancient right of way through a pop star's new estate; the exposure of the Council's attempt to conceal the Saxon burial site under a proposed multi-storey car park; and the jailing of the director and two nurses behind the sadistic regime at Rosecroft psychiatric hospital.

In recent years, however, the position had changed dramatically. The growth of the Internet and effects of the Recession had dealt the paper a double blow from which it was doubtful it would ever recover. There were only so many pages that the paper could lose before it lost its purpose. In the past, Duncan had been able to assign a two-man team for two months to a single story; now, with a skeleton staff, he could barely afford to send one man for a day *on patch*. The news team spent as much time paraphrasing press releases as filing their own reports. Without the resources to hold the police and the Council to account, the paper was as tame as it had been in his father's day, although the imperative now was economic rather than social. It sometimes felt as if the journalists' sole function was to supply copy in order to sell advertising. But advertising revenue had fallen by seventeen per cent over the past year. Classified adverts had migrated to the web, where they would be up and running in an hour rather than the week it took at the *Mercury*, and display adverts, once a guaranteed moneymaker, had been hard hit by the cuts in public spending and dearth of job vacancies.

Turning to his mother, who was chiding him for the dead bulbs in the chandelier, Duncan felt a pang of unease. His sustained attempts to spare both her and Alison the full extent of the paper's decline would make today's disclosures all the more shocking. They were granted a temporary reprieve when Sheila brought in tea and digestives, Duncan noting with relief that she had abandoned the broken-biscuit assortment, which, penny-wise, she had taken to buying at the market. Adele, whose coolness towards her husband's pretty young secretary had survived both his death and Sheila's lost looks, complimented her on a hairstyle that had not changed in a decade. Alison, with the solicitude she could afford on a flying visit, asked after her mother, flinching at the vehemence of the response.

'I did everything I could to keep her at home. The doctor said I'd end up being put away myself. Duncan will tell you … I'm sorry.' Clasping her hand to her mouth, she fled from the room.

'Did I miss something?' Adele asked.

'I presume she's finally put the old witch away,' Alison replied. 'Not a moment too soon if you ask me.'

'That's a dreadful thing to say. I wouldn't wish it on my

worst enemy,' Adele said, breaking off as though to evaluate the hyperbole.

'She had no choice. Her mother's behaviour grew more and more deranged. She buried all Sheila's dolls in a flowerbed. They might still be there if her neighbour's dog hadn't dug up a bone. She ordered vast quantities of maternity clothes to be sent to her here at the office, although how much of that was madness and how much malice I wouldn't like to say.'

'So where is she now?' Alison asked.

'Castlemaine. The old Regis Hotel next to the golf course.'

'A dreadful place,' Adele said. 'One of the residents fell and was found screaming in agony. But she had liver cancer, so they just upped her morphine without even bothering to give her an X-ray. It was six months before they discovered she'd broken her hip. Chris told me. I asked Duncan to put it in the paper. That was a genuine scandal – not like the filth he prints now.' Duncan shook his head as Alison gazed at him nonplussed. 'But no, he's afraid of offending the staff in case they refuse to take me!'

'What?' Alison said.

'Where's all this coming from, Mother?' Duncan asked. 'Castlemaine is a psychiatric geriatric home. No one's suggesting that you need psychiatric care.'

'Or geriatric care, I hope,' Alison added.

'Well, she does have Chris.'

'He's my housekeeper,' Adele said, reclassifying him to suit the occasion. 'I can't be expected to run Ridgemount all alone.'

'I agree. Which leads us neatly to the matter in hand. You both have a copy of the accounts.'

'Do we have to look at it all, dear?' Adele asked, as reluctant as if it were a list of fatty foods.

'Not unless you want to. It doesn't make for pleasant reading. For the third year running we've registered a loss.'

'Surely that's just on paper?'

'Well, everything's on paper, Mother. But we owe the bank in the region of £400,000. We took out a five-year loan, which we're due to repay in January. That won't be possible, though I'm confident we can negotiate a deferment. Even with the slump in property prices, this building is excellent collateral.'

'How could you let everything slide?' Alison asked.

'We're hardly unique,' Duncan said, bridling at her tone. 'Do you have any idea how many local papers have gone under in the last few years? At least we're still here.'

'Just!' Alison replied.

'No one predicted the rise of the Internet. We thought we'd see it off the same way that we saw off local radio and the free press in the Nineties. Plus, the economic downturn has wiped out our advertising.'

'I've always said that there are too many adverts in the paper,' Adele interjected.

'Yes, Mother, but we operate in the real world. Anyway, it's nothing new. I was looking through the archives. In the very first issue, great-great-grandfather published a list of all the hotel and lodging-house guests in Francombe, presumably in the hope that they'd each buy a copy. I've been thinking of reviving the practice – although no doubt it's in breach of some EU privacy law.'

'And I don't suppose that anyone today would choose to broadcast their presence in the town.'

'Nonsense, darling,' Adele said crisply. 'Now that the carpet factory has been shut down, the sea is perfectly safe.'

'But the web has hit more than advertising. The management consultants I brought in – '

'I don't suppose they came cheap,' Alison said.

'No, but highly recommended. They told me that local newspapers were of no interest to the young. "That's not such a problem here," I said, "Francombe has an ageing population." "By young," one replied, "we mean anyone under sixty."'

'That's young to me,' Adele said.

'So did these highly paid consultants come up with any solutions?' Alison asked.

'Nothing that I hadn't already considered and discounted.'

'Such as?'

'Selling out to one of the conglomerates. Along with ninety-five per cent of the local press. Becoming a four-page insert in a generic paper produced in Ipswich or Basingstoke. Turning back the clock to when great-grandfather bought syndicated stories from London *off the shelf.*'

'But would it solve the problem?' Adele asked. 'Would they pay?'

'They'd pay something. The title has value, as does the building, although as I said they'd switch production elsewhere. I can't see them keeping on any of the staff except maybe Brian. When you tot it up, there's almost a hundred and fifty years of loyalty in that office. I can't just chuck it away.'

'They'd be given decent settlements, surely?' Alison said.

'That depends on the deal. One thing I know for certain is that I'd be first for the scrapheap.'

'Nonsense,' Adele said. 'You do a marvellous job. Everyone says so. Regional Editor of the Year.'

'In 1994, Mother. The only award we've had since then was second prize in the "Britain in Bloom" Business Category last summer.'

'Maybe it'd be for the best if we did sell up,' Alison said gently. 'Especially for you, Duncan. While there's still time for you to try something else.'

'It's not just the staff I'd be letting down. What about them?' Duncan asked, pointing at the portraits. 'How can I walk away from everything they achieved?'

'They're dead! Besides, what do you think will happen after you're gone? I can't see Jamie sacrificing himself to save the paper – always supposing there's still a paper to save. And would you want him to waste his life the way you've done?'

'Waste my life?'

'I didn't mean that. You know what I mean. You were a talented kid; you wanted to write. I still remember that sketch show in Cambridge. Instead, you chose to moulder in this two-bit town.'

'You can be very hurtful sometimes,' Adele said. 'Francombe dates back to before the Conquest. It's twinned with Cadiz.'

'What choice did I have? Do you think I wanted to abandon my friends and my studies and my hopes and ambitions and practically everything else that makes life meaningful at twenty-one … no, not just at twenty-one, but for ever? If I hadn't come back and sorted out Father's mess, the paper would have gone under. Your shares would have been worthless. I'd have managed; I'd have got a grant to finish my degree and then, who knows, maybe a traineeship with the BBC? But what about you and Mother? What would you have done?'

'If you want to play the martyr, that's your affair, but please leave me out of it. I never asked you for anything.'

'It was spring 1986. Ring any bells? You were training for Wimbledon. I was so proud of you; we all were. I was determined to make sure you'd have nothing else on your mind.'

'That was very kind of you. And I'm sorry if I didn't appreciate it. But as you'll remember, my own career didn't go exactly to plan. Besides, it was nearly thirty years ago. What does it have to do with what's happening now?'

'Not once in all that time have you offered to give up – or even reduce – your dividend.'

'I'm not a mind reader, Duncan. Why didn't you let me know how serious things were?'

'I tried, but every time the occasion arose, you started talking about your own expenses. The crippling cost of sending two boys to school and then to university, of keeping up the flat in London and the house in Oxfordshire and the villa in Umbria.'

'That was a bargain. It was practically a shack when we bought it.'

'You made me feel that, far from asking you to cut back, I should be offering you more. My marriage suffered; Linda said that I always put you and Mother first.'

'Don't you dare lay that on me! Cause of break-up? Cruelty. Husband's? No, sister-in-law's!'

'I'm just trying to make you understand. And, yes, maybe the fault was mine. I was too proud; I didn't want to lose face in front of my big-shot sister. Even so, you should have been more aware. You may not come here that often, but you're not blind. You've seen the size of the paper and the state of the building; you've seen me. Look at me! I pay myself less than I pay my junior reporter. The only reason I'm not dossing in one of the hostels is that I'm living above the shop.'

'That isn't amusing, Duncan!' Adele interjected. 'I've told you before.'

'I'm sorry, Mother, but there's more at stake than your sensibilities.' Duncan turned to Alison. 'These clothes aren't fit for a scarecrow. Is it any wonder my son's ashamed to be seen with me?'

'That's not the reason,' Alison said.

'What?'

'Nothing. I don't know why I said it.'

'That's enough now, both of you,' Adele said.

'Tell me! What did you mean?'

'Believe me, it's nothing. Just something he said when we met at the Science Museum: how he pretended that you were his teacher rather than his father, because you insisted on reading out all the labels and quizzing him on every exhibit. You never let things be fun.'

'He said that?'

'It's not important. Remember how embarrassed we used to be about Dad.'

'Your father was always impeccably dressed,' Adele said.

'He wouldn't have dreamt of leaving the house without a buttonhole. And I was the only one he allowed to pin it on. You'd do well to take a leaf out of his book, darling.'

'Thank you, Mother, I'll bear it in mind. Now, unless either of you has anything to add, I vote that we approve the accounts.'

Three

Disturbing Incidents at Nature Reserve

by Rowena Birdseye

Thursday, 17 October 2013

Sussex Police and Francombe Borough Council Rangers are stepping up their patrols of Salter Nature Reserve following complaints from visitors who have suffered unwelcome advances in the woods.

Steve Flanders, 27, of the Sussex Orienteering and Wayfarers Society (SOWS) reported that during an all-day event on Saturday, 5 October one of their members, who did not wish to be named, became detached from the main group after slipping on a stile. While removing his jogging bottoms to examine his leg, he received several inappropriate offers of assistance.

In a separate incident, June Holder MBE, Honorary President of the Sussex branch of the International Mycological Association, was inspecting a newly discovered Bearded Tooth Fungus on the evening of Tuesday, 8 October. She returned to her car when she was spotted by a friend out walking his dog. As they chatted through the window, he was accosted by a middle-aged man who asked if there were 'any decent action inside'.

Miss Holder and her friend took some moments to realise what he meant. 'When we did, we were most upset,' she said. 'My friend gave him the rough edge of his tongue and he slunk off with his tail between his legs. Salter Woods are home to many rare fungi – not just the Bearded Tooth but the Pepper Pot and twenty-eight species of waxcaps. It would be a tragedy if this precious natural resource were threatened by the activities of a few degenerates.'

Asked by the *Mercury* to comment on the incidents, Len Barber, 62, Parks and Open Spaces Manager, Francombe Borough Council, stated that 'I and my staff are fully committed to protecting the biodiversity of Salter Nature Reserve and to ensuring that all sections of the community are able to enjoy its facilities. Following these distressing reports, I myself paid two visits to the woods, the first at dusk on Friday and the second on Sunday afternoon. I'm pleased to say that I witnessed no improper behaviour and, although I was dressed in bright clothing, no one approached me apart from a vigilant Ranger.'

Poring over the new issue of the paper, which Sheila had placed on his desk together with a piece of her home-made gingerbread, as long-established a ritual as his mother's pinning of his father's buttonhole, Duncan felt confident that it was worth 80p of anyone's money. Even in a quiet week for news, there was a disturbing report on the youths stealing alcohol hand gel from the Princess Royal lavatories, sensitively written by Ken who, ever since his daughter's death, had kept all hospital-related items for himself. There was a second such story, also by Ken, of a woman on Incapacity Benefit who, having been referred to a review panel, swallowed a cocktail of drugs to lend credence to her claim. She misjudged the dose and was now on a life-support machine facing the prospect of permanent brain damage. Contrast was provided by heartening features on the Francombe Talking Newspaper's autumn tea party for its clients and the Hedgehog and Garden Bird Rescue Team's round-the-clock care for an orphaned hoglet.

His sole reservations concerned the front page. Should he have opted for Brian's report on the successful trial of seagull-proof dustbin bags on the Pudsey Road estate, rather than Rowena's on the continuing problems at Salter Nature Reserve? On balance, he had decided that, whatever the benefits for residents who would no longer wake up to rubbish-strewn lawns, the bin bags were too parochial and, notwithstanding his mother's charge that he was wallowing in filth, had ventured back into the woods. This had the additional virtue of mollifying Rowena, who had complained of being given fewer lead stories than the unseasoned Brian, hinting darkly that she might have a case for gender discrimination.

After reading the paper from cover to cover and finding only one glaring typo in the description of the St Anselm Over Sixties Ladies' Bowling Champion as 'unbearable' (he waited grimly for the howls of protest), he made his way into the reporters' room.

'Great work this week, everyone. Lovely splash on the Nature Reserve, Rowena.'

'It'd have been a damn sight better if the copy hadn't been hacked to bits,' she said, scowling at Stewart.

'Come on! You did go a little OTT on the debris,' Stewart replied. 'It read as if it had spilt out of one of Brian's dustbin bags.'

'It wasn't me; it was the fungus woman. She said there were places you couldn't move for condoms. A couple of times she thought she'd found some exotic mushroom which turned out to be a spunk-filled johnny.'

'She said that?' Stewart asked.

'I paraphrase.'

'Look on the bright side,' Brian said. 'At least they're practising safe sex.'

'Oh yes, laugh at everything, why don't you?' Brian assumed an air of injured innocence. 'I don't want to come on all Mary Whitehouse, but it isn't only plants that are being harmed. Look at that tramp!'

'There's no news yet on Dragon's assailants,' Duncan said. 'The police are keeping an open mind.'

'Too open if you ask me,' Rowena replied. 'It's a no-brainer. After his crusade against cruising.'

'I never had you down as a closet homophobe,' Brian said.

'Oh, grow up! But why can't they screw around in private like everyone else?'

'It's not just gays who gather in the woods,' Ken said. 'It used to be a popular spot for kids to make out.' Duncan blushed as a torrent of long-forgotten memories – New Year's Eve, Daisy Clarke, dampness first on the ground and then on his groin – engulfed him. Across the room, he heard Brian mutter something about being 'a good boy, tucked up by ten with the latest Jane Austen', but the subsequent banter was lost in the thrill of his recollections. He was sixteen and home for the Christmas holidays, struggling to re-establish old friendships after two years at Lancing. One of his friends – it might even have been Geoffrey Weedon, but he suspected that that was his mind creating patterns – had thrown a party and Daisy, already a notorious nymphet, had chosen 'the posh boy' to help her see in the New Year. Revelling in the resentment of boys he had planned to appease, he accompanied Daisy to Salter, the long trek punctuated by regular gulps of cider. The romance of the woods soon faded as they tripped over concealed roots, flinched at sinister murmurs and shivered in the cold. Any advantage he might have gained by offering Daisy his jacket was squandered when, in a rush of ardour, he compared her to Titania and she accused him of smut.

With a modesty that belied her reputation, she declared French kissing to be vile and at first denied him any greater licence than to fondle her breasts through her blouse, but when he threatened to walk away and leave her she relented, agreeing to take off her bra provided that he took off his pants. His delight in her gentle breasts was matched by her disgust at his rigid penis. Refusing to believe that it was involuntary, she charged him with 'cheating'. She allowed him to stroke her nipples, pushing him away when he grew too ardent, but refused to touch his penis, claiming that it was dirty. He begged her to hitch up her skirt but, hissing with outrage, she insisted that he wasn't going 'to get two for the price of one'. They appeared to have reached an impasse when, telling him to 'get on with it then if you're going to', she lay back and pulled down her knickers, clenching her thighs so tightly that all he could do was rub his face in the silky threads of her pubic hair. Almost at once he felt a starburst in his blood and fell back, gasping. Granting him no respite, she jumped up, adjusted her clothes and gazed at him in triumph, as if her pleasure derived not from desire or even contact but from witnessing his loss of control. 'You happy then?' she asked, which struck him as the cruellest question he had ever heard.

'You're smiling, Duncan,' Sheila said approvingly, as she entered the room with a plate of broken biscuits.

'Am I?' He felt the muscles in his jaw tighten and wondered

how an experience that had been so wretched at the time could be so affecting in retrospect. 'I suppose I am.' He had rarely seen Daisy after that, as the distance between Francombe and Lancing lengthened and his old friendships descended into polite indifference or, in Geoffrey's case, bitter rivalry. Twenty years on, they had briefly resumed contact when Linda, intent on a home delivery, selected Daisy as her midwife. Daisy's manner towards him was so relaxed that he started to wonder whether he might have dreamt the entire episode. Nevertheless, he had thought it only right to tell Linda who, far from feeling threatened by their past intimacy, maintained that it validated her choice. Full of respect for Daisy's professionalism, he had to admit that there was a kind of symmetry in watching the birth of his first child alongside the woman with whom the whole adventure had begun.

'If it is, then it's the boys who put pressure on them,' Rowena was saying. Duncan made an effort to concentrate on the exchange. 'Don't you remember that headmistress describing how girls as young as ten were being bullied into giving boys blowjobs on the grounds that they weren't real sex? What do you think?' she asked Sheila, stifling her usual contempt for her views in a bid for female solidarity.

'Oh, you know me,' Sheila said, looking ruffled. 'I'm just an old fuddy-duddy. In my day, blowjobs were something you got at the hairdresser.' Brian sniggered; Ken and Stewart laughed; even Jake cracked a smile. After a moment of confusion, Sheila assumed a knowing expression as if to claim credit for the joke. 'Minds like sewers! I'm surprised at you, Brian Gannon,' she said, simpering at her favourite, oblivious to the biro he was holding on which a busty blonde lost her bikini every time that he tipped it up. 'Don't let these reprobates lead you astray.'

'Not me,' he said. 'Innocent as a lamb.'

Sheila raised an eyebrow, the effect of which was to set her blinking uncontrollably. 'Now I can't stand here gossiping all day,' she said. 'Don't forget the children will be here at two. Mary's coming in at noon to give the place a good clean. It looks like a pigsty.'

'Great,' Stewart said, as she left the room. 'So now it will smell like one too.'

'That's not kind,' Duncan said.

'Come on, Duncan. You may shut your eyes to what's happening in the woods,' Rowena said, refusing to let the matter drop, 'but you can't ignore what's under your nose.'

'Literally,' said Jake, laconic as ever.

'You'd have thought things would improve when her husband gave up his boat,' Stewart said.

'But it's not a fishy smell,' Brian said. 'More like carpet glue.'

'That's enough!' Duncan said. 'You should be ashamed of yourselves. Mary has more to worry about than a spot of BO. For her last birthday I bought her an M&S cardigan. Sheila caught her taking it back and exchanging it for food.'

Cheered by their chastened expressions, Duncan returned to his office, where he set out to read the FA report into racist chants on Francombe FC terraces, but his mind remained fixed on the Nature Reserve. Rowena might attack him for wilful blindness, but her wild speculation about Dragon's attackers made him all the more determined to stick to his editorial code. Dwindling circulation notwithstanding, exposure in the *Mercury* had the power to destroy livelihoods, even lives. Unlike civic corruption or corporate fraud, sexual impropriety did not warrant the risk. Nothing in his sorely debased profession disgusted him more than the tabloid tactic of pandering to prurience under the guise of upholding morality. So when the duty manager of the Metropole Hotel had rung with the story of a TV weatherman who spent the night with a hostess from the Sugarbaby nightclub, he put down the phone, just as he did when a disaffected Liberal activist alerted him to the party chairman's affair with the Labour leader's wife. The dilemma had been more acute when a police contact brought him a list of local paedophiles during the furore over the Hawksey Road Children's Home but, with the fate of Bert Ponsonby's mother in mind, he had deemed the threat of vigilantism to be greater than that of the men's reoffending and refused to publish their names. Linda was outraged, repeatedly asking what he would have done had Jamie been one of the victims. He replied that his gut reaction would have been different but his decision the same. The *Mercury* was Francombe's conscience, not its judge and definitely not its executioner.

The visit of a group of sixth-formers from Francis Preston High School gave him the opportunity to canvas the views of the next generation. With the exception of Brian, who enjoyed showing off to his near contemporaries, the staff regarded such visits, of which there were four or five a year, as both an intrusion and an embarrassment. To Duncan, however, they were a far more agreeable part of the *Mercury*'s outreach programme than the editor's surgeries, where he was at the mercy of every crank who harangued him on the paper's failure to highlight the menace of chewing gum residue on pavements, or the piles of foreign-language pamphlets in the library, or even a next-door neighbour's overgrown privet hedge. While his ultimate aim was that an insight into the workings of the paper should encourage the pupils to become readers, his immediate one was that they should become contributors. It was hardly surprising that the *Mercury* held little appeal for the young when they were barely mentioned outside the sports section. In conjunction with their English teachers, he had adopted a policy of offering each visiting group a features page to fill with any topic of their choice. Although this had so far resulted in a series of earnest pieces on overpopulation, genocide and global warming, rather than the first-hand concerns for which he had hoped, he valued the experiment and planned to extend it.

Duncan welcomed the group in the opulent entrance hall

that had once doubled as an enquiries office but was now used largely for deliveries. Their relief at being out of school mixed with resentment at remaining constrained, the eight girls and six boys milled around the hall as if defying him to excite their interest. After a brief conversation with their teacher, Pete Daniels, a slight man in his late twenties with haunted eyes, a wispy beard, bolo tie and canvas belt with *Wolverine* embossed on the buckle, Duncan was ready to take up the challenge.

'Good afternoon, everyone. I'm Duncan Neville, the *Mercury*'s editor, and I'd like to welcome you to your paper. That's neither an empty phrase nor an advertising slogan. My great-great-grandfather founded the paper. My family and I are the proprietors, but you are the owners.'

'Aren't they the same thing?' asked a girl wearing three of the colour-coded jelly bracelets that Rowena had analysed in a recent feature. Duncan trusted that she had chosen the black, blue and green bands for aesthetic effect rather than sexual symbolism.

'A thesaurus would tell you yes, but I beg to differ. In a very real sense, the paper belongs to Francombe. You're the ones who read it, who advertise in it, who ring in with stories and complaints and yes, sometimes even with compliments. So I say again you're the owners. We're merely the guardians.'

'Which bit's mine then?' asked a boy with his collar button undone and his tie knotted halfway down his chest.

'The bit you buy for 80p every Thursday,' Duncan replied.

'You must be joking!'

'So how many of you do read it?'

The silence was broken by a red-haired girl with translucent skin and freckles. 'I sometimes see it at my nan's,' she said. 'She gets it to find out who's died.'

'That's a perfectly valid reason,' Duncan said, cutting into the laughter. 'It's part of life in a community. In today's world, too many communities are splintered. Some of you may not know your neighbours.'

'Some of us may not want to,' the boy with the open collar remarked.

'A community needs a voice and, at the *Mercury*, we try to provide it,' Duncan said, careful to avoid the 'losing its voice losing its heart' analogy after his encounter in the spring with the daughter of a sign-language user.

'My dad used to get it,' a girl said. 'But he stopped when you banned an ad for a BNP rally.' Duncan looked at the girl, whose pasty face and flaxen hair took on a sinister hue. 'He said it was censorship.'

'For the greater good,' Duncan replied, remembering his battles not just with Trevor Vale, the advertising manager, for whom scruples belonged to papers with healthy balance sheets, but with Ken Newbold, a staunch libertarian, who held that extremists had the right to damn themselves from their own mouths.

'Aren't the BNP part of the community?' asked a solemn-looking boy.

'Individually, of course,' Duncan said, 'but I'd maintain that, collectively, they're out to destroy everything community is about.' He wondered whether the two Asian pupils might wish to add something, but both stood studiedly impassive. 'In the end, it's my job as editor to take the tough decisions. And I hope that you might be able to persuade your father to give us another chance,' he said to the flaxen-haired girl.

'Like he listens to me!'

He ushered the pupils upstairs to the boardroom where, because there were too few chairs, he suggested that some sit at the table and the rest on the floor. 'Perhaps we should work on the principle of ladies first?' he said to three boys who had scrambled for seats.

'That's sexist,' one of the girls said, plumping herself down on the carpet.

'I'm sorry. I didn't realise,' Duncan replied. Catching sight of his father's portrait, he felt a surge of sympathy for the man

whose old-school courtesies, however self-serving, had made
for a gentler world. With a glance of irritation at Pete Daniels
who, having ceded responsibility for his charges, had wandered over to the window to check his texts, Duncan outlined
the history of Mercury House.

'It was built in the 1920s by my grandfather to accommo-
date both the offices and the presses. Back then he had a staff
of around forty: reporters, secretaries, printers and so on.
Every inch of the premises was occupied. The foundry and
presses were in the basement (nowadays the paper's printed
off-site). On the ground floor, where you came in, were the
switchboard and mailroom, the advertising department' –
he swallowed the words for fear of a further challenge – 'and
storage space for the huge rolls of newsprint. On the first
floor, as well as this boardroom, there was the reading room
where we still house the archives. On the second floor, which
we're about to visit, were the reporters' room and the editorial
offices (that's the only area that's remained much the same),
and the case room where the linotype operators set the page.
On the third floor was the art department, along with a bookbinding and design studio, which was a separate business. On
the top floor was a small executive flat where the editor could
stay overnight.' He refused to admit to these children that it
had become his permanent home. 'At the very top were the
turrets. You can't have missed them; they're a local landmark.
Any ideas what they were for?' He held the silence for longer
than was comfortable. 'Pigeons.'

Hoping for a response, Duncan had to settle for a repeti-
tion. 'Pigeons?' asked a gawky boy with green-tinged teeth.

'Yes. Don't forget, in the Twenties phones were scarce.
Pigeons were used to file stories till the end of the decade.'

'You mean they trained them to speak?' the boy asked, to
general derision.

'Sure,' one of his companions replied. 'They said: "I am a
retard."' The second burst of laughter prompted Pete Daniels

to look up briefly from his phone and utter an ineffectual 'Hush!'.

'No,' Duncan said gently. 'Reporters would take them to football matches and send them back with copy in cylinders attached to their legs.'

'Didn't they bite?' The gawky boy's attempt to redeem himself led only to further jeers.

'The birds' legs, dumbo, not the reporters',' a pug-nosed boy interjected. 'Can we climb up to the top?'

'I'm afraid not. The staircases aren't safe. After the pigeons were axed – not literally,' he added, seeing the Asian girl's widening eyes, 'we used one of the turrets as a dark room, but now we no longer have a photographic department it's fallen into disrepair.'

'Was that where the pervert worked?' asked a girl with a disconcertingly deep voice.

'I beg your pardon?' Duncan asked.

'The paedo,' the girl replied, as even the most listless faces around her grew animated. 'My mum said he was done for taking porno pictures of kids and he hanged himself before his trial.'

'His name was Bert Ponsonby and he was an outstanding photographer,' Duncan said, determined to give him both his identity and his due. 'No matter where you sent him, he instinctively knew how to get the best shot – even group portraits that can look so dreary.'

'But he was a paedo,' she insisted.

'He had a weakness,' Duncan replied to the girl, whose doe eyes and full lips would undoubtedly have played to it. 'I'm really not happy discussing it, but if gossip is still doing the rounds after twenty years you ought to know the facts.'

'Why?' the pug-nosed boy asked.

'Because there's more than one side to every story,' Duncan replied, taken aback. 'And Bert's ... Ponsonby's story' – he quickly added the surname for fear of sounding complicit

– 'is a constant reminder to me of that. It's true that Bert took photos of girls – young women – in inappropriate poses.'

'You mean like this?' One of the first boys to grab a chair now leant back in it, with his legs splayed and a finger inserted in his pouting mouth.

'Something like that,' Duncan said, above the wolf whistles. 'The vast majority of them were in their late teens and early twenties, but a couple were underage. Up in the dark room, he was able to develop the pictures undisturbed. One girl – or it might have been her parents, I forget – contacted the police. After a lengthy investigation they decided not to press charges.' He turned to Bert's principal accuser. 'That's where your mother was wrong, there would have been no trial. I kept Bert on. In retrospect it was a mistake, but I accepted the police line that he hadn't coerced – let alone, interfered with – any of the girls. Indeed, given his medical condition' – he gulped – 'that wouldn't have been possible. But there was another paper in Francombe at the time, the *Citizen*, which liked nothing more than to disparage the *Mercury*. They covered the story in the most scurrilous way, insinuating that we knew and even condoned Bert's … Ponsonby's actions. An unholy alliance of parents, feminists, church groups and the National Front held a series of protests outside the building, haranguing my staff as they came to work. Worst of all, the *Citizen* published Bert's address and a gang of thugs firebombed his house. The only person in at the time was his mother.'

'Was she killed?' a moon-faced girl asked, in between chewing a hank of hair.

'Not in the fire, no, but she had a heart attack and died in hospital a week later. The morning after her funeral, Bert drank bleach.'

'Then he really was a weirdo,' said the girl with the jelly bracelets.

'It wasn't for pleasure!' Duncan replied in amazement.

'Quite the opposite. There were plenty of his mother's pills in the bathroom that he could have swallowed, but he seems to have wanted to suffer.'

'That's what I said. A weirdo!'

The conversation having taken an unforeseen turn, Duncan was eager to move on. He led the pupils to the second floor where he introduced them to the reporters, the lack of response to his suggestion that they might have seen them around town a reflection less of the children's apathy than of the reporters' increasing confinement to their desks. His assertion that staffing cuts had resulted in a leaner, closer-knit team was challenged when one of the boys noticed the Readers' Response chart pinned to the wall.

'What's this?' he asked.

'It's a record of the number of letters, phone calls and emails each of the news team have received,' Brian said.

'Who's Rowan?'

'Rowena!' she corrected him sharply. 'The token woman.'

'You've not got half as many ticks as Ken and Brian.'

'That's because I'm not given half as many big stories,' she replied, poised to break ranks.

'Or else because young Brian here gets all his friends to write in,' Ken said quickly.

'That's libel,' Brian said. 'And I'll be calling you lot as witnesses.' Some of the children looked worried. 'But then our venerable news editor knows all about libel, don't you, Ken?'

'Private joke,' Ken said, looking unamused.

Several of the boys gravitated to the sports desk where Jake, with rare loquaciousness, expounded his pet theory that sports journalists had a unique insight into human nature at its most primal. Meanwhile, two of the girls were inspecting Humphrey. Brian lost no time in regaling them with the bear's history, before offering to take a picture of one of them sitting on its lap. 'Though you're wasting your time, sweetheart. You'd have more fun sitting on me.'

Her frosty stare triggered Duncan's fears that Brian had confirmed the paper's reputation for depravity.

'It stinks!' she shrieked, jumping away.

'Behave, Dawn!' Pete Daniels said, finally putting down his phone.

'It stinks of puke.'

'It's old,' Stewart said, as Ken looked away. 'We keep it on for sentimental reasons.'

'Gross!' Dawn said, frenziedly rubbing her face.

Duncan strove to rescue Ken from the shame that was visibly engulfing him. 'I don't want to sound boastful,' he said, 'but at the *Mercury* we see ourselves as the first line of defence for local democracy. Who's going to hold the Council and the police and big business to account if we don't? Not the national press with its metropolitan bias and celebrity culture. Not Internet bloggers who are subject to little or no scrutiny. Not the large media groups whose loyalty is to their share-holders rather than their readers. To take one example, Ken here spent two months undercover as a porter at Rosecroft psychiatric hospital in order to expose its brutal treatment.'

'Didn't they realise?' asked a boy in a jacket two sizes too small for him.

'Realise what?' Ken replied.

'Who you were.'

'As far as they knew, I was on the staff.'

'So you got two pay packets?' the boy said. 'Cool.'

'The commitment of our journalists is the *Mercury*'s great-est resource and, if I may say so, it's also one of Francombe's. Ken's been with us for over forty years. He joined the paper straight from school, just like Brian.'

'Are you going to stay here that long?' Dawn asked Brian.

'They'd have to nail me down by the ... by the fingertips.'

'Brian's going to be whisked away to Fleet Street,' Ken said. 'You'll see, in two years' time he'll have his own column in the *Sun* and be hosting makeover programmes on Sky.'

'At least I won't be a sad old alkie drinking to forget where his life fell apart.'

'You must have noticed a great many changes in your time here, Ken?' Duncan interjected.

'The journalists who were here when I arrived were giants, not like the pygmies they send us now.' Ken glared at Brian. 'My first news editor was a man called Frank Brocklehurst. He knew every street – every house – in Francombe. He was respected by one and all from the local villains to Lord Cradwyck at Seacombe Court. A hard drinker and chain smoker, he'd sit at his desk with his hip flask and his packet of Players. He used his typewriter as an ashtray. Clouds of smoke would rise up as he pounded the keys. I thought it was magic. I still do.'

'What about Health and Safety?' a soft-spoken girl asked.

'That's right, love. What about them? What the bloody hell about them?'

Ken pushed through the clustered pupils and left the room. Brian lifted an invisible glass to his lips, provoking a few nervous giggles.

'As you see, the news desk is nothing if not lively,' Duncan said. 'Creative tension's the name of the game. I don't know if any of you are considering a career in journalism, or if anything you've seen today may have encouraged you...' His voice trailed off in embarrassment.

'How much do you get paid?' the deep-voiced girl asked.

'It's not a profession you go into for the money.'

'What do you go into it for then?' the boy with the green teeth asked.

'Job satisfaction. The chance to make a difference. I'm sure that Mr Daniels would say the same about teaching.'

Mr Daniels looked unconvinced.

'But how much do you get paid?' the girl insisted.

'It all depends. Top Fleet Street columnists can earn fortunes. Salary levels at the *Mercury* are more modest. If you start straight from school, it's around £12,000.'

'Is that all?' one of the boys asked. Two of his companions spontaneously edged away from Brian, who stared at his feet.

'Maybe those of you who are putting together the features page for next month will feel differently. I'm really looking forward to seeing what you come up with. But there are other ways to get involved. I'd encourage you all to send us letters.'

'On what?' the girl with the jelly bracelets asked.

'Anything you feel passionate about.'

'Then you can write about Bilbo,' said a boy with a prominent Adam's apple, before playfully punching his undersized neighbour.

'Matters you think are of public interest. We get far too few letters from anyone under twenty.'

'We get far too few from anyone under fifty,' Brian said, in a vain attempt to restore his standing.

'How much do you pay for them?' the deep-voiced girl asked doggedly.

'We don't. You get the pleasure of seeing your name in print and knowing that you're contributing to the community.'

'Why? We're not on probation,' one of the boys said. Duncan forced a laugh, breaking off abruptly when the boy's affronted expression showed that he was serious.

The visit over, Duncan escorted the pupils to the main entrance where several put on headphones as if needing the security of their self-regulated worlds. As he returned to his office, his fears for the future extended far beyond that of the *Mercury*. Age might have warped his perspective and memory his perceptions, but the children seemed so inert, devoid of the hope and enthusiasm that had marked his own adolescence. Depressed by the encounter, he was determined to do everything he could to motivate Jamie, the occasion presenting itself barely an hour later, when he drove to Francis Preston for the parents' evening.

On his arrival at the school two years before, Jamie had been horrified to learn about the *Mercury* visits, making him swear never to invite groups from his year, a vow from which he trusted that he would be released before it was put to the test. Meanwhile, Jamie had even tried to deter him from attending tonight, maintaining that 'Mum should come on her own, since she's the one who sees me do my homework'. To Duncan's relief, Linda had demurred and was waiting for him now at the school gates. Apologising for the traffic, he kissed her cheek, a greeting that seven years after he had lost the right to greater intimacies still felt forced.

A sense of regret enveloped him, as it did for the first few minutes of every meeting with his former wife. He was grateful that Linda, who had once been so attuned to his slightest mood, now seemed oblivious to his distress.

'You're looking well,' he said, with a pang of guilt. It was undeniable that, despite the strain of looking after Rose, she had blossomed since the divorce.

'You might have made more of an effort,' she said quietly. 'That jacket should have gone to Oxfam years ago.'

'I offered, if you remember.'

'I'm sorry. Forget I mentioned it.'

It was not just his wardrobe he had offered to change in a last-ditch attempt to keep her from leaving. He had promised to spend less time at the paper and at Ridgemount and even, with a resolve that she had discounted, to enrol on a basic DIY course.

'We've both tried, Duncan,' she had said. 'But it's not working.'

'I've not tried hard enough.'

'It's not you that's the problem. It's us.'

He knew, of course, that she was right. He had been told as much when they announced their engagement, not only by his mother and sister but by impartial observers like his Cambridge writing partner, Angus Carmichael, who described them as 'the original odd couple: he's very *mot juste* and she's very just a mo', a jibe that had sounded even more cruel when he was forced to spell it out to Linda. She, however, shrugged it off with her usual good grace, suggesting that they nick-name each other 'Justin' and 'Mo', a riposte that had even impressed Angus. She was so beautiful and passionate and full of life that he was astounded when she accepted his pro-posal. Although she refused to admit it, he was convinced that she had been influenced by her mother, for whom mar-riage to the editor of the *Mercury* promised the prestige and security denied to the owner of a seafront souvenir shop. So the reality of his sixteen-hour days and permanent financial worries, not to mention his Klinefelter Syndrome, must have struck her a severe blow.

A stronger and more self-confident man or simply a more aggressive one – the KS at work again – would have fought harder to save his marriage, but his overriding desire, as he explained, was that she should be happy.

'You're the kindest man in the world,' she said. 'You'd better watch out; you'll be fighting off the women once they know you're back on the market,' a prospect that would have alarmed him had he not found it risible.

'What about you?' he asked. 'How are you going to fight off all the men?' It was then that, having sworn there was no one else involved, she told him about Derek.

He may have lost her love but he was determined to retain her affection. Against both his solicitor's and his accountant's advice he made her an unduly generous settlement. It was not until he realised that this was the same policy he had adopted with his redundant printers that he felt the full force of his self-disgust.

When his mother reproached him with profligacy, he insisted on the need to maintain good relations with Linda for Jamie's sake, but privately he knew that it was for his own. As they made their way down the drive, looking every inch the established couple, he comforted himself with the thought of the many occasions on which they would meet as parents: sports days and speech days, wedding day and christenings;

breaking off abruptly when he remembered that the failure to live in the present had been one of Linda's recurrent charges against him. They walked into the entrance hall, its drab plasterwork relieved by a huge collage of brightly painted inner soles. He stepped up to inspect it more closely when Linda pointed to Jamie, who was lurking behind a frosted-glass partition.

From his expression it was clear that he did not entertain any sentimental notion that his parents would get back together. On the contrary, his life seemed to be predicated on keeping its disparate elements apart. Duncan gazed at his son and wondered how it was that so surly a face and clenched a body could unleash such a torrent of love in him. He longed to hug him but knew that the contact, barely tolerated in private, was utterly taboo in public. So he contented himself with reaching out to squeeze the nape of his neck, but Jamie's simultaneous recoil meant that, instead, he clipped his ear.

'What was that for?' Jamie asked indignantly.

'I'm sorry. I didn't mean ... I was just trying to squeeze your neck.'

'Why?' Jamie asked, staring at him with even more than the usual dismay.

'I'm sorry.'

'Don't worry, darling,' Linda said. 'You know your father's all thumbs. Come on, we're due at the science lab in five minutes.'

They made their way down a battleship-grey corridor and into a large concrete yard surrounded by assorted classrooms and subject blocks. Spotting a couple peering forlornly at a rudimentary plan, Duncan considered asking Jamie to direct them, but the absence of their own child, combined with Jamie's protest that only 'nerds and dweebs' accompanied their parents to these evenings, dissuaded him. They entered the lab where the chemistry, physics and biology teachers sat at adjacent desks like rival politicians at the hustings. As they headed for Mr Lawson, the chemistry teacher, they passed a couple being led away by a boy whose pustular face and gangling demeanour seemed to bear out Jamie's claim.

'Isn't this ghastly?' the woman said gaily. 'Almost like being back at school yourself.'

'I know,' Linda replied. 'I feel as if I'm the one being judged.'

Duncan wondered whether he were alone in welcoming these events, which offered some acknowledgement of his role in his son's life. He still bridled at the memory of having to beg the Headmistress for a copy of Jamie's report. Francis Preston held two parents' evenings a year, the first in October to discuss how the children were settling in and the second in March to review their progress. Tonight, he and Linda were to see eight of Jamie's teachers, all for the first time.

'It's quite different from my own school,' Duncan said. 'Parents were actively discouraged from participating in their sons' education. They had to make do with a skimpy report at the end of term where academic results jostled with height, weight and general behaviour. Each subject master was allotted a single line, but some confined themselves to a single word. The classics master wrote his in Greek!'

'Let's go, Dad!' Jamie hissed. 'We're next.' With a nod to his fellow parents, Duncan followed his son past a row of sinks, as pristine as those in a kitchen showroom. 'Why do you have to do that?'

'Do what? I was just making conversation.'

'Yeah, about how you went to public school.'

'I never mentioned Lancing.' He turned to Linda. 'Did I mention it?'

'Hurry up,' she said. 'Mr Lawson's waiting.'

Lawson, a genial Scot whose soft burr might have been designed to reassure anxious parents, lavished praise on Jamie's work and the meeting went well, or so Duncan thought until they were back in the yard and Jamie upbraided him for once again speaking out of turn.

'Why did you have to tell him chemistry was my favourite subject?'

'Isn't it?' Duncan asked, recalling their various experiments in Adele's garage when even she played a part, feigning terror at the thermite-and-ice explosion.

'Maybe, two years ago.'

'So what is it now?'

'Why should I have one? I'm not a kid.'

'Don't be rude, Jamie,' Linda said. 'Your father's only asking.'

While appreciating her support, Duncan resented the intervention, which made him feel even more of an encumbrance, like an elderly uncle whose whisky breath and whiskery kisses Jamie had been ordered to endure. He had heard, not from Jamie himself but from Ellen, whose son Neil was in the same class, that they had been assigned a local history project. He had offered Jamie the run of the *Mercury*, proposing that they explore the archives together, only to learn that he had already spoken to Derek, who had agreed to help him with the evolution of the wheel park. Every attempt that he made to bond with his son was similarly thwarted. Sometimes, to ease the pain, he pretended that he had, after all, sent him to boarding school and that his truculence was emotional reserve. It rarely worked.

They headed for the language lab where two French teachers sat at either end of an airy room flanking a German colleague. Duncan's disappointment that Jamie was not being taught by the glamorous young woman, whose looks and smile would inspire diligence in even the most indolent teenage boy, was compounded by the discovery that his actual teacher, Mr Berwick, had a heavy lisp, which did not bode well for his pupils' pronunciation. He declared Jamie's grammar and comprehension to be satisfactory but his vocabulary deficient, at which Linda remarked that, while hopeless at languages herself, Jamie's father was bilingual and she had suggested that they speak French to each other. For once, Duncan shared Jamie's horror. They found it hard enough to communicate in English without venturing into French.

The session was cut short by Mr Berwick's alarm, which, while ensuring that he stuck to his schedule, seemed to convey his contempt for the entire exercise.

'So who's next on our dance card?' Duncan asked, as they hurried past the German teacher, who was loudly berating an inept pupil in front of her hapless parents and several onlookers.

'Maths,' Jamie replied.

'That was always my worst subject,' Duncan said.

'That doesn't mean it has to be mine! Isn't it bad enough that I've got your ears – and other things?'

Duncan sat through the meeting with the maths mistress in a state of creeping anxiety. Jamie looked both surprised and grateful that he failed to object when Linda questioned the need for him to be set so much homework. All he could hear was that ominous coda echoing in his ears. His earlier irritation that Jamie had bungled the arrangements, leaving them with a twenty-minute gap between maths and ICT, was replaced by relief that it afforded him a chance to talk to Linda. So, asking Jamie to give them a moment in private (a request that was accepted with predictable alacrity), he joined her at a scuffed Formica table in the canteen.

'So he knows about the KS?' he said.

'Why do you ask?'

'That "and other things" he slipped into the conversation. Or do I have more characteristics that he finds repugnant?'

'No,' she replied quietly. 'It's the KS.'

'He does know that it's not been passed on? He does know that we took the tests? He does know that he's in the clear?'

'Yes, he knows all that.'

'Then why did he say it?'

'Just to be hurtful. You know what he's like.'

'No, not really. That's the trouble; I don't.'

'I sometimes think he makes himself as obnoxious as possible in order to challenge us.'

'Well it works. So who told him: you or Derek?'

'It wasn't like that. We were having a discussion about Rose and genetics, and why you and I had no other children.'

'Then it was you?'

'No, it was Derek.'

'Of course. Any opportunity to emasculate me in the eyes of my son.'

'That's not true! He's not like that. Besides, if anyone feels emasculated, it's him. By Rose.'

'You've always told me how good he is with her.'

'He is. He'd do anything for her. He spent all last weekend making two new pages for her chart.'

'There you are then.'

'Though it's not the same as doing things with her. He'll do everything he can to help her communicate, but he communicates so little with her himself.'

'We each of us play to our strengths,' Duncan said, surprised to find himself defending Derek.

'I feel disloyal talking to you like this,' Linda said, 'but who else is there? My mother wouldn't understand and my girlfriends would gossip.'

Duncan would have felt happier about keeping a place in her life had it not been that of elder brother. It was clear that neither she nor Derek regarded him as a threat.

'It was Ellen who gave us the idea for the new pages, one on Rose's guinea pig and the other on *Shrek*. She's worked wonders with Rose in just an hour a week. And I gather she's made her mark elsewhere.'

'Did she tell you that?'

'Who else? I'm not your mother with a network of spies that would put MI5 to shame! I think it's great.'

'What's great?'

Duncan looked round to find that Jamie had returned.

'That Dad has gone out on a couple of dates with Rose's speech therapist.'

'Pass the sick bag,' Jamie said, adding vomiting noises for good measure.

'They weren't dates,' Duncan said, amused by Jamie's reaction. 'We walked up to the Old Lighthouse and went to the cinema.'

'So I heard,' Linda said.

'She mentioned the film?'

'I'm not sure that *Firehawk 2* was top of her list.'

'Those multiplex schedules are so hard to follow.'

'I warned her that anyone who went out with you had to double-check all the details. I learnt that on our honeymoon.'

'You didn't tell her that!'

'Tell her what?' Jamie asked.

'You know the story: how we got to Heathrow and your father found that his passport had expired. So we ended up going to Penzance instead of Rome.'

'Still, it worked out all right,' Duncan said.

'Yes, it did,' Linda said, smiling.

'Ellen's here tonight, with her son Neil,' Duncan said. 'I'm surprised we haven't bumped into them. I've promised to drive them home at the end.'

'Why?' Jamie asked.

'Partly because her car's being serviced and partly because I want to. Strange as it seems, I miss you when you go back with your mother and Derek.'

'So you'll take him instead?' Jamie asked angrily.

'Of course not,' Duncan said. 'I'm taking his mother. He's just "along for the ride".'

His cowboy drawl failed to lighten the mood.

'He's a dickhead,' Jamie said. 'Good luck to him. I wouldn't be seen dead in that heap of junk.'

'Don't be mean,' Duncan said, relieved at the return to a routine grievance. 'I know you're fond of the old girl really.'

'It's a dinosaur, Dad. It's twenty years old. And it's an it, not a she!'

'Don't let Rocinante hear you say that!'

'Who names a car after a horse? Who names a car after anything? You're so lame!'

'That's unkind, Jamie,' Linda interposed.

'And you're a hypocrite!' he replied, leading Duncan to wonder what she had said about the car. 'Come on then if you're coming; we'll be late!'

Jamie strode out of the canteen and down the corridor, checking at intervals that his parents were following.

'I'm sorry,' Linda said. 'He's tired. We were up half the night with Rose. I tried not to wake him but...'

'He can always come and stay with me if it helps.'

'No, that would be even more disruptive. Besides, he'd see it as a punishment. And it's not his fault.'

Startled, Duncan wondered whether Linda meant what she had said or if lack of sleep had taken its toll on her too. They made their way into the computer room for the regulation ten minutes with the ICT teacher, whose plaudits for Jamie's first forays into web design led Duncan to quip that they could do with him at the paper, to Jamie's undisguised disgust. As they walked back to the science lab, this time to see the biology teacher, Duncan waved at a vaguely familiar figure, only to realise that she had featured in the *Mercury* after being sprinkled with her dead husband's ashes. Watching her trail behind a girl, presumably one of her vengeful daughters, he felt a surge of sympathy for a parent even more beleaguered than himself.

On leaving the science lab, they returned to the main building for their final three appointments, with the geography, history and English teachers. After two hours, the strict time slots had been abandoned, inducing forced smiles and frayed nerves on all sides. There were worse places to wait, however, than the brightly coloured geography room with

its patchwork of flags covering the ceiling and alphabeti-
cal posters, from the Arctic to Zanzibar, dotting the walls.
After an encouraging session with the geography mistress,
who praised Jamie's start to his ecotourism coursework, and
a depressing one with the history master, who lamented his
failure to come to grips with the Industrial Revolution, they
moved to the English room, where Duncan greeted a lesbian
couple whom he had championed in his column when a hate
campaign forced them to withdraw as classroom helpers at
their younger daughter's primary school. He nodded to Irma
Lewis, one of Linda's oldest friends, who walked in a few
minutes later with her son, a contemporary of Jamie's. To his
surprise, after giving them a guarded smile she crossed to the
opposite side of the room.

'Is she embarrassed to see us together?' Duncan asked
Linda.

'No. Why should she be?'

'I wondered if she'd bitched about me after the divorce and
now she's worried you'll say something.'

'She bitched about you when we were married and I told
you at the time. In fact she's just a prize bitch,' Linda said in a
stage whisper. The two English teachers looked up and two of
the parents looked round. Irma stared intently at a wall chart
of tricky plurals.

'I thought she was one of your closest friends.'

'She was, until Rose.'

'I see.'

'Do you? Yes, of course you do. You'd have seen straight
away. It took me a little longer. She had Kate at about the same
time. She was terrified I might want them to play together. I
don't suppose even she could have thought that cerebral palsy
was catching. So it must have been a fear that she'd cramp her
style.'

Distressed by the pain in Linda's voice, he reached for her
hand, heedless of what Irma or anyone else might think. They

sat in silence until called up by Mr Brighouse, who introduced himself while stirring his tea with a marker pen. The
session started badly when he referred to Jamie, whom he
had been teaching for the past six weeks, as Jeremy, and grew
worse when he dismissed Duncan's concerns about Jamie's
grammar with the claim that apostrophes, prepositions,
double negatives and the like might be left to the computer
style check. Conflict was narrowly averted when Linda, well
versed in Duncan's views, hustled him away. As they walked
back to the school gates, where she had arranged to meet
Derek and he to meet Ellen, he inveighed against the decline
of standards.

'You get what you pay for,' Jamie said. 'If you wanted me to
have a decent education, you should have sent me to Lancing.'

'Where's that coming from?' Duncan asked, astonished. 'I
thought you wouldn't be seen dead in a public school.'

'I'm just saying ... Tim and Graham went to Wellington.'

'Aunt Alison and Uncle Malcolm have much more money
than I do. Besides, it's against my principles.'

'Right. Just don't blame me when I fail my GCSEs.'

'Now you're being childish.'

'Here we are,' Linda said, as they arrived at the gate to
find Derek shouting into his mobile. Without drawing
breath he kissed Linda and high-fived Jamie. Then, removing his headset, he held out his hand to Duncan. 'How's it
hanging, young man?' he asked, a question that Duncan at
first assumed was addressed to Jamie.

'Fine, thanks,' he replied. 'And you?'

'Can't complain. So how did it go, Jamie? Straight As, I
hope.'

'The teachers were very pleased with him,' Linda said.

'Though there's room for improvement,' Duncan added, to
his instant regret.

'Well, we can't all be as brainy as our dads. I remember
when I used to take home my end-of-term report (none of this

touchy-feely-meet-the-teachers stuff in those days). I'd always
try to find ways to get rid of it. One time I told my mum that
the dog had eaten it. Which would have been fine except that
we had a cat.'

Duncan was unsure whether to be more depressed by
Derek's joke or Jamie's laughter. He longed for them to leave
him in peace to wait for Ellen, but Derek seemed to sense his
discomfort and spin it out.

'It's been a busy day at the office,' he said. 'Geoff showed
me the plans for the pier, hot off the drawing board. I know I
shouldn't say anything in front of the press – '

'Oh, I switch off sometimes,' Duncan said.

'But they'll cause quite a stir. I can see my man here is
already getting ready to pounce. Don't worry, we won't take
it personally.'

'I hope not.'

Even as he voiced the hope, Duncan knew that it was in
vain. However hard he tried to separate his personal and
professional dealings with the Weedons, Geoffrey made it
impossible. It was not Linda's affair with Derek that had set
them at odds, but his own alleged betrayal of their boyhood
friendship when he went away to school. For all Geoffrey's
claims that he was just a businessman, Duncan sometimes
suspected that his whole career had been driven by a desire
for revenge on the social and cultural values that Lancing
represented, and from which he felt excluded. A true child of
the Eighties, for whom price was the only measure of worth
and free enterprise of free choice, he had bought a series of
ailing companies and tumbledown properties and, through
a mixture of shrewd deals and sharp practice, turned himself
into Francombe's leading entrepreneur. Whenever Duncan
condemned a world in which cops no longer chased robbers
through the woods and shot them with pointed fingers but,
instead, sat in a video arcade and zapped them with heavy
weaponry, or families no longer splashed and swam in the

Olympic pool but gorged themselves on junk food while watching BMX races in the wheel park, Geoffrey launched a counterattack, accusing him of being out of touch, narrow-minded and, most damning of all, elitist.

'I look forward to seeing the plans,' Duncan said.

'You do that,' Derek replied. 'But a word to the wise. This is Geoff's biggest project to date. He won't take kindly to interference.'

'Say goodbye to your father, Jamie,' Linda said. 'We're late picking Rose up from Granny.'

'I'm hungry,' Jamie said.

'Then say goodbye … Look, there's Ellen.' Linda waved at Ellen, who walked towards them with Neil.

'I work with teachers every day,' Ellen said, after a brief exchange of greetings. 'But the moment I come here as a parent, I feel like a little girl again.'

'I'm the same with nuns,' Linda said, 'and I'm not even Catholic.'

'Still, the important thing is that they're happy with this one,' Ellen said, stroking Neil's hair.

'Leave it out, Mum!'

'Well done, Neil,' Duncan said. 'It can't be easy moving to a new school where they all know each other. Still, they're a friendly lot here, aren't they, Jamie?'

'You said we were going home, Mum,' Jamie said, his slighting of Duncan almost as marked as his coldness to Neil. 'I'm starving.'

'Of course. Growing boy alert! 'Bye, all.'

''Bye, Jamie,' Duncan called out as his son rushed into the street. 'See you on Sunday.'

'You said you'd speak to him!' Jamie stopped short and turned to Linda.

'It's your father's day,' she replied.

'But me and Craig are going cycling.'

'It's your father's day.'

'Your grandmother's looking forward to seeing you,' Duncan said.

'Oh great!'

Jamie stalked off, followed by Linda, who remonstrated with him, and Derek, who answered his phone.

'Boys,' Duncan said, shrugging. 'Not you,' he added quickly to Neil, who failed to respond. 'Shall we go? I'm afraid the car's a couple of streets away. I can drive it round.'

'I'm happy to walk,' Ellen said. 'How about you, Neil?'

'Not bothered.'

'We're all agreed then,' Ellen said brightly.

They made their way out of the yard, past the patchy lawn lined with pollarded trees, and into the ill-lit street.

'Good day?' Duncan asked, as he steered Ellen clear of a pothole.

'So-so. The family of one of my clients on the Edmund Hillary estate are being harassed by neighbours because two of the kids have learning difficulties. I spent all morning with their case worker and the Health and Housing team trying to get them moved.'

'Any luck?' Duncan asked.

'In principle. The problem is finding them somewhere safer. But this afternoon was great: my regular Thursday drop-in for kids and their parents. We had a real breakthrough with one little girl who managed to brush her teddy's teeth.'

'Big deal,' Neil said.

'It was for her. Now I'm shattered. I'd no idea that coming back to work would be so intense. It's not just that I'm older (which of course I am), but the job's changed. There's a whole lot more to fit in: home visits; conferences; reporting … We never used to write up so much. Plus there are the new health regulations. You can't just chuck toys in a drawer at the end of a session. Everything has to be carefully wiped.'

'The last thing you need is to go home and start cooking.

What do you say to some fish and chips? Do you like fish and chips, Neil?'

'Everyone likes fish and chips.'

'But Francombe fish and chips are special. The fish is freshly caught and the chips: well, they're special too. And the Mr Wu Fish Bar is the best in town.'

'Sounds good to me,' Ellen said. 'We must get a portion for Sue.'

'*Andiamo*...! Oh, just a sec.' Duncan stopped to inspect a flyer tacked to a lamp post.

'Is it an appeal for witnesses?'

'No, for a missing dog. Sorry, old habits die hard. My father taught me never to pass a lost pet notice without jotting down the details. Nine times out of ten it'll come to nothing, but you may get a decent human interest story – you know, the little kid who's lost the kitten she was given for Christmas, or even a bona fide scoop, like when we spotted that several Staffordshire bull terriers had disappeared and helped the police to break up a dog-fighting ring.'

They reached Duncan's Volvo Estate, which proved as obdurate as ever.

'How old is your car?' Neil asked.

'I bought her in 1992. You do the maths.'

'You're kidding me! My dad drives a Porsche Panamera.'

'I'm impressed,' Duncan replied, eliciting a grateful look from Ellen. The image of her former husband in his Porsche turned his own struggle to start up Rocinante into precisely the kind of virility test that he found ludicrous in others, the comparison growing more pronounced as he pumped the accelerator so hard that it risked flooding the engine. Finally, the car juddered into action and they headed for the Front.

'Are there a lot of blind people in Francombe?' Neil asked.

'Not that I know of,' Duncan said. 'Though there are certainly plenty who don't read newspapers. Why?'

'Look!' Duncan glanced in the mirror to see where Neil was

pointing. 'That's the second man today I've passed walking with his hands out like that.'

'They're drunks. You'll come across many more if you're in town on a Saturday night – which I don't recommend. They stretch their arms out in front of them to protect themselves when they fall.'

'So this is the kind of dump you've brought us to,' Neil said to Ellen.

'It's not that bad,' Duncan said. For all its tawdriness, he retained an affection for his home town. Yet, as they drove along the Front, past the rows of Victorian villas that had been converted into DSS hostels, their once elegant façades as run-down as their residents, he pictured how it must look to a newcomer. Unemployment, bankruptcy and drug use in Francombe were among the highest in Britain. Moreover, the influx of refugees and asylum seekers had created a host of social problems in a town where, previously, the only black faces had been in the minstrel shows on the pier.

'It's no wonder the kids lose hope,' he said, speaking his thoughts aloud. 'With youth clubs and other facilities cut, they gather out here with bottles of cheap supermarket booze, waiting for trouble. There's a group of them now.'

'Stop the car!' Ellen screamed.

'Is something wrong?'

'Just pull over, please.' Duncan did as she asked. 'Look, Neil! Isn't that your sister?' Duncan followed her gaze. He had not met Sue but if he had identified the right girl, the boy with whom – or rather round whom – she was entwined was Craig. She could not have picked a more inauspicious introduction to the youth of Francombe. Although too loyal to admit it, Linda clearly mistrusted her stepson. She had once let slip that she never left him alone with Rose after he expressed an unhealthy interest in her toilet arrangements. Duncan wondered if he had targeted Sue as the one girl who was ignorant of his reputation. He must have moved fast since he had known her only a few weeks. He winced as he realised that this was as long as he himself had known her mother.

Ellen leapt out of the car and Duncan followed a few steps behind, uncertain whether she would view his presence as an intrusion or as a support.

'You should be at home,' she said to the dark-haired girl wearing overemphatic eye make-up and lime-green leggings.

'Well, I'm not,' Sue said, emphasising her defiance by swigging from a bottle.

'Is that beer?' Ellen asked.

'No, it's Fanta,' Sue replied, to general mirth.

'Get in the car at once, please.'

'I'm with my friends, Mum!'

'You were supposed to be doing your homework.'

'I'm with my friends!' She took another swig from the bottle and swung on the balustrade.

'You're making a spectacle of yourself.'

'Look who's talking!'

As mother and daughter glared at one another, Craig greeted Duncan. 'Evening, Mr N.'

'You two know each other?' Ellen asked.

'Craig's Jamie's stepbrother; Linda's stepson; Rose's half-brother.'

'Don't worry, it's not as pervy as it sounds,' Craig said, grinning.

'Then perhaps you'll tell my daughter to come home since she's taking no notice of me.'

'Mum! I can make my own decisions.'

'You heard the little lady,' Craig said to Ellen. 'No can do.'

'I'm sixteen. Old enough to appear in porn.'

'What?'

'I don't think that's true, actually,' Duncan interposed.

'Who are you?' Sue asked.

'He's Mr N. Aren't you, Mr N?'

'What porn?' Ellen asked, her voice ringing with alarm.

'I didn't say I'd done it. See what she thinks of me!' Sue appealed to her friends who, bored with the altercation, were staring out to sea. 'What kind of sicko are you?'

Ellen stood stock still, as if wondering how she had come to be the one under attack. 'Well, now you're here, you may as well enjoy it,' she said, sounding strained. 'Just so long as you promise to be back by ten and not to drink any more alcohol.'

'Whatever,' Sue said and, swaying perilously on the rail, flung her arms round a startled Craig.

Duncan and Ellen returned to the car, where Neil was slumped in the back seat.

'Would you drive us straight home, please,' Ellen said, shaking.

'What about the fish and chips?' Neil asked.

'You didn't really want them.'

'Yes I did.'

'Another time. We'll have a pizza at home.'

'Just great!' Neil said, kicking the back of Duncan's seat.

'Don't worry,' Duncan said to Ellen. 'She'll be fine.'

'How can you be sure? Did you see her clothes? I didn't buy them. Where did she get the money? Has she said anything to you?' She turned to face Neil.

'She never tells me anything. She hates me. They all do.'

'If your sister's in trouble, I'm relying on you to let me know. You're the man of the house now.' Duncan questioned the wisdom of placing such a burden on a thirteen-year-old boy but he knew better than to interfere.

'I don't want to be. It's supposed to be Dad.'

'You know that's not possible.'

'It's your fault.'

'How? I didn't commit a multimillion-pound fraud.'

'He did it for you. So you'd have money to buy things. You wanted a new kitchen.'

'Maybe, but only when I thought he'd earned it. If I'd had my way, I'd have torn out every piece of granite.'

'You're a bitch!'

'You've no right to speak to your mother like that,' Duncan said, unable to hold back any longer.

'And you've no right to speak to me at all. You're not my father. Just because you're fucking her.'

He stumbled over the word as if it were as hard for him to say as for them to hear. After a shocked silence, Ellen asked him where he had learnt to talk like that and ordered him to apologise to Duncan. Duncan, insisting that no apology was needed, experienced a welter of emotions: sympathy for Ellen and her two disturbed children; fear that Neil's misreading of their relationship would seal its fate; doubt that he could help with her adolescent son given his problems with his own.

No sooner had they turned into Ellen's drive than Neil flung open the car door, ran into the house and up the stairs.

'Come in,' Ellen said wearily, as she led him into a sitting room dominated by a biscuit-coloured sofa designed for a far larger space. 'Can I get you anything? A glass of wine?'

'If it's no trouble.'

'There's a bottle open in the fridge.'

They were distracted by heavy footfall overhead. 'Don't worry. He'll run out of steam. He's not as strong as his rage.'

'Is there anything I can do?'

'Other than turning back the clock? I won't be a moment.'

As she went into the kitchen, Duncan surveyed the room, trying to glean as much about her as he could. He glanced at the brass firedogs and antique bellows beside the log effect fire, the pewter mugs and Capodimonte figurines lining the windowsill, and the illustrated books in the alcoves, as decorative as the knick-knacks that held them in place, before resting his gaze on the framed Magritte exhibition posters from Vienna and New York, intrigued to know whether she had bought them there or here.

'Chateau Sainsbury, I'm afraid,' Ellen said, returning with two glasses.

'Fine by me. I'm the opposite of a connoisseur. I was trau-matised by my father who regularly sent wine back, even at my great-aunt's funeral.'

'I swore to myself that when I had kids, I'd do things dif-ferently from my mother. But they've turned against me just the same,' Ellen said, to the echo of Neil's clomping. 'I'm sorry you had to witness that.'

'Don't worry. She'll be home soon. A sore head in the morning should teach her a valuable lesson.'

'I meant Neil. Such ugliness.'

'The sad thing is that it's not even true,' Duncan said warily.

'That's the story of my life.'

'Stories change. New chapters and so forth.'

'Well, we have moved to Francombe.'

'That's just a change of setting; I was referring to charac-ters. The tall, sandy-haired divorcee, slightly frayed at the edges, who's been introduced as the love interest. Ring any bells?'

'It might if it weren't for the "frayed". He seems in remark-ably good shape to me.'

'Thank you.' Duncan felt dizzy. 'I assure you that the feel-ing's mutual.'

'Even so, I'd hate to rush things. Believe me, it has nothing to do with Neil. We've known each other such a short time. Are you sure we're ready?'

'I'm one hundred per cent sure, but I'm sure enough to wait. Take as much time as you need. Well, as long as there's still an "r" in the month.'

'We have to be honest with everyone: Linda … the kids. After Matthew, I couldn't bear to do anything furtive.'

'What's furtive?' He moved towards her. 'The lights are on; the curtains are open.' He put his arms on her shoulders and, giving her every chance to break away, kissed her full on the lips. He felt her whole body tremble before she relaxed into the embrace. After a while he withdrew and, holding her face in his hands, gazed deeply into her eyes. All at once they both burst into laughter, which he silenced with a second, more confident kiss.

'Where's my pizza?' Neil's voice rang through the house, forcing them apart.

'Duty calls,' Ellen said.

'I know the feeling. Do you want me to leave?'

'Yes … no … yes … no. Why not stay for some pizza?'

'Do you have enough?'

'It's a twenty incher. Don't laugh!'

Four

Charlie is Our Darling

by Brian Gannon

Thursday, 31 October 2013

Charlie Lyndon wants to be cloned. While there is currently no risk of one of the country's most unique talents being duplicated, the BAFTA award-winning actress claims that it needs at least two of her to cope with her hectic schedule.

'Although with my luck,' the pint-sized star says with a mischievous twinkle, 'she'd turn out to be a younger, prettier, more talented and certainly taller version of yours truly and end up putting me out of work.'

Lyndon, known to millions as the Reverend Penny Herring in the BBC sitcom, *The Vicar's Husband*, is appearing at the Crystal Room of the Metropole Hotel on Sunday, 3 November in *Dear Mistress*, her highly acclaimed one-woman show about Dr Johnson's close friend, Hester Thrale.

I met Lyndon at her elegant Georgian home in London's fashionable Spitalfields. She spoke of her pleasure at returning to Francombe, which she came to know in the mid 1980s, and her sadness at the recent decline in the town's fortunes. 'That's why I'm happy to give this performance in aid of the Francombe Pier Trust.

'I fell in love with the raffishness: the salty tang in the air; the peeling façades – and that's just the buildings; the day trippers out for a taste of candyfloss and how's your father,' she says with her trademark chortle. 'I suppose the rot set in with all the package holidays to Spain. But then I should know about that,' she adds, referring to one of her rare flops, in ITV's *Costa Packet*.

Lyndon, who is currently filming the role of Mrs Noah for the BBC's updated Genesis series, relishes the chance to return to Mrs Thrale in a play that she co-wrote with *The Vicar's Husband* mastermind, Angus Carmichael, and has performed in cities across the globe.

'Hester was a fascinating woman. I first discovered her at Cambridge. I was immediately drawn to the fact that she was only four foot eleven! For nearly twenty years she was Dr Johnson's hostess, confidante and, in all probability, his mistress. In one of his letters he asks her to keep him "in that form of slavery which you know so well how to make blissful".

'The Mrs Grundys of the literary world would have us

believe that the slavery was symbolic,' she says dryly. 'But it's plain that theirs was a deeply erotic relationship. Though don't worry, I only talk about it in the play. I'm not sure that Francombe is ready for the sight of me in a PVC catsuit cracking a whip!'

Mrs Thrale fell from grace when, as a forty-three-year-old widow, she married her daughter's Italian music teacher. Lyndon herself is no stranger to scandal after the *Daily Mail* revealed that she lived in a *ménage à trois* with the writer, Jasper Gurney, and the architect, Brian da Silva. 'First they tried to make out that I was a scarlet woman and then that Brian and Jasper were gay, and I was their beard. Just think of us as Mormons but in reverse,' she says with a smile.

Such candour failed to disarm those critics who held that her lifestyle made her inappropriate casting for the role of the nation's favourite vicar. 'They claimed to be offended by me but they were really offended by Penny. These were people who loathe the mere idea of women priests but they don't want to admit it. So they went for the soft target.' Her sunny features cloud over. 'You wouldn't believe some of the letters we received. Scratch the surface of this green and pleasant land and you find yourself knee deep in filth!'

That moralistic minority may be relieved, but her vast army of fans will be dismayed to learn that there are no plans for a seventh series of *The Vicar's Husband*. 'If the Church of England Synod ever votes to allow women bishops, we might do *The Bishop's Husband*,' Lyndon says, smiling.

She has much else to keep her busy. After Mrs Noah, she returns to Stratford to play Juliet's Nurse and Mistress Quickly. 'I know what you're thinking,' she says, daring me to object, 'it should be Juliet! Perhaps you could start a campaign to persuade the director to recast?' There are also several TV projects in the pipeline.

Meanwhile, the actress has one burning ambition. 'I want to do a rom-com,' she says. 'I want to be snogged by a Hollywood hunk before I hit menopause. Why should leggy blondes have all the fun? Surely it's the turn of a forty-something roly-poly dwarf?'

From everything Ellen had told him, Duncan expected to see a woman in a tie-dye shirt, silk bandana and patchwork pantaloons but, as he strained to glimpse her through the windscreen, he saw a statuesque sexagenarian soberly dressed in a grey-and-white Fair Isle sweater and black ankle-length skirt, her one concession to hippiedom the tangle of chains round her neck. Ellen had asked him to remain in the car to avoid awkward introductions, but her mother, who seemed to be as intrigued by him as he was by her, had followed her to the front door.

Prior to her arrival earlier in the week, Ellen had given him a detailed account of Barbara, whose insistence that she call her by her first (never Christian) name had distressed her as a girl but was now a blessing, since it freed her from any undue filial sentiment. She was born in Dorking, the only child of a chartered surveyor and a school secretary, and one of the many grievances that Ellen bore her mother was that she had cut her off from her grandparents. With no sense of inconsistency, she heaped scorn on their conformism while expecting Ellen to respect her own less orthodox but equally predictable lifestyle. From an early age she possessed a talent for painting, which her parents encouraged until, at the age of eighteen, she announced that she wanted to go to art school rather than university. Her father proposed a compromise whereby he would support her to study commercial art at St Martin's. Her disenchantment at having to design beer mats, cereal packets and railway posters, while her contemporaries on the fine art course were taught painting by Gillian Ayres and sculpture by Anthony Caro, vanished after graduation when the training that her father had viewed as the passport to a job at J. Walter Thompson thrust her into the heart of late-1960s counter-culture.

At a happening in the basement of Better Books, a radical bookshop a few steps from St Martin's, she met two young Americans who were setting up *Black Eagle*, an underground magazine whose objectives of cultural subversion, anti-capitalism and social and sexual liberation were not then seen as incompatible. Discovering her grasp of Letraset and lithography, they asked her to join them and she quickly became an integral member of the team. Although she later admitted to Ellen that she never understood why her design expertise was a better foundation for washing dishes and making tea than the literary background of her male colleagues, she flourished at the magazine. *Black Eagle* ran for seventeen issues before being shut down by the police in 1971 after it published the names and addresses of twenty-five Tory MPs whom it deemed to be justified targets for the Angry Brigade's bombing campaign. Meanwhile, she had moved into a squat in Hyde Park Mansions among an ever-shifting population of musicians, actors, buskers, anarchists and impoverished aristocrats.

While roundly scorning the bourgeois notion of couple-dom, she fell in love with Richard Houseman, an Old Etonian performance poet who was given a six-month jail sentence for burning a copy of *Burke's Peerage* in the House of Lords public gallery during a debate on the Misuse of Drugs Act. On his release, she persuaded him to move with her to Wiltshire where Olivia Meridew, the bubble-wrap heiress, had set up a commune in a derelict stately home. Although she subsequently told her daughter that her sole aim had been to rescue Richard from the hard drugs scene to which he was increasingly drawn, Ellen suspected that a secondary one had been to distance him from the hordes of female admirers for whom his good looks and poetic flair were now enhanced by public notoriety. They stayed in the commune for seven years, although they never moved into the house but lived in one of the caravans dotted around the lake, largely because Olivia's belief that the restoration should be carried out by the residents themselves in order to maximise the flow of chi meant that it was left unfinished. Ellen was born during their first year and while, with a few exceptions, Barbara kept Richard away from other women, she failed to keep him off the drugs. Whereas the rest of the commune smoked pot, took LSD and ate home-grown magic mushrooms, Richard, convinced that it was the way to revive his waning creativity, consumed ever greater quantities of amphetamines, barbiturates and cocaine. He suffered a massive stroke, and one of Ellen's earliest memories – certainly her most vivid – was of returning to the caravan to find him slumped on the floor, his right cheek collapsed into his chin.

Richard never recovered. After several months in hospital, he was moved to his family home in Berkshire. Barbara took Ellen to visit him every week, thereby acquainting her with her paternal grandparents who had disowned their son after his parliamentary protest. Then, without warning, their visits ceased. While assuring Ellen that her father was not dead, Barbara offered no explanation for the change and it was many years before the truth emerged. Blaming Barbara for Richard's drug use (which, as they knew full well, had long pre-dated their meeting), his parents claimed that she was an unfit mother and applied to the court for custody of Ellen. Aided by Olivia's barrister brother and a precipitate move from the caravan to an estate cottage, Barbara won the case. The Housemans retaliated by saying that, if she wanted them to provide the round-the-clock care for Richard that was way beyond her means, she must break off all contact with him. To Ellen's lasting resentment, Barbara agreed.

Over time, Richard regained sufficient movement in his right arm to reach for the ancient scimitar that hung above his bed and slit his throat. Barbara knew nothing of his death until after the funeral when his sister, defying her parents' wishes, sent her a small parcel of his personal effects including a silver pentacle necklace that Ellen still treasured. Her father's most significant legacy, however, was to have ignited her interest in speech therapy. While keen not to overstate the connection, she was convinced that the sight of someone she loved struggling to communicate had inspired her choice of career.

Soon after Richard's death Barbara left the commune, taking the six-year-old Ellen to Lyme Regis, where they moved in with Rupert Thring, a middle-aged violin maker, whom Ellen credited with sparking her love of music but who otherwise remained a shadowy presence in her life. After five years Barbara, whose confidence had been restored by the success of her glass paintings, left Rupert to live with a series of unsuitable men, one of whom, Roman, a Polish puppeteer, took an excessive interest in the now pubescent Ellen, although she was quick to point out that this was manifest in nothing more than suggestive remarks, protracted hugs and unwanted mugs of late-night cocoa. Dismissing her daughter's protests about her affairs, Barbara insisted that every woman had the right to a fulfilling sex life. Eager for Ellen to enjoy that right, which she presented as almost a duty, she took her to have a coil fitted at the age of fifteen. To her chagrin it wasn't needed for another four years, by which time Ellen had left home to study speech and language therapy in Sheffield.

It was there that she met Matthew while on placement at the Northern General Hospital, working with adults who had feeding problems after surgery. Once a week the consultant led a ward round that he attended. He was intelligent, good-looking, self-possessed and serious, and one of the few junior doctors not to add a U, either mentally or manually, to the SLT notices in the common room. They fell in love, or at least she did (she could no longer be sure of anything about Matthew), and married two years later, after her graduation and his appointment as a senior registrar.

If, as Ellen came to suspect, part of Matthew's attraction for her was his distance from her mother's world, then Barbara's response was unsurprising. With her New Age contempt for allopathic medicine, she failed to share Ellen's conviction of his brilliance. Moreover, long before the revelation of his crimes, she detected a ruthlessness behind his reserve. To her credit she stuck to her promise not to interfere in her daughter's marriage, her antipathy to Matthew, along with the demands of an ever-expanding business (she now employed four painters to execute her designs), restricting her visits to a couple of weekends a year. Her only prolonged stay came in the summer of 2006 when, having failed to cure herself of cancer with a regime of juices, Chinese herbs and chanting, she was recovering from the removal of her left breast. She refused any reconstructive surgery, which, true to form, she turned to her advantage when, on her return to Dorset, she met a retired archaeologist whose predilections had been shaped by his late wife's mastectomy.

She was as candid with her grandchildren as she had been with her daughter. Matthew had been outraged to come across her showing nine-year-old Sue and six-year-old Neil her postoperative scars. Although she rarely gave them presents, preferring to plant trees in their names for birthdays and Christmas, they both loved her. Sue, who never voiced approval of anyone over thirty who lacked a media profile, even pronounced her 'cool'. So it was with mixed feelings that Ellen greeted her newfound interest in her family. In the eighteen months since Matthew's arrest she had visited them as often as in the previous six years. Ever mistrustful of her motives, Ellen suspected that she was driven less by affection than the belief that her daughter would be lost without her help.

'Why do grandparents and grandchildren get on so well?' she had asked Duncan when, after profuse – and redundant – apologies for boring him, she concluded the story.

'Is this a riddle?'

'No, it's a joke. At least it's supposed to be. I was told it by one of our paediatricians.'

'I don't know. Why do grandparents and grandchildren get on so well?'

'They share a common enemy.'

To be fair, Barbara did not look hostile as she waved expansively to him from the front door, although Duncan was unsure how much this was a genuine greeting and how much an attempt to disconcert Ellen. He considered waving back but feared that Ellen might view it as a betrayal. So he contented himself with flashing a broad smile in her direction, even though it was too far away for her to see.

Ellen stepped into the car, filling it with a gentle fragrance.

'You smell delicious,' Duncan said after kissing her.

'Thank you. It's a new perfume my mother brought me, made by one of her friends.'

'She should market it.'

'Though as always with my mother there's a catch. It's not just a perfume; it's a floral remedy, made from jasmine and roses and ylang ylang and heaven knows what else, designed to boost confidence, diffuse anger and promote well-being. I thought I'd put it to the test by wearing it when I met Matthew.'

'In which case, shall we make a start?'

'Please.'

Try as he might, Duncan could think of no less romantic date than driving a recent divorcee to visit her ex-husband in prison. Yet no sooner had Ellen mentioned her trip to Bedford than he offered to take her. If their relationship were to grow, he needed to share in all aspects of her life, both the good and the bad. Matthew's trial had been national news and while Nugent was an unremarkable name and Martin Casey, the only person in Francombe to know of the connection, was sworn to silence, she lived in permanent fear of exposure. Duncan had at least been able to assure her that there would be no mention in the local press, even though it was a matter of legitimate interest, given that one of the hospital trusts Matthew had defrauded was East Sussex.

Duncan remembered the case well. After fifteen years as a consultant neurologist, Matthew had left the NHS to set up a locum agency with a chain of bogus offices across the South. Capitalising on the chronic understaffing of hospital accounts departments, he submitted duplicate and inflated invoices, which over a four-year period resulted in a demonstrable loss to the NHS of £400,000, although the true figure was reckoned to be ten times higher. In court, Matthew blamed the discrepancies on errors by the locums, hospital billing clerks and his own staff, but the jury was not convinced and found him guilty on three charges of false accounting and two of fraudulent trading. He was sentenced to five years in prison, ordered to pay £200,000 in costs and disqualified from acting as a company director for ten years. Two months later at a disciplinary hearing of the GMC, he was struck off the medical register.

Although both the trial judge and the district judge who subsequently granted her divorce accepted that Ellen knew nothing of Matthew's malpractice, public opinion was less generous. Friends who had enjoyed their hospitality were especially quick to condemn her. She saw no way to defend herself without relating a history of subservience that she feared would make them despise her all the more. Duncan was, therefore, doubly grateful for her readiness to confide in him. On a windswept cliff with the herring gulls screaming in sympathy, she described how within months of their marriage Matthew had taken control of every detail of her life. Having ordered her to give up work when she was pregnant with Sue, he refused to let her return once Neil started school, accusing her of seeking to humiliate him. Charm itself so long as his wishes were obeyed, he sank into baleful silence the moment they were defied. Her spirit was so crushed that she sometimes even longed for him to hit her. At least a bruise might embolden her to fight back.

Today's visit, the first since her move to Francombe, was at Ellen's request. Although his elderly parents, who continued to assert their son's innocence, saw him regularly and wrote her lengthy reports in the hope that, the divorce notwithstanding, she would take him back on his release, she wanted to verify that he was both well and well-treated. More importantly, she needed to be sure that he was no longer a threat. It was four years since a chance discovery by the audit manager at Basildon Hospital led the police to launch their investigation into Safe Cover: four years during which she felt that she would never be able to trust anyone again, including herself. Now she had been given another chance with Duncan. For that to succeed she had to confront her past, in the person of her former husband, one last time.

'Would you like some music on?' Duncan asked, when fifty minutes into the journey the companionable silence grew strained.

'I'm sorry; I didn't think I'd feel this nervous. I'm very glad you're here.'

'So am I … that is I'm glad to be with you.'

'I couldn't have done it on my own. Barbara offered, but her show of sympathy would have been worse than blame.'

'What about the kids? Doesn't Matthew want to see them?'

'He didn't ask. Then again, he would never set himself up for rejection. I sounded them out. Sue refused point-blank. But that has nothing to do with her anger towards her father and everything to do with her passion for Craig. The latest is that she wants his name tattooed on her thigh.'

'Surely she's too young?'

'She's too young to have one without my consent. I know I'm not best placed to talk about self-respect – and I'm terrified that she may have learnt from my example – but you don't have to be a card-carrying feminist to object to a girl having her boyfriend's name branded on her body.'

'She's clearly besotted,' Duncan said, wondering whether they had slept together and worrying in an undefined way about Jamie.

'She wants to make a deal. If I allow her to have the tattoo, then she won't have sex with him,' Ellen said, as if reading his mind.

'Some deal! Either you let me mutilate my body or I'll let him break my hymen. Sorry,' Duncan said, catching her grimace.

'No, you're right. She's desperate to show her commitment. I explained that he was her first boyfriend and that she wouldn't be with him for ever – which drew the predictable response.'

'Is Craig equally serious about her?'

'He's a sixteen-year-old boy: you tell me! The one advantage of the relationship is that it's reconciled her to moving to Francombe. I wish I could say the same for Neil. He's not as openly antagonistic towards me as his sister; he can't bear to see me in tears. Though I suspect that it's less out of genuine compassion than because it makes him feel insecure.'

'Maybe it's both?' Duncan said, trying to blot out the memory of Neil's tirade against his mother on parents' evening.

'He's the more disturbed by everything that's happened. Boys need their fathers.'

'True.' Duncan wondered if she had forgotten his own separation from Jamie or assumed that, because he was not incarcerated, their relationship must be close.

'He's become so aloof. When he's not at school, he spends most of the time holed up in his room. He's never been what you'd call an outgoing boy, but he used to enjoy cycling and chess and gardening – he had his own flowerbeds in Radlett and heaven help the gardener if he touched them. Now he shows no interest in anything. He's punishing me for bringing him here because it's easier than punishing his father who's the reason we came, although of course the person he's really punishing is himself.'

'Does he read?'

'If only! He's glued to his computer. It's as though he can

only engage with the world when it's at one remove and in two dimensions.'

'How about friends?'

'None to speak of, or at least that he speaks of. I knew that the first few weeks at a new school would be tough but things haven't improved. Then again, he's so prickly, such a mixture of bitterness and aggression and envy and spite, I'm not sure I'd want to be his friend. It's hard enough being his mother.'

Duncan thought of asking Jamie to take him under his wing but feared that it would do more harm than good. 'I know it's not a solution, but if he'd like the odd game of chess … I play every Thursday with Henry Grainger of St Edward's. He beats me hands down. I could use the practice.'

'That's really kind. Of course I'll ask, though I don't hold out much hope. But there is one thing. I hesitate to mention it when you already have so much on your plate. The other evening you were saying how you were hurt that Jamie was doing his local history project on the wheel park – '

'Oh lord, I hope I wasn't moaning.'

'This is me you're talking to! Anyway, I wondered if you'd consider helping Neil. He told the teacher that he knew nothing about Francombe and asked if he could do his project on Radlett, specifically the Victorian mental hospital that recently shut down at Shenley. But the man was adamant that "local" meant local to them. Somehow it's come to stand for everything Neil hates about moving down here. If you could give him a hand with the history of the *Mercury* … It wouldn't have to be too in-depth, just pointing him in the right direction.'

'I'd be delighted.'

'Really?'

'Of course.'

'That's wonderful. I know that it's not the same as doing it with Jamie.'

'I'll still enjoy it, and it'll be a chance to get to know Neil.'

Even as he spoke, Duncan felt a fraud. Had he agreed to her request out of sympathy for Neil, to prove himself to Ellen, to compensate for Jamie's collaboration with Derek, or, given that clear-cut motives rarely existed outside books, from a combination of the three?

Reaching Bedford early, they had an all-day breakfast at the Titanic Café. Visiting time was from 3.15 to 4.15, but Ellen had been told to arrive half an hour beforehand, so at 2.30 they walked to the prison where she touched up her lipstick and added a dab of powder to her cheeks. 'War paint,' she said ruefully, before disappearing into the gatehouse, which with its two-toned brickwork, gabled roof and white portico might have passed for a faculty building in a new university, were it not for the razor wire on the adjoining wall.

Having planned to spend the afternoon exploring the town, Duncan chose instead to stroll round the perimeter of the prison, which, like all such institutions, exerted a strong pull on both his conscience and his imagination. While he had long since abandoned the 'Property is Theft' sloganising of his teens, he harboured deep reservations about the efficacy, expense and, above all, the justice of locking up so many people. 'The rich man in his castle' and 'the poor man at his gate' might have been omitted from modern versions of the popular hymn (although not without a struggle, as Henry had discovered at St Edward's), but the rich man on the bench and the poor man in the dock remained an integral part of the social order.

Never had he been more aware of this than at Cambridge, where, in his second – and, as it turned out, final – year, a group of students looking for an original party venue fixed on a country house near Newmarket, which one of their number, John Fitzsimmons, a distant cousin of the owners, knew to be empty apart from an elderly housekeeper. So, preceded by John who had slipped a Nembutal into the housekeeper's tea, thirty or so of his friends turned up and, boosting their supply of alcohol with several choice bottles from their hosts' cellar, proceeded to make merry. In the early hours the police, alerted by a neighbouring farmer, arrived to investigate, but John's patrician tones and plausible story swiftly satisfied them and, apologising for the intrusion, they drove off. The revellers then carried on until dawn when they returned to Cambridge by car, bike, motorcycle and, in the case of the ever-flamboyant Julia Flitton, on a white stallion. The house-keeper, either mollified by the large tip left on her chair or terrified of the owners' response to her negligence, kept silent and nothing more was heard of the incident. Duncan put it from his mind until the following term when he listened to his bedder's tearful account of her son who, in revenge for being thrown in the Cam by a gang of rowers, had set fire to the Pembroke boathouse. He was convicted of arson and jailed for eight years.

For weeks, Duncan agonised over whether to report his own crime in order to highlight the inequity, finally deciding that it would be futile, doing nothing for the wretched arson-ist and incriminating his friends. But he never lost his sense of outrage and, in his first year at the *Mercury*, he commis-sioned a series of articles on conditions in the three prisons – Lewes, Blantyre House and East Sutton Park – that served the Francombe area. In several hard-hitting leaders he decried the inadequacy of the prisoner's discharge grant, which, at a few pounds, was an open invitation to reoffend, and he upbraided the Council for the lack of jobs and facilities for ex-inmates. More controversially, he questioned the basic prin-ciples behind judicial policy, arguing that white-collar crime, which was perpetrated by well-off, well-educated people and motivated by greed, should be dealt with more severely than burglaries, assaults and even rapes, which were perpetrated by inadequate, damaged and deprived people in need of help rather than punishment.

Duncan trusted that it was revulsion at Matthew's crime,

a cynical attack on the most revered institution in the country, which reconciled him to his sentence, and not Ellen's anguished expression when she emerged from the gatehouse, conspicuous among a group of women whose drabness seemed designed to reassure their husbands of their fidelity.

'Quick, let's escape!' she said, grabbing his arm with unexpected force. 'How did it go?'

'I'd rather you didn't ask questions,' she said, only to answer his tacit ones unbidden once they were back in the car and heading out of town. 'I don't know what to think. Last time he barely spoke to me; he was as distant as some of my most damaged kids. Today it was the opposite; he never stopped talking. But it wasn't to me. Not really. I might as well have been his mother or even a prison psychiatrist monitoring how well he's settling in.'

'Isn't that good? An acceptance that things have changed?'

'I suppose so. I know I shouldn't mind, but we've driven all this way and he didn't ask me a single question about myself or the job or the house or Francombe or even – and this is what hurt the most – the children. When I mentioned them, he seemed almost indifferent.'

'Maybe it's self-defence?' Duncan said, angry at making excuses for a man who, no matter how hard he tried to block him out, cast a permanent shadow over their relationship. 'He knows he can do nothing for them so he's withdrawing emotionally. I find it hard enough being apart from Jamie and I'm not in jail.'

'Do you think so? Yes, of course. Thank you. I couldn't bear it if the one real thing – the only real thing – we've ever had meant nothing to him. He spent the entire visit chattering about his cellmate, what they watched on TV, the bowl he was making in the prison workshop, his weight loss course – '

'I didn't know he was fat.'

'He is now. After almost an hour of telling me about table tennis and music appreciation and the over-forties gym sessions and how his fellow inmates distrust the prison doctor so they come to him for a diagnosis, I felt sure he was putting on an act – talking big as he always has, desperate to prove he's top dog. Then he let slip that he's due to be transferred to a Category C prison – '

'When?'

'No idea. Neither has he. But it could be any day now and he isn't pleased. He claims he couldn't bear to start again from scratch, but that's a smokescreen. The truth is that he thrives on all the rules and regulations. He doesn't want to go into a more relaxed regime.'

'But that's perverse!'

'And swindling an institution you described as "criminally underfunded" isn't? Sorry, I'm still on edge. I listened to him and suddenly everything fell into place: the blind rage when one of us used his coat peg; the cast-iron timetables that turned the simplest journey into a military campaign; the desperate need for order to keep all his demons at bay.'

'What demons?'

'I wish I knew. If I did, I might have been able to help. But I'm convinced that the fraud was part and parcel of it. Why steal all that money? We didn't need it; we didn't use it. Sure, there was the house and the cars and the holidays and the parties (not that he showed much sign of enjoying them). But by getting away with it all for so long, he could fool himself that he was in control.'

'He'll have a job doing that now.'

'Exactly. And, when I saw him looking more content than he has done in years, I realised that he no longer has to pretend. Far from being a punishment, his sentence is a kind of relief. The prison walls are nothing compared to the ones he built around himself.'

'I'm struggling to take all this in.'

'Do you think I'm on the wrong track?'

'I don't know; I don't know him.'

'The truth is that neither do I. How is it possible to live in the same house, to share the same bed and make love to a man for sixteen years and have so little idea of what's going on inside his head? I suppose it would be the same if I'd found out he was having an affair. When the police first came to interview me, I assumed that's why Matthew had done it. It was the only logical explanation. Now I know better than to look for one.'

Her voice cracked and Duncan was afraid that she was about to break down. 'You're free of him now,' he said.

'Am I? It's not just the kids. I can push him to the back of my mind but I doubt I'll ever push him out of it.'

'I do understand.'

'Of course. You and Linda get on so well, I sometimes forget you were ever married.'

'Ah yes. The poster couple for divorce.'

'From the outside, you seem so compatible that it's hard to see why you ever split up. Sorry, I don't mean to pry. Well, that's not true, actually.' She smiled for the first time all day.

'You're not prying. It's very simple. I'm sure there were lots of subsidiary reasons but there was one overwhelming one. She wanted another child, which I couldn't – well, a mixture of couldn't and wouldn't – give her.'

The bitter irony was that her much longed-for second child had been born severely disabled. He wondered whether, had Rose been his daughter (and, given his genetic make-up, it was a possibility he had often considered), their relationship might have been strengthened. He would have loved Rose so much; indeed, in moments of self-reproach he feared that her dependency would have made her easier to love than Jamie. Suppressing the thought, he asked Ellen to hand him a butterscotch from the packet in the dashboard. She unwrapped it with delicious intimacy before taking one herself. They savoured their sweets in silence, united, he suspected, by memories of their pasts.

In retrospect, it was clear that he should never have married

Linda. They met when she had just turned twenty and was widely held to be the most beautiful girl in Francombe: a verdict confirmed by the judges of the annual Seafood Festival who crowned her Queen. Fellow guests at a Chamber of Commerce reception for national travel agents, they sought refuge from the tedium, scarcely leaving one another's side all evening. Over the next few months Duncan invited her out whenever he could and, on occasions when he was working late, brought her to the office, heedless of the smirks of the staff. She was funny and vibrant and sweet-natured, and far cleverer than her constant self-deprecation might suggest. Despite her protests, he was eager to introduce her to his university friends, but after a meal with Angus and Miles following a live recording of *The Carmichael Report*; a weekend in Jarrow with Alice and her new husband, Lesley, the area dean; and, most painfully, a reunion in Devon with the cast members of *Cambridge Marmalade*, he resolved to make a complete break with the past.

When they married after a two-year courtship, Duncan felt as though he were making a commitment not just to Linda but to Francombe, turning his back on the metropolis and pledging himself to the coast. By any standards – not least those that he had observed as a boy – their first years together were happy. Linda, while continuing to work in her parents' shop, relished her connection with the *Mercury*, which, having fought off the challenge of the *Francombe Citizen* and BBC Southern Counties, was once again solvent. But for all her pride in his achievement, he knew that he had failed her in the one thing that mattered. Every christening mug and romper suit and rattle that she bought for a friend's baby brought it home. Nothing in her life, even her love for him, could compare with her longing for a child.

Although he shared Linda's hopes of parenthood, Duncan knew that it would not be easy. At the start of their relationship he had confessed that he suffered from Klinefelter

Syndrome, but he had been so frightened of scaring her off that having explained he was still able to produce some viable sperm he had failed to emphasise how few. It was not a subject on which he cared to dwell. He had been diagnosed at fifteen after two years as the butt of changing-room jokes about eunuchs and castrati. He had never felt so alone. With a father who made virility the yardstick of his identity and a mother who was repulsed by the least physical defect, he found little sympathy at home. The Germanic name and extra X chromosomes made him desperate to conceal the condition from his friends, who would have shown him no mercy. Even the medical dictionary in the school library – more often consulted as a masturbatory aid – produced only the threat of further hideous and degrading symptoms. Fortunately, an enlightened housemaster reassured him that he was a late developer while encouraging him to take up running, for which his rangy body was perfectly formed. As ever at school, sporting prowess held the key to acceptance. When he finally reached puberty the following year, he was so keen to display himself in the dormitory and showers that he risked fresh notoriety. Since then he had been determined to turn the condition to his advantage. Not only did his light beard free him from daily shaving but it brought unexpected success with women, for whom the Burt Reynolds look had lost its appeal. And whatever the medical dictionary might say about his low sex drive, he had striven to make up for it in performance.

Linda came off the Pill as soon as they were married, but her fervent conviction that 'Nature will find a way' was put to the test when, four years later, she was still not pregnant. For the first time in his life Duncan was faced with the full force of female obsession. They saw their GP, whom Duncan suspected of trivialising the issue with his sketch-show advice that he should stop cycling to work, wear boxer shorts instead of Y-fronts, and give up eating curry. When those failed to achieve results, he proposed that they try surgical sperm retrieval coupled with testosterone therapy. The treatment was not without risks, including liver failure, heart attacks and strokes, and Duncan was shocked by how readily Linda brushed them aside. In the event he suffered little more than sore gums, a foul taste in his mouth and the acne that he had escaped during adolescence. He was also prone to fits of anger, particularly with Linda, although he was unsure how much of that was due to the drugs and how much to his dismay at her cavalier attitude to his health.

His sperm were extracted and implanted one by one in her eggs, in a procedure that seemed scarcely less miraculous than birth itself. When she finally fell pregnant, their elation was tinged with anxiety that if it were a boy he would inherit KS, and in a more acute form than his father. It was not until the tests revealed him to be clear of abnormalities that they could breathe freely. Then Jamie was born, so perfect that for the first time since childhood Duncan was tempted to see his life as divinely ordained. He hoped that Linda would feel the same sense of completion, but her boundless love for her baby made her all the more determined to try again. When he pointed out that they might have another boy who in turn might have the rogue chromosomes, she accused him of being more concerned about the dangers to himself. But it was her health that he was protecting as much as his own. She had suffered badly from overstimulated ovaries and mood swings during the treatment. The example of Gillian Canning, who had been so scarred by IVF that Stewart left her, should give them pause.

For her part, Linda grew convinced that his denial of her greatest desire was proof that he no longer loved her. Then at Geoffrey and Frances Weedon's wedding she met a man who did. Whether or not Geoffrey's aim in choosing Musclebound, the 'Ultimate Eighties tribute band', to play at the reception was to keep Duncan off the dance floor, it had that effect. Meanwhile Linda, enjoying a rare chance to revisit the hits of her youth, and Derek, shrugging off the ticklish role of his ex-wife's new brother-in-law, boogied through the night. Shortly afterwards they embarked on an affair, which, with a logic that would have been laughed out of any court but a divorce court, Linda maintained had been justified first by Duncan's indifference to her needs and then by his blindness to her infidelity.

Feeling his mood darken and worried that it would infect Ellen, he asked her about her plans for the rest of the weekend, to which she replied wryly that, unless he had had any better offers, she was expecting to accompany him to the gala evening at the Metropole. Flustered, he seized on her request to sketch out his relationship with Charlie Lyndon, recounting how they had performed together in several Footlights Smokers and an outdoor production of *Cyrano de Bergerac*. He glossed over their subsequent fling, even though, of all his Cambridge girlfriends, she was the one for whom he retained the deepest affection. Wary of begging favours from his famous friends, particularly after the outcry over Miles Dorset's act in the fund-raiser for the Fishermen's Museum, he knew that he was safe with Charlie. He had written to her in January, soliciting her support for the FPT. She immediately offered to bring Mrs Thrale ('all I need is a first class train ticket and some hot and cold running waiters'). The first date that she had free was 3 November and, although the pier had since been sold, she insisted on honouring the commitment, with the proceeds earmarked for any legal challenge to the development plans.

So it was with a heady sense of anticipation that he made his way to the Metropole to meet her on Sunday afternoon. As he walked into the fusty vestibule he felt a flicker of unease. After the *Mercury*'s splash on a recent *Good Hotel Guide* report that there was not a single hotel to recommend in Francombe, the manager had accused him of setting out to destroy the town's tourist industry and declared him persona non grata. Yet, far from berating him, he was the soul of deference, greeting him warmly and escorting him to the conservatory to meet the celebrity guest. Duncan felt the stardust lighting on him when, with the most effusive 'darling' he had heard in years, Charlie clambered out of her seat to give him a hug. He had forgotten how small she was until the cameo pendant perched on her bust rubbed against his waist. She sat down, still clasping his hand, and summoned a waitress, whose excitement was palpable. To Duncan's surprise, Charlie ordered nothing but a pot of Earl Grey.

'Don't tell me you've given up cake?'

'Don't be absurd, darling. It's strictly temporary. I'm filming a bedroom scene next month.'

'Not the rom-com at last?'

'I wish! I'm playing a gay nymphomaniac for Sky. Cue tastefully lit shots of the Lyndon boobs.'

'How are Brian and Jasper?' Duncan asked, aware of the eavesdroppers.

'I trust that's a non sequitur,' Charlie replied with a chortle. 'Tickety-boo. They send their love. At least Jasper does. He's at some Frank Lloyd Wright symposium in Chicago. I've barely spoken to Brian for days. He's in Halifax ministering to his aged mother. She's in shock after discovering that the *barrister* her favourite granddaughter's living with is actually dishing out coffee in Starbucks. Isn't it priceless?'

'Absolutely,' Duncan replied, confused. 'Any news of the old gang? I'm so out of touch.'

'Best way to be. You're so lucky to live in such a wholesome atmosphere – and I don't just mean the sea air.' Duncan smiled as she extolled Francombe, confident of the return ticket to Waterloo tucked in her bag. 'I see Angus and Ross regularly, of course. And I was at a party last Sunday for Miles's fiftieth.'

'Really?' Duncan frowned at the mention of Miles, whose

savage mockery of his 'Well-loved Caretaker Retires' headline still rankled.

'It'll be us before you know it. Oh, I remember what I wanted to tell you. I saw Alice last month in Cambridge.'

'Was there a reunion?' Duncan asked, swallowing his hurt.

'No, just the Union. Baboom! We were guests speakers in the debate: This house believes in the biblical definition of marriage.'

'I presume you were on opposite sides.'

Charlie wrinkled her nose. 'From the way she talks, you'd think she'd written the Bible, not just followed it. Whatever happened to the biggest tart in Newnham?'

'She found God and Lesley, not necessarily in that order.'

'You might have expected her to keep a low profile after all that business with her son. But no, she's used it as an opportunity for more of the "hate the sin, love the sinner" bilge she spouts in her columns.'

The waitress brought two pots of tea along with a cake stand filled with meringues, éclairs, macaroons and doughnuts. As Duncan considered his choice, Charlie stretched across and grabbed the éclair with a look that dared him to comment.

'I'm saying nothing.'

'Dykes aren't body fascists. I can always claim I put on weight for the part.'

For two hours they chatted without constraint, interrupted only by a bashful fan requesting an autograph for Lindzee ('with a "z" and two "e"s'). At six o'clock Charlie went up to her room to prepare. 'A line-run with my stage manager and some emergency repair work to the façade. And no, I'm not talking about the stucco. How wicked of you to send that luscious young man to "do" me!' she said with studied ambiguity. 'You knew he'd break down all my defences.' Duncan protested his innocence and she promised to forgive him as long as he laughed loudly at the jokes and brought Ellen, whom she was longing to meet, for a glass of champagne after the performance. He hurried home to change, feeling a deep satisfaction that nearly thirty years on he could still fit into his Cambridge dinner suit. Forty minutes later he was once again waiting for Ellen outside her gate, although now for reasons of haste rather than discretion.

'You look stunning,' he said, as she appeared in a strapless ivory gown, with her hair in a braided bun.

'Do you mean that?' she asked hesitantly.

'Stunning!' he repeated, kissing her lightly on the lips.

'I bought a new dress. I didn't want you to be ashamed of me.'

'No one could ever be ashamed of you.'

'Try my daughter!'

They drove to the Metropole where, having found their names on the seating plan, they walked into the Crystal Room, its lustre dimmed now that the last of the chandeliers had been removed. Temporary waiters in starched linen jackets stood stiffly as the four hundred guests took their places. Threading his way through the tables, Duncan was hailed by Geoffrey Weedon who, as usual, turned a handshake into a trial of strength. He was sitting with his wife, brother, sister-in-law and four friends, among them Lorna Redwood, Chair of the Council's Leisure and Recreation Committee, who smiled sheepishly at Duncan as though he had caught her raiding the fridge. After kissing Linda, he introduced Ellen to Frances who, flouting both taste and convention, wore a crimson mesh dress slit almost to the navel, exposing a wide triangle of fake tan.

'Congrats on the turnout,' Geoffrey said to Duncan. 'Shame it's all for nothing. I trust you're arranging to give these good people their money back now that the FPT's washed up.'

'On the contrary, we'll need the cash more than ever if we have to fight your plans.'

'Come on, you know the game's up! Your only hope now would be to prove some impropriety in the contracting process.' From the corner of his eye, Duncan glimpsed Lorna Redwood shift in her seat. 'Which you can't.'

'Well, I mustn't keep you,' Duncan said. 'Your prawn cocktail will be getting cold.'

He escorted Ellen to their table, where he introduced her to their fellow diners: Glynis Kingswood and her husband Bill, a former classics master whose loathing of children had long pre-dated his retirement; Ralph Welch, branch manager of Barclays, typecast as treasurer of several local charities including the FPT, and his wife, Bella, a woman so obsessed with her prize borzois that it came as a shock to learn that she had three daughters; Lea Brierley, a Salter artist best known for her paintings of womblike caves, who, permanently unattached, had brought along her taciturn teenage son, Noah. Noah's embarrassment at sitting next to his mother was shared by Duncan, although he trusted that he hid it better. Some weeks after Linda's departure he had spent a disastrous night with Lea, which, unaccountably, she had been eager to repeat. For months she plagued him with invitations that he gently declined. He finally lost patience when she rang one press day with the news that 'My fanny's very dry this morning'. 'What do you expect me to do about it?' he snapped. 'Hold the front page?' She had never spoken to him since.

After a meal marked by Lea's caustic asides to Ellen who, unaware of the history, looked baffled, Duncan was heartily relieved when the waiters removed the remains of the tiramisu and the play began. Heralded by a short blackout and a blast of Handel, Charlie, wearing a powdered wig and grey Brunswick gown, made her entrance to rousing applause. With minimal props and a set consisting solely of a lacquered screen, ladderback chair, writing desk and two stone urns commandeered from the hotel conservatory, she evoked an entire eighteenth-century world. Her consummate portrayal of a woman of whom few had heard held the audience spellbound throughout. In one especially felicitous touch she quoted Johnson's celebrated analogy between women preachers and dogs, alluding to her TV persona without ever stepping out of character. At the end of the ninety-minute monologue when Mrs Thrale posthumously read her own obituaries, Duncan wondered whether he were alone in thinking that the tributes to her talent, eccentricity, wit, generosity and spirit might well apply to Charlie herself.

The curtain call was duly rapturous, after which Glynis Kingswood, as gauche as a child at a primary school prize-giving, stepped up to the stage and presented Charlie with a large bouquet before delivering an equally florid vote of thanks. Wickedly insinuating that Glynis's confusion of a 'perfectly simple' and 'simply perfect' evening had been deliberate, Charlie in turn thanked the audience for being so 'laughable'. Then, waving the flowers above her head – a moment that Duncan, now doubling as the *Mercury* photographer, failed to capture – she swept out, an effortless blend of eighteenth-century hostess and twenty-first-century star.

Bidding a hasty goodbye to their dinner companions, Duncan led Ellen up to Charlie's suite. 'Are you decent?' he called through the half-open door.

'That depends if you read the *Daily Mail*,' she replied. 'Just changing. Come on in; make yourselves at home.' They entered a sitting room that was so impersonal as to render the phrase redundant. A moment later Charlie emerged dressed in a black kimono, having removed her wig but not her make-up, as though half of her remained in the world of the play. 'You must be Ellen,' she said, hugging her ebulliently. 'I say "must", yet knowing Duncan he might have picked up somebody else since tea. Don't look at me like that, darling; I'm giving you a brilliant write-up. Make yourself useful and open the champagne.'

As he eased out the cork Duncan feared that Ellen, who had confessed to being daunted by Charlie's celebrity, would be further disconcerted by her manner. He poured the champagne and handed it round. 'A toast!' He raised his glass. 'To Charlie! Thank you for an amazing performance.'

'To Charlie!' Ellen echoed.

'To all three of us!' Charlie replied. 'Old friendships and new loves.'

'Don't push it!' Duncan said, with a glance at Ellen. 'We've only known each other six weeks.'

'Who said I was talking about you? Typical man!' She gave a throaty chortle. Then, insisting that she was bored with the sound of her own voice, she asked Ellen to tell her everything about speech therapy.

'I've only been back in the profession a few months,' Ellen said nervously.

'So it'll be fresh.'

Ellen needn't have worried since no sooner had she begun than Charlie interrupted with the story of a friend who was undergoing gender reassignment ('we're all PC now') and so seeing a speech therapist to help raise the pitch of his voice. 'He sounds like Mrs Thatcher with mumps.'

'I'm afraid I only deal with children,' Ellen said.

'Don't be afraid, darling. I'm sure it's wonderfully reward-ing. But I'm old school: never work with children and animals!'

'Do you have children of your own?'

'Christ, no! I'd have been the world's worst mother – well, worst but one. When I was nine, my mother told me I was so disgusting that not even a paedophile would want me.'

'How dreadful!' Ellen said.

'And now she wonders why I haven't spoken to her for twenty years! I've had two abortions. People think I did it for my career but the truth is I did it for my sanity. I know I'm supposed to beat my breast and say that the memory will haunt me till the day I die, but it isn't true. Best thing I've ever done. Saving your presence, of course.'

'Not at all,' Ellen replied, gulping.

'Still out to *épater* the rest of us,' Duncan said. 'You should take care – too much champagne on an empty stomach.'

'Too much? I've barely had a thimbleful. You're neglecting your duties.' She held out her glass for a refill. 'Don't get me wrong, Ellen. The world must be peopled and all that. Just not by me. You two should have children. Lots of gorgeous children.'

'Really?' Duncan said, sensitive to Ellen's discomfort. 'I told you, we've only just met.'

'Which is why you mustn't waste any time. We're none of us getting any younger. Don't let him slip away, darling. Take it from me. I did, and I'll always regret it.'

'I'm flattered,' Duncan said, 'but it was nearly thirty years ago.'

'You're still the best, the most passionate, the most considerate lover I've ever had. Don't you agree, Ellen?' Since by her own admission, Ellen had only had two boyfriends before marrying Matthew, to whom she remained faithful for sixteen years, she had little scope for comparison. Fortunately, rather than pressing her for a reply, Charlie launched into an account of his behaviour during her breakdown. 'I was in the funny farm for three months during my second year at Newnham. Tons of friends came to visit (I was the first of our lot to crack up, you see). They brought fruit and flowers and chocolates, all the usual. But not Duncan. Do you remember what you did?'

'Yes,' he said softly.

'He arranged for me to see a hairdresser, not the hospital hack but a stylist from town. He found the perfect way to make me feel better. No one's ever done anything so beautiful for me before or since.' She stood up and moved to him with tears in her eyes. 'You have the memory of my youth on your face.' Just as his own eyes started to fill, he wondered if she were quoting a line from a play and the spell was shattered.

Afraid that she was growing maudlin, he told her that they had to leave. 'Sorry, but I have an early start in the morning.'

'You can't! You've only just arrived. How can I finish all this fizz by myself? Who am I trying to kid?' She grabbed a second bottle, prised off the cork and filled her glass, oblivious to the cascading foam. With promises on both sides to meet again soon that were all the more poignant for their sincerity, Duncan kissed Charlie and led Ellen to the door.

'One moment!' Charlie said, running into the bedroom and coming out with the flowers. 'These are for you.' She handed them to Ellen.

'No really, I couldn't!'

'Don't be silly. I'll only be leaving them for the chambermaid.'

'Oh well, in that case … Thank you.'

With a backward glance at Charlie, Duncan followed Ellen into the corridor where the strong smell of damp reinforced his sense of exile. They walked slowly to the lift.

'Did you hate her?' Duncan asked.

'Not at all,' Ellen replied. 'She's so … feisty. You wouldn't think she'd spent the evening on stage.'

'That's the adrenalin. It takes time to come down after a show.'

'Of course,' Ellen said. 'It was very kind of her to give me the flowers.' She led the way into the lift.

'They smell marvellous,' Duncan said, as a stray lily brushed his nose.

'They're heavy.'

'I'd offer to carry them, but if we bump into anyone we know, they might think I'm taking them back to the florist's for a refund.'

As it turned out, Duncan spotted a familiar face as soon as they reached the vestibule. Chris, Adele's carer, wearing a dinner suit with exceptionally wide lapels, stood beside an older man in black tie and a bright red cummerbund. Introductions were effected, causing Duncan to wonder how much weight to attach to the 'friend'.

'I didn't realise you were coming,' Duncan said to Chris.

'Oh, we never miss a gala, do we, Paul?' Chris said, his words belied by the whiff of mothballs issuing from his jacket.

'We never miss Miss Lyndon,' Paul said. '*The Vicar's Husband* is my all-time favourite sitcom. I've worn out my DVDs.'

'Not to mention your friends. Go on, show him your doll.'

'No, I couldn't.'

'Go on! You know you want to.'

Coyly, Paul opened his bag and took out an eighteen-inch, flame-haired doll dressed in a cassock and surplice, which, despite the blandness of the embroidered face, bore a definite resemblance to the Reverend Penny.

'It's uncanny,' Duncan said. 'What do you think, Ellen?'

'Did you make it yourself?' she asked.

'Of course,' Paul said testily. 'I've made hundreds. All my favourite stars. The Queen. Princess Diana.'

'You should see his front room,' Chris said. 'You think your mother's bad! I've told him, you wouldn't get me dusting in there.'

'In your dreams! I wanted to give this one to Miss Lyndon. But the stuck-up bitch at reception – pardon my French – says they're not allowed to accept any unauthorised packages. Security.'

'Who'd bother to blow up this dump?' Chris asked.

'Why not take it up yourself. No one need know. She's on the third floor, room 317.'

'Really? She won't think it's an awful cheek?'

'She'll be thrilled,' Ellen said.

As Chris and Paul sidled through the vestibule in a manner calculated to arouse suspicion, Duncan and Ellen made their way outside.

'Do you think Charlie really will be pleased with that doll?' Duncan asked. 'I'd find it creepy.'

'She can always leave it for the chambermaid.'

'You know she didn't mean it like that.'

'No, I'm sure. I wish you'd told me you'd had an affair. That's twice in one night! I felt such a fool.'

'I'm sorry,' Duncan said, stroking her arm. 'It was so long ago I didn't think it mattered.'

'Do you ever regret leaving that world behind?'

'Of course.' Duncan shrugged. 'But then I also regret not qualifying for the four hundred metres final at the 1982 English Schools Championships.'

'You wouldn't have been happy.'

'With a gold medal?'

'You know what I mean.'

'Maybe not, but I'd like to have given it a go. I sometimes wonder, if my father hadn't died and I'd moved to London with the rest of the gang, would I have made it writing sketches or plays or even novels? I could have brought in an editor for the *Mercury* and contributed my own weekly column: "Notes from the Metropolis". I might have done something with my life.'

'You've done more than something. How would Francombe talk to itself without its paper?'

'That supposes it has anything worthwhile to say. Listen to me! I even feel futile admitting my own futility. I'm as preposterous as Uncle Vanya.'

'The play?'

'Right. He believes that he's wasted his life slaving away for people who don't appreciate him. He claims he could have been another Schopenhauer or Dostoyevsky. When I first saw it in my twenties, I thought that was his tragedy. Now I see the real tragedy is that he's deluding himself. He's as third-rate as everyone else.'

'But not you, Duncan. If you won't take my word, ask Charlie.'

'Come on,' he said, clasping her hand. 'I'll drive you home. I wasn't joking about the early start.'

Five

The Poison in Our Society

Comment

Thursday, 7 November 2013

The arrest earlier this week of two boys aged ten and twelve on suspicion of poisoning Dragon Greenslade has sent shock waves through Francombe.

Mr Greenslade, who has now been released after several weeks in the Princess Royal Hospital, was found unconscious, his dog dead at his side, in his hut in Salter Nature Reserve on 28 September. Doctors subsequently discovered substantial traces of weedkiller in his stomach.

Although the arrest of the boys, who cannot be named for legal reasons, brings the extensive police investigation to a close, it raises urgent questions for the entire community. Youth crime in the area has increased dramatically over the past decade. Figures obtained by the *Mercury* show that, during 2012, Francombe and Salter police arrested 316 offenders under the age of eighteen on a total of 2,042 charges.

Older residents on the Stafford Cripps and Edmund Hillary estates claim to be living in a state of siege, terrified of attack by local gangs who require prospective members, some as young as eight, to commit burglary, arson and assault as part of their initiation.

Small shopkeepers describe being forced to pay protection money to teenagers who brazenly ransack their shelves. Staff at chain stores report repeated raids by 'hoodies' using eight- or nine-year-old children as decoys, safe in the knowledge that they cannot be charged. Visitors to the Promenade or Jubilee Park at weekends witness the dispiriting spectacle of drunken youths vomiting, urinating and generally misbehaving. Anyone who, like the editor of this newspaper, attempts to remonstrate with them risks being subjected to a barrage of threats and abuse.

So who bears the blame for this delinquency? Discussion of the current case has already exposed a deep divergence in public opinion. There are some who maintain that despite their youth the boys knew exactly what they were doing and should face the full penalty of the law. After all, the argument goes, even if they did not appreciate the toxicity of the weedkiller, they could scarcely have overlooked the skull and crossbones on the can.

Others maintain that the fault lies with society as a whole, which has failed to provide young people with a set of fundamental values, including respect for the rights and – in the case of Dragon

Greenslade, the differences – of others. According to this view, if children grow up seeing reckless, ruthless and even criminal behaviour glamorised in the media and rewarded in the City, it's unsurprising that they should come to mimic it themselves.

At the *Mercury*, while acknowledging the importance of personal responsibility, we support those who apportion the guilt more widely. We do not believe that young people today are inherently more selfish, violent or, to use an old-fashioned word, wicked than they were in the past. Here in Francombe, we suffer from some of the worst rates of poverty, unemployment and family breakdown in the country. Although crime is not an inevitable consequence of social deprivation, it must be obvious to all but the most partisan observer that it's a common one.

Nevertheless, the Council has seen fit to slash its spending on youth clubs, sports clubs and drop-in centres, leaving the most vulnerable youngsters, often banished from home in the evenings by hard-pressed parents, with nowhere to congregate but the streets. What message does it send when the only communal spaces open to them – the amusement arcades, wheel park and even the cinema – are beyond their means? Why are we shocked when they threaten, rob, attack and, in the most extreme case, poison us in order to earn the respect of their peers in a world that otherwise disowns them?

Let us treat this latest incident as a wake-up call. Next time it may not just be a dog that dies.

Duncan left the bank in a daze. Ralph Welch, a loyal ally in the fight to save the pier, had proved to be less supportive of the *Mercury*. He had summoned Duncan to discuss the company's £400,000 loan, which was due for repayment in January. Duncan, who had hoped to renegotiate the loan or, failing that, to discuss new methods of finance, was stunned by the bluntness with which Ralph – their first-name terms now seemed risible – told him that the old business model was obsolete and refused to accept Mercury House as collateral when so many buildings in the town centre stood empty. He urged Duncan to consider the takeover bids from Newscom and the Provident Group, adding that the only alternative was to find a philanthropic tycoon with a love of both print journalism and the local community. Trying to keep the bitterness out of his voice, Duncan pointed out that, in the unlikely event such a saviour existed, he would not be found in Francombe.

Anxious to clear his head before returning to work, Duncan walked briskly up the Parade and through the suburban sprawl to Ellen's house, where he had arranged to drop off her watch. Given her reluctance either to let him stay the night until the children knew him better or to leave her thirteen-year-old son alone for long in the evening, they were reduced to snatching odd hours at his flat between her cooking the family dinner and enforcing the ten o'clock curfew. Having likened their plight to the plot of a chic French film, he took to answering the doorbell in the voice of a Parisian concierge (or, at any rate, with an Inspector Clouseau accent) and once even put a copy of *Le Monde* on the pillow; but it did not feel chic, let alone sexy, to have to make love with one eye on the clock and defer their post-coital chat until she rang from home two hours later. It was no surprise, therefore, when she called this morning to say that she had forgotten her watch, adding, in a phrase that promised more than it delivered, that she felt 'naked without it'. She declined his offer to take it round to the Centre while she was still on probation, which made him feel even more hole-and-corner than her veto on overnight stays. So he had slipped the watch in a jiffy bag and brought it round to the house.

Holding open the letter box to push the bag out of reach of any opportunistic burglar, he heard voices, which for a moment convinced him that thieves were already at work. When he identified one of them as Sue's, his anxiety took a new turn. All his resentment at her refusal to babysit her brother faded as he simultaneously banged the door and pressed the bell, but the only effect was to plunge the house into silence.

'Sue, is that you?' he asked, bending to peer through the flap. 'It's Duncan Neville. Are you all right? Please open the door.'

The ensuing flurry of giggles was not what he had expected. Offended, he banged harder. 'I'm quite prepared to stay here all day,' he said. 'So you may as well answer me.'

Two pairs of legs entered his field of vision and the door opened abruptly to reveal Sue and Craig. Both were bleary-eyed and blinking, as though emerging from a cave.

'Hey there, Mr N,' Craig said. 'Have you dropped something?'

Sue giggled as Duncan sprang up. Craig smiled smugly at them both.

'Craig, I didn't expect to find you here. Nor Sue, for that matter.'

'We're on a study period,' Craig said.

'That's right. We're on a study period,' Sue repeated flatly.

'And you're allowed to come all the way back from school?'

'We're encouraged. It's called "Giving the children respon-sibility",' Craig said snidely. 'But what brings you to these parts, Mr N? Out drumming up subscriptions?'

He tempered the insult with a winsome smile that Duncan knew he was rare in resisting. Once again he feared for Craig's influence on Jamie. This was a boy who, answering a question on obesity in a human biology exam, had chosen to write – allegedly in graphic detail – about fat admirers, men who fed and fetishised grossly overweight women. His outraged teacher gave him an F until his mother, from whom he had acquired both his confidence and his conceit, threatened to appeal to the LEA unless the paper were marked 'objectively', whereupon it was upgraded to a B.

'I've come to return Sue's mother's watch, which she left when … when we had dinner earlier in the week.'

'Was the food tough?'

'What?'

'Did she take the watch off to get a better grip on her fork?'

'You're not funny, Craig.'

'No?' Craig asked, glancing at Sue who was giggling inanely. As the confrontation dragged on, Duncan detected an odour that was instantly recognisable, even after twenty years.

'What's that smell?'

'What smell?' Craig asked.

'That pungent, composty smell?'

'Oh that! That's just our raging teenage hormones,' Craig replied. This time Sue did not laugh.

'Have you been smoking pot?'

'No!' Sue said, reddening.

'Scout's honour,' Craig said. 'Search me if you don't believe me.' He pouted and raised his arms provocatively.

'You do realise the damage you're doing to your brain cells?' Duncan asked, staring at Sue and wondering what, if anything, Ellen had told her of her grandfather.

'A million die every day, so what do a few more matter?' Craig replied.

'Poppycock! Where on earth did you pick that up?'

'On the Net. Which is why we should get back to our work while we've still got some left.' As Craig put his arm round Sue's shoulder and turned away, Duncan remembered why he had come. 'Sue, don't forget your mother's watch!'

Craig grabbed the jiffy bag from him. 'No sweat. We'll make sure she gets it. Always a pleasure, Mr N.'

'Wait...' Duncan said as Craig slammed the door, exercising a prerogative that was all the more painful for its being denied to him. After a moment's hesitation he hurried down the drive for fear of losing his composure, which was never more tested than during an encounter with one of the Weedons. Craig might have acquired his conceit from Frances but he had been schooled in its use by Geoffrey.

Returning to the office, Duncan was plunged into a frenzy of activity that wiped out all thoughts of debts and takeovers and drugs and truancy. Sheila was sifting through the competition entries for tickets to the Switherton Players' production of *The Crucible*. Forty-six readers had submitted seventy-three answers to the question: 'Which famous film star did playwright Arthur Miller marry?' If they wanted to waste their time on candidates such as Groucho Marx and Lassie, that was their affair, but he never ceased to be amazed by the lengths to which the likes of Mr/Mrs/Miss/Ms Victor/Victoria/Vicky/Vick/Vee Brown/Browne/Browning would go to send multiple entries for prizes that were worth less than the stamps. He had no compunction about rigging the results. The competitions, however paltry, were all that remained of the paper's power of patronage and he was determined to wield it on behalf of the worthiest (in other words, *neediest*) members of the community. So whenever possible, the winning entries should come from one of the housing estates and be written in a pensioner's neat copperplate or spidery scrawl. In recent years the system had broken down only once: when Brian Gannon, supposing that Seacombe Court was a high-rise block on the coast between Salter and St Anselm, had awarded 'a day's pampering' at the Diamond Health Spa to Frieda Cradwyck.

Having picked the three winners, Duncan wandered into the reporters' room where, unusually for a Monday afternoon, no one was out *on patch*.

'So how long will this meeting last?' Ken bawled down the phone, as he solicited the Director of Housing's response to a leaked memo outlining proposed Council rent increases, which, given the cap on welfare benefits, would cause real hardship to children, the elderly and other vulnerable tenants. 'Last winter they had to choose between food and heating,' he said after truncating the call. 'This year it'll be between food, heating and a roof over their heads.'

'Look on the bright side. If they don't have a roof over their heads, they won't need to worry about heating,' Brian said. 'Just a thought,' he added, ignoring Ken's glare.

'Remember the old girl at the WRAC group when I asked how they coped with rising prices?' Ken said. '"I skip meals," she replied without an ounce of self-pity. "I skip meals." Jesus wept!'

'But it's a story we've run so often,' Stewart said, looking up from his screen. 'If it's going to be this week's splash, you'll need a punchy headline.'

'So find one!' Ken said.

'How about "Blood on their Hands"?' Rowena asked, continuing to type.

'Too loaded,' Ken said, newly circumspect after the libel case. 'Town Hall would go ape-shit.'

'Just "Genocide" in a 150-point font?' Stewart asked.

'That might work,' Duncan said.

'It sounds like Rwanda,' said Rowena who, for all her complaints about male egos, chafed at the least rebuff.

'The average life expectancy of a Rwandan man is fifty-two,' Jake chimed in, incongruous as ever.

'And for women?' Rowena asked. 'Or don't they count?'

'Fifty-five. it's gone up twelve years over the last decade.'

'Pity it's not the same in Francombe,' Brian said. 'I wouldn't have to cosy up to any more centenarians.'

'Don't be so modest!' Ken said. 'Think of the joy you bring them. Better than the telegram from the Queen.'

'"I've always kept myself busy," said Jessie Potts, who celebrates her hundredth birthday this week.' Brian read out the piece in the clipped tones of a newsreel announcer. '"My back gives me gyp but I still do all my own housework." On the great day, Jessie will be up at seven as usual making lunch for some of the nine children, twenty-four grandchildren, forty-seven great-grandchildren and nine great-great-grandchildren who will be spending it with her. "I've just had a new carpet in my front room. I mean to stick around and get my money's worth," she said with a twinkle in her eye.'

'Can you think of another word for "twinkle"?' Duncan asked.

'I can think of plenty but they wouldn't be printable.'

'While I remember,' Duncan said, turning to Ken, 'we need someone to review the Switherton Players' production of *The Crucible.*'

'When does it open?'

'Thursday.'

'Rowena?' Ken said, trying to couch an instruction in an interrogative.

'No way,' she replied. 'Besides, I'll be out on the Marsey Road.'

'Have things got that bad?' Brian asked with mock solicitude.

'Very funny! I'm with the police reporting their clampdown on kerb crawlers. So be warned.'

'On my money? Fat chance!'

'Brian'll go,' Ken said to Duncan. 'Keep him out of mischief for one evening.'

'But isn't that the play about witches? You want to save it for yourself, mate. You being such an expert and all that.'

'Sort it out between you,' Duncan said quickly. 'I don't mind who goes so long as it's covered.'

Listening to their bickering, he had an uneasy sense that what had once been friendly competition had hardened into genuine antagonism. The constant strain of the shoestring operation was starting to tell.

'Any gems in this week's post bag?' he asked Stewart, who was laying out the letters page. Unlike his father for whom they had been a source of cheap copy, he saw the readers' responses as integral to the *Mercury*'s attempt to foster a communal conversation.

'Much the usual. There's yet another one from the East Sussex humanists, accusing us of pandering to ignorance and superstition by printing Henry's column.'

'Any specifics?'

'No.'

'Bin it!'

'This one may be a wind-up. It's from a bloke who asks: "Does no one else share my horror on observing an elderly member of the fair sex stooping to pick up her dog's doings in the park?"'

'Doings?'

'His word, not mine.'

'What colour ink?'

'It's typed. On blue Basildon Bond paper with an embossed address.'

'Check the name with the electoral register. If it tallies, run it. What about Mr Jonley? Don't tell me there's nothing from him this week!'

'Two. One asking whether queue jumping has become a permanent feature of Francombe life and the other deploring the rudeness of bus drivers on the 101 route. Which should I go for?'

'You decide. I can't stand the excitement.'

'Here's one that's more to your taste. A letter complaining about letters of complaint. It ends: "When will Francombe learn to be more tolerant?"'

'I love it! Let's make it Letter of the Week. No feedback from my leader?'

'None that you'd want to use. Several objecting (if that's not too mild a word) to your remark about the dog. Here's one: "Shame on you for suggesting that an innocent creature who never harmed anyone" – I thought it'd bitten several ramblers but never mind – "is less precious than a dirty tramp whose way of life is an affront to the entire town…" Shall I go on?'

'I get the gist. Send over the proof when you're done.'

Duncan left the room, dismayed that once again the communal conversation had descended into name-calling. Rather than return to his office, he went downstairs to the archives, seeking solace as so often in the large leather-bound volumes lining the shelves. As reverently as a priest lifting up the Gospel, he took down the volume for the second half of 1913, turning to the issue of 20 November in search of a suitable item for next week's 'On This Day' column. He found it at once in the front-page report of the suffragettes arrested for daubing red paint on the statue of Queen Victoria. Quite apart from its inherent interest, the story gave him a sense of validation. Even if the *Mercury* no longer played a defining role in Francombe's present, it was the principal repository of its past.

Refreshed, he went back to his office and embarked on his long-deferred letter of apology to Sam Vernham. When, after weeks of rumour and speculation, the fire investigators announced that a melted paraffin stove and scraps of bedding had been found in the charred shell of the Winter Garden, their chief had laid the blame for the inferno on vagrants who had broken through the security fence to seek shelter. While resolved to keep an open mind, Duncan thought it a fitting moment to celebrate the service's achievements and arranged for Brian to spend three days shadowing a crew at the Oswald Street Fire Station. The subsequent feature, complete with photograph of the intrepid reporter sliding down a pole, contained a faulty link, directing readers wanting to learn more not to www.eastsussexfire.co.uk but to www.eastsussex.fire.

co.uk, the site of a male strip troupe who promised to 'light your fire' and 'send the temperature soaring' at 'hen nights, birthday parties, girls' nights out and other special occasions'. Vernham who, unknown to Duncan, had been fighting for years to have the offending website shut down, had taken the misplaced dot as deliberate mockery and threatened to sue.

Cloyed with humble pie, Duncan turned to the window, where his gaze fell on a solitary figure on the far side of the road. His taut body and shuffling feet would have made him a sinister presence even if his face had not been obscured. Catching sight of Duncan he pulled down his hood, revealing that he was in his late teens or early twenties, with the distinctive mixture of aggression and vulnerability that shorn hair brought to soft features. Lifting a hand from his anorak pocket he beckoned to Duncan, who stepped swiftly out of view. If he wanted to speak to him, why hadn't he rung the bell? Was he afraid of being recognised? Had he read – or, more likely, been told about – last week's leader and come to sell inside information on one of the gangs? Eager to find out, Duncan walked to the door, only to double back and, with an instinct that shamed him even as he surrendered to it, placed his wallet in his desk.

Pausing at Sheila's door, he debated whether to tell her where he was going, 'just in case', but anticipating a fraught exchange about risks and knives and psychopaths designed, he suspected, to titillate herself as much as to safeguard him, he carried on without a word, exited the building and crossed the road, where the young man greeted him with grim satisfaction.

'I knew you'd come.'

'You did?'

'I have powers, see.'

'Not really, no.' He feared that the warning he had attributed to Sheila would prove to be timely.

'I wanted you, and here you are.'

'Do I know you?'

'No one knows me. I know you, though. You're Mr Neville,' he said with strange formality.

'Guilty as charged.'

'Are you taking the piss?'

'No.'

'You don't want to mess with me, mate. I'm dangerous; I've been through the courts.'

The claim made him seem all the more vulnerable. 'Aren't you cold?' Duncan asked.

'What's that? No, I ain't cold.' He unzipped his anorak to reveal a flimsy T-shirt covering a puny chest.

'Well, I am. So I'm going back indoors.'

'Wait! I'm talking to you. Ain't you ashamed of yourself?'

'What for?' Duncan asked, more perplexed than ever.

'The way you treat women of course,' he replied, as if it were self-evident.

Duncan ran through a quick list of the women in his life: Ellen; Linda; Adele; Alison; Sheila; Rowena. With the possible exception of the last, he could not imagine any of them having denounced him. 'Do you mean in one of our articles?' he asked, although it would be hard to envisage a less prurient paper. They had barely featured a swimsuit all summer.

'I'm talking about Mary.'

'Mary? Mary who? Do you mean Mary the cleaner?'

'Is that all she is to you? A cleaner? To scrub your floors and pick up your rubbish and … and … and …'

He broke off, unable either to think of any other domestic tasks or to contemplate Mary undertaking them. 'Who are you?' Duncan asked.

'Jordan!' The question was answered by Mary herself, who raced down the road towards them. 'Jordan,' she said, fighting for breath, 'what are you doing here?'

'I told him – didn't I tell you? – that if he didn't treat you right, I'd kill him.'

Although it was the first time that death had been mentioned, Duncan thought it wiser not to quibble.

'I'm so sorry, Mr Neville,' Mary said. 'Jordan, love, you shouldn't have come here. Let's go.'

'You know him then, Mary?' Duncan asked.

'I'll tell you later. I'm really sorry. Really. Come on, love.' She put her arm round Jordan's shoulders and dragged him away. As he went, Jordan turned back and pointed two fingers at his own eyes and then at Duncan, the effect undermined by his squint.

Duncan returned to his desk and the letter of apology, but the curious encounter preoccupied him. The name Jordan struck a chord and he wondered whether he were a nephew or cousin of Mary's or, given his reference to the courts, an associate of her son Norman. He felt a pang of guilt, aggravated by Jordan's charge, that she might have mentioned him one day while cleaning and he had drowned out her voice as if it were the drone of the Hoover. He impatiently awaited her arrival but when she knocked on his door, she was so on edge that he was obliged to spend several minutes assuring her that he did not hold her in any way responsible for Jordan's threats. He insisted that she sit down and would have offered her a cup of tea had he not feared that she would see it as the prelude to bad news.

'He says I'm his muse,' she finally conceded.

'What?'

'That's like the inspiration for his painting.'

'I know,' Duncan said, more confused than ever.

'Yes, of course you do. I'm sorry.'

'No, I am.' Suddenly everything fell into place. Henry had mentioned a young man doing community service in the church hall. 'He's the one painting the Garden of Eden.'

'I'm his Eve,' she said with a blend of bashfulness and pride. Although without precedent in his experience of Eden, Duncan saw no reason why Eve should not be a fleshy earth mother as much as a willowy Venus. Even so, he struggled with the image of a naked Mary before realising that, as a graffiti artist, Jordan would in all probability have used caricature. 'I've always thought it must be the most wonderful thing in the world if you can paint,' Mary said. 'But I never realised how wonderful till I watched Jordan. The look on his face when he's working. It's like he can tell everything about you and at the same time you're not there. I've never seen that look before except...'

'Yes?'

'Perhaps on Bob's face when ... you know, we were first married.'

'I can't wait to see the result. How long till it's finished?'

'It's finished now. At least I think so. Jordan's never satisfied.'

'The quest for perfection.'

'Sometimes I look at it for hours on end and I make out I'm looking at all the details, but I'm really looking at me. Isn't that dreadful?' The glint in her eyes belied the question. 'He's made me so beautiful. And I don't know how. It's the same face I've always had. And the same body. A body I didn't even like showing to the doctor. Now it's up there for everyone to see. And I'm not afraid and I'm not ashamed.'

'He really has put you in Eden,' Duncan said, moved.

'I told him you'd understand.'

'But why did he target me?' Duncan asked, as the memory of Jordan's tirade flooded back.

'That's my fault. I'm really sorry. I told him you were always putting your foot down, making me come in early and stay late. I had to, else he never would have given me a moment's peace. He says he can only work if I'm there. But I have people to see to at home.'

'Surely he appreciates that? Doesn't he have a mother of his own?'

A shadow crossed Mary's face and for a moment Duncan

feared that he had misconstrued their relationship. 'His mother has MS,' she said. 'She's in a wheelchair. He has to do everything for her, even things that ... well, I wouldn't want my Nick or my Norman doing them for me. He hasn't had it easy, poor love. His dad buggered off when he was a kid. He's been her main carer ever since.'

'Henry – Father Henry – said he had trouble at home, but he didn't elaborate.' Once again Duncan found himself in a world of stark polarities. No matter how serious the domestic problems among his acquaintance, they would never land any of them in court.

'All the stress meant that he fell back at school, except for his art. He always came top in art. Then he left and he didn't even have the art lessons any more. He had nothing: nowhere to paint; nowhere to set down all his thoughts. That's why he wrote his tag – that's like his signature – all over the shelters. He knows he's been given a second chance. He's done twice the hours of his community order. He's still on probation for nine months. He has to pay off his fine and make sure he keeps his nose clean or else the prison sentence will be activated. But the vicar's promised to bring people to see the picture, people who'll help him get to college. He's worried what'll happen to his mum, but I've told him how she wouldn't want to hold him back. Now he has to think of himself first.'

Duncan was suddenly conscious of the time. Thanking Mary for putting him in the picture, which made her laugh, he prepared to leave work, first looking in on the reporters' room where Ken, still waiting for the Director of Housing to return his call, informed him that Jake was at the Ley Park bowls tournament, Brian at the Council Licensing Committee, Rowena interviewing a teenager who had delivered his baby on the kitchen floor, and – he added censoriously – Stewart gone home early to oversee the installation of a new Jacuzzi. Dismayed by Ken's tone, Duncan hurried out and popped his head round Sheila's door, but his 'quick goodnight' was predictably drawn out as she announced that she was off to see her mother in Castlemaine, where there was great excitement among the more lucid female residents ever since the arrival of Dragon Greenslade had doubled the number of available men.

Duncan unlocked Rocinante and drove to Granary Lane, a journey he could have made blindfold and which, gazing misty-eyed at the well-loved landmarks, he rather wished that he had. Parking outside Swallows' Nest, he fought the familiar urge to scratch out Swallows' and replace it with Cuckoo's, in a nod to Derek. While he had encouraged Linda to stay on in the house so as to minimise the disruption to Jamie, he had been surprised by Derek's compliance. He longed to know – although after so many years it was impossible to ask – whether Linda had told him of the months they spent when first married knocking down the scullery wall and extending the conservatory. Had a childhood of wearing Geoffrey's hand-me-downs made him doubt his own taste? Apart from the miniature golfer teeing off on the lawn, its only obvious expression was in the shelving unit in the sitting room that held his home cinema.

The door was opened by Gabriela, the Argentinian au pair, whose request for *Durex*, which turned out to be Spanish for sellotape, had become a staple of Derek's comic repertoire. Ever uneasy with Duncan's nebulous role in the household, she led him into the sitting room where Rose was watching a cartoon featuring psychedelic elephants. Her neck was twisted and her arms and legs were flailing, which he had once compared to the fluttering of a butterfly but which now looked more like the death throes of a prisoner in an electric chair. She seemed to smile when she saw him, although with her mouth in spasm it was hard to tell. After kissing her cheek and stroking her tousled hair, he stood watching a short sequence in which the elephants, now a nuclear family, perched on stools around a dinner table, looking as awkward as Rose herself. Respecting

Linda's demand that no one should talk down to her (which wasn't easy when she was four years old and her head level with his thigh), he crouched beside her and explained the difference between African and Indian elephants, whereupon she slowly, almost imperceptibly, shifted her gaze back to the screen.

'Just wait till they all go to the seaside. That's the best bit, isn't it, angel?' Linda said as she walked into the room. Duncan stood up to kiss her cheek, which was less yielding than Rose's. 'I'm afraid Jamie's not home yet,' she added. 'I've left two messages on his mobile but he hasn't replied.'

'Never mind, I expect I'm early. Besides, it gives me a chance to catch up with Rose.'

'We've spent the afternoon gardening, haven't we, angel?' Having named her before her diagnosis, Linda had been doubly delighted by Rose's affinity with flowers.

'Was it fun?' Duncan asked Rose, who gurgled and dribbled with pleasure. Linda adjusted the wheelchair tray, bringing the communication book closer to Rose, who pointed the middle finger of her right hand to a smiley face above the word 'happy'.

'You were happy!' Duncan said, at which Rose nodded her head.

'What did you do?'

Rose laboriously turned the laminated pages until she reached one marked Garden. Like everyone who came within her orbit, Duncan was familiar with her book, its first page of key words (I, it, he, she, you, mine, Mummy, Daddy, Jamie, Craig, drink, eat, like, see, feel, hurt, play, want, help, listen, good, bad, happy, sad, big, little) followed by pages relating to specific topics, such as Family, House, School, Stories, Food, Clothes and Television. Each time he asked her a question, she would point to one or more symbols, building up a sentence for him to repeat, whereupon she would either nod her head if he had interpreted correctly or shake it if he had misunderstood. He asked her what she had seen and she pointed in turn to Worm, eat and Butterfly, an improbable sequence that, observing the etiquette, he nonetheless repeated. 'You saw a worm eating a butterfly?' he said, replacing his scepticism with excitement. As her tongue rolled about and her head wobbled like a toy dog on a dashboard, he was uncertain whether she were nodding or shaking, smiling or frowning, and felt deeply ashamed.

'Don't be a silly sausage, Uncle Duncan,' Linda said, gently lifting Rose's hand and directing Duncan to Bird, drink, and Pond, in each case one symbol to the right.

'You saw a bird drinking from a pond? Of course. I'm such a ninny,' Duncan said stiltedly.

'It's a new page and we haven't fully got the hang of it yet,' Linda said. 'Who made it for you, angel?'

Rose pointed to one of the stock symbols on the left-hand side of the page.

'Daddy!' Linda said. This time Rose's smile was unequivocal. 'Though if I were to ask her who read it with her,' she added under her breath, 'it would always be Mummy.'

Duncan wondered how to respond to another hint that all was not well in Linda's marriage. There was a time when, despite his protestations, nothing would have pleased him more than for her to admit that their divorce had been a mistake and ask him to take her back, not just for Jamie's sake but for Rose's. That time, however, had passed.

'I saw Ellen this week,' Linda said.

'Don't you see her every week?' Duncan asked, startled by the mention of her name at this juncture.

'Must you always nitpick?'

'I'm sorry.'

'In fact I've seen her twice. She's conducting a series of language assessments on Rose for the LEA.'

'How's she doing ... Rose, I mean?'

'Excellently I think – no, I know. Mummy isn't worried

about her clever little girl, is she, angel?' she asked, drawing no response from Rose, whose gaze remained fixed on the TV.

Rose would turn five in June and start primary school in September. That she was the first child with cerebral palsy ever to attend Ley Park nursery owed everything to the tenacity of her mother, who was now limbering up for the even tougher fight to keep her in mainstream education. The local authority wanted to send her to Haycock Road where she would receive customised care, but Linda was adamant that she should not be confined to a 'special-needs ghetto'.

'The nursery school teachers report that she's not very bright. But that's precisely because they don't take the trouble to listen to her. Ellen's tests prove that she understands far more than you'd think. She's about to start with her first VOCA. You'll be seeing a tremendous change.'

'Fingers crossed.'

'No, that's not good enough! We can't leave anything to chance.' Linda's voice betrayed a desperation that Duncan had not heard since she pleaded with him to start the testosterone treatment. 'Ellen'll set out the results of her tests, but she could still conclude that Rose needs a level of support she'll only get at a special school. I've even read of kids in wheelchairs being refused places in regular schools because they're a fire risk!'

'I suppose that must be a consideration.'

'What? How many school fires have you heard of lately?'

'Well, none that – '

'Exactly. I've told them how much time I'm prepared to put into the school – in the classroom too if they can't afford enough teaching assistants. Our buying the VOCA will already have saved them five thousand quid.'

'Of course,' Duncan said, wondering whether she expected him simply to be a sympathetic listener or to deploy the power of the press.

'That's why I hoped you'd sound Ellen out on her recommendations. I know she's on our side … not that it's a question of sides. But she works closely with the local authority, so she's in a tricky position.'

'I promise I'll do what I can,' Duncan said warily. 'But she's a professional to her fingertips. I'm not sure she'd welcome my interference.'

'You're right. Forget I mentioned it!' Linda said, moving to wipe the saliva from Rose's chin. 'I might have a word with Craig,' she said, refusing to let the matter drop. 'He's the last person I'd choose to ask for a favour, but he's going out with Ellen's daughter, Sue. Of course, you already know that. Small world!'

'Or just a small town?'

'I'm not proud; I'm ready to try anything. I won't let Rose be written off. She may not be the next Stephen Hawking, but she deserves a chance.'

Rose, alert to her mother's agitation, moaned and thrashed about. Linda hurried to her. 'Don't worry, angel. It'll soon be time for your tea. Where do you suppose that naughty brother of yours has got to? Oh look,' she said, pointing at the screen. 'Lollipop and Aniseed are playing beach ball.' Calming herself as well as her daughter, she turned back to Duncan.

'I'm sorry. I know how you hate fuss.'

'That's not fair.'

'It wasn't a criticism. I expect it's why you hit it off so well with Ellen. You still are, aren't you?'

'Yes,' Duncan said, unable to resist a smile.

'That's great. Truly. I so want you to be happy.'

'Thank you. It's early days yet. We're both afraid of rushing things. She's not long out of a disastrous marriage.'

'That's not your problem, I hope.'

'You know it's not. I don't understand how she stuck it for so long. Matthew – her ex – was a brute.'

'Maybe that's why she's gone for a man who's the opposite?'

'Is that why you went for Derek?'

'I asked for that, didn't I? I don't know; I've never analysed it.'

'No,' Duncan said, recalling an attraction that, perhaps to spare his feelings, she had described to him as 'chemical' but to a mutual friend as 'magnetic'. In retrospect he knew that he should have fought harder to keep her, but not only was it not in his nature, it wasn't in his code. Having encouraged her to open new doors, he felt unable to stand in her way when she chose the one marked Exit.

Jamie's arrival put an end to his soul-searching. Ignoring his parents, he made straight for Rose, planting a squelchy kiss on her cheek and asking whether she had had a good day.

'Earth to Jamie,' Linda said. 'Has a magic spell turned us both invisible?'

'Can't you see I'm talking to Rose?' He followed her hand, interpreting the symbols effortlessly. 'You saw a bird drinking from the pond? Cool!'

'Your father's been waiting half an hour. Don't you think you owe him an explanation?'

'I'm sure there's a very simple one,' Duncan said mildly.

'I left two messages on your mobile,' Linda said. 'Why was it switched off?'

'I was in detention, all right?'

'What did you do?' Duncan asked.

'It wasn't my fault. Why can't you both get off my case?'

'We'll talk about it later,' Duncan said. 'We'd better make tracks. Granny's waiting.'

'Oh no,' Jamie said, turning to Linda. 'Craig said he was coming round tonight.'

'So he's seeing his father and you're seeing yours,' she replied. 'Now go and clean yourself up. I don't want your grandmother saying I sent you off looking like a tramp.'

Jamie went out, dragging his heels and muttering.

'I heard that,' Linda said.

'Did you really?' Duncan asked as soon as Jamie was out of earshot.

Linda shook her head. 'But it's as well to keep him guessing.'

While Linda consoled Rose on the loss of her playmate, Duncan brooded on Jamie's fixation with Craig. Was it simply deference to the elder brother he had never had, or did it represent something more sinister?

'I wish I felt warmer towards Craig,' he said tentatively. 'This morning, I caught him playing hooky with Sue. I'm fairly sure they were smoking dope.'

'I wouldn't be surprised. Francis Preston's drowning in the stuff.'

'You don't think Jamie…?'

'No, I'm sure not. But it's only a question of time.'

'You're being remarkably sanguine. Shouldn't we talk to him?'

'And say what? It was easy for our parents. They'd never smoked anything stronger than Senior Service. But our kids know that we have. Remember the night you, Miles and Sanjay liberated the chickens from the factory farm in Devon? It'd be the pot calling the kettle black.'

'No pun intended,' Duncan said, as her baffled expression confirmed that it wasn't. 'But the dope is so much stronger these days. It does real damage.'

'Sure, that'll be the clincher! Sorry, kids, it was safe when we took it, but not any more.'

'Even so, it'd be irresponsible not to point out the risks.'

'They have drugs advisers at school. Not that they seem to be much use.'

'Exactly. There are some things that come best from a parent.'

Although he still winced at the memory of his own father who, ignoring the evidence of his KS, had assumed that he was sexually active at the age of twelve and given him a lengthy pep talk on the use of condoms, few aspects of Derek's usurping of his paternal role had galled him more than his pre-empting of the sex chat after catching Jamie with a pile of Craig's top-shelf magazines. If Derek had warned Jamie against confusing flesh-and-blood girls with pornography (apparently as great a danger in the Internet age as getting them pregnant), then he would be the one to warn him against the equally bogus attraction of drugs. So what if he had to admit to certain youthful indiscretions? The odd blush was a small price to pay for protecting his son.

'Look who I found lurking on the stairs,' Derek said, walking in with his fist pressed casually to Jamie's skull. 'How are my two favourite girls?' he asked, moving first to kiss Linda, who appeared indifferent, and then Rose, whose face crinkled with joy. 'Evening, young man,' he said, raising his right hand in preparation for a high-five and, when Duncan failed to respond, tracing an arc in the air. 'How's the world treating you?'

'Oh, I've given up worrying about the world. I've enough problems on my doorstep.'

'It's an expression, Dad,' Jamie said, sighing. 'You don't have to take it literally.'

'Actually, it's a cliché, which is why I did.'

'The editor speaks! That's telling us, isn't it, son?' Derek said with studied ambiguity.

'You should go now, Jamie,' Linda said. 'Your grandmother will be waiting and I've got to cook supper for Craig.'

'I'm sorry love; he's not coming,' Derek said. 'I meant to ring but it slipped my mind. He texted to ask if he could make it another night. He's doing something with Sue.' He turned to Duncan. 'She's his ... of course, you know. She's your new girlfriend's daughter.'

'Gross!' Jamie said.

'Take no notice,' Linda said to Duncan. 'He's delighted for you really.'

'Like I care.'

'Actually, I saw them both this morning,' Duncan said to Derek. 'I had to drop a parcel off for Ellen and they were at the house. Craig said they had a free study period, which seemed unlikely.'

'For fuck's sake, Dad, how can you be such a grass?'

Duncan was taken aback by Jamie's outrage. 'I was concerned about Craig and thought it only right to warn his father. The same way I hope he'd tell me if he was concerned about you.'

'No chance of that, is there, sport?' Derek asked, brushing Jamie's head with enviable licence. 'I mean there's no chance that you'd do anything to worry me.'

Seeing the easy rapport between stepfather and stepson, Duncan reflected bitterly that his initial fears of their mutual resentment had been replaced by envy of their intimacy. Yet he of all people should understand why, missing Craig, Derek had turned to Jamie. He hinted as much when he was finally alone with his son on the way to Ridgemount.

'Derek must be hurt at Craig crying off.'

'He's cool. Some dads want their kids to have a good time.'

'Some dads want to have a good time with their kids,' Duncan said, affecting nonchalance.

'Yeah, right! Still, there's always a bad vibe when he comes round. Mum gets pissed that he refuses to eat with Rose. He says it's like feeding time at the zoo.'

'That's very cruel.'

'It's true. Sometimes she even gets food stuck at the back of her throat. Mum has to put her fingers in her mouth to stop her choking. It's disgusting.'

'I'm disappointed in you,' Duncan said, glancing at Jamie, his face aptly jaundiced by the street lights. 'You've always been so good with Rose.'

'So? People change. Are you the same guy you were when you were thirteen?'

'I hope I'm still as loyal to my sister,' Duncan replied, conscious that he had yet to tell her about his meeting at the bank.

'Aunt Alison's a tennis champion; Rose is in a wheelchair. It's not the same. Anyhow, what are you getting at me for? I didn't blow you off.'

'I know, and I'm very pleased to see you. So give me a rundown on what you've been up to.'

'Boring!'

'All right. We'll save it till we get to Granny's.'

'Why do we always have to go to hers?'

'You're the one who complains that my flat's too cramped.'

'It's wrong that everyone else lives in smart houses and you're squashed in a cubbyhole.'

'It's a very convenient cubbyhole; I'm never late for work. Still, I'm touched that you're so concerned about your old dad.'

'Who says I'm concerned? It's just embarrassing.'

'Try to make an effort with Granny,' Duncan said, as they waited in a lengthy tailback on Bartholomew Road. 'She may not always show it, but she lives for you children.'

'She should get out more.'

'That isn't kind.'

'If she lives for anyone, it's Tim and Graham. She never stops talking about them.'

'I'm sure she talks to them about you.'

'When? They never come here. They've got more sense. She's always criticising me. And making sly digs at Mum. "I don't suppose that's the way things are done in your house, is it, darling?" "Whoever taught you to use the word *serviette*? Oh, I'm sorry, was it Linda?"'

'You're quite right to stick up for your mother, but don't be too hard on your grandmother. She hasn't had the easiest life.'

'Because her dad was a Nazi?'

'Whatever you do, don't say that to her! In any case he wasn't; he was a fascist sympathiser. He was culpably naïve and he suffered the consequences. What I meant was her life with your grandfather.' Having previously glossed over his parents' differences, he judged that Jamie was old enough to understand that two generations of marital discord need not lead to a third.

'I thought he was Mr Popular.'

'Mr Too Popular if you were his wife! When I was your age, I could never figure out why the editor of a Francombe newspaper had to spend so many nights in London.'

'So why did he?'

'He didn't.'

'Then what?' Jamie laughed coarsely. 'You mean he was a dirty old man?'

'The polite word is roué.'

'There's always a polite word like "napkin" and "serviette", but it's the same thing underneath. Mum said that Granny made up half the things that were wrong with her so you'd feel sorry for her. She said if it weren't for her, the two of you would still be together.'

'What? That's nonsense. I don't believe Linda would have said that.'

'She so did!'

'Then you must have misunderstood. Either way it's not true.'

'So why did you split up? It can't be because of the two of you. You always get on so well. You row far less than Mum and Derek.'

'But then we see each other far less,' Duncan said, striving to be fair.

'Michael Phillips's mum cut his dad out of all their wedding photos. Pete Limkin's mum accused his dad of trying to rape her.'

'Not all divorces are like that.' Duncan ached for his son's lost innocence.

'So if it wasn't because of Granny, then it must have been me.'

'What?' Duncan asked, as the lights changed and the cars surged forward.

'Mum said you didn't want another kid. Which means you didn't want another one like me.'

'Where on earth...? Who told you that?'

'No one. They didn't have to. I can work things out for myself.'

'You couldn't be more wrong. True, I didn't want another kid. But it had nothing to do with you. I'd have had ten more if I'd known they'd turn out like you. Good and clever and healthy.'

'What sort of healthy? You mean not like Rose?'

'No, not like me. We really can't have this conversation now,' Duncan said, in response to a salvo of hooting from behind.

'You're driving too slow, Dad.'

'The needle's dead on thirty.'

'So? There aren't any speed cameras around.'

'That's not a reason for breaking the law. Look, forget the cameras. I'm talking about you, or rather me. You know I was born with a slight – very slight – chromosomal imbalance?'

'Whatever.'

'And you know you haven't inherited it?'

'Uh-huh.'

'But if you'd had a brother, he mightn't have been so lucky. I'm very low on the KS spectrum. Some men who have it are born with learning difficulties and grow such large breasts that they have to go for regular mammograms.'

'Dad, please! I don't want to talk about it. All right?'

'It's not my favourite topic of conversation either. But if there's one thing I want you to remember – if it's the only thing you ever remember – it's that you're in no way to blame for what went wrong between your mother and me. On the contrary, you were the best thing we had then and you're still the best thing we have now. Do you believe me?'

'Suppose.'

'"Suppose" isn't enough.' Duncan parked the car at the bottom of the Ridgemount drive. 'I'm not going to let you out until you promise that you believe me.'

'I promise, OK? I'm hungry.'

'And not a word of this to your grandmother. She'd be mortified to think that you or your mother or anyone else blamed her for my divorce. I tell you what: you be on your best behaviour tonight and next week I'll book us a table at Vivien's. I'll ask her to make us her seafood pasta. Deal?'

'Deal.'

For all that he disapproved of bribing children to do what they should do willingly, Duncan was prepared to make an exception. With a spring in his step, he walked up to the house, past the algae-choked pond and the clump of chestnut trees, their conkers rotting on the ground like a mockery of childhood. Standing beside his son in the cluttered porch, he tentatively placed a hand on his shoulder and, to his delight, it was not shrugged off. Chris answered the door, scuttling back inside to warn Adele of their arrival.

'You didn't say he'd be here,' Jamie hissed.

'Is it a problem? He's a big-hearted man, devoted to Granny.'

'He gives me the creeps.'

They crossed the beeswax-scented hall to the drawing room, where Adele was crocheting a giant bedspread for Alison and Malcolm's silver wedding in June. 'I'll never have the energy to make another one,' she had said to Duncan. 'So it's some comfort to know I won't have to.'

Bending to kiss her cheek, Duncan caught whisky fumes on her breath, but any hope that the drink might have mellowed her was quickly dashed.

'I thought I must have muddled the day,' she said.

'No, Mother, the new counter-flow system on Bartholomew Road caused a massive snarl-up.'

'Don't blame me if the dinner's burnt.'

'We won't,' he said, making way for Jamie whom she greeted with heartening enthusiasm.

'I invited Chris to join me for a small scotch after all his hard work,' Adele said, as if to justify his presence in the room.

'Maybe he'd like to stay to dinner?' Duncan asked, to be met by three distinct looks of horror.

'That's very kind but I wouldn't want to muscle in,' Chris said. 'Mrs Neville doesn't see this handsome young man often enough.'

'True,' Duncan said, trusting that his smile would offset Jamie's glower. 'How are things, Chris? I haven't seen you since the Metropole.'

'Now that really was a night to remember. I told you all about it,' Chris said to Adele, who smiled indulgently. 'Miss Lyndon – she said to call her Charlie, but we couldn't – was everything you'd expect and more. I never knew you were such good friends.'

'She stayed here several times,' Adele said. 'Scruffy little thing. She wore her bra outside her blouse.'

'That was the fashion, Mother.'

'Telling no tales, but she said you'd had an affair.'

'You had an affair with Charlie Lyndon?' Jamie asked incredulously.

'It was a long time ago. I was still in my teens ... that is I was nearly twenty – '

'Do you have any proof?'

'Why would I want proof?'

'For me to show to the guys at school when they take the piss out of you and your lame paper. How many of their dads have slept with a celebrity?'

'She wasn't a celebrity then.'

'So?'

Chris stood up to leave and Duncan accompanied him into the hall, where he could scarcely refrain from thanking him. While trusting that a thirty-year-old fling would not be his sole claim on his son's respect, he had not seen Jamie so proud of him since they launched their home-made rocket two years ago. Chris, meanwhile, intimated that he had something on his mind.

'I hope I'm not speaking out of turn, but I'm worried about your mother.'

'In general or something specific?'

'She's getting so morbid: always quizzing me about my gran's dementia. When the doc came yesterday, he wanted to give her a pneumonia jab but she refused. She said the first sign she was losing her marbles and she'd be sitting outside in the rain with "Do Not Resuscitate" pinned to her chest.'

'The fact she can talk that way shows that her mind is as sharp as ever, but I'll have a word with her and see what I can find out. Now you go home and relax. Be sure to give my best to Paul.'

After sending Chris off with a handshake that would not have disgraced Geoffrey Weedon, Duncan returned to the drawing room to find Jamie holding up a hank of yarn that Adele was winding into a ball.

'I hope he hasn't been giving away any secrets,' she said suspiciously.

'Not at all,' Duncan replied, flushing. 'He's just concerned about you.'

'He's a very sensitive young man. Well, they all are.'

'Who's they, Granny?' Jamie asked.

'Gay homosexuals ... Don't snigger, Jamie. That's what they like to be called. He says I remind him of his grandmother. Before she went cuckoo, of course. He still visits her twice a week in the bin.'

'It's a very well-run residential home, Mother.'

'Says who? He's had to stop taking her out ever since she had a turn in Jubilee Park, screaming that he was kidnapping her and' – she looked at Jamie – 'another time. The keeper rang the police, who arrested him. But he's devoted to her.'

'She brought him up,' Duncan said.

'Still, I don't know many young men who'd do as much for their grandmothers.'

'You're embarrassing Jamie.'

'Oh darling, nothing could be further from my mind. I'm well aware what a busy life you lead. I'm just grateful you can still spare an evening for the old girl.'

'Shall we eat, Mother?' Duncan said firmly. 'I don't know about you two, but I'm famished.'

He led the way into the dining room where he and Jamie sat on either side of Adele at the long Biedermeier table she had inherited from her grandparents. He pretended not to notice Jamie's frown when Adele, who never thought to ask whether his tastes had changed, pointed to the prawn-topped avocados laid out in their moulded glass dishes and declared them to be his favourite.

'How's your poor little stepsister, darling?' she asked after a few mouthfuls.

'She's my half-sister, Granny.'

'Isn't it the same thing?'

Having explained the difference to her countless times, Duncan suspected that she wanted to dissociate her grandson from any blood link with Rose's disability.

'No, it's not. And she's fine. Great,' Jamie said, as always playing down Rose's problems to outsiders. 'Mum's taking her for some Botox injections.'

'Really? I know she's no beauty, but isn't that rather drastic?'

'They're not for her face! She has a lovely face. They're to relax the muscles in her arms and legs. She still won't be able to walk but they may help her hold things better. Otherwise she'd have to have an operation.'

'Such a tragedy,' Adele said, chewing.

'She's already got to have one on her salivary glands so that the drool runs the right way down her throat.'

'That's not a word to use at the dinner table, darling.'

'What word, Granny?' Jamie asked disingenuously.

'Drool.'

'I'm sorry. So much slobber – is that better? – pours out of her that the skin around her mouth and on her neck and chin is really raw.'

'That's enough now, Jamie. Tell your grandmother what's going on in your life while I clear these dishes and fetch the pie.'

A debilitating mixture of arthritis and affectation exempted Adele from serving the dinners over which she presided. Duncan was happy to fill in, not least because it offered a temporary respite from both his mother's chatter and the ghosts who surrounded him at the table. Depositing the avocado dishes in the sink, he drained the peas and took the chicken-and-ham pie out of the oven, its golden-brown crust a testament to the care that Chris had lavished on the baking. He loaded the trolley and pushed it into the dining room, where his mother's face presaged trouble.

'Did you know about this, Duncan?' she asked the moment he stepped through the door.

'About what, Mother?'

'That the children at Jamie's council school are going to be taught in Arabic and Kurdish as well as English?'

'What?' Duncan turned to Jamie, who was the picture of innocence. 'He's pulling your leg, Mother.'

'What for?'

'It's a joke, Granny.'

'Not to those of us who knew Francombe in the old days. Enid Marshall told me last week that Wavell's has been replaced by a halal food store.'

'Pie, Mother?'

'Just a small – not that small, dear! An inch more. I'll leave what I can't manage.'

Duncan served Jamie and himself, and sat down to eat. 'This is delicious,' he said after a couple of bites. 'Chris is an excellent cook.'

'The pastry's a touch soggy, but he does his best.'

'What do you think, Jamie?' Duncan asked, hoping for greater enthusiasm.

'I'm eating it, aren't I? Do I have to write an essay on it as well?'

'Don't snap, darling,' Adele said. 'Your father's entitled to ask. And do take your elbows off the table. As my old nanny used to say: "All joints on the table should be carved."'

'Why? Was her father a butcher?'

'Jamie!'

'I'm surprised Linda allows it. Though I don't suppose she notices.'

'Mother...' Duncan said, longing to give up the role of family conciliator.

'When she has to devote so much time to Rose,' Adele said sweetly. 'What did you think I meant?'

'I've no idea. May we just enjoy the meal?'

They each concentrated on eating.

'You could learn a thing or two from your cousins,' Adele said to Jamie, breaking the silence. 'They have perfect manners.'

'It's not the be-all and end-all, Mother,' Duncan said, remembering the time she told a one-armed salesman to take his hand out of his pocket. 'It's what's inside that counts.'

'Not that I'm blaming you. One of the worst mistakes of your father's life – and there've been many – was not sending you away to school.'

'How often do I have to explain? I didn't want Jamie being taught to repress his emotions.'

'You always were a cold fish, dear. You can't blame that on Lancing.'

'No? What about the letter I wrote you from the Prep? I was all of nine years old and threatening suicide.'

'You're still here, aren't you?'

'Only it was spelt "s o o y s i d e". Alison told me you read it out over breakfast and said that, if nothing else, school would teach me to spell!'

'Go ahead. Blame me if it makes you happy. I'm the one who ought to kill myself, then you'd all heave a sigh of relief.' She whimpered.

'Look what you've done!' Jamie said to Duncan. 'Don't cry, Granny; Dad didn't mean it.'

'Thank you, darling. I knew you'd understand.'

'Oh, for heaven's sake!' Duncan said, as she clasped Jamie's hand, proving that while not quite Ellen's 'common enemy', grandmother and grandson shared a common scapegoat. Refusing to sit and watch, he jumped up, grabbed their plates and piled them on the trolley.

'I wanted seconds,' Jamie said.

'There's a pudding.'

Duncan wheeled the trolley into the kitchen. After loading the dishwasher and taking the trifle out of the fridge, he returned to discover Adele and Jamie comparing notes on *The Simpsons*, of which Adele was an unlikely fan. 'I've always found cartoon characters more engaging than actors,' she said. 'At least they don't have their squalid private lives splashed all over the newspapers.' Duncan spooned out the trifle, which Adele devoured with her customary relish.

'Are you enjoying it, darling?' she asked Jamie.

'It's sickening.'

'Don't be so rude, Jamie!' Duncan said, thinking much the same himself.

'That means it's good!'

'Really? How are we supposed to know?' Adele asked.

'We're not,' Duncan said. 'The Tower of Babel has nothing on Jamie and his friends. They treat words like the Keep Out stickers on their bedroom doors.'

'So? They're our words.'

'Tell that to Shakespeare and Milton and Dickens.'

'Words change, don't they? We have to look up half of *Julius Caesar* at the back.'

'Yes, but gradually, by a process of association. Not by

turning the richest language in the world into a series of private codes.'

'Give me a break!'

'There are districts of Francombe where you no longer hear English spoken,' Adele said. 'Soon we'll all be left talking to ourselves.'

'First sign of madness,' Jamie said smugly. 'Can I have some more? It's spiffing,' he added with cut-glass vowels.

'That's better,' Adele said. 'Of course.'

No sooner had Duncan spooned out Jamie's second helping than his phone rang. Ignoring his mother's admonitory sniff, he answered it to find Ellen in a panic about Neil who, having come home from school with his face bruised and blazer torn, had rushed straight to his room, where he was lying in the dark refusing to speak to her.

Touched that she should appeal to him, he offered to go round at once. For all his concern about Neil, it was the ideal opportunity to prove himself to Ellen, whose fears for her children constituted the greatest threat to their relationship. Bidding a hasty goodnight to his mother, who in return extracted his promise to come again on Thursday, he bundled Jamie into the car and drove him home.

'I wanted to stay longer,' Jamie said petulantly.

'Two hours ago you didn't want to come.'

'You're supposed to be spending the evening with me, not Neil Nugent.'

'What do you have against him? He seems a perfectly pleasant boy to me. He's just finding it hard to settle. I wish you'd try to be friends.'

'Why? There are a hundred and fifty kids in my year. I can't be friends with all of them.'

'I can't go into details – I promised his mother – but Neil hasn't had things easy these past couple of years.'

'You mean cos his dad's in jail?'

'How do you know about that?'

'Sue told Craig. It's not like he was a kiddie fiddler or a rapist. He stole some money from the NHS.'

'Several million pounds to be precise.' Duncan realised that there was no longer any call for reticence.

'Craig thinks it's cool. Everyone steals from the state. He just did it big-time.'

'Till he was caught. Now he's in prison for five years.'

'Which means he'll be out in two. And they only made him pay back a couple of hundred thou. So he'll be rolling in it.'

'I'm speechless! You're thirteen years old. How did you become so cynical?'

'Practice!'

Duncan fell silent. While aware that Jamie was goading him, just as he had done Adele over the Arabic lessons, he feared that contact with the Weedons was warping his values.

'Are people picking on Neil because of his father?' he asked as he turned into Granary Lane.

'Who's picking on him?'

'His mother said that he came home in a dreadful state but wouldn't tell her why.'

'He'd better not grass!'

'Come on, Jamie, there are more important things at stake here than the schoolboy code.'

'Like what? Even his sister makes fun of him. He's so gay!'

'Really? Of course. It's all starting to make sense.' Having blamed Jamie's contempt for Chris on his insecurity, he could not ignore its extension to one of his classmates, least of all Neil. 'But that's why it's even more important you stand up for him against the bigots.'

'Let me out, Dad, please!'

'We're not home yet,' Duncan said, reducing speed.

'I'll walk; I'll crawl! I thought you were in a rush.'

'I want to tell you a story.'

'I'm not listening,' Jamie said, sticking his fingers in his ears.

'Yes you are,' Duncan said, pulling away his right hand. 'There was a boy in my dorm at Lancing, an unpopular, unprepossessing boy, whose one passion in life was ornithology. He had a large collection of birds' eggs, which for some unfathomable reason he brought to school. But – and you'll have guessed the rest already – not everybody shared his enthusiasm. Three boys from the year above – mini Flashmans – came in after lights out and smashed the eggs one by one in front of him, while the rest of us looked on. Whether it was that we disliked the boy or feared the bullies or were simply mesmerised by the violence I don't know. It was thirty-odd years ago and I've had much to regret in my life since then but nothing that's left me with such an acute sense of shame.'

'Yeah, well, just because you bottled it doesn't mean I will. You wanted to know why I was in detention this afternoon. OK then, it was because Mr Grieve caught me scrapping with two blokes who called you a loser on account of what you wrote about us all being druggies and hoodies.'

'You shouldn't have fought them, Jamie. There are other ways to make your point,' Duncan said, dumbfounded by the news that his son had defended him.

'Don't worry, I won't do it again. Not for you and certainly not for Neil fucking Nugent,' Jamie said, wrenching open the car door and running up to the house.

Duncan resisted the urge to follow, but as he gingerly reversed down the lane, he resolved to ring at lunchtime and thank him for the support. After a short drive he arrived at Ellen's, to find her waiting at the front door. 'What it is to be wanted!' he said, hurrying towards her.

'I'm keeping an eye out for Sue. She should have been home half an hour ago. But I'm very pleased all the same,' she said, returning his kiss distractedly. 'I feel awful; I didn't mean to interrupt your dinner.'

'There are compensations.'

'What? Oh don't.' She ran her fingers through her hair. 'I'm a mess. Come into the sitting room. What can I get you to drink?'

'Nothing. Honestly.'

'Please, I've dragged you all this way.'

'Well then, a brandy. Just a small one if I'm driving home.'

Ignoring the hint, she busied herself at the sideboard. Then, after handing him a glass, she explained about Neil. 'He's still not settled in at school. At first I thought it was teething trouble but it's been two months. His head of year rang to ask me why he wasn't doing any homework, but I've supervised him myself. When I challenged him, he clammed up. Finally he admitted that some of the boys in his class were stealing it. Why? He made me promise not to tell anyone. He said he'd … do something dreadful. It terrified me. But I can't stand idly by. I went to see the headmistress, who clearly thought I was blowing things out of proportion. She all but accused me of being clingy. Why are they doing it, Duncan? Is it because he's new? Because his accent's different? I know he's not the easiest of boys. I've told him that if he wants to make friends, then he has to make an effort. But even if he's a misfit, surely with so many kids in his year there must be other misfits for him to latch on to?'

With Jamie's words fresh in his mind, Duncan feared that Neil had been targeted on account of his sexuality. He had no idea whether he were innately gay or going through an adolescent phase – if such a thing were still possible in a world where sex had become a branch of marketing. Either way he should be free to experiment without adult intervention, however well-intentioned. So he resolved to say nothing to Ellen. Instead, he would ring the headmistress in his professional capacity, claiming to have heard of several homophobic incidents at the school and demanding that she put her anti-discrimination policy into effect or face exposure in the press.

'Duncan?'

'Yes?'

'Don't you have anything to say?'

'I was weighing up the options.'

'I'm at my wits' end. Neil was livid that I'd been to the school. He punched me in the stomach (don't look so horrified! I was only winded). He said I'd made things ten times worse and maybe he's right. If you'd seen him when he came home this evening, all battered and bruised.'

'You mustn't blame yourself. You did what any mother would.'

'Would any other mother have brought him here, cutting him off from the life he knew, all for the sake of her stupid pride? He wasn't the one accused of complicity in his father's crimes.'

'Would you like me to have a word with him? I can't promise it'll do any good but he might find it easier to confide in someone outside the family – and a man.'

He was surprised by how avidly she seized on his offer. So with no chance to prepare what to say, he headed upstairs, identifying Neil's door by the brass rubbing of a medieval knight who, on closer inspection, turned out to be crossing his legs as if waiting for a privy.

Receiving no answer to his knock, he edged open the door to find Neil lying flat on the bed, his face buried in the pillow. He felt a stab of sympathy on recalling his own adolescence, when the gulf between his sense of self and his place in the world had been greater than at any time before or since.

'Do you mind if I switch on the light?'

'Fuck off!'

'Sure, if that's what you really want. But I'm here now. Won't you spare me five minutes?' Taking the silence as a yes, he turned on the light and was immediately struck by the neatness of the room. Other than the sour smell and the posters of racing drivers on the walls, there was nothing to indicate that it belonged to a teenage boy. Either Ellen was stricter about mess than both Linda and himself or else Neil was tidier than Jamie. Hesitating between the chair and the bed, he opted for the latter, perching so close to the edge that he risked slipping to the floor.

'What do you want?' Neil asked, sitting up abruptly.

'Just to talk.'

'Did my mum send you?'

'She asked me, but I came of my own accord.'

'Why?'

'To see if there was anything I could do to help.'

'Why?'

'Because I was worried about you.'

'Why?'

'Because you don't seem very happy.'

'What do you know about how I feel?'

'I'd know more if you told me,' Duncan said calmly. 'I imagine it must have been hard, moving down here, leaving your friends.'

'I didn't have any friends.'

'Not at your old school?'

'Who'd want to be friends with me?'

'Lots of people.' Duncan resolved to make another appeal to Jamie. 'And in time,' he said, carefully avoiding genders, 'there'll be special friends, people who won't just like you, they'll love you.'

'Oh yeah? They go for ugly, do they?'

'Who says you're ugly?' Duncan asked, resting his hand lightly on Neil's shoulder. 'I certainly don't.'

'And inside? What do you know what I'm like inside? I'm sick, just like my dad.'

'This isn't about your dad; it's about you. You're your father's son, not his shadow. I know what's behind all this and I promise you you're wrong. Being gay isn't sick.'

'What are you on about?'

'It's quite natural,' Duncan said, feeling Neil tense beneath his touch. 'Gay or straight, I'm here for you.'

'Fuck off!' Neil jumped up and grabbed his pillow, pummelling Duncan in an assault that only confirmed his impotence. 'Barbara was right; you're a pervert. Go on, fuck off!'

'Of course. I don't want to impose – '

'Fuck off!'

'Can't we talk about this?'

'Fuck off!'

Ruffled, Duncan returned downstairs where Ellen was waiting in the hall. 'I heard shouts,' she said.

'It was all going so well when he suddenly turned on me. I don't understand. Did your mother tell him I was some kind of pervert?'

'Oh no! Oh, I'm so sorry.' Ellen cupped her hand over her mouth as if she were the one who had maligned him. 'Come in here.' She grabbed his hand and pulled him into the sitting room. 'My bloody mother! My bloody, bloody, bloody mother! Trust me, Duncan, this is about me not you. I'd no idea that Neil had overheard but then he's always snooping around. He thinks it's the only way to find out what's going on.'

'Overheard what?' Duncan asked anxiously.

'With her usual faith in my judgement, she warned me to be on my guard against you because men – paedophiles – sought out vulnerable women with kids – '

'She thinks I'm a paedophile?'

'She's never met you; she knows nothing about you. It's me she's getting at: punishing me for marrying Matthew. In other words, how can any man – any decent man – be attracted to someone like me who had no idea that her husband was a swindler?'

'What utter crap! In any case she can't talk. What about her Roman boyfriend who came on to you?'

'Polish. It's just his name that was Roman.'

'Either way.'

'I agree, and when I put it to her she accused me of being vindictive and told me to see a healer.'

'The bitch! I know she's your mother, but still … She can say what she likes about me but she has no right – none at all – to denigrate you. What's her number? I'll ring and set her straight.'

'There's no point.'

'I can be very persuasive.'

'No, I mean her phone will be off. She's on a week's retreat in Carcassonne to find her inner goddess.'

'On current form, it'll be Kali.'

With a laugh that turned swiftly into a wail, she slid into his arms. He nuzzled her hair and stroked her back until her tears subsided. 'I don't know about you,' she said, a sob lingering in her voice like damp in the air, 'but I could murder another brandy.'

'Good idea. I can always leave the car here and ring for a cab.'

'If you want. But after tonight what do we have to lose? I'd like you to stay.'

She poured the drinks and they sat holding hands on the sofa, transfixed by the flickering of the artificial fire. Duncan felt a deep sense of tranquillity, which was shattered by the opening of the front door.

'Just one moment, young lady!' Ellen jumped up and hurried into the hall to confront Sue. 'Where have you been?'

'Out!' From the sound of her voice, she was already halfway up the stairs.

'Do you have any idea what time it is?'

'Do you get a kick out of ruining my life?'

'You're managing that well enough on your own. Just look at you! You're a beautiful girl. Why make yourself so grungy?'

'Oh yes, like I'm going to take fashion tips from you!' Duncan, a reluctant eavesdropper, moved to the sitting-room door in a show of support for Ellen. 'No! It's so not fair! You're allowed to be with your boyfriend, but I can't be with mine.'

'You know perfectly well that it isn't the same.'

'Why not?'

'I'm not going to argue. For the next two weeks you're grounded. If you want to see Craig, you'll have to ask him here.'

'Oh sure! Like he's going to come to this dump!'

'He didn't seem to mind this morning,' Duncan interjected.

'What?' Ellen asked.

'When I dropped off your watch. They were here during a study period.'

'What study period? You don't have one on a Monday.'

'Yes we do,' Sue said defiantly.

'And why come all the way back? It's a twenty-minute walk. Oh no, Sue! Please tell me you weren't sleeping with him.'

'You're sick, Mum, do you know that? That's all you ever think about: sex!'

'I think they might have been smoking pot,' Duncan said hesitantly.

'What?' Ellen asked.

'Thanks a bunch, creep!' Sue said.

'I can't say for sure.'

'Why didn't you tell me?'

'I didn't want to worry you. You had enough on your plate with Neil.'

'I have two children, Duncan. It's my job to worry about them.'

'I know, but under the circumstances…'

'No one keeps anything about my children from me. No one. I think you should go. I have things to discuss with Sue.'

'But you said – '

'I need to talk to her in private.'

'Yes, of course.' Taking a gulp of brandy, he placed the glass on the hall table. He moved to kiss Ellen but thought better of it. 'Shall I call you tomorrow?'

'Please do that.'

Opening the door, Duncan turned back to face Sue and realised that it was the first time he had seen her smile.

Six

'Notes from the Pulpit'

by the Reverend Henry Grainger

Thursday, 28 November 2013

'And God said, Let there be light.' And with light came colour. And with colour came art. And through art mankind reaches closer to God.

Over the past few months we at St Edward's have watched with mounting excitement as a vision of paradise has filled the church hall. Ever since I came to the parish six years ago I have dreamt of refurbishing the hall but, as regular readers of this column will know, we have struggled to fund the essential repairs to the church itself without turning our attention to the outbuildings.

But God moves in a mysterious way. In July, nineteen-year-old Jordan Maplin was convicted of spraying graffiti on three seafront shelters. He was given a six-month suspended prison sentence, a 150-hour Community Order and required to pay £500 towards the cost of the damage.

Jordan claimed that he was protesting against the drabness of the shelters (which have been criticised in many quarters, including this newspaper). This is not the place to argue the merits of street art in general or Jordan's work in particular, but it is worth noting that, in his character witness statement, Jordan's former art master described him as a highly gifted pupil who, in happier circumstances, would have won a scholarship to art school.

Meanwhile, the Probation Service had approved my request to make the renovation of the church hall a Community Payback project. By a stroke of providence, Joel Lincoln, one of our churchwardens, had been in court for Jordan's trial. Recognising Jordan among the team, he proposed that we ask him to paint a mural.

Despite an initial reluctance to be singled out, Jordan accepted that this was the perfect opportunity to demonstrate his talents. His probation officer granted permission for him to work alone under the supervision of Joel, who gave me a private assurance that if the painting were a disaster he would cover it over himself.

Fortunately, no such redress was necessary. Jordan's insistence on working in secret provoked some misgivings within the parish, but when the mural – a highly charged depiction of Adam and Eve in the Garden of Eden – was revealed, the doubting Thomases were confounded.

The mural is to be unveiled by the Bishop of Lewes at 3 p.m. on Thursday, 5 December. Everyone is welcome to attend, and there will be further opportunities to view it over the coming months when our popular weekend teas are served in the hall.

'As every man hath received the gift, even so minister the same one to another, as good stewards of the manifold grace of God.' 1 Peter 4:10

In Duncan's view, everything one needed to know about Trevor
Vale was summed up in his formula for the perfect woman:
'somebody half my age plus seven'. Having first assumed that it
was a joke, he was appalled when Trevor's quest for a Russian
mail order bride no older than twenty-five (and therefore more
like a quarter of his age plus ten) had shown him to be deadly
serious. Trevor was the sole survivor of a once vibrant advertising team, which had been decimated by the decline in the
paper's fortunes. Over the past decade, the twin forces of the
Internet and the Recession had reversed the paper's traditional
48 per cent editorial to 52 per cent advertising balance. Property
adverts, previously as popular with curious neighbours as with
serious buyers, had moved on to designated websites. Motoring
and recruitment, the other mainstays of the classified pages, had
been all but wiped out and, for the first time in living memory,
the annual 'In Memoriam' supplement had been dropped. Long
gone were the days when Trevor could wine, dine and otherwise
entertain prominent retailers, his huge expense claims justified
by the full-page display ads he secured. Now he was reduced
to making cold calls, offering cut-price rates and promising
regular advertisers positive feature coverage.

The need to toady to his clients made him all the more com-
bative with his colleagues, and Duncan had come to dread
the Monday morning meetings when, invoking the spectre of
bankruptcy, Trevor sought to win his approval for his more
reckless schemes. The latest was that they should link the
news and advertising on the website by, for example, selling
sidebar space to life insurers after a fatal car crash or sailing
accident. Duncan, who was as keen as anyone to exploit their
web presence but not at the expense of common decency, dismissed the idea out of hand, whereupon Trevor accused him
of turning his back on the twenty-first century, a theme to
which he returned when Duncan yet again refused to accept
adverts for massage parlours, among the few local businesses
to have weathered the slump.

'Shall we call a brothel a brothel? I may be the last person in Francombe to think of this as a family paper,' Duncan said, trying to ignore the razor burn on Trevor's neck, 'but I hope I'm not alone in seeing it as an honourable one. How could we run, say, Rowena's story about the Estonian and Ukrainian women lured here with the promise of hotel jobs and forced to work as prostitutes, and at the same time take money from their pimps?'

'Not everything's so black and white. I've spoken to the police; they're all for it so long as there's no mention of anyone's age or race. They see it as a way to keep tabs on operations they don't know about.'

'Let them do their own dirty work! My father – not to mention my grandfather – would turn in his grave.'

'Which means they're not in the market for buying papers. If even half the rumours about Weedon's plans for the pier turn out to be true, you're going to have to change your tune or lose the biggest new source of advertising revenue in town.'

'It's a small price to pay for preserving our principles.'

'Let's hope your principles pay for my pension,' Trevor said, unable to contain his anger. 'Meanwhile, if you want to hold on to what advertising we have, I suggest you start coming up with some good news stories for a change. "Hoodie helps widow find cat". "Study shows sea air cures cancer" – whatever. No business wants to be associated with an endless deluge of doom and gloom.'

Stung by Trevor's charge, Duncan waited impatiently for him to leave before picking up the flat page to assess the balance of stories in the next issue. While much of the paper remained to be set, including the first three pages, which, barring an attack on the Town Hall, would be devoted to the presentation of the pier development plans, there was enough material for him to make a fair appraisal. Opening his notepad, he drew two columns headed Negative and Positive. In the first, he put the children taken into care after a

rat infestation on the Edmund Hillary estate; the landlord of
the Cod and Lobster found guilty of branding his wife; the
£500,000 cocaine haul at the Salter and St Anselm yacht club;
and the baby left alone on a tower block roof while her mother
went out drinking. In the second, he put the entrants for the
Pet Idol competition; the four generations of the Heathcote
family who were running a charity marathon for Save the
Rhino; the South-East lightweight bodybuilding champion
whose name had inspired one of Stewart's happier puns ('Everything's hunky dory for hunky Dorian'); and, most heartening of all, the leukaemia patient at the Princess Royal who,
having received a perfect bone marrow match from a man
who turned out to be her brother, had been reunited with the
mother who gave her up for adoption at birth.

While the general tenor of the paper was more cheerful
than Trevor had claimed, Duncan agreed that even without
the commercial imperative they should take every opportunity for optimism in such troubled times. To that end, he
headed into the reporters' room and spoke to Stewart.

'This *nib* about the close call from the car crash: can you
add a hundred words and put it above the fold?'

'No probs. There's space on page eight. We'll need a photo.'

'I'll handle that. I'm off for a sneak preview of Henry's
mural. I can go via Hawksey Road.'

'What was it?' Rowena asked. 'Another joyrider?'

'No,' Stewart said. 'A woman drove her Polo into a lamp
post. Only the bumper was scratched.'

'You're kidding me!' Brian said. 'Is that it? Forget "Small
Earthquake in Chile. Not many dead". Try "Car Collides with
Lamp Post. Neither damaged".'

'Yes, that's it,' Duncan replied. 'Maybe in the august pages
of *The Times* the earthquake wouldn't have rated a mention,
but our remit is different. Strange as it sounds, there are times
when we have to think small. "Car collides with lamp post" is
part of the fabric of local life. A rich tapestry if we're lucky; a

MICHAEL ARDITTI

frayed patchwork if we're not. Either way, it's our job to record it.'

He left the office and drove to Hawksey Road where, unable to spot even the slightest scratch at bumper level, he chose a lamp post at random and, in a wide-angled shot that Bert Ponsonby would have commended, framed it against a street sign, a privet hedge and a passing toddler on a tricycle. He returned to Rocinante and made the short trip to St Edward's vicarage. Built to house a mid-Victorian family with its Sextus, Septimus and even Octavius, the three floors and warren of corridors was too large for the previous incumbent with his four young children, let alone for the unmarried Henry. Anywhere else in the country it would have been divided into flats or sold to a private care consortium and Henry dispatched to live among the Sunday morning car washers on a modern estate, but property values in Salter were so low that, its sea view and rambling garden notwithstanding, it remained in the hands of the Church.

Approaching the door, he found Brandy in his usual vantage point, poised on the back of a battered chaise longue against the hall window. His neck was encased in a white conical collar, as though his double on the HMV logo had caught his head in the throat of the gramophone horn by his side. Emitting only a token bark at Duncan's knock, he hung back when Henry opened the door, seemingly ashamed to let his old friend and walking companion see him in such a sorry state.

'What is it, boy?' Duncan asked, stretching across Henry to stroke him. 'Have you been in the wars?'

'No, the vet's,' Henry said. 'I had him spayed three days ago.'

'No wonder he's so subdued. No little Brandies to carry on the line.'

'Don't! I feel bad enough already. I held off as long as I could, but he was becoming a liability.'

■ 192 ■

'With the local bitches?'

'Well, with some of my female parishioners,' Henry said with a laugh. 'Hayley Ridley's mother threatened to remove her from confirmation class after Brandy molested her leg. Still, at least it was only canine abuse. Let's go through. Shall I take your coat?'

'I'll keep it on for now.' Wishing that the East Sussex humanists who regularly attacked clerical privilege could spend a day in the draughty vicarage, Duncan followed his host to the kitchen. He took his place at the table, while Henry stirred the soup and Brandy, who usually sat at his feet waiting for an illicit titbit, retreated to his basket unable even to lick his wounds.

As the meal progressed it became clear that Henry was as downcast as his dog. When Duncan asked the reason, he explained that he had just returned from visiting two elderly parishioners, Roy and Marjorie Tattersall. Although he recognised their names, Duncan failed to place them until Henry added that they had had a daughter with paranoid schizophrenia who was discharged in March after several years in psychiatric care. Eager to reintegrate her into family life, they had persuaded their more circumspect son and daughter-in-law to allow her to babysit their children. At first all had gone well, but in May she had sneaked her six-year-old nephew out of the house, taken him up the cliff and thrown him off before jumping herself. To add to her parents' anguish, their son and daughter-in-law held them responsible, publicly denouncing them at the funeral (one of the most harrowing Henry had ever taken) and refusing to let them see their two remaining grandsons.

'Six months on and they're in despair, although they would never describe it as such. When I told them they had every right to rail at God, they were shocked. Instead, they look for comfort in the very place where they ought to be laying blame.'

'Surely if they find it, that's all that counts?' Duncan said, more concerned with the emotional than the metaphysical impact. 'Doctors don't torment themselves over the placebo effect, so why should you?'

'To know that a piece of sugar or starch can have the same effect as a highly sophisticated pill must make any self-respecting doctor question his skill; his practice; his whole identity. At least it would me. Do you remember the fuss when I introduced incense and benediction to St Edward's? I explained that they were designed to induce a sense of mystery. Now I wonder if they're not a smokescreen to hide the horror beyond.'

Despite Duncan's best efforts, Henry's spirits remained low throughout lunch, lifting only when they entered the church hall, in whose whitewashed brick interior Duncan had spent many long evenings perched on a tubular chair listening to the competing sounds of the gurgling pipes and the tinny upright. The first thing to strike him, even before Henry switched on the lights, was the riot of colour suffusing the room. The second was the sheer size of the mural, which filled an entire wall: not just the paintwork but the joists, junction box, ventilation ducts and skirting board. Transfixed, he wavered between stepping up to study it in detail and standing back for a panoramic view.

Settling on the latter, he examined the picture, which, far from the envisaged caricature, put him in mind of both Douanier Rousseau, who had employed the same vibrant colours, bold lines and stylised figures, and Stanley Spencer, who had sanctified his home village. This Eden was not a garden but a beach, and one that bore more than a passing resemblance to Salter Cove. Might Jordan, like Duncan himself, have stumbled on the nudist beach as a child and seen it as an image of paradise? On closer inspection the childhood resonance grew stronger, since the lions, tigers, bears, penguins, rabbits and other animals scattered about the landscape were not, as he had supposed, naïvely drawn but rather depictions of cuddly toys. Moreover, the yellow-and-pink striped snake, curled on a distant rock, a threat to neither man nor beast, was a knitted draught excluder. Was Jordan making a complex theological point about the frailty of evil or merely using a model that was close to hand?

The question of intent was even more pertinent when Duncan turned to the two humans. He knew, of course, that Eve was based on Mary – albeit a Mary he would never have suspected lay beneath her overalls – but not that Adam was a self-portrait: a slight, fresh-faced adolescent whose penis, either as a challenge to centuries of Church teaching or in literal self-aggrandisement, was disproportionately large. The older, fleshier Eve sat beside him, a hefty arm wrapped pro-tectively round his shoulder. While Henry rhapsodised about the way in which, consciously or not, Jordan had portrayed Eve as an archaic mother goddess and Adam as the embodi-ment of the younger Judaeo-Christian tradition, Duncan struggled to tear his eyes away from Mary's – or, rather, Eve's – heavy breasts.

'Is there any reason she's holding such a large apple?'

'Probably because it's a mango! When I told him that the Bible never named the fruit, he decided to choose his favourite.'

'I didn't know what to expect; I certainly didn't expect any-thing as extraordinary as this.'

'Such talent,' Henry said wistfully. 'I hope now that he's paid his debt to society – disgusting phrase! What about soci-ety's debt to him? – he can use this as a calling card for art schools. He affects not to be interested: "Why would I want to sit around all day smoking dope with a load of wankers?" But he's just trying to protect himself against rejection.'

'I doubt there's anyone who wouldn't be impressed by this, whether or not they know his story. Look, even Brandy's engrossed!' Duncan pointed to the dog who was sitting three feet away from a pair of rabbits, his ears pricked as if ready to pounce.

'It's the same whenever I bring him. But then, as one untainted by Original Sin, he has a unique affinity with the prelapsarian world. Of course if St Augustine's right and Original Sin is rooted in our genitals, that affinity's just increased.'

Henry's flippancy, which seemed to spring from somewhere deep in his conflicted nature, alerted Duncan to the fact that the painting's eroticism, which spoke so eloquently to him, might dismay several of the hall's regular users. He could not help wishing that Jordan had chosen an equally colourful but less contentious myth such as Noah's Ark.

'You are prepared for the inevitable backlash? I'm afraid that some of your parishioners will be of the fig-leaf persuasion.'

'Some of my parishioners would be of the niqab persuasion if they weren't such racists! It's high time they had their eyes opened. There's an innocence to Jordan's style that's the perfect reflection of its subject. The Church says no far too often. For once it's saying yes.'

As he drove away from St Edward's, Duncan mulled over Jordan's story. In his column Henry had described his churchwarden's presence in court as a stroke of providence, but even if things had been otherwise and Jordan forced to serve his Community Order whitewashing the walls along with his fellow offenders, he would have done so with the soul of an artist painting *White on White*. As the spraying of the shelters had shown, he would always find some means of self-expression. For years Duncan had consoled himself with the thought that, but for his father's untimely death, he would have become a writer. Seeing the mural had taught him that it was not propitious circumstances that he lacked (and perhaps not even talent) but will: the will that against the odds had driven Jordan to make his mark on the world.

Had he needed confirmation, it was waiting for him on his

return to the office in the Post-it note that Sheila had stuck on his desk. No matter how often he explained to his mother that the demands of his job precluded his being at her beck and call, she paid no attention, citing the example of his father who, despite 'editing a far bigger paper', had always found the time to deal with problems at home. Stifling any reference to a guilty conscience, he invariably gave way and so, ignoring the pile of proofs waiting for his approval, he rang the courier company to ascertain the whereabouts of a fridge that he had urged her not to buy in the first place. After the obligatory burst of Vivaldi, a robotic voice informed him that he had called at a busy time and might prefer to try again later. Resolved to prove that what he lacked in willpower he made up for in perseverance, he continued to hold for an adviser who, when she finally answered, committed the dual solecism of addressing him by his mother's Christian name.

Conceding that the ill-suppressed agitation in his voice and Adele's details on her screen excused the error, he gruffly corrected her and arranged a 'delivery window' for Wednesday morning. He was about to ring off when she asked if he would be willing to take part in a customer satisfaction survey. Despite his belief that such surveys proliferated in direct proportion to the decline in service, he agreed and a recorded message invited him to rate the likelihood on a scale of 1 to 10 of his recommending Parcel4U to a friend. Stung that even an automaton should suppose him to be the kind of man who discussed courier companies with his friends, he was about to press 1 when a pang of sympathy for the adviser prompted him to press 8.

He put down the phone and picked up the proofs of the sports pages, which he had barely begun reading when Mary knocked on the door, bringing thoughts of Jordan and the church hall flooding back.

'I've just returned from St Edward's,' he said at once. 'I saw the mural.'

'Did you like it?'

While ignorant of the appropriate tone to adopt with an employer who had recently seen one stark naked, Duncan doubted that it was girlish pride. 'A remarkable achievement by any standards, let alone for someone untaught.'

'He got an A* in his GCSE,' she said defensively.

'I meant with no formal training.'

'He has all these pictures in his head. You just need to mention something – even something he's never seen – and he knows straight off how it ought to look.'

'He's captured you remarkably,' he said, keeping his eyes fixed on her face.

'It's the best thing that's ever happened to me, bar none,' she said. He wanted to ask whether that included her husband and children but was afraid of the answer. 'I'm bringing the whole family for when the bishop comes on Thursday.'

'Are you sure that's wise?'

'Father Henry says he's going to introduce us.'

'The picture is very intimate.'

'You mean because I'm naked?'

'In part, yes.'

'But I'm not.'

'Really?'

'I'm nude. Jordan explained the difference.'

'Do you think Bob will appreciate it?'

'Him! His idea of nude is a Page 3 girl licking an ice cream. He's not got an artistic bone in his body.'

'I'm worried for you,' Duncan said, flinching at the note of contempt that had crept into her voice. 'I know he has a temper. What if he gets the wrong end of the stick?'

'Now what end might that be?' she asked teasingly.

'I think Jordan may have a crush on you,' he replied, finally voicing the suspicion that had nagged at him ever since he saw the picture.

'Oh Mr Neville, you're priceless! I'm sorry; I don't mean

to laugh. Jordan's in love with me, and I am with him.' Her radiant smile rendered any makeover show redundant.

'Why that's wonderful,' Duncan said, trying to match his expression to his words.

'You don't mean that, but thank you anyway. Have I shocked you?'

'A little.'

'I'm sorry, but I'm glad – a little.'

'Perhaps you should sit down,' Duncan said, finding the conversation strained enough without her standing clutching a bottle of bleach.

'Are you going to sack me?' she asked, her voice cracking.

'No, of course not! Why ever…? Not for a single moment!' Duncan reached an arm towards her, only to draw it back at the memory of Eve's encircling Adam. He turned to the window, where the shimmer of silvery-blue on the horizon looked more than usually enticing.

'I've never shocked anyone in my entire life. Not even as a kid.'

'There's still time.'

'You're thinking he's younger than me. He is. He's younger than my kids. But that makes it all the more easier.'

'It does?'

'If he'd been my own age or older, like Ken – '

'Ken Newbold?'

'He's always trying it on. Didn't you know?'

'I had no idea.'

'Water off a duck's whatsit! But with Jordan it's like I'm living in a fairy tale. He doesn't make me feel young; he makes me feel like age doesn't count. With any other lad I'd be shy – worse … I've had four kids. But he's an artist; he sees things different.'

'I know it's none of my business – feel free to slap me down – but have you … do you mind my asking if…?'

'If we've made love? Oh yes! Isn't it obvious?'

'Probably to everyone who looks at the painting.'

'You see! Other men would have made it a smutty joke; he makes it art.'

'But where?' With neither having the money to rent a room, he pictured them trekking up to the Nature Reserve or, in a further irony, sneaking into one of the seafront shelters that Jordan himself had sprayed. 'Surely you don't stay in the church hall? It's so cold and uncomfortable – and public.'

'How can you think that? I could never do that to Father Henry.' Now it was her turn to sound shocked. 'We go over to his. His mother can't make it down the stairs, so we're quite safe. But I don't like it; it feels like we're taking advantage. I won't be happy till we're in a place of our own.'

'What? Are you planning to leave Bob?'

'Of course, it's only right. When Jordan goes to college, I'll go with him.'

'You'll apply to art school?'

'Bless you for that!' she said, with a peal of laughter. 'Look at me!' She held out her raw hands. 'Just about fit to ice a cake. Still, they do well enough for cleaning. I'll get a job. He'll need someone to support him while he's doing all his studying.'

Duncan tried to share Mary's excitement, but despite her claim to be living in a fairy tale she would still be scouring lavatories and scrubbing floors, even if it were now on behalf of her prince.

'Have you thought what happens if you go off together, somewhere full of bright young people, and he – either of you – finds someone else?'

'Then we've still had each other. That can't change. Do you know what it's like when you've never lived, Mr Neville? No, of course you don't. My mum, she's sixty-two and the only time she's ever sat in a decent car was at my dad's funeral. I'm not going to be like her. I'm not!' She clenched her fists as if to reinforce her resolve. 'But I can't spend all day nattering.

There was something I came in to ask. Oh yes! Do you want me to change your sheets?'

'They've only been on a few days.' He suddenly felt grubby. 'On second thoughts, why not? And Mary,' he added as she opened the door. 'I am on your side. I wish you all the luck ... all the happiness in the world.'

'I've got that already. I just need it to last.'

Mary left and Duncan turned back to the proofs. He was so confused that he would have found it hard to focus on an exclusive report of Geoffrey Weedon's bankruptcy, let alone Jake's interview with the president of the Salter and St Anselm Over-Sixties Ladies' Bowling Team. A muffled knock brought a welcome distraction. 'It's only me,' Sheila said, inching open the door. 'Am I disturbing you?'

'Not at all.'

'I've brought a young gentleman to see you,' she said, ushering in Neil with a distinctive blend of deference and unease that marked her out as childless.

Duncan's initial hope that he had come as Ellen's emissary vanished at the memory of their appointment. 'Neil's in the same form as Jamie at Francis Preston,' he said, choosing the simplest reference point. 'He's here as part of his local history project.'

'He's certainly come to the right place.'

'Anything you want to know about the *Mercury*, just ask Sheila,' Duncan told Neil, who hung back as if to distance himself from the discussion. 'What's history to you is memory to her.'

'I'm not sure I like the sound of that, Duncan,' Sheila said, smiling. 'Do you want a piece of gingerbread, young man?' she asked Neil. 'It's home-made.'

'I'm not six!'

'Maybe another time.' Hiding her hurt, she went out.

'Is she drunk?'

'No,' Duncan replied, choking back his annoyance. 'What on earth makes you think that?'

'Her breath stinks of mints. My dad says that drunks suck mints to cover up the smell.'

'But some people just like the taste. I'm very glad you've come. I want you to make this place work for you. Feel free to roam around, but the obvious place to start is the archives. It's my favourite room in the building … one of my favourite rooms,' he added, recalling Geoffrey Weedon's jibe about his living in the past. 'Do you read a newspaper yet?'

'No and I'm not going to. Everything they print is lies.'

'I know that's the fashionable viewpoint, but fortunately it's not true or else the libel lawyers would rake it in even faster than they do now.'

'Did you see what they wrote about my dad?'

'Some of it.'

'Mum tried to hide all the papers, but Sue and I bought them with our own money. Even the photographs didn't look like him! But they were more like him than the words. "Cruel", "wicked", "heartless", "unashamed", "evil". And those are the words that people will have to remember him with for ever, like they were carved on his grave. Our RE teacher said we should never call anyone evil, only the things they've done. What do you say to that?'

'Let's go downstairs.'

As he shepherded him down the corridor, Duncan felt Neil's shoulders quiver with rage either at the press's betrayal of his father or at something he found harder to articulate: his father's betrayal of him. He feared that in seeking explanations for her son's behaviour, Ellen had lost sight of the most basic: his deep-seated ambivalence towards the "cruel", "wicked", "heartless", "unashamed", "evil" father whom he felt honour-bound to defend to everyone but himself.

Passing the photographs of the annual *Mercury* sports days on the stairs, Duncan contemplated his own father. The paternalistic editor presenting trophies to his workers had been less solicitous at home. Would their lives have been happier if

Adele, tiring of his infidelities, had left him in the Seventies? Probably. But she had been so scarred by her parents' divorce and her mother's subsequent breakdown that her overriding concern was to spare her children a similar ordeal. Duncan never knew his maternal grandmother, but his father had painted a grim portrait of a woman who vented her marital grievances on the entire male sex and whose overprotective-ness towards her daughter (she fed the teenage Adele senna tea every Friday night to keep her away from boys) was the source of her lifelong frigidity.

With no one to authenticate the portrait – certainly not Adele, who refused to hear a word against either of her parents, not least those that they had exchanged in court – Duncan suspected his father of embellishing it in order to justify his conduct. In the event, his philandering proved to be as dam-aging as his mother-in-law's prudery since Duncan was so determined not to follow in his footsteps that several women, including Linda, had accused him of coldness. He wondered whether, on an unconscious level, that might have been his father's wish since, Oedipus and his complex notwithstand-ing, it was clear that the greater resentment in the 'family romance' was felt by fathers for the sons who displaced them, first in their wives' affections and then in the wider world. But before he could make up his mind, they arrived at the reading room.

'After you,' he said, ushering Neil inside and switching on the lights. 'This is where you'll find a copy of every issue from day one. Apologies if it's a little gloomy; it's a constant battle to replace all the bulbs. But there's plenty of light on the table in the corner, plus a socket if you want to bring your laptop.' As Neil walked along a row of shelves, skimming his fingers over the dusty spines, Duncan was struck by the image of him slashing them with a penknife.

'Smells like mushrooms,' Neil said, sniffing his fingers.

'And new-mown hay. And wood. And almonds. Sorry,

I'm getting carried away. To me, it's the most evocative smell in the world. That's the advantage you have over your class-mates. They'll need to search out history; you hold it in your hands. Why not pick a volume – it doesn't matter which – and see what you find.'

Neil staggered, as he edged a volume off the shelf. 'Fuck! That's heavy.'

'Please take care. They're fragile.'

'You could of warned me!'

'What have you got here?' Duncan examined the date. 'July to September 1916. I think someone's been cheating.'

'What do you mean?' Neil asked indignantly.

'It's not hard to work out what was making the headlines then.'

'What? Why?'

'World War One? The Battle of the Somme?'

'We've only done the Nazis.'

'Let's try our luck with the most recent volume,' Duncan said quickly. 'Put that one back first, will you? It's easy to mix them up.' Neil pushed the volume back on the shelf. 'April to June 2013, fresh from the binders.' He opened it in the middle. '16 May 2013. Slope Street lavatories closed after … That's not particularly interesting. How about this? John Hitchings's obituary.'

'Never heard of him!'

'I doubt many of our readers have, but that's the point. He was a milkman in the Falworth Road area for forty years, and there aren't many of those left in the twenty-first century. For thirty years he kept a dray horse in a stable behind Plover's Yard. See, there's a photo of them together.'

'So what?'

'When Brian – he's one of our reporters – went to interview his widow, she assumed he was joking. She couldn't under-stand why anyone should be interested in her husband. But he got chatting to her and gleaned some fascinating stories. Like this! As a schoolboy during the war – that's the war against the Nazis,' he said pointedly – 'he helped a friend whose father was a haberdasher to steal silk from the barrage balloons that were sent up to stop German bombers flying low over the harbour. As his widow says: "there was no lack of fancy knickers in Francombe during the war."'

'She was right. Who's interested?'

'You'd be surprised. Obituaries regularly top the poll for the most popular section of the paper. But more than that, they're an invaluable resource for the future. Who else is recording this stuff? I don't suppose John Hitchings kept a diary; he wasn't the literary type. His wasn't the sort of life to rate a mention in the national press. Which is why I always tell my writers that they're social historians as much as hardcore reporters. In a hundred years' time, anyone who wants to find out what Francombe was like in 2013 will pick up this volume, just as we picked up the one for 1916.'

'That's ninety-seven years.'

'I beg your pardon?'

'From 1916 to 2013 is ninety-seven years, not a hundred.'

'I think you know what I meant.'

'Why are you helping me?'

'What?'

'You said it'd give me an advantage over the other kids. One of them's Jamie.'

'He's chosen to do a project on the wheel park with his stepfather.'

'You're not mine!'

'What?'

'You're not my stepfather, not now and you never will be.'

'I never said – '

'You said he was doing a project with *his* stepfather, like I was doing one with mine.'

'You're making something out of nothing,' Duncan replied. 'Nobody's forcing you to come here, Neil. If you'd rather tackle something else...'

'Like what? The decline in Francombe's fish stocks?'

'In which case, you must decide what line you're going to take and follow it through. You could look at changes in the *Mercury*'s coverage of a particular area – '

'Like Falworth Road?'

'You could of course make it geographical, but I was thinking more of something thematic: sport or tourism or the Town Hall.'

'The Mayor and that?'

'Local government in general. Or you could look at broad feature coverage. When I took over in 1986, there were far more of what we called "gold clock stories" – people who retired after fifty years with the same firm.'

'Losers!'

'That's not how we saw it then. Their jobs gave them status and security. They crossed over into their social lives. At the *Mercury* we had a cricket team and a drama club. We took works outings to London: football matches at Wembley; West End shows.'

'So what changed?'

'The world – the whole world – and this little corner of south-east England couldn't remain unscathed. We had a Prime Minister who told us there was no such thing as Society and set about proving it. And though many of us were happy to see an end to some of the dottier things that had been done in the name of Society with a big S, we soon found that she and her friends were destroying society with a small s too. Or as I'd rather think of it: community. That's something you'll hear a lot of around here. A couple of years ago the staff set up a swear box for every time I used the c word. It cost me dear but I wasn't surprised. Community's what we're all about.'

'What about trials?'

'What about them?'

'I could write about the changes in how you cover trials.'

'You could,' Duncan replied uneasily. 'You'd learn a lot

about the shift in social attitudes from the way court cases are reported. Fifty years ago, people routinely referred to the "criminal classes". They talked about "wastrels" and "ne'er-do-wells" up before the magistrates for being drunk and disorderly fifteen times in as many months. Nowadays, offenders are treated with more respect.'

'Why?'

'Because they're still members of the community.'

'One pound, please!'

'What?'

'For the swear box.'

'Nice try! That was scrapped after a few weeks, before I went bust. Besides, it was 10p. Now I must get back to my desk. You have a rummage around in here. Work out if the trial idea is feasible. I'll help you as much as I can. You're free to come here any afternoon after school, though I should warn you that Tuesdays and Wednesdays are press days so they're manic. If you want somewhere more comfortable, I'll lend you the keys to my flat. The one thing I ask is that you let either Sheila or me know whenever you leave the building. This evening you've got till 6.30, when I'm taking your mother to the pier consultation at the library. I don't suppose it's your thing, but you're very welcome to tag along.'

Duncan's supposition was correct and, after finding a 'sick' story about a Salter man who, on divorcing his wife in 1998, sued her for the return of the kidney he had donated to her six years earlier, Neil took the bus home, leaving Duncan to lock up and collect Ellen. Although she had forgiven him for his silence over Sue, he had barely seen her over the past three weeks when she had stayed in every evening with the children. To Duncan's surprise, this turned out be a blessing since, with their meetings limited to two rushed lunches and a blustery walk on the cliffs, they had fallen back on late-night phone calls in which they voiced their mutual longing more freely than they had done face to face. Not since Linda had he found someone with whom he was so sexually compatible. Anxious to refute the charge of coldness, he had too often placed his partner's needs above his own, leaving him frustrated and, in the case of Lea Brierley, physically repulsed. With Ellen, however, he had nothing to prove.

In a sign of her newfound confidence, she had allowed him to meet her at the Child Development Centre, the much maligned 'mushroom building' in north Francombe. The Centre, with its red-and-white speckled roof and cylindrical frame, which according to its architects put the requirements of its young clients above those of its staff (and according to its critics those of awards committees above both), consisted of a large circular foyer surrounded by a series of therapy and consulting rooms. Ellen let him in and he felt a boyish thrill at finally being admitted to her place of work, even though her colleagues had already gone home.

Clasping her to his chest, he kissed her with both passion and relief. 'Thank you,' Ellen said, gazing deeply into his eyes. 'Just what the therapist ordered.'

'There's plenty more where that came from.'

'Well then?'

He kissed her again, feeling her breath recharge every cell in his body, before she broke off to yawn.

'Oh dear! Was it that bad?'

'I'm sorry. I've had the day from hell.'

'They're still not cutting you any slack?'

'The trouble is it's just as tough for the guys who've worked here for years. It'd be one thing if we only had to deal with the kids; the real problem's the parents. They expect us to wave a magic wand and, hey presto, their kids will start to talk.'

'You can see their point of view,' Duncan said, remembering Linda's ambitions for Rose.

'Maybe, but it's the kids' point of view that counts. Just because we're *speech* therapists doesn't mean we regard it as the be-all and end-all of communication. I had a mother this morning who demanded – and that's putting it politely – that I give her severely disabled son vocal exercises.'

'And did you?'

'Of course not. I explained, as gently as I could, that the pressure she was putting on the boy was making things even harder for him and that we needed to work together to find him the right AAC – sorry, that's alternative and augmentative communication aid.'

'Did she agree?'

'You're joking! She accused me of wanting to turn her son into a robot and swore that she'd never let him become dependent on technology. A minute later she took out her BlackBerry and wrote a memo to herself. You couldn't make it up.'

'Linda told me Rose is about to get her first VOCA.'

'You're out of date; she got it last week. It's a simple entry-level model, like a communication book on a screen. But it's still a quantum leap.'

'I look forward to seeing it. How's she coping?'

'It's early days. She's easily flustered and hits the wrong keys, so we're reducing the number of symbols per page until she gets the hang of it. On Friday she threw a strop and refused to go on, but eventually we coaxed her into trying again. Linda said she'd never seen her so excited as the first time she heard herself – OK, the synthesiser – speak her name.'

'She's a brave kid – and a bright one,' Duncan said, seizing the chance to fulfil Linda's commission. 'I'm sure she'd thrive within the right educational environment.'

'I hope you're not fishing, Duncan. You know I can't talk to you about that.' She eyed him sharply, as if weighing up his loyalties to Linda and to her.

'Of course not. But I gather that after the disappointing report from the nursery school your assessment is vital if she's to stay in mainstream schooling.'

'Then you'll also have gathered that it's strictly confidential. You wouldn't want to see me struck off?'

'Not for the world!'

'That's a relief. There's a limit to how often I can pack up and leave a town in disgrace.'

Linking arms, she led him out of the Centre. They drove to the library, heading straight for the Reference Section where the architectural drawings for the renovated pier were newly on display. Duncan edged through the room to inspect the intricate floor plans, elevations and cross sections, with the seemingly innocuous labels: Revue Bar; Museum; Cinema 1. Turning to the crowd, he spotted Glynis and Bill Kingswood looking like the agents for a defeated parliamentary candidate; Ken Newbold holding an ominously empty glass; Vivien Pilling taking a rare evening off from her café; and Henry Grainger in animated conversation with his Methodist counterpart. Conspicuous at the centre was a trio of Weedons: Frances, exuding her unique brand of sprayed-on glamour, talking to a dumpy woman in a sari; Geoffrey subtly deferring to two sober-suited businessmen, whose very anonymity gave cause for alarm; and Derek showing a large polystyrene model of the proposed reconstruction to Ralph Welch.

Scenting conspiracy, he sought out the one Weedon he could trust. 'Is Ralph Welch your bank manager?' he asked.

'I've no idea,' Linda said, bristling at the brusque greeting. 'I bank on line.' She turned to Ellen with whom, to Duncan's surprise, she was now on kissing terms.

'You weren't sure you'd find a sitter,' Ellen said.

'My long-suffering mum. I had no choice. It's Derek's big night.'

'Not to mention Geoffrey's,' Duncan said.

'Try not to pick a fight with him, Duncan, please.'

'Ladies and gentlemen, may I have your attention.' Lorna Redwood's voice sputtered over the microphone, accompanied by a loud whistle. 'If you'll take your seats, we're ready to start.'

'Catch you later,' Linda said, as she moved to join Derek.

Eschewing his usual choice of a middle-row seat, Duncan escorted Ellen to the front, where they sat opposite the Weedons like feuding in-laws at a wedding.

'To anyone who doesn't know me,' Lorna said smugly, 'I'm Lorna Redwood, Chair of the Council's Leisure and Recreation Committee.' This triggered a lone cheer from one of the librarians, of which she feigned disapproval. 'I'm delighted to have been asked to chair this meeting, but I must stress that I'm here in a purely private capacity. While the Council has been eager to seek the widest possible consultation on a matter of such intense public interest, it has no power to impose one, and, indeed, it has played no part in organising this evening's event. Now without further ado let me pass you over to Geoffrey Weedon.'

There was a smattering of applause dragged out by Derek, while Frances kept her hands in her lap as if they had just been manicured. Geoffrey stepped up to the microphone and Duncan took some satisfaction from seeing that, for all his success, he still felt the need for a comb-over.

'Thank you all for coming. It's great to have such a large turnout. As Lorna said, we're under no obligation to hold this meeting, but at Weedon's we've always believed in transparency. So whatever you may have heard, this is no PR stunt. The designs aren't set in stone. Miss Nisbett and her team have kindly agreed to display them here for the next four weeks. There are message boxes sited throughout the room.' Derek stood up and pointed them out as if they were emergency exits. 'Yes, thank you,' Geoffrey said, visibly irked by the interruption. 'So please do have your say. I guarantee that every comment will be taken into account before we submit our final plans to the Council.

'As you know, a lot of water has flowed under the bridge – or should that be on to the beach?' – he paused for a laugh that was not forthcoming – 'since the pier was closed in 2008. The FPT has fought hard to maintain it as a public amenity and I commend their efforts, but it was never a viable proposition. Like other outmoded Francombe institutions, the structure needs a complete overhaul.' Duncan could not decide whether Geoffrey was looking directly at him or merely in his direction. 'Our feasibility study proves that it's impossible to retain the pier as an all-purpose family recreation complex. Quite apart from the enormous costs involved – at a conservative estimate, around £50,000,000 – where are the families we'd have to attract? I'll tell you where: sitting in front of their home entertainment systems, eating takeaway pizzas, watching satellite TV, playing video games and listening to iPods. They don't want variety shows, fruit machines, winter gardens or tea rooms. The old-fashioned family pier is as obsolete as the old-fashioned family.

'The FPT has described the pier as a community asset. But the world has moved on and it's our kids who are leading the way. They don't have communities; they have networks. Their friends are as likely to live in New York or Sydney as in the next street. Far from being an asset, the pier is a liability: a white elephant – or should that be a beached whale?' Once again he paused to no avail. 'So do we leave it to rot: a blot on the landscape and a drain on the public purse? Or do we think outside the box? Do we find our USP and transform it into Britain's first X-rated pier?' He allowed time for the collective gasp. 'Think about it! Seaside resorts have always been a bit edgy – a bit risqué. Look at Donald McGill postcards and What the Butler Saw machines. We're just taking it a stage further. So we'll replace the ghost train with a love train and the variety shows with erotic revues. We'll sell latex and lingerie instead of rock and toffee apples. We'll put a tantric therapist in the fortune teller's booth, pole dancers in the fun fair and a sex museum in the Winter Garden. We'll have strip shows, adult cinemas and naked volleyball – remember, we're the ones who brought women wrestlers to Francombe. We'll cater for stag and hen nights, swingers, and the respectable end of the fetish market. We'll sell Kiss Me Quick hats that mean what they say. You don't need me to tell you that Francombe needs a facelift.' Duncan sneaked a glance at Frances, whose smile was as stiff as her skin. 'With the carpet factory closed, there's no more light industry. Our fishermen are drowning in EU regulations. The only thriving tourist facilities are the caravan parks, and how much income do they generate for the town? At last we'll give people a reason to come here. And they won't just be day trippers. With our late-night entertainment, they'll be wanting to stay. No wonder the Chamber of Commerce and the Hoteliers Association are backing us every step of the way. I'm counting on all of you to do the same.' Duncan raised his hand. 'Well, maybe not all of you,' Geoffrey said with a thin smile. 'I'd hoped that even our most diehard opponents would take a moment to reflect. But at least have the courtesy to hold fire until Archana Nayar has shown us her drawings ... You'll know Archana by reputation,' he said, neatly wrong-footing the ignorant. 'Not least for her prize-winning contribution to the 2012 Olympic Park. We're honoured to have her on board.'

Acknowledging the applause, Archana stepped on to the dais, and Duncan understood why Frances had been so attentive to a woman whose dowdiness would otherwise have dismayed her. After thanking Geoffrey for his generous tribute and insisting that it was she who felt honoured to be associated with such an innovative and exciting project, Archana asked for the lights to be dimmed (which in practice meant switching off the fluorescent bar nearest the screen). Then, in a deft display of computer graphics, she led the audience on a virtual tour of the remodelled pier, explaining the various shaded areas as clinically as an oncologist.

'It's easy to be sentimental about the pier,' she said. 'Contrary to popular belief, it's only the steel frame that dates back a hundred and forty years. Everything else has been rebuilt, often several times: the Moorish pavilion (which some might regard as a relic of cultural imperialism) after the fire of 1954; the Winter Garden after the roof collapsed in the early Seventies; the bandstand after the great storm of 1987. Even the decking was completely refurbished in the mid 1990s. So please, let's hear no more about the architectural integrity. What about environmental integrity? Throughout the design process, I've been at pains to integrate the pier with its surroundings so that for the first time it will both enhance the vista from the bay and reflect the existing seafront. Thank you.' She returned to her seat amid warm applause. 'One thing I forgot to mention,' she added from the floor. 'The entire site will be disabled-friendly.'

'Haven't they suffered enough?' Duncan whispered to Ellen, who shushed him. 'Seriously, does it just mean ramps and extra-wide doorways or will there be special cars on the love train and booths in the erotic revue bar? How about lower nets on the volleyball court?' he added, warming to his theme. 'Or would that be the disreputable end of fetishism?'

'They're watching us!' Ellen hissed.

Duncan looked at the stony faces of Geoffrey Weedon and Lorna Redwood as the latter announced that she was opening the floor to questions. 'Duncan Neville from the *Mercury*,' he said, shooting up his hand.

'I'm sure you need no introduction, Mr Neville,' Lorna said, admitting him to that select band of luminaries in which she had recently placed herself.

'Thank you. Can you tell us if the Council knew about these proposals when it agreed to sell the pier to the developers?'

'For the last time,' Lorna said with a sigh, 'I'm not here tonight to speak on behalf of the Council. The proposals will go before the Planning Committee, which will rule on them in due course.'

'Why, when everyone knows it's already a done deal?'

'If you'll allow me, Madam Chairman,' Geoffrey said, rising to his feet. 'I've emphasised the economic benefits of the development, but many experts see our regeneration of the pier as an end in itself. I have here a letter from the National Piers Society endorsing the project. Even the Victorian Society has given us its blessing now that we're committed to retaining the original frame. I'm happy to pass both letters on to Mr Neville and expect that, in the best tradition of independent journalism, he'll print them in full.'

Duncan sat tight-lipped, trusting that other objectors would fare better. He was reassured by the first name that Lorna called.

'Dr Kingswood.'

'May I ask if Mr Weedon appreciates the weight of opposition to his cultural vandalism?' Glynis said.

'Of course our plans won't be to everyone's liking, any more than they would if we rebuilt the pavilion as a hotel or a casino. Just because those who oppose the scheme make a lot of noise doesn't mean there aren't hundreds – thousands – who support it. I'm a great believer in the silent majority.'

'Shouldn't that be the apathetic majority?' Glynis asked.

'If you say so. Personally, I have more respect for my fellow townspeople,' Geoffrey replied to a murmur of approval that in other circumstances Duncan would have echoed.

'But why the pier?' the Methodist minister asked. 'Build your pornographic theme park if you must, but build it somewhere without such a rich history.'

'First, let me assure Your Reverence that it won't be in any way pornographic. All the attractions will be strictly policed and no one under eighteen will be admitted. Second, it's precisely because of its history that I've taken on the project. I grew up with the pier and I want to preserve it.' His eyes narrowed. 'Isn't it odd that the people who make the most fuss about Francombe's decline are the first to cry foul at anyone who tries to reverse it? They call themselves conservationists; I call them dinosaurs ... well, I call them something else, but not in public. Just because they choose to live in the past, do they have to drag the rest of us back with them? I don't want to personalise the debate but it's no secret that the opposition to this scheme – along with almost everything else I've done for Francombe – has been orchestrated by the *Mercury.*' Feeling Ellen tense beside him, Duncan clasped her hand. 'It didn't take a genius to realise that the old arguments would resurface tonight so I've done a little digging and you might be interested in what I've found. How many of you know that the very facilities Mr Neville is now so anxious to restore were once bitterly attacked by his paper? In the 1920s the *Mercury* denounced the owners of the pavilion when they proposed to turn it from a concert venue into a dance hall. In the Seventies it was back on its high horse when the new owners – or maybe they were the same? I don't know – turned it into a roller-skating rink. And in the 1980s it waged a war of words when, in a final transformation, the rink became a disco. This is from one of its leading articles: "Has any engineer studied the effect on the pier's foundations of hundreds of young people leaping into the air to the beat of the latest *popular music* hit?" And, yes, ladies and gentlemen, popular music is in italics.'

'That was written by the previous editor,' Duncan interjected.

'Who was, of course, your father. Three cheers for nepotism!' Duncan felt Ellen's fingers digging into his palm. 'I've been painted as a johnny-come-lately, an opportunist out for all he can get and, frankly, I resent it. I love this town. True, Francombe has been good to me, but I like to think I've been good to it in return.'

'Hear hear!' a voice shouted from the back of the room.

'Now I want to do more. This development is the biggest opportunity to come our way since the building of the railway in the 1860s. Do we grab it and make Francombe proud again, or do we let it slip and condemn ourselves to terminal decay? It's your call. Are you with me?' His appeal prompted a surge of 'yeses' and a solitary 'no', which Duncan took to be a mis-understanding rather than genuine dissent.

Geoffrey sat down, and Duncan knew that he was beaten. The nepotism jibe had stripped him of even the dignity of defeat. As the applause swelled around him, Geoffrey signalled to a young man crouching at the edge of the dais, who flicked a switch, flooding the model pier with hundreds of minuscule lights.

Seven

£3,260 raised in *Mercury* Christmas Toy Appeal

by Brian Gannon

Thursday, 19 December 2013

*M*ercury readers have dug deep in their pockets to raise a magnificent £3,260 for our fifteenth annual Christmas Toy Appeal.

The money will be used to buy toys and presents, which will be added to the bumper sacks of goodies, including dolls, jigsaws, board games, colouring books, dressing-up clothes and DVDs that have arrived at Mercury House and our various collection points across town over the past few weeks.

Among the last donors to contact us before Saturday's deadline were two big-hearted schoolgirls, Hayley and Tanya Watson. Francis Preston pupil Hayley persuaded her younger sister to join her in raiding their piggybanks after reading about our appeal.

Hayley, 11, said: 'It made me sad to think that there are children who won't be able to have any presents at Christmas. I thought we should give them our pocket money so their mums and dads can buy them some presents.'

Tanya, 6, who attends St Columba's primary school, said: 'We opened up our money boxes to help the poor children. I hope now they can have a doll's house and a bicycle.'

The £3,260 is made up of £180 deposited in our collection boxes, £440 sent in by readers, and £2,640 contributed by local businesses. Topping the list of donations are £200 from Francombe Numismatics; £250 from Tesco's, Bartholomew Road; and £1,000 from Weedon Investments.

Mercury editor, Duncan Neville, said: 'Once again there has been a fantastic response to our appeal, and I would like to thank all our readers and local businesses for their support. In the fifteen years that the appeal has been running, we have been able to help more than 6,000 underprivileged children in the Francombe area. I am delighted that we will be able to do so again this year.

'It is at Christmas that we realise how lucky we are to be surrounded by our loved ones. But in the current economic climate many people are facing a bleak future. Thanks to the goodwill of the local community, their children will be able to wake up on Christmas morning with a smile.'

Despite the shampoo dripping down his forehead and sting-
ing his eyes, Duncan leapt out of the shower to silence the
radio the moment that Elvis Presley at his most lachrymose
launched into 'If Every Day Was Like Christmas'. Even in
such an overcrowded field, it must win the prize for the most
fraudulent lyric of all time. The festive season was gruelling
enough on an annual basis. With neither a strong faith nor a
young family to give it meaning, he felt secret sympathy for
Scrooge.

This year there would at least be the compensation of
spending his first Christmas since his divorce with Jamie and
his first ever with Ellen. In the meantime he had to endure
various official functions, starting with the staff Christmas
dinner in two hours' time. The three-course set meal at the
Metropole, complete with selected wines, was a far cry from
the Christmas parties of his youth: dinner dances in the Pier
Pavilion, which his mother allowed him to attend on condition that he stand behind her in the conga line to shield her
from the printers' wandering hands.

Even without the financial considerations, he would have
balked at holding a dance for a staff of eight, or rather six
since Trevor was going to his newly divorced brother's
freedom party and Mary had been kept at home by Bob.
While shedding few tears over Trevor, who routinely confused drunkenness with conviviality, he would miss Mary,
who was fighting to save her marriage. Bob's response to the
mural had been chilling. Far from celebrating his wife's portrayal, he had railed against the public humiliation, giving her
the biggest black eye Duncan had ever seen outside a comic
strip. When she turned up for work three days later claiming
to have 'walked into a door', with no 'it's my own silly fault for
drinking too much/not looking where I was going/not buying
new glasses' to corroborate her story, she seemed to be daring
him to challenge her. But when he did, reminding her of her
plan to move in with Jordan, she described it as a menopausal

fantasy, adding that she deserved whatever Bob gave her after destroying the one thing that he had left: his pride.

In a further setback, Henry rang the next morning with the news that the figures of Adam and Eve in the mural had been defaced, purportedly by Jordan himself, who was found with two empty cans of acrylic paint beside a graffiti-daubed fishermen's memorial. Whatever his motives for the attack, Duncan refused to believe that he had acted of his own volition. He must have been intimidated either by Bob or Norman, who had lately been released from Ford, with one or other of them driving him into town and forcing him to vandalise the monument, before tipping off the police. Jordan himself gave nothing away. In court he spoke only to confirm his name and address, and plead guilty, whereupon the magistrates activated his suspended sentence, jailing him for six months. No doubt all those readers who had complained of his being mollycoddled after the front-page photograph of him shaking hands with the bishop would feel vindicated.

All else being equal, Duncan would have preferred to hold the meal at Vivien's but he feared that some of the staff would feel cheated. So, after calling in at the café to drop off a present for Connor, his four-year-old godson, he proceeded up the Parade, where the annual orgy of consumption lacked even a fig leaf of festivity since the major retailers, citing the Recession, had refused to pay for Christmas lights. Several of his correspondents, together with Brian and Jake, who confounding expectations took the Elvis Presley view of Christmas, proposed that the *Mercury* should initiate a boycott of the offending stores. But, mindful of the outrage provoked by the recent 'Tide of Filth' story on the state of Francombe beaches, he was reluctant to alienate any more powerful interests (or, as Trevor put it, potential advertisers), not least when he would need their support to stem the tsunami of filth that Weedon's was preparing to unleash on the town.

Further evidence of the Recession was to be found in the

half-empty Crystal Room. The sweep of white linen, unrelieved by the gleam of silverware, cast a pall over proceedings as Duncan led in his guests, all except Ken having observed the smart-casual dress code that Stewart described as the only oxymoron he would ever let pass. They had scarcely sat down when Sheila insisted that they pull their crackers, at which Brian, ignorant of the history, declared that Stewart was 'firing blanks' after his failed to pop. Exhorting everyone to put on paper hats, Sheila made Rowena swap, first with Jake and then with Ken, to find the one that best matched her cardigan and Duncan relinquish his mitre for her own 'more appropriate' crown. 'Ever the office manager,' Ken said, defusing the tension, which rapidly built up again when Jake read out the jokes.

Duncan, whose sense of social obligation was not shared by the rest of the table, struggled to keep the party flowing. The veto on talking about work left them painfully aware of how little they had in common. In a welcome distraction, Jake, announcing that soup made him sweat, removed his jacket to reveal a knitted woollen waistcoat with a border of pigs. Sheila, already on her third glass of wine, stretched across Ken to stroke what she declared to be the prettiest pussies she had ever seen, whereupon Brian snorted so hard that his nose began to bleed. As the scarlet stain spread across his napkin, Rowena and Ken bickered over whether he should bend his neck backwards or forwards; Stewart suggested dropping car keys down his shirt; and Jake claimed that his mother used to swear by running a butter knife along the spine. Sheila, professing to have such poor circulation that her hands were like ice, offered to rub his back, at which the bleeding abruptly stopped.

Brian's choice of main course kept him at the centre of attention since, while everyone else had ordered crown of turkey with herb stuffing, cranberry compote and sprout puree, he had chosen venison. Ken, moved more by antipathy than tradition, compared it to asking for shellfish at a bar mitzvah, whereupon Sheila, telling him not to be such a bully, assured Brian that if he wanted stuffing he could have some of hers. 'Next she'll be asking if he's a leg or a breast man,' Rowena hissed in Duncan's ear.

Swiftly changing the subject, Duncan enquired about everyone's Christmas plans, but even that was not without risk since only Stewart, who was taking Laura to Lanzarote, was looking forward to the break. Ken would be entertaining his widowed sister-in-law, whom he had loathed for forty years but whose presence he tolerated since it gave him the necessary excuse to escape from his wife for a few hours. Brian would be with his family, his primacy threatened by the return of his younger brother from London. Jake would be at his lodgings, although banished upstairs in deference to his landlady's children. Rowena would be paying her annual visit to her sister in Canterbury, where the solicitude of her three nieces would underline her daughter's disaffection.

Duncan's greatest concern was Sheila, so much so that despite an already crowded table he had resolved to invite her to Ridgemount for Christmas lunch when she forestalled him by announcing that she had volunteered to help out at Castlemaine. Jean Davison, the manager, whom she knew from a folklore class, had seized on the offer of an extra pair of hands and she herself was glad to have found a way to spend Christmas with her mother. Moreover, it would allow her to assess the deterioration in her behaviour that the staff had ascribed to Dragon's arrival at the home. Defying hopes that he would interact with the other residents, he had remained as reclusive as in his hut, even shunning a belly-dancing display by the cook's daughter. The problem was that the acute gender imbalance put his presence at a premium. According to Jean, on some unconscious level (the only one on which most of them still functioned), the women interpreted his indifference as rejection. Egged on by Sheila's mother, they had ganged up on him: mocking and mimicking him like feral five-year-olds. Witnessing it for herself, Sheila would have a chance to reason with – or, at any rate, constrain – her mother before things spun out of control.

'I hope you'll give yourself a little Sheila time as well,' Duncan had said when she outlined her arrangements.

'Why? What would I do with it?' she replied, extending his concern beyond Christmas.

The meal ended with brandy for everyone except Sheila, who with rare self-awareness announced that she was 'already a bit squiffy', and Jake, who had offered to drive her, Rowena and Brian home. Advising them with deceptive flippancy to cash the cheques before they bounced, Duncan handed out their Christmas bonuses. Sheila then gave him a present from the staff, which custom obliged him to open on the spot.

'A plant!' he said, his relief after last year's James Bond cufflinks tinged with fear that he would let it die.

'Not just any plant, a money plant,' Sheila said. 'Your office needs cheering up. And we all know that finances are tight. I've read up on the feng shui, so I can show you exactly where to put it. In the left-hand corner opposite the door.'

'It's very kind of you all. Thank you,' Duncan said, struggling to conceal the leaf that he had ripped off with the wrapping paper. 'When I was a boy, my mother used to tell me that money doesn't grow on trees. Let's hope this proves her wrong.'

Holding the pot at arm's length like a baby with a full nappy, he returned to Mercury House. He knew that he should be grateful not just for the gift but for the coded acknowledgement of his plight. Instead he felt pained that they should suppose, even jokingly, that it might be relieved by recourse to an ancient superstition. The bank loan was due for repayment in less than a month. With no white knight on the horizon, he and Dudley Williams were engaged in detailed discussions with executives, lawyers and accountants from both Newscom and Provident. He was no longer in any doubt that he would have to sell the company to one of these two local media giants, and that he and his family would receive next to nothing for their shares. His principal objective was to reach a deal that would preserve the title, protect the staff and, above all, guarantee their pensions.

At half past twelve it was too late for his nightly call to Ellen, so he rang her as soon as he woke up. Busily packing for Sue's Caribbean trip, she did little more than confirm that she and Neil would come round at seven for dinner with him and Jamie. It was a meal that filled him with a mixture of excitement and dread. After dithering over the menu, he had opted for pizza as both adolescent-friendly (he would even let them eat out of the box if it helped) and cheap. The need for frugality depressed him. He promised himself that as soon as Christmas was over, he would reveal the full extent of his debts to Ellen. If there were the slightest chance of their sharing a future, he had to warn her that it might not be as rosy as she had supposed. His fear was not that she would leave him – she had experienced the emptiness of colour-supplement living during her marriage – but that she might feel duty-bound to stay.

Struggling to stave off the gloom, he set out to collect Jamie, although ten minutes of scraping the frost from Rocinante's windscreen and another five of coaxing her temperamental engine to start did little to relieve his apprehension. It was not only their first Christmas together since the divorce but their longest period under one roof since Alison had turned her house in Umbria into holiday lets three years earlier. Although he and Linda had agreed to alternate custody at Christmas, it had seemed churlish to force the issue when Jamie might be staying with his mother, stepfather and Rose (not to mention the all-important Craig) at Geoffrey's villa in Antigua. This year, however, things were different. If his relationship with Ellen were to succeed, it was essential that their sons become friends and Christmas offered the perfect opportunity.

Jamie, of course, had rebelled: threatening to run away, go on hunger strike and even phone Childline. When that failed, he printed out evidence from the web on the importance of sunlight for children's bone development, melatonin balance and mental well-being, to which Duncan replied that the first would be achieved by a healthy diet and the second and third by regular sleep and exercise. Changing tack, Jamie outlined the educational benefits of immersing himself in a Third World culture. When Duncan wryly assured him that he would learn more by spending one day helping out at the Morley Road refugee centre than ten issuing instructions to Geoffrey's housemaids and pool boy, Jamie accused him of being a sad loser and ruining his life.

He was particularly incensed that, while he was being kept at home, Craig was taking Sue. For his part, Duncan was astonished that Ellen had allowed her to go, not least after Frances's announcement that she would be giving her a bedroom with Craig since they were both sixteen and she refused to be kept awake by creaking floorboards. With a persistence that put Jamie to shame, Sue wheedled and pleaded, screamed and insulted and threatened to cut herself, until Ellen was browbeaten into submission.

Linda too would be spending Christmas away from her daughter. Duncan's surprise at her willingness to let him have Jamie had paled beside the news that she was going to Antigua without Rose. The red eyes and puffed cheeks with which she greeted him at the door attested to the wrench.

'Come on in,' she said, leading him through the hall. 'Forgive the mess,' she added, although the three suitcases, pile of gift-wrapped presents and crate of disability aids were neatness itself to one accustomed to the *Mercury* reporters' room.

'What time are you flying tomorrow?' he asked.

'Nine thirty. But Derek's determined to take advantage of the hotel meal deal, so he wants us there by six tonight.

Meanwhile I have to finish packing, deliver those presents to my parents, shut up the house and take Rose to respite.'

'Can't Derek help?'

'Yes, of course. But he's chosen this morning to have his hair cut. Don't ask.'

'Well, at least I can take Jamie off your hands. Is he ready?'

'As much as he'll ever be. I asked if he wanted me to do his packing. He said he never wanted me to do anything for him again.'

'No change there then!'

'Still, I've got more important things to worry about than Sir's moods. I've...'

She had no need to finish the sentence since Duncan knew that, other than a weekend in Newcastle two years ago when she had accompanied Derek to his cousin's wedding, it would be the first time that she had ever spent more than an afternoon apart from Rose. Despite all the hazards of travelling: from being hoisted on to the plane like cargo, through the tortuous sanitary arrangements, to the curiosity and even hostility of their fellow passengers (most blatant in the woman who held up a flight for an hour after claiming that Rose was 'an ill omen'), Linda had insisted on including her in every trip. This time, however, Derek, who by his own avowal knew better than to oppose his wife where their daughter was concerned, was adamant that she needed a complete break. Not only was the relentless strain of caring for a paralysed four-year-old taking its toll on her, but she would require every ounce of strength for the forthcoming battle with the LEA.

The first salvo had been fired a fortnight earlier when the Chief Education Officer sent them a draft copy of the revised statement of Rose's educational needs, which, despite Ellen's report, concluded that she would be best served by the greater classroom and therapeutic support available at a specialist school. They were given fifteen days to make representations, after which the LEA would review the evidence and issue a final statement. If, as seemed likely, that upheld the original verdict, they had the right of appeal. Knowing Linda, Duncan was certain that she would not rest until she had exhausted every avenue; knowing Ellen, he was equally certain that she would support her all the way, notwithstanding her private admission that there was little hope of the tribunal's ruling against the Local Authority.

'Come and say hello to Rose,' Linda said, 'and I do mean "say". She's been waiting all morning to show you her new talker.'

He followed Linda into the living room where Rose was sitting in front of her bright-red VOCA. 'How's my favourite girl?' he asked. 'I hear you've become quite the chatterbox.'

Rose turned towards him, with her neck thrust back and face screwed up as though a wasp were circling beneath her chin, in what Linda had assured him was an expression of pleasure.

'You're looking very pretty this morning, Rose. Are you excited about your stay in the country?' Duncan asked, careful to choose one of the yes/no questions in which she was practised.

'Wait for it!' Linda said.

Rose pressed a key on the VOCA, which responded with the phrase: 'My name is Rose.' Despite the science-fiction flatness of the voice, Duncan realised that, except for nebulous vowels and hacked consonants, these were the first sounds he had ever heard her produce.

'Hello, Rose. My name's Duncan,' he replied, eager not to betray his emotion.

'We've transferred all the symbols from her communication book to her talker. And Derek's made her a new page specially for Christmas: tree, present, card, turkey, cracker – not that she'll ever be able to pull one. We tried it out last Sunday at my parents'. At first Mum was thrilled, but then she suggested we add another couple of symbols for "please" and "thank you"!'

'Same old Brenda!'

'Ask her who she went to see last week,' Linda whispered.

'Who did you go to see last week, Rose?' Duncan asked.

With an effort that made him ashamed of his idle chatter, she pressed another key, sending the symbols gliding slowly across the screen. Even so, they moved too fast for her to control and, as she stopped at the turkey instead of Father Christmas, her back arched and her head twisted, her arms and legs stiffened, and her jaw clenched in frustration.

'Don't worry. We all make mistakes,' Duncan said. 'My newspaper does it the whole time.' He tried to think of an example, but the only one that sprang to mind was Rowena's report of the Council's new 'meretricious' rather than 'meritorious' community composting scheme, which he half suspected had been deliberate and which in any case would mean nothing to a four-year-old. 'I remember,' he improvised. 'Last week, we put "a doggy day" instead of "a foggy day".'

Rose's head jerked, her eyelids fluttered and her tongue rolled in her mouth. 'Yes, darling, it is funny,' Linda said.

Duncan was framing another question when Jamie marched in. 'OK then, are we off?' he asked.

'Good morning, Jamie. It's good to see you too.'

'Yeah, whatever.'

'Are you sure you've got everything you need?' Linda asked.

'Like you care!'

'I dare say he'll scrape by,' Duncan said.

'Well then, you'd better say goodbye to your sister,' Linda said.

''Bye Rose,' Jamie said. 'Have a nice time in kennels.'

'Jamie!' Duncan said, grateful for once for the ambiguity of Rose's reactions.

'That's a cruel thing to say.' Linda's eyes welled with tears.

'You're the one who's cruel,' Jamie said. 'Leaving us here while you swan off to the sun.'

'I'm a wreck, Jamie.' Linda's voice was as raw as her eyes.

'Don't worry; it's nothing serious. I just need to recharge my batteries.'

'You should apologise to your mother,' Duncan said.

'Don't worry about me,' Linda said. 'How about saying sorry to your sister?'

Jamie's façade of indifference crumbled as he approached Rose, dropped to his knees and put his arm round her shoulders. 'Bye-bye, Rose. Have a great Christmas. I'm sure you'll make loads of new friends.' He kissed her on the lips before walking to the door.

'What about me?' Linda asked. 'Don't I get one?'

'No.'

With a commiserative shrug, Duncan moved to Linda, knowing that the light kiss he planted on her cheek was no compensation for her son's rebuff. 'Have a wonderful holiday. And you too, Rose. Don't forget I'm bringing Jamie to see you on Boxing Day.'

He followed his son out to the car. As they drove off in an unusually tractable Rocinante, Jamie switched on the radio, destroying any chance of conversation. Arriving at the flat, he shut himself in his bedroom, not emerging until lunch: Sainsbury's sweet-and-sour chicken, the first of the ready meals that would be the staple of his stay.

'So what would you like to do this afternoon?' Duncan asked. 'I've looked in a certain local paper and there's not much on at the cinema. But do check in case there's something I've missed. Otherwise, at 4.30 the Local History Society is joining forces with the East Sussex Paranormal Association for a ghost walk in the castle ruins. It's billed as suitable for children of ten and over.'

'Ten!'

'And over. That just means it's too frightening for little kids.'

'Sorry, Dad, but I might be scarred for life. Anyway, I've arranged to meet up with some friends.'

'You never said.'

'You never asked.'

'Do I know them?'

'Are you a paedo?'

'What?'

'Then why would you know them?' Jamie's tone mellowed. 'They're just guys from school.'

'I know this wasn't the holiday you planned,' Duncan said, trying a new approach. 'But we're going to have fun. I want us to use this opportunity to grow closer.'

'There you go again,' Jamie said. 'Why must you spell it out? It makes everything harder.'

'I feel we're drifting apart. There are great swathes of your life I know nothing about.'

'What do you expect? I don't live with you. When I talk to Mum, it's natural. She asks about school, what I've done today, stuff like that. With you, it's like "So tell me what you've been doing since I saw you last week?" and I have to think of something special. We have to discuss things like we're in a book.'

'Everything you do is special to me.'

'No, it's not. That's dumb! You mean like every time I take a shit?'

'You're deliberately misunderstanding me.'

'No, I'm not, Dad. Honest! It'd be easier if I was.'

'Well, you're here for the next two weeks. Let's hope we can have the kind of casual conversations you have with your mum.'

'Will you pass me the soy sauce please?' Jamie asked, enunciating every word.

After an uneasy lunch, far from feeling hurt by Jamie's departure, Duncan was glad of a few hours to himself before what threatened to be an even more strained evening. He was in the middle of washing up, adding his light tenor to the darker tones of Leporello's Catalogue Aria on the radio, when Jamie poked his head round the kitchen door. 'I'm off then.'

'Be sure to be back by 6.30. We have guests.'

'Who?'

'It's a surprise,' Duncan said, choosing to defer the risk of an outburst.

'Typical! You say you want to spend time with me, then you fill the house with strangers.'

'Wait and see. Surely you're not going out like that?' He looked askance at Jamie's bomber jacket and jeans.

'What should I wear? A suit and tie?'

'A coat. There's a force 10 gale blowing outside.'

'I haven't got a coat.'

'What?'

'I mean I haven't brought one.'

'Wear mine,' Duncan said, chiding himself for not having checked earlier. 'It'll swamp you but...'

'You're joking, right? I'd rather get frostbite. I'd rather my fingers fell off and my toes fell off and my nose fell off and – '

'I get the picture. Then at least wear a scarf. If you haven't brought one, take mine from the hall cupboard.' Jamie grimaced. 'I mean it.'

Jamie went out and a moment later Duncan heard the reassuring squeak of the cupboard door.

'Fucking hell!'

'What's wrong?' Dropping his cloth, Duncan dashed into the hall to find Jamie holding a Francis Preston cap. 'I thought you'd done yourself an injury.'

'What's this? No, whose is it?'

'It belongs to Neil.'

'Neil Nugent?'

'He left it here last week. I've told you he's doing his local history project on the *Mercury*. I'd far rather have done it with you, of course.'

'But he's the next best thing?'

'You know perfectly well it's not like that.'

'How do you know what I know. Are you a fortune teller?'

'Don't you mean a mind reader?'

'Do you pick him up on every word too?'

'Why compare yourself with him? I'm just trying to give him a helping hand. I've become close – very close – to his mother. You've met her: Rose's speech therapist.'

'Is she teaching you new swallowing techniques too?'

'That's disgusting, Jamie. You're not a child.'

'That depends, doesn't it? On what you want from me at the time.'

'I want you to understand what I feel for Ellen,' Duncan said, wounded by the charge. 'I love her.' For all the awkwardness, it felt fitting that the first person in whom he confided should be his son.

'So? You loved Mum, didn't you?'

'Most definitely.'

'And that fucked up.'

'In the end, yes. But we had thirteen – well, ten – happy years. In any case I'm older now. We both are. Maybe not wiser.' He laughed uneasily. 'But more experienced. So's Ellen. She's been through a lot.'

'Big whoop!'

'It's early days, but when you know something's right, as right as this is, then the usual rules don't apply. I want to marry her.'

'You can't!'

'It may look like I'm rushing things, but I promise you to me it feels more like holding back.'

'I'm not listening.' Jamie clamped his hands to his ears like a four-year-old protesting against bedtime. Duncan wondered whether to prise them away, extending the movement into a hug, but he was afraid of feeling his son's body tense up against him. Besides, Jamie could still hear every word.

'That's why I want you to make a special effort to get along with Neil.'

'He'll never be my brother.'

'No, but I hope he'll be your stepbrother.'

'What about Craig?'

'Exactly like Craig. Though on my side of the family.'

'No freaking way!'

'I'm not asking you to fall in love with him,' Duncan said, immediately regretting his choice of words, 'just to make an effort to get along.'

'This is the worst Christmas ever!' Jamie said, stomping out of the flat and down the precipitous stairs. For once Duncan was grateful for the slam of the front door, which showed that he hadn't broken his neck. He grabbed his coat and was about to follow when he decided that, despite the arctic conditions, Jamie needed time to recover. At least the intensity of Jamie's fury proved that beneath the defiance and contempt he still cared for him. Or was it just the selfishness of a child who snatched back a discarded toy the moment that it was claimed by somebody else?

As the hours passed with no word from Jamie, he grew increasingly anxious. He left messages and sent texts and even contemplated going on a reconnaissance mission around town, but with such a hazy view of his son's life he had no idea where to start. In desperation, he debated whether to ring Linda for a list of Jamie's close friends, but he was loath to worry her, and any innocent explanation for the request, such as throwing him a surprise Christmas party, sounded lame. At six o'clock he called Ellen to cancel dinner, saying only that Jamie had picked a quarrel with him and stormed out of the flat. On impulse he asked whether Neil knew of any classmate he might be seeing. She went upstairs to find out, returning after several muffled shrieks and bangs with a tight-lipped 'no'. Assuring him that she knew 'the territory', she offered to come over and wait with him, but he reluctantly refused, fearful of Jamie's reaction when he finally arrived home.

At 8.30, with the 'when' in Duncan's calculations looking dangerously like 'if', he texted Jamie that unless he heard from him within ten minutes he would call the police. His gamble that Jamie, unfamiliar with investigative procedures, would fail to detect the hollowness of the threat paid off when he received an instant reply: 'At Stu's. Back 10.' With relief bordering on euphoria, he rang to tell Ellen before devouring half of a sixteen-inch seafood pizza. He left the rest in the oven for Jamie, who sauntered in at 9.58 as though determined to extract every last ounce of drama. Far from the frozen and bedraggled waif Duncan had envisioned, he was warm, dry and even, having eaten with Stu and his family, well-fed.

Claiming to be too tired to talk, Jamie went straight to his room, not even emerging to brush his teeth – although perhaps, Duncan thought bitterly, he had done that at Stu's house too. He remained equally tired, or at any rate taciturn, throughout Sunday, barely speaking except at meals and even then confining himself whenever possible to one-word answers. He refused to discuss, let alone meet, Ellen and Neil, saying that having to spend Christmas Day with them would be bad enough. And while grudgingly observing the ban on texting at table, he reached for his phone the moment that they stood up.

'Do you ever have a thought you don't share?' Duncan asked on Sunday evening, when Jamie sat glued to his phone during a TV thriller that he had insisted they watch.

'Lots! With you.'

Given Jamie's instant rejection of every proposed activity, Duncan decided to go in to work on Monday. He sat at his desk, savouring the peculiar calm of the one week in the year when the paper was not produced – even if this year it was tempered by the fear that the respite might prove to be permanent. The full staff would be back in a week's time for an issue that could practically write itself, with stories of Christmas Day babies, the Francombe Dolphins' Boxing Day Dip and any local resident who featured in the New Year Honours list. Meanwhile, as on every holiday in living memory, Ken had volunteered to man the news desk, fuelling Duncan's suspicions that he and his wife Pamela were one of those couples who for years had communicated only by notes.

In mid-morning they were joined by Sheila, whose claim that 'I thought you might need some company' would have held more conviction without the rider that 'You won't even know I'm here'.

'Aren't you supposed to be helping out at Castlemaine?' Duncan asked.

'After yesterday, Jean thought it best if I left it till Christmas Day. She says that Mother's always worse when I'm there. She plays up in order to punish me.'

'Surely not?'

'Why should she change the habits of a lifetime? Sorry. Just once before she dies, I'd like some acknowledgement: a sign that I'm more than just a spare pair of hands. But no doubt she'll be so sedated that she'll make even less sense then than she does now. Or else I'll sit by her bedside for days and she'll slip away while I'm in the loo. Out of spite! Or she'll cling on and on till I'm even madder than she is.' Sensing that his editorial duties now stretched to a hug, Duncan took a step towards her, but she put up her hand to check him before rummaging in her bag for a mint, which she popped in her mouth. 'Don't mind me, it's just all the excitement of Christmas,' she said, adding that she would spend the day sorting out the petty cash.

On Tuesday the office was closed, and Ken and Sheila were left to their own devices. Duncan spent the morning buying presents, panic as ever a great inspiration. He returned to the flat to find Jamie sprawled on the sofa, scrolling through the TV channels and complaining about the lack of Sky.

'No friends to chat to?' Duncan asked disingenuously.

'They're all doing boring things with their families.'

'You don't need the boring.'

'What?'

'If they're with their families, the boring's understood.'

'Is that supposed to be funny?'

'If you've no better offers, you can always come and be bored with me this afternoon.'

'I'm bored with you now.'

'It's my annual stint as Father Christmas, delivering toys from our appeal to the children at the Princess Royal.'

'No way! Any case, aren't they meant for the poor? What if some of the kids are rich? Or do only poor people get sick at Christmas?'

'They're for the poor and *needy*. Any child who's in hospital at Christmas is in need of cheering up. Why not come and see for yourself? You might find it moving. If we can track down a costume, you can be an elf.'

'An elf?' Jamie asked, the crack in his voice accentuating his outrage.

'It's not the same as a pixie. Aren't there elves in *Lord of the Rings*?'

'You really are losing it!'

After lunch Duncan made his way, alone, to the Princess Royal, where he donned a Father Christmas costume that was redolent of the doctor who had worn it for the Santa Fun Run in Jubilee Park the weekend before. Following last year's embarrassing exchange with a scornful boy who had spotted his wandering beard, he had brought his own spirit gum. Once his transformation was complete, he presented himself to Sister Bennett, who led him onto the ward where their noisy welcome confounded her hope that he would not 'over-stimulate the patients'. Flanked by two nurses, one Filipina and the other Nigerian, he handed out gifts to tiny tots who fervently believed in his existence and older children who judiciously suppressed their scepticism. He ho-ho-hoed till he was hoarse, chatting with each one in turn and promising that he would visit them at home next year. He answered familiar questions about Rudolph and Mrs Claus, along with new ones about the number of toys he made in a day and how he would cope if his computer crashed (in the past it had been his sleigh). He faltered only twice: first, at the sight of a bald girl lovingly stroking the hair on her new Barbie; and second, when a clammy, red-faced boy, wondering why he was so much thinner than his picture, asked if he had lupus too.

Leaving the ward to the echo of Sister Bennett's 'three cheers for Santa', he returned to the sluice room to take off his beard and costume before heading home in a state of profound unease. While the courage and resilience of the children were as uplifting as ever, he felt as if he had colluded in a giant confidence trick extending far beyond the existence of Father Christmas to the festival itself. How could anyone celebrate the birth of a God who permitted the suffering of so many children? It was no coincidence that the Nativity had been followed by the Massacre of the Innocents, for which neither He nor His apologists had ever expressed one word of remorse.

Rarely had he felt less in the mood for church. Yet ever since childhood, when his father maintained that it was 'best to get all the holy stuff over with so that it doesn't spoil the day', he had attended Midnight Mass on Christmas Eve, first with his parents and sister, and now just with Adele. It was one of the few occasions for which she still left the house, trusting no doubt that both God and the congregation would applaud the effort. Duncan escorted her, swathed in moth-eaten mink, to a pew next to the crib, which, as she never ceased to remind him, had been donated by her mother. Then, concealing his parcel in the parish newsletter, he walked shyly down the nave and under the organ loft to the sacristy, where he had arranged to call on Henry before the service.

'I brought you this,' he said, as Henry ushered him in. 'Just a little something ... nothing really.'

'I'm afraid I don't have anything for you,' Henry said with a smile. 'Mm, I wonder ... what can it be?' He shook the parcel, whose shape, size and solidity left little room for doubt.

'I wasn't expecting anything,' Duncan said. 'It's only a review copy. But the moment I saw it I thought of you.' He felt a tinge of apprehension, as in the musty, dimly lit sacristy, *Make the Most of Your Time on Earth* no longer seemed the most appropriate choice for a vicar. 'I won't stop. You'll need some time to prepare.'

'No, I'm all kitted out and ready for battle. We've no choir tonight and only Joel Lincoln serving. He's busy clearing up vomit from the font.'

'Too many mince pies?'

'Too much Christmas spirits! Still, we all need something to get us through the night. I'm ready to drop.'

'Only three more services and then you can unwind.'

'It'll be time off but I doubt there'll be much unwinding. My cousin Charles and his wife invite me to stay out of duty – not Christian duty, mind, since Charles tells me at least twice every visit that he doesn't believe in God. I think he expects me to respect his sincerity.'

'Maybe he's embarrassed by your faith?'

'He's embarrassed by me, period! I'm nothing but an inconvenience to them both. They have to push lunch back to five o'clock so I can make it after the family service. Last year I was in such a rush that I was stopped for speeding. After failing the breathalyser, I explained that I was a vicar who'd been obliged to consume the leftover Communion wine.'

'Did the policeman believe you?'

'He let me off. Maybe he thought anyone who could make up a story like that deserved a break.'

'Was it made up?'

Henry gave Duncan a cryptic glance, which he took as his cue to leave. He rejoined his mother who, having shifted her attention from the crib to her fellow worshippers, was affronted by the lack of reverence, notably from a trio of youths beneath the lancet window who were quaffing cans of lager.

'Christ turned water into wine, Mother.'

'But not to the best of my knowledge into beer.'

Preceded by Joel, Henry entered with the air of a priest in a more majestic procession. As the service began, Duncan derived the same pleasure from listening to the familiar lessons and carols as he did from looking at old family photographs: the meaning may have been lost, but the associations were rich. The one discordant note was struck by Adele's sobbing during 'The First Noël'. He waited until they were walking back to the car before asking her what was wrong.

'You'll think me silly.'

'Try me.'

'Some weeks ago I was going through your grandfather's papers. I found the commission for a new arrangement of 'The First Noël' for Hereford Cathedral in 1932. It was a great success.'

'Do you still have the score? I'm sure Henry would be happy to use it next year. Of course he doesn't have the cathedral's resources.'

'I don't intend to beg, Duncan. Your grandfather won't be the first prophet without honour in his own country.'

Resisting the temptation to point out that, a few dubious Scandinavian folk music circles apart, Stafford Lyttleton was no longer honoured anywhere, Duncan drove her back to Ridgemount, where his hopes of a swift getaway were dashed by the need to reassure her about the full house for Christmas lunch.

'You used to love entertaining.'

'That was when I had staff.'

'One maid, Mother,' Duncan said, anxious to puncture her pretensions before she offended Ellen as deeply as she once had Linda.

'Poor Duncan,' she replied. 'You always did have such a literal mind.'

Duncan returned home, where the chink of light under Jamie's door emboldened him to knock. Greeted by a less aggressive (or merely more drowsy) 'What?' than usual, he entered and was further cheered to find that, rather than listening to his iPod or playing with his computer, Jamie was reading.

'Just seeing if there's anything you want.'

'A cheque for a million pounds.'

'It'll be in your stocking tomorrow.'

'How was the service?'

'You should have come.'

'Why? I don't believe in it, same as you. At least I'm not a hypocrite.'

'You can believe that something has value even if you don't believe that it's true.'

'It's late, Dad!' Jamie replied with a groan.

'I wish you'd come to the hospital this afternoon,' Duncan said, sure that with Jamie by his side he would have felt less disenchanted.

'Those kids must be really sick if they thought you were Father Christmas.'

'I remember when you were young – '

'Oh no!' Jamie said, pulling a pillow over his face.

'You must have been five or six,' Duncan said, gently lifting off Jamie's fingers. 'Some bright spark at primary school had told you that Father Christmas was a made-up person – at least that was how you put it to us later. We managed to convince you he was wrong.'

'See, you were lying to me even then!'

'But the next morning when you opened your presents, you looked at your mother wide-eyed and asked: "Why does Father Christmas use the same wrapping paper as you?"'

'I'm tired, Dad. What does it matter?'

'It matters because you're my son. I like to remember the funny things you used to say.'

'Get a life!'

Duncan felt a rush of gratitude that Jamie was here with him and not in Antigua or, worse, the Princess Royal. He bent to kiss the crown of his head and for once Jamie didn't flinch. Bone-weary, he prepared for bed where, despite telling himself that Christmas was not a time for introspection, he was tormented by the thought of everything that he might have done to preserve the *Mercury* for his son. Sleep, when it finally came, brought no relief since he was plunged into a nightmare where the money tree in his office shot up like a pantomime beanstalk, filling the entire building and forcing him to transfer the archives to Geoffrey's sex museum on the pier. In order to consult them, he had to stand in a line of seedy-looking men, only to be told on reaching the turn-stile that he could not be admitted until he was eighteen. 'I'm forty-eight!' he protested in an unconvincing treble. The next moment the museum was engulfed in flames and he woke up trembling. Since it was almost seven, he crept into the kitchen where he sat with a pot of Earl Grey, listening to Berlioz's *L'Enfance du Christ* on the radio. At 8.30 Jamie walked in, the buttons of his pyjama jacket touchingly misaligned, and gave him his first unsolicited kiss in years.

'Orange juice?' Duncan asked, not trusting himself to say more.

'Presents!' Jamie replied, a child again if only for one day.

'Just a moment.' Duncan went to his bedroom, returning with a parcel that he handed to Jamie, who ripped it open, indifferent to the inept wrapping.

'But these are the ones, Dad!' he said, rubbing a pair of trainers against his cheeks. 'The new Lebron X. You're a star!'

'You're very welcome.'

'They cost a shitload of cash.' Jamie looked anxious. 'Are you sure you can afford them?'

'I've kept the receipt. If it were me, I'd get a refund, buy a cheaper pair and spend the difference on something else.'

'No way! These are the best. Just wait till I text Craig.' He rushed to his room, returning not with the expected phone but with a parcel. 'This is for you.'

'Thanks very much. You're a far better wrapper than I am.' Jamie laughed. Duncan pulled the paper off a small book, struggling to sustain his smile as he read out the title. *'Le Mot Juste.'*

'Have you got it already?'

'No, not at all. I'm delighted.'

'It's a dictionary of loads of foreign and old-fashioned phrases. Mum suggested it.'

'I thought so,' Duncan said, wondering if she had meant it as a joke or a rebuke. 'She told me you'd set your heart on the trainers too, so she's done us both a favour.'

At 11.30, with Jamie proudly wearing his new trainers, they drove to Ridgemount to be greeted by Chris, flaunting a flashing bow tie and a Michelangelo's *David* apron, the muscular torso taut across his flabby chest. Duncan handed him a bottle of whisky and nudged Jamie to do the same with the box of chocolates that he had bought on his behalf.

'Happy Christmas,' Jamie said, looking at his feet.

'I didn't expect … You shouldn't have spent your money on me. I'm sorry,' Chris said, rubbing his eyes. 'Too much cooking sherry!' He scurried back to the kitchen.

'Was he crying?'

'He was touched. What did I tell you?'

'What a dork!'

They entered the sitting room where Duncan curbed an impulse to switch off the lights, which were all on despite the clear blue sky and string of Victorian lanterns on the Christmas tree. The tree, neatly trimmed with woodland fairies and red-and-gold glass baubles, was the only seasonal decoration apart from a solitary row of cards, two of which came from his mother's hairdresser and dentist, the latter instantly identifiable by the sketch of Santa drilling Rudolph's teeth.

Chastened by the reminder of her dwindling acquaintance, he planted a kiss on her forehead and gave her his present, which, after effusive thanks, she asked him to place under the tree, where it was dwarfed in both size and splendour by the elegant packages from Alison, Malcolm and their sons.

'Happy Christmas, Granny,' Jamie said, brushing his lips against a cheek that he had just described as 'soggy', and handing her his gift.

'Is this for me, darling? How naughty! I told you last week that having you here for Christmas was the only present I wanted. Now I have a little something for you.' She gave them each an envelope.

Jamie tore his open as if expecting a cheque. 'A book token! That's great, Granny … Will you buy it off me?' he mouthed at Duncan.

'I think I've got one too,' Duncan said quickly. 'No, what is it?' He took out a card. 'An IOU?'

'You're always so impossible to buy for. I'd rather you chose something special for yourself. On my account.'

'Thank you, Mother.'

While Duncan poured drinks and Jamie inspected the pile of parcels, Adele relayed greetings from Alison and Malcolm, who were spending the day with their neighbours in Oxford-shire, one of whom, as she never tired of repeating, used to play polo with the Prince of Wales. Duncan passed Jamie a bowl of peanuts, which he proceeded to toss in the air and catch in his mouth, until Adele asked with glacial sweetness if he were training for a job in the circus.

'Maybe.'

'Why are you sitting so far away? Come somewhere I can see you!' Jamie lumbered across the ancient carpet to a chair by her side. 'That's better. Now be honest. Wouldn't you rather be here than halfway across the world? A barbecue at Christmas isn't natural.'

'It's great,' Jamie muttered.

'So tell your old Granny all the exciting things you've been doing.'

'None.'

'God blessed you with the power of speech, darling. You needn't be so monosyllabic.'

'Antidisestablishmentarianism.'

'What?'

'Saved by the bell!' Duncan said, as a sharp ring interrupted the exchange. 'That'll be them. Now remember both of you, best behaviour!'

'That's telling us,' Adele said.

'They're the guests. They're the ones who should behave,' Jamie said.

Duncan hurried into the hall, narrowly missing Chris. 'I'll get it. I hope you'll join us for a drink before lunch.'

'A woman's work is never done.' Chris scratched a sculpted pectoral as he returned to the kitchen.

Duncan opened the front door to reveal Ellen, with Barbara and Neil on the step below. Refusing to let her mother's presence inhibit him, he kissed Ellen full on the lips. 'You look lovely,' he said, charmed by the blush on her cold cheeks.

'Happy Christmas,' she said, the blush spreading.

'How are you, Neil?' he asked, squeezing his shoulder. 'Happy Christmas.'

'Can I come inside?' Neil said gruffly.

'Yes of course,' Duncan replied, taken aback.

'He's missing his sister,' Ellen said.

'I am not! It's so not fair that she's in Antigua while I'm stuck here.'

'You should talk to Jamie,' Duncan said, eager to foster any bond between them, however negative. 'Hello, I'm Duncan.' He held out a hand to Barbara, who ponderously removed a mitten to shake it.

'Barbara,' she replied curtly.

'Delighted to meet you,' he said, determined to allay her

remaining doubts about his motives. 'Please come in.' He led them into the sitting room, trusting that his mother would not notice or, at any rate, comment on the pink streak in Barbara's raven hair.

'It's very kind of you to ask us,' Barbara said on being introduced to Adele. 'I'm sure you'd rather have been alone with your family.'

'Not at all. We have a long tradition of inviting waifs and strays. Lovely to see you again, my dear,' Adele said to Ellen. 'It's the first time Duncan has brought one of his lady friends here since Linda.'

'No pressure there then,' Duncan said.

'I'll take it as a compliment,' Ellen said to Adele.

'This is Neil, Mother.'

'A pleasure. Oh, what icy hands! Are you a friend of Jamie's?'

'No,' Jamie and Neil replied in involuntary unison.

Barbara extracted a small picture from her shopping bag and gave it to Adele. 'I've brought you this. I don't believe in wrapping. Did you know that in Britain alone we produced 40,000 tons of extra paper waste last Christmas?'

Duncan shot a glance at Ellen, who raised her eyebrows.

'A painting! How exciting,' Adele replied, oblivious to Barbara's indignation. 'Where are my glasses?' She picked them up off her work basket. 'It's a cliff.'

'Durdle Door in Dorset.'

'And it's on glass. How unusual! Have you seen, Duncan?'

'Yes, Mother. It's beautiful.'

'It's one of mine,' Barbara said.

'Really? But won't you miss it? Or are you, in that wretched phrase, "downsizing"?'

'I painted it!' Barbara replied fiercely.

'You did? How silly of me! You never told me we had an artist coming, Duncan.'

'Barbara has a gallery,' Neil said.

'Who's Barbara? Oh yes, of course. He calls you Barbara?'

'It's my name. What else should he call me?'

'Granny.'

'That's not a name; it's a label.'

'Oh dear. I'm afraid I'm an old stick-in-the-mud but I rather like labels, don't I, darling?' Adele appealed to Jamie.

'Yes, Granny.'

'Won't you all sit down while I see to drinks?' Duncan asked, suspecting that his fears about the two boys' animosity would have been better directed at their grandmothers.

'I have presents for you and Neil,' he told Ellen, as he poured her a glass of sherry.

'I hope you've stuck to the £10 rule.'

'Not entirely,' he admitted, picturing the lavish perfume bottle in his bag.

'Me neither,' she said with a smile.

'Have you always been an artist?' Adele asked Barbara.

'That's another label I try to avoid. I believe we're all artists. Just that some of us are lucky enough to be given the opportunities.'

'And the talent,' Adele replied tartly.

'Barbara used to be a hippie,' Neil said.

'Really?' Adele said. 'You warned me that she was a vegetarian, Duncan. I'd no idea she had so many other distinctions.'

'You make it sound like play-acting,' Barbara said to Neil. 'I was part of a Utopian community. We were out to create a new world. It was the late Sixties.' She turned back to Adele. 'You'll remember: Grow your own; make your own; build your own! The personal is political.'

'Not in Francombe,' Adele replied with a shudder.

'Very wise,' Ellen said. 'Like every other Utopia, somebody always ends up left out.' Duncan wondered whether she were alluding to her father or herself.

'Sometimes I see my parents in you so clearly,' Barbara said.

'For those of you who don't know, that's a bad thing,' Ellen explained. 'Moving swiftly on, did Rose get off all right, Jamie?'

'Expect so.'

'Such a brave little thing,' Adele said. 'I don't know how I'd have managed if she'd been mine.'

'You'd have put her in a home, Mother,' Duncan said, to his instant regret.

'You can be very hard, Duncan,' Adele replied. 'Jamie, please don't monopolise those nuts.'

'Her mum's put her in a home,' Neil said. 'She's taken my sister instead.'

'That's not true!' Jamie said. 'The journey's too much for Rose. Any case, my mum needs a rest.'

'She didn't take you either,' Neil said to Jamie.

'I wanted to stay with my dad.'

'That's not what I heard.'

'That's enough now, Neil,' Ellen said. 'I don't know what's got into you. It's Christmas.'

'You mustn't blame him,' Adele said smoothly. 'Christmas can be so hard when your parents are divorced. Divided loyalties. Having to choose who to spend it with.'

'Neil doesn't have much choice,' Jamie said.

'Jamie…' Duncan warned him.

'It's a time when all the problems of a broken marriage come to a head,' Adele said, leaving Duncan uncertain whether she had conveniently forgotten her own parents' divorce or held that her father's genius made it a special case. 'My husband and I were together for twenty-five years. He died two months before our silver wedding anniversary. Of course we had our ups and downs. Who doesn't? But we worked through them. Nowadays, marriage is as instantly disposable as everything else. We might as well be Jews – or is it Arabs? – "I divorce thee; I divorce thee; I divorce thee." And it's the children who suffer. No continuity in their lives; no real sense of their place in the world.' She turned to Jamie and Neil. 'My heart bleeds for you both.'

'Stop it, Granny, please,' Jamie said, squirming.

'Yes, stop it, Mother,' Duncan said. 'Surely it's better for children to grow up seeing their parents happy than stuck in a miserable marriage for the sake of appearances?'

'I'm well aware of what you're implying, Duncan, but you're wrong. It wasn't for appearances; it was for you.'

Duncan floundered as he realised that far from forgetting her parents' divorce, Adele remembered it only too well. She had once told him that shortly after they moved to Francombe, her mother had made her write to her father accusing him of destroying her life and demanding that he cease all correspondence. Might she even suspect that her letter had contributed to his death? It put her brusque dismissal of his own schoolboy 'sooyside' threat in a new light.

'I just wish Sue would get in touch,' Ellen said. 'I've sent her umpteen texts.'

'There's a four-hour time difference,' Duncan said.

'It shows she's enjoying herself,' Barbara said. 'You'd hear soon enough if she weren't.'

'She's enjoying herself all right,' Jamie said. 'I've had a photo from Craig.'

'Really? Did she look happy?' Ellen asked.

'See for yourself. I've got it here.' He took out his phone to show Ellen.

'Are you sure it's not private, Jamie?' Duncan asked, suspicious of his sudden eagerness to please.

'They're on a public beach,' he replied, scrolling through his photos. 'Here you are.'

'She's naked!' Ellen said.

'Show me.' Barbara grabbed the phone from her daughter. 'Nonsense, she's just topless.'

'How can you tell?' Ellen asked. 'The picture's cut off at the waist.'

'You're disgusting,' Neil said to Jamie.

'I'm not the one flashing my tits!'

'There's nothing disgusting about the female body, Neil,' Barbara said. 'Sue's sixteen; she has beautiful breasts. Why shouldn't she show them off?'

'But in front of all those West Indians?' Adele said. 'You hear such terrible things about what they do to white girls.'

'Mother!'

'It's no use burying your head in the sand.'

'Who else has Craig sent this to?' Ellen asked Jamie.

'Just me. He sends me everything.'

'Please delete it.'

'No way. This is a free country.'

Jamie snatched back his phone and slipped it in his pocket just as Chris entered, apron removed but bow tie twinkling. 'C'est servi, Madame! Grub's up for those of you who don't parlez français.'

'This is Chris, my Man Friday. I'd be lost without him,' Adele said. 'He's gay,' she added proudly to Barbara.

'Not that they'd have known,' Chris said, dropping a curtsey, which drew a thin smile from Barbara and snorts of derision from Jamie and Neil. He then moved to help up Adele, whose degree of incapacity bore a direct relation to the assistance at hand. She led her guests into the dining room where she apologised for having to put two men beside each other, despite – or perhaps because of – being the only person present who cared. With everyone seated, Duncan poured the wine, his relief that it was only cava dulled by the suspicion that it was indifference rather than economy that had caused his mother to forgo the customary champagne. He proposed a toast to Absent Friends, which was echoed more mutedly than expected, before wishing them Bon Appétit as they ate their starter: slices of melon wrapped in parma ham (or, in Barbara's case, garnished with kiwi fruit). When Chris returned to the kitchen to check on 'the bird', Duncan asked Jamie to help him clear the plates, which he did with such bad grace that Adele called out 'Do take care, darling. This service was a wedding present from the Cradwycks.'

Duncan made his way to the kitchen, where he struggled to find a place for the crockery. 'Should I put these straight in the dishwasher?'

'No, I'll have to do them by hand,' Chris said.

'We can help.'

'This is the worst Christmas ever,' Jamie said, stomping in and depositing his plates in the sink.

'Believe me, it's not,' Chris replied with grim certitude. 'I once spent it with a dying friend who did nothing but ask when his parents were coming.'

'And did they?' Jamie asked, intrigued in spite of himself.

'No, most decidedly, absolutely, fucking not! Don't mind me, I'm getting maudlin.'

'Cooking sherry again?' Duncan said.

'Right.'

At Chris's insistence, Duncan and Jamie returned to the dining room where they found Barbara in the middle of a sneezing fit and Adele blessing her religiously. Five minutes later Chris pushed in a trolley laden with the turkey and all its trimmings, including bread sauce, which Duncan had watched congeal, untouched, through every Christmas lunch since his father's death but which Adele nonetheless insisted on serving. 'Humour me on this one, will you, darling?' she had asked as if it were a unique event. Duncan took charge of the carving, while his mother heaped praise on his father, describing him with a nod to Barbara as 'an artist with a knife'.

Chris, meanwhile, went back to the kitchen to fetch a small lattice-topped tart. 'A special dish for a special guest,' he said, with a flourish of which Barbara looked wary.

'What is it?' Neil asked.

'Toffee and roasted walnut tart.'

'Toffee!' Duncan and Barbara exclaimed in the same breath.

'That's what you asked for,' Adele replied.

'*Tofu*, Mother. Tofu or nut roast. Tofu, not toffee.'

'Aren't they the same thing?'

'Is this some kind of joke?' Barbara asked.

'Yeah, it's hilarious,' Jamie said.

'You'll be quite happy with the vegetables, won't you, Barbara?' Ellen urged. 'Such an assortment: sprouts, parsnips, peas, carrots and potatoes.'

'I refuse to be blamed,' Adele said to Duncan. 'I wrote down exactly what you told me. I'm not used to faddy diets.'

'There are over three million vegetarians in the UK,' Barbara said, another figure at her fingertips.

'Maybe, but you'd think they'd take a break at Christmas,' Adele replied.

Barbara sneezed.

'Bless you.'

'How about I just consider myself blessed?'

'Do you have an allergy?' Duncan asked.

'In this chemical factory? I started wheezing as soon as I stepped through the door. Furniture polish and silver polish and glass polish and air freshener and bleach.' She turned to Adele. 'What is it you're so afraid of?'

'Forgive me. If I'd known I was entertaining a hippie, I'd have left out some dirty clothes and kitchen slops.'

'Mother, please!'

'I'm sorry, Duncan, but I won't be insulted in my own home.'

'You shouldn't call Barbara a hippie,' Neil said. 'She just said she doesn't like it.'

'That's enough, Neil,' Ellen said firmly. 'You'll ruin all our appetites. I for one want to enjoy this wonderful meal, this deliciously moist turkey Chris has cooked.'

'And the toffee tart.'

'Thank you, Jamie,' Duncan said.

Everyone focused on the food and an uneasy hush

descended, which was eventually broken by Jamie. 'What do you think they have for Christmas lunch in jail?' he asked.

'Really, darling,' Adele said, 'some of us are still eating.'

'Mind if I start clearing away?' Chris asked. 'That pudding's been steamed to within an inch of its life.'

'Don't you know?' Jamie asked Neil.

'Why should Neil know?' Adele asked. 'He's not an expert on prison menus, is he?'

'No, but his dad is.'

'That's enough now,' Duncan said.

'It's no secret,' Barbara said. 'My daughter's ex-husband was a fraudster and a thief.'

'Not just an ordinary thief,' Jamie added. 'He stole from people in hospital.'

'I said that's enough!'

'The suspense is killing me,' Chris said, 'but that pudding won't switch itself off. Fill me in later.' He hurried out of the room.

'Don't let it upset you, Neil,' Ellen said. 'It's not worth it.'

'Of course it's not,' Barbara said. 'You'll make your own life regardless of your parents. What your father did has no bearing on you.'

'Sure, it does,' Jamie said. 'It's why he's so gay!'

'Jamie!' Duncan jumped to his feet. 'That's quite out of order. Neil's sexuality has nothing to do with his father. It's innate – he was born with it – and he's entitled to our respect.'

'What are you on about?' Jamie asked.

'Duncan, I think you may have misunderstood – ' Ellen said.

'No, I understand only too well. I've fought against prejudice all my life. I know I'm not your father, Neil, but I hope you'll feel able to come to me if ever you're being mocked or bullied. You're only thirteen; your feelings may well change. But whether you end up gay or straight or both, you can count on my support.'

'This is a fucking nightmare,' Neil said, banging his head on the table.

'Do take care, dear,' Adele said, 'that glass is Lalique.'

'Stop there!' Barbara said to Duncan. 'What gives you the right to speak to my grandson like that? It strikes me you take far too much interest in his sexuality.'

'What?'

'Are you mad?' Ellen said to Barbara. 'I'm so sorry, Duncan. I warned you, she's a sick woman.'

'Someone has to look out for you,' Barbara replied. 'You're obviously incapable of doing it yourself. You've just escaped from one disastrous marriage and here you are, ready to throw yourself into another and to a man you've only known for a few weeks.'

'Marriage?' Adele asked. 'Did you say "marriage"?'

'How much do you really know about him?' Barbara asked Ellen. 'He may seem credible enough, but have you seen the figures for the respectable middle-class men who prey on single mothers?'

'Not more statistics!' Duncan said.

'Yes, I'm sure you'd prefer to gloss over them. But Ellen's a vulnerable woman with two teenage children. They need protecting.'

'You mean the way you protected me?' Ellen asked.

'I always took care of you. I always put you first.'

'The sad thing is you believe that.'

'Is this why you made me spend Christmas here?' Jamie asked Duncan. 'So's I could listen to this crap?'

'I'm sorry, I was wrong. You should have gone to Antigua.'

'Why not stand up for yourself: tell her where to get off?' Jamie turned to Barbara. 'This is my dad you're talking about. He's a great dad. The best.'

'Oh yeah,' Neil said. 'So how come your mum has to pay you to stay with him?'

'Shut the fuck up!'

'Jamie, please!' Adele said. 'We have guests.'

'Deny it if you can! She gave you two hundred quid.'

'That was for Christmas, Neil,' Ellen said. 'You're always telling me you'd rather have cash.'

'He got an iPad. You were there when Sue told us. She heard it from Craig. His mum gives him money loads of times when he has to come here.'

'You have to be bribed to visit me?' Duncan asked Jamie, as the rest of the table fell silent.

'You know kids,' Ellen interjected, 'out for whatever they can get. My two won't even clean up their rooms without the promise of a couple of pounds. It's hardly a bribe.'

'You have to be bribed to visit me?'

'Why can't you all just leave me alone?' Jamie ran out of the room, colliding at the door with Chris, who was holding a flaming Christmas pudding.

'Watch out!' Chris said. 'No, it's still burning. Lucky I went overboard on the brandy. Can everyone see?' he asked, bewildered by the lack of response.

'Yes, thank you,' Duncan said, the words like acid in his mouth. 'It's spectacular.'

'Shall I serve now or wait for Jamie? He looked desperate to get to the you know where.'

'Are there any coins in the pudding?'

'No, after last year I thought it best to be on the safe side.'

'Then there's no need to wait.'

Eight

Pier Proprietor Honoured

by Ken Newbold

Thursday, 2 January 2014

Local property developer and entrepreneur, Geoffrey Weedon, has been awarded the OBE in the 2014 New Year Honours list.

The controversial businessman whose company, Weedon Investments, owns a string of properties in the area, along with Francombe Pier, the Excelsior Wheel Park and various entertainment outlets, has been recognised for services to urban regeneration and charity.

On leaving school, Weedon worked for his parents in the motor trade before branching out on his own. In 1972 he founded his property empire by buying up disused guesthouses and hotels, and renting out rooms to DSS claimants from around the country. Responding to criticism of the scheme, which was later widely emulated, he claimed that even the most disadvantaged members of society should have a chance to benefit from the Francombe climate.

He caused outrage in 1984 when his subsidiary company, Excelsior Leisure, demolished a row of listed Regency shopfronts on Flood Street in order to expand their flagship amusement arcade. Then in 1994, having bought the Olympic pool out of receivership, he reneged on a commitment to restore it to its former glory, transforming it instead into a wheel park. The Council's failure to take action in either case led to unsubstantiated allegations that both councillors and Council officers were in his pocket.

Weedon is currently engaged in what he has described as the 'crowning glory' of his career: the restoration of Francombe Pier and its transformation into an adult entertainment complex. Plans for the project, which has provoked widespread opposition, are due to go before the Council's Planning and Regeneration Committee later this month.

In recent years Weedon has combined his business activities with charitable work: setting up a drugs advice centre for the under twenty-fives; sponsoring the annual Seafood Festival after Birds Eye withdrew; chairing the Forward Francombe initiative; and sitting on the board of the Princess Royal Hospital, for which he ran a £2,000,000 appeal to equip the Len and Doreen Weedon Dementia Unit.

Asked for his reaction to the award, he replied by phone from his holiday home in Antigua: 'I'm over the moon. The first I knew of it was when I received an official envelope postmarked London. For hours I didn't open it, since I was afraid it was another spanner in the works for the pier.

'When I finally plucked up courage, I couldn't believe my eyes. I feel honoured and very humbled to be on a list with such distinguished men and women who have contributed so selflessly to their community. In business, as in my private life, I've tried to stick to the principle that you have to give back ten times more than you take out.'

For the full story, as well as public reaction to the award, see next week's Mercury, *out on Thursday, 9 January.*

Although by nature neither superstitious nor sentimental, Duncan had resolved to propose to Ellen on New Year's Day. Encouraged by an exceptionally clement New Year's Eve, he invited her for a walk on the cliffs, where he envisaged going down on bended knee against the romantic backdrop of sea, sky and the ruined Martello tower. But an overnight down-pour rendered the paths impassable and the grand gesture, which in any case risked absurdity in a man approaching fifty, would have caked him in mud. Instead, they retreated to his flat where, sitting so companionably on the sofa that the ques-tion was almost a formality, he asked her to marry him.

'You don't have to give me your answer at once. Not for weeks. Take as long as you like,' he said, terrified that despite all their efforts to settle the differences both within and between their families since the Christmas Day debacle, she would regard the antipathy between their sons as an insuper-able barrier.

'Yes,' she replied, without any show of hesitation or attempt to draw out the suspense.

'What?'

'Yes. Yes, thank you. Yes, I will. Yes. Isn't that what you wanted to hear?'

'Yes.' Such a tide of joy and relief engulfed him that he scarcely trusted himself to kiss her. For several minutes he could do no more than trace his fingers over her cheeks as if he were blind, although his sight, along with the rest of his senses, had never seemed so sharp.

'This calls for a celebration,' he said. 'I've got a bottle of champagne in the fridge.'

'Someone was very sure of himself.'

'No, not at all. Quite the opposite,' he said, failing to read her smile. 'It's been tucked away at the bottom for years waiting for the right occasion.'

'A likely story!'

'It's true,' he said, unwittingly providing confirmation

when he uncorked the bottle without a pop. 'Oh no, it's gone flat! I'm so sorry.'

'Don't worry. I never like the bubbles anyway. They go straight up my nose.'

Refusing to toast their future in stale champagne, he offered to run to the mini-mart for a fresh bottle, but she claimed that she was intoxicated enough already and would prefer a cup of tea.

The whistling kettle was their cue to discuss practicalities. Within minutes they had fixed on the when, where and how of the wedding (late spring, St Edward's, as quiet as possible). Neither relished having to break the news to incredulous family and friends. Ellen's confusion at Duncan's joke that they should take out a full-page advert in the *Mercury* both charmed and humbled him. They agreed to tell no one before their children, which, to avoid misunderstanding (Duncan privately added resentment and rage), they would do at exactly the same time a week or so after their return to school, giving them less time to brood.

Term began on 6 January, but events on both sides conspired to delay the announcement. Rumours of the takeover having leaked out, Duncan was left to reassure the staff, stall creditors and negotiate with the two rival bidders, at the same time bringing out the paper as usual. Ellen, meanwhile, was preoccupied with Neil, who had been threatened with suspension for insulting two Iraqis. She was summoned to see the headmistress, who explained that, although Neil's domestic circumstances had disposed her to overlook his behaviour last autumn, her patience was wearing thin. He must learn to engage with his classmates. She therefore asked Ellen to stop sending him to school with sandwiches and to encourage him to eat in the canteen. Shocked, Ellen replied that she never made him sandwiches but had a standing order for his lunches with ParentPay.

As soon as he arrived home that afternoon – making his usual beeline for the kitchen to guzzle a bowl of cereal – Ellen confronted him with the headmistress's allegations, starting with the racist abuse. After vehemently denying it, he admitted, between sobs, shrieks and charges of disloyalty that he had called them 'Camel Jockeys', but only after they had called him far worse (precisely what he refused to say). He maintained that he had been routinely bullied and had kept away from the canteen after other children, girls as well as boys, put salt in his water and spat in his food. Horrified both by his ordeal and her own obtuseness, Ellen promised to go to the school the next morning and demand that the culprits be rooted out. This made him so hysterical that she backed down in return for his undertaking to report any further incidents himself.

'And if anyone calls you names, ignore them,' she said. 'You're too good to stoop to their level.'

'Yeah, you can't go any lower when you've got your head slammed on the ground,' he replied.

Every day since then she had given him a bag filled with sandwiches, fruit and a muesli bar, which he placed in his backpack without a word.

'Do you have any idea how it feels to know you can't protect your child?' she asked Duncan, after relating the story over dinner. He had to answer 'no', since however remote he felt from Jamie he had never for a moment doubted that he was safe. With a concern for Neil that was now independent of his love for his mother, he declined coffee and headed upstairs to talk to him. Ignoring both the derision that greeted his knock and the groans that greeted his entry, he stood as far away from the bed as the confines of the room would allow and asked what he could do to help.

'Go fuck yourself!' Neil said.

'Well, I could try,' Duncan replied lightly. 'But I'm not sure it'd do you much good and I might end up in traction.'

Neither his levity nor his support made any impression on Neil. Trying another tack, he urged him to return to Mercury House to complete his history project, trusting that there at least he could keep an eye on him. When his warning that the imminent sale of the paper might restrict his access to the archives was met with a terse 'Who cares?' he admitted defeat and returned downstairs, where he spent a further hour persuading Ellen that, whatever the difficulties, she had been right to move to Francombe, using every argument except the clincher: if she had stayed in Hertfordshire, she would never have met him.

Switching on his mobile as he left the house, he picked up two new messages from his mother about Chris's unexplained absence for the second day running. From her voice, it was clear that her initial irritation had been replaced by anxiety, which turned out to be warranted when, shortly after returning home, he received a call from Paul, informing him that Chris was in the Princess Royal, recovering from an attack in Salter Nature Reserve.

Duncan's horror was compounded by the realisation that the story had been under his nose the whole time. On Monday morning Ken had briefed him on a weekend queer-bashing at the reserve. Convinced that his readers were as weary of the murky goings-on in the woods as he was himself and afraid of fanning the flames of prejudice, he told Ken that there was no need to follow up the story, which he consigned to a hundred-word *nib* on page five outlining that a male in his thirties had been mugged and was being treated in hospital. Now that the male had a name and a face and a voice, he felt deeply ashamed. He was, however, able to ring his mother first thing the next morning and assure her that Chris was being well looked after, while taking care to blur the details of the attack, since experience had shown that her acceptance of homosexuality was dependent on its remaining clothed.

He promised to visit Chris in hospital and report back to her as soon as he had put the paper to bed that afternoon. So at four o'clock he drove to the Princess Royal where, ignoring the poster exhorting him to 'Burn Calories Not Electricity', he took the lift up to the Balmoral wing. Stepping charily over a toddler racing a toy bus in the direct path of the swing doors, he made his way across the packed ward to Chris, whose bed was at the far end between a grizzled old man with a withered goitre clutching a bag of oranges to his chest and a young Arab sporting a pair of giant headphones, deaf to the two women in sequined niqabs keening softly by his side.

Chris was lying propped up on pillows, his bruised cheeks looking as if they were designed for the Rorschach inkblot test. His left hand was bandaged, the three middle fingers in a splint and a drip attached to the wrist, with his right arm resting in a sling.

'These are from my mother,' Duncan said, handing Chris a bouquet of yellow, orange and pink gerberas.

'The petals are so bright, they look dyed.'

'Just forced. I don't suppose they'll last.'

'Then they've come to the right place. Would you...?' He gestured with his bandaged hand to his locker.

'Yes, of course,' Duncan said, placing the bouquet on the top. 'I'll ask a nurse for a vase. How are you feeling?'

'I've been better. I suppose you know what happened.'

'Paul told me.'

'And Mrs Neville?'

'Not the full story. But then my mother rarely knows the full story about anything.'

'I'm glad. I don't think I could bear it if she...' His eyes watered.

'She won't. Have they given you any idea how long they'll keep you in?'

'Till my finger clears up. Ironic, isn't it? With a broken collarbone and cracked ribs, it's a pesky little finger that's holding me back.'

'Was that broken too?'

'Just where he stamped on it. They inserted a wire but the infection had already spread. That's the reason for the drip. They're worried I might get an abscess on the bone.'

'Does it hurt?'

'Not so much as the humiliation. You see, appearances to the contrary, my life isn't just about swapping knitting patterns with your mother.'

'I should hope not. But Salter Reserve in the dead of winter...' The memory of his teenage escapade with Daisy flooded back. 'Apart from anything else, it's so bloody cold.'

'That's nothing compared to the cold you feel inside. I'm sorry if I embarrass you, but you have no idea. The hunger for another man's flesh. The hope against hope it'll lead to something more.'

'The power of Eros?'

'I expect it sounds better in Latin.'

Duncan bit his tongue. 'I thought you and Paul were an item.'

'Paul!' Chris laughed and slid his right hand on to his ribs. 'No, I mustn't. We're sisters ... You winced.'

'No, I didn't,' Duncan replied, afraid that a blush would betray him.

'Have it your own way. But that's who I am. I like chintz and scatter cushions and Judy Garland and all the other things that gay men are supposed to have junked.'

'There must be thousands like you.'

'But do they like me? Do I like me? Don't get me wrong. I don't mean do I like me inside? I can see you ticking the box for Self-hating Faggot. Oh no, inside I'm fabulous. But on the outside ... You must have read – no, I don't suppose you have – all the contact ads for "no fats, no fems, no fairies". Where does that leave me?' He started to cough.

'Would you like some water?'

'Just a frog in my throat. Who knows? Perhaps it'll turn into a prince?'

'Have the police got any leads on the bastards who did this to you?' Duncan asked.

'If they do, they haven't told me. An officer came to take my statement. You should have seen him struggling to stick to his diversity awareness training. Given half the chance, he'd have charged me instead.'

'That's not very fair.'

'Funny but I don't feel fair. There were four of them: two boys and two girls; although one of the girls ran off. It was dark. I only saw the first guy's face. He can't have been more than twenty. I thought he was alone, but then his friends jumped out and...'

'You couldn't have known.'

'I should have realised. What would a gorgeous young hunk like that want with a minger like me. Quite frankly, I deserved everything I got. Not for being gay; not for being out there; not for being so desperate I was willing to let my dick get frostbite. But for being so bloody fucking dense!'

Duncan was grateful that the two keening women appeared not to understand English. 'The more you beat yourself up; the more you do their work for them. Save all your energy for getting well. Meanwhile you have my word that the *Mercury* will keep up the pressure on the police to hunt down the perpetrators.'

'When I was at school I wanted to be a journalist.'

'Really?'

'Well, to be honest I wanted to be a showbiz reporter. I pictured myself sitting on a leopard-print sofa interviewing Ann Margret. But I didn't get the A levels.'

'Not everyone can be academic.'

'Especially not when they have their homework ripped up on a daily basis.'

'Is that what happened to you?'

'Along with being punched and spat on and having my books nicked and my clothes torn and being force-fed laxatives. There's no need to look so appalled. It was twenty years ago.'

'Yes, of course,' Duncan said, fearful that Neil was suffering a similar fate now.

'Hark at me: Moaning Minnie! Don't worry,' he said wryly, lifting his splint. 'It gets better.'

'Didn't you tell your parents? Oh, I forgot; I'm sorry. They were dead.'

'My parents are alive and well and living in Hastings.'

'But you said you were brought up by your grandmother.'

'So? They threw me out when my mother found a couple of skin mags under my mattress. They were so innocent, scarcely a dick in sight and that easily passed the Mull of Kintyre test. But it was still too much for my Bible-stroke-child-bashing parents. I was fourteen and homeless. My gran took me in and my parents never spoke to her again. But, as she said, I needed her more than she needed them.'

'She sounds like a very special lady.'

'Don't get me started. She's the kindest, wisest, most loving, most caring person I've ever met. But even she would have rather I were straight. She worried I'd have a miserable old age – ironic when you think what her own's been like! I was more worried about my miserable youth. I had so much love in me; I wanted to share it with someone. Not to be told I had beautiful buttocks by an antique dealer.'

'I can see that wouldn't be much fun.'

'Then I met Jay. He was a trainee chef at the hospital where I worked. He was everything I ever wanted; he still is. He said he loved me, and not just when we were in bed. We were together for three years. Gran thought the world of him. But then he fell for Gina, one of the ward clerks, or at least for the sort of life he could have with her. And everyone was happy for him. Even Gran, the one person who was always on my side, thought it best that he was "settling down with the right girl". That's when I realised that in your heart of hearts all of you – even the nice, kind, sympathetic ones – despise us.'

Although stung by the charge, Duncan refused to argue. A lifelong victim of bigotry, Chris had every right to feel bitter. His physical injuries were nothing compared to his psychic scars. So, promising him again that the *Mercury* wouldn't let the story drop, Duncan left the ward. The following morning, after ringing a police contact who admitted that the investigation had so far drawn a blank, he put it out of his mind while spending the day with the regional director of Provident and his team. Then, at six o'clock, back at his desk writing an 'On This Day' column about the first electric tramlines in Francombe, he received a phone call from Ellen that stunned him. She had returned from work to find Neil locked in the bathroom where, according to Sue, he was scrubbing the word 'Twat' off his forehead. Scouring his bedroom for clues to this latest assault, she had come across his unlocked phone and, scrolling through the messages, opened one with the subject: 'You next, gay boy!' Attached was a fuzzy video clip, which at first looked like three men wrestling underwater but gradually revealed itself as two thugs beating up a man in the woods.

Telling her to do nothing without him, Duncan left the office and sped through Francombe as though the alarm bells ringing in his head had been transformed into a siren on his car. Arriving at Ellen's, he no sooner stepped through the door than she handed him the phone. Trembling, he studied the grainy grey-green footage of two youths attacking an older man, first kneeing him in the groin and wrenching his shoulder, then stamping and spitting on him as he rolled on the ground. A girl fleetingly grappled with one of the youths, who pushed her aside. Confounding expectations, the victim, who made shockingly little attempt to defend himself, was the only one who was hooded, but when the camera picked out the line of spittle on his cheek, it was unmistakably Chris. The next moment a leering face approached the lens and, despite the darkness and distortion, it was equally unmistakably Craig. The focus then shifted abruptly and, to judge from the peal of laughter, inadvertently, to a swaying treetop where the clip ran out.

The attack had been as brief as it was brutal: one minute
fifty-two seconds according to the timecode display; but they
were the one minute and fifty-two most sickening seconds of
Duncan's life. He stared at the phone in his palm as if it were a
deadly spider that had injected its venom into his bloodstream.
Unbidden, Ellen handed him a glass of whisky, which he took,
grateful not just for the drink but for the excuse not to speak.

'That was Chris. I visited him in hospital yesterday,' he
said, finally breaking the silence.

'I thought so. I was frightened to look too closely.'

'And Craig.'

'Yes.'

'The girl who tried to pull him off…?'

'I can't be sure … yes, I can. That top. The way she screamed
at him. It was Sue.'

'So she did the right thing; she tried to stop it. And, as you
told me on Tuesday, they've split up.'

'They most certainly have! If I have to lock her in her room;
if I have to send her to school in Scotland, she won't see that
boy again!' Ellen said with a steeliness that Duncan had never
heard in her before.

With Craig and Sue accounted for, Duncan pondered the
identities of the rest of the gang and the harrowing possibility that one of them was Jamie. Size alone ruled out his
having been the second assailant (never had he felt so grateful for the double-edged 'Squirt'), but there was nothing to
prevent his having been behind the camera, filming the attack
to impress his friends – and intimidate Neil. The climactic
laughter sounded girlish but might it have come from a boy
with a breaking voice? Reluctant to replay the sequence, he
asked Ellen if she would fetch Sue.

'And then what? Do we pretend it never happened? Do we
go to the police?'

'I don't know.' He tried to picture his response were the
clip to land on his desk without his knowing any of the

participants, but the leering face and the saliva-coated cheek, to say nothing of the unknown cameraman, made it impossible. 'If we cover it up, we'd be complicit ... accessories.'

'Oh God! That's all my kids need. Two criminal parents! And why was it sent to Neil?'

'I'm as much at a loss as you.'

'There's only one way to find out.' She walked into the hall and called, 'Sue! Sue, will you come down here a minute?' Receiving no answer, she went upstairs and returned moments later.

'She's on her way.'

When Sue walked in, she looked somehow smaller. It was not just that her hair, which had been bunched on top of her head, hung limply round her face, but her body, which had been thrust out at the world, seemed turned in on itself. She stood behind the armchair, gripping the back, as if the storm raging round her were real.

'I thought you said he wasn't coming here on school days,' she said. And, in the substitution of 'school' for 'week', Duncan glimpsed the contract that Ellen had made with her daughter.

'We need to talk to you about something very serious,' Ellen said.

'Don't tell me; you're getting hitched!' Sue said with a sneer.

'No, of course not,' Ellen replied, at which Duncan caught his breath. 'We've watched a piece of film on Neil's phone.'

'If it's on Neil's phone, then ask Neil. What's it got to do with me?'

'It shows a man being mugged in Salter Nature Reserve,' Ellen continued resolutely. 'We think you may know something about it.'

'Well, that's where you're wrong, see! I've never been to any nature reserve. Can I go now?'

'You're not in any trouble ... quite the opposite. But the man was badly injured.'

'No!' Sue's face paled.

'It's clear that one of those involved was Craig.'

'Then why are you asking me? Craig and me have broken up.'

'Yes, but this occurred on Saturday night: the last night you went out with him; the night you came home so upset.'

'Don't do this, Mum. It wasn't me, honest!' Sue burst into tears.

'I know, darling; we can see you tried to stop them. But you have to tell us the truth.' She moved to Sue. 'Let's sit down.' She led her to the sofa where Sue laid her head on her shoulder and wept. Duncan caught Ellen's eye and made as if to leave the room, but she shook her head. 'Now take your time and tell us exactly what happened.'

Through her tears, Sue explained that she and Craig and another couple had gone to the woods to 'drink and smoke and make out'. Duncan's relief that Jamie had not been one of the party was checked by a glance at Ellen, struggling to conceal her dismay at her daughter's weekend pursuits. Sue explained that Craig had gone behind a tree for 'a piss' and then shouted at them all to come quickly because he was being 'felt up by a queer'. Everything had happened so fast, but she remembered that Craig and Alan began punching the man while yelling at Rosalie and her to film it on their phones.

'I tried to pull Craig off, but he kept on punching him. It's like he was possessed. They say the woods are haunted. It wasn't really him, Mum, honest. I know what he's like. I really, really love him.'

Her voice splintered into sobs as her mother stroked her hair and consoled her.

'But you said you'd broken up,' Duncan said, at which her sobbing grew louder.

'Come on, darling. Let's go upstairs and wash your face.' She turned to Duncan. 'Make yourself at home. I won't be long.'

Duncan poured himself two fingers of whisky and mulled over what to do. Was this the only footage of the attack in existence? In which case, if he were to delete it would the two boys be in the clear? For all his antipathy to Craig, he had never suspected him of violence. The shock of Chris's advances on top of the drink and drugs must have unbalanced him. There was no reason to suppose that he would ever behave so brutally again. On the other hand, had he (or Alan or Rosalie) still been intoxicated when they posted the clip the next day? Far from expressing remorse, the threat to Neil suggested that they were ready to strike again. Yet something failed to add up. He thought back to the aftermath of Christmas lunch and Jamie's explanation that 'gay' had become an all-purpose insult, irrespective of a person's sexuality. So why had they muddled the two in the message to Neil?

Defeated, he moved to the sideboard but just as he was about to refill his glass Ellen walked in with Neil, his hair drenched and forehead raw but eyes blazing.

'Mum says you've got my mobile.'

'I have.'

'Give it back! It's thieving. Else I'll report you to the police.'

Duncan smiled at the thought of how neatly that would solve his dilemma.

'What's so fucking funny?'

'Neil!' Ellen interjected, matching her tone with a pained glance at Duncan.

'Nothing, I'm sorry. It's just that we want to talk to you about a crime. Who sent you the film?'

'What film?'

'The one of the man being beaten up.'

'Yeah, wouldn't you like to know?'

'It's no good protecting them.'

'I'm protecting me. Me! If I grass, they'll kill me.'

'You mustn't say things like that!' Ellen said. 'We'll put a stop to this bullying once and for all. I'll talk to the headmistress, to the teachers, to the governors if necessary.'

'You think they're like the counsellors at your Centre

having cosy case conferences over tea and biscuits? You don't know squat!'

'Then tell us,' Ellen said.

'I want to go now. Just give me back my phone.'

'I'm afraid I can't,' Duncan said. 'It's evidence.'

'What if I need to call an ambulance for an old lady who's been mugged?'

'You mean like the man in the clip?' Duncan asked, wondering whether Neil had studied the face closely enough to recognise Chris.

'I'm not gay!'

'I didn't say you were. But somebody obviously thinks you are. And he or they are using it to menace you. How do you get on with your sister's ex-boyfriend, Craig?'

'I hate you!' Neil shrieked. 'You want to know who sent me the film? It was Jamie.'

'Jamie?' Ellen asked.

'My Jamie?' Duncan asked.

'Don't you know your own son's number? You freak! I hate you!' Neil repeated as he fled the room.

Duncan and Ellen stood in silence listening to his heavy tread on the stairs.

'Jamie,' Duncan said.

'He may just be saying that to hurt you,' Ellen said.

Duncan took out his phone, comparing the number on Neil's text with that in his contacts. 'I wish he were.'

'I'm sorry,' Ellen said, mechanically rubbing her ring finger as if grateful that it was still bare. 'What do we do now?'

'I don't know,' Duncan replied, feeling chopped in two. 'Jamie's only thirteen.'

'He wasn't with them in the reserve.'

'No, but he sent the clip. And the message.'

'I'm sure he didn't mean anything by it,' Ellen said, and Duncan felt that he had never loved her so much. 'It's like the poison-pen letters girls send each other at school.'

'Except in this case the poison's real. A man was badly injured: a man he knows. Though to be fair, he may not have realised that. And he's used it to terrorise another boy. How could he? That's not the Jamie I know. I suppose I've answered my own question.'

'You'll have to ask him.'

'What's the time?'

'Ten to eight.'

'I'll drive over to Linda's and tackle him. What's more, I'll talk to Derek about Craig. Let's not forget he's the main offender. Do you want to come with me?'

'My place is here with my children.'

'Yes, of course,' Duncan said, feeling a chill seep through him. He went out to his car where, with an editor's instinct, he forwarded the clip to his office mailbox before setting off. As he made his way to Granary Lane, all the fears that the whisky had dulled came sharply back into focus. He had no plan other than a grim determination to seek out the truth, which crumbled the moment he saw Linda.

'Duncan,' she said. 'Is something wrong?'

'I'm afraid so,' he replied, remembering to kiss her. 'Is Jamie at home?'

'He's in his room. Why?'

'Can you call him?'

'You're scaring me. Is he in trouble?'

'Yes, but not as serious as some. Will you ask him to come down?'

'Of course. Go on through. Derek's watching TV.'

As Duncan walked into the living room, two shots rang out on the screen. From the corner of his eye he saw a half-naked woman in black fishnets and four-inch stilettos slump to the floor.

'Duncan, my man, to what do we owe the pleasure?' Derek asked, standing up and tucking in his shirt.

'I'm afraid this isn't a social call.'

'Sounds ominous! Just a mo while I find the remote. Switch off this rubbish.'

'Let me guess, she's a tart with a heart who's informed on her gangland lover but still has to atone for her past.'

'Is it a repeat?' Derek asked, looking perplexed.

'Not that I know of,' Duncan said, envious of a world where morality was defined by wardrobe.

'Grade A crap, but it hits the spot. Fact is we've had a rough day. A meeting with Rose's educational psychologist, the one who wrote the damning report. Seems like he won't budge. And if he won't, neither will the LEA. Linda's a bit low.'

'I'm sorry to hear that,' Duncan said, conscious that he was about to drag her down further. 'Is Craig – ?'

Linda walked in followed by Jamie, who looked worried by his father's surprise visit. Although he had tried to make up for the horrors of the Christmas Day lunch by being both cordial and compliant during the remainder of his stay, he knew as surely as Duncan that something had changed for ever in their relationship.

'What are you doing here, Dad?' he asked.

'I suggest that we all sit down.'

'Will you please stop being so mysterious and tell us what's going on?' Linda said.

'It concerns Jamie.'

'What have you been up to now, Sport?' Derek asked casually.

'But not only him,' Duncan said, taking a chair and waiting for them to follow suit. 'I've come straight from Ellen's.'

'So what else is new?' Jamie asked.

'Jamie…' Linda said.

'I saw the film clip you sent to Neil.'

'The knob end!' Jamie said, jumping up. 'He showed it you? The little grass. I'll kill him.'

'He didn't show it me. His mother found it.'

'What film is this?' Linda asked.

'He should have deleted it.'

'No,' Duncan said, struggling to contain himself. 'You shouldn't have sent it.'

'What film is this?' Linda repeated, standing as though for emphasis.

'It shows Craig and a friend beating up my mother's carer in Salter Nature Reserve.'

'Chris?' Jamie asked.

'Yes.'

'Craig?' Derek asked. 'My son Craig?'

'Yes.'

'I don't understand,' Linda said. 'When was this?'

'Last Saturday. Chris is currently in the Princess Royal.'

'The fucking idiots!' Derek said.

'Is he badly hurt?' Linda asked.

'Bad enough to have been kept in all week.'

'Were you there?' Linda asked Jamie.

'No!'

'So how come you have the film?'

'Craig sent it to me.' Jamie's boast that 'he sends me everything' resounded in Duncan's head.

'I don't understand.'

'One of the girls filmed it on her phone.'

'Fuck! Fuck! Fuck!' Derek said, moving to pour himself a drink.

'No, Derek,' Linda said. 'Remember Dr Matthews.'

'What were they thinking of?' Derek asked, ignoring her.

'You sent the film to Ellen's son,' Linda said. 'Why?'

'He's gay,' Jamie mumbled.

'What?' Linda asked.

'It was a joke.'

'A bloody sick joke if you ask me,' Derek said.

'It's not any kind of joke,' Linda shouted. 'A man's in hospital.' She walked over to Jamie, who was perched on the edge of the sofa, and slapped his face.

'Mum!' he cried.

'What's happening to you?' she asked.

'I didn't do anything. All I did was send it. I'm sorry, right!'

'Explain it to me slowly, Jamie,' Derek said. 'Craig and his friend were in the reserve with some girls and they beat up this bloke who works for Adele?'

'No … I don't know. Ask him. I wasn't there.'

'But he told you what happened?'

'Suppose.'

'So how about you tell us?'

'There's nothing to tell. Craig and Alan went up to Salter on Saturday night with their girlfriends to … I don't know.'

'But it was freezing on Saturday,' Linda interjected. 'Don't you remember when we went to Nana and Granddad's?'

'They had booze and stuff. I don't know. Anyway, Craig went to take a leak and this queer – Chris – pounced on him and tried to fiddle with him, and maybe because they were wrecked … Look, it was stupid, I know, but I wasn't there!'

'You mean the guy molested him?' Derek asked.

'He grabbed his dick,' Jamie said with growing confidence. 'The sick fuck!'

'Derek, please,' Linda said.

'That puts a very different slant on things.'

'Why?' Duncan asked.

'Why do you think "why"? Craig's a kid. If some pervert comes on to him, he has a right to defend himself.'

'Couldn't he just have said "no"?'

'Yes, of course. Let's be civilised about it. That's your answer to everything, isn't it?'

'You two squabbling will get us nowhere,' Linda said.

'He's lucky he's only in hospital. He could have been sent down for years. Banged up with all the nonces.'

'And that's the attitude you've taught Craig?'

'What would you have done if it'd been Jamie?'

'That's totally different.'

'I see. Your boy's sacred but mine's fair game?'

'No, Jamie's thirteen and Craig's sixteen. And, as luck would have it, he'd stumbled on a gay cruising spot.'

'Maybe he missed the signs? Like the ones on the swifts' breeding ground. Only I forgot; they don't breed, do they? They just fuck. Day and night, like animals.'

'Says the man who plans to open Britain's first sex pier.'

'At last! I wondered when you'd get round to that. Any chance you can find to point the finger at the Weedons! Well, you know what I think? Craig was right to batter the bloke.'

'You don't mean that, Derek,' Linda said.

'Don't I? He did us all a favour.'

'Be sure to say that to the police,' Duncan said.

'What police? Why?'

'There's a criminal investigation. We can't withhold evidence.' Derek's outburst had removed all Duncan's doubts about how to proceed. Any hope that he might leave the father to discipline the son had vanished with the realisation that the father was part of the problem.

'Now wait a minute – '

'And the evidence is conclusive. You talk about Craig defending himself. Take a look at this.' He pulled out Neil's phone, found the clip, clicked Play and handed it to Derek.

'Can I go now?' Jamie asked.

'No,' Duncan said.

'It's not your house any more!'

'No,' Linda echoed.

Duncan fixed his eyes on Derek as, grey-faced, he watched the footage. The one minute fifty-two seconds seemed longer than they had at Ellen's. Finally, Derek put down the phone and drained his glass in silence.

'Well?' Duncan asked.

'May I see it?' Linda asked.

'No!' Derek said. 'How does this thing…?' He searched the phone. 'There! Deleted. Gone for ever. So much for your evidence!'

'How do you know he didn't send it to someone else?' Duncan said, giving thanks for his instinct.

'Did he?' Derek asked Jamie, who shrugged wretchedly.

'Or that I didn't make a copy?'

'Did you?' Duncan nodded. 'You shit!' Derek clenched his fist and punched the arm of his chair.

'Blood pressure, Derek!' Linda said.

'Look, I'll bollock Craig. I'll give him the biggest bollocking he's ever had. I'll make his life a misery. That's enough, isn't it?'

'You know it's not. You saw what he did. If you have any sense of justice, you can't hush it up.'

'He's sixteen years old! He's never done anything like this before.'

'And I'm sure the police will take that into consideration.'

'And if they don't? He'll go on trial. He could be sent down.' Derek's voice cracked. Linda put her arm round his shoulders but he shrugged her off. Jamie sat with his head in his hands.

'Which is why he must give himself up. It'll count in his favour.'

'And if he doesn't?'

'I'll wait till this time tomorrow, then I'll go to the police myself.'

'You're enjoying this, aren't you? Mr Whiter than White. Mr "Anyone who drops a sweet wrapper on the beach should have his hands chopped off".'

'I think you should go now, Duncan,' Linda said.

'Believe me, if there were any other way.'

'Of course there is. I've fucking told you what it is.'

'No.' Whatever Derek might think, he took no pleasure in accusing Craig. Nonetheless, he refused to defend him by blackening Chris's name. However differently Chris might behave in the dark, he did not believe that someone who cared so tenderly for Adele would have accosted a total stranger without encouragement. 'An innocent man is hooked up to a drip in hospital.'

'Just go please,' Linda said. 'I'll ring you as soon as we've decided what to do.'

'Of course.' Duncan moved to the door. 'Goodnight, Jamie.'

Jamie sank his head deeper in his hands without replying, and Duncan returned home. The following afternoon Linda called to say that, after a family conference, Derek and Frances had taken Craig to Falworth Road police station, where he confessed to his part in the assault, implicating Alan and Rosalie but absolving Sue. He explained how, high on a cocktail of vodka and marijuana, he had lost control when Chris lunged at him. Determined to make a clean breast of it, he showed the officers the mobile phone footage, but the filming itself turned out to be instrumental in the CPS decision to charge him. He was given police bail to appear before the magistrates the following week. His solicitor was optimistic that in view of its being a first offence and his previous good character they would refer him to a Youth Offending Panel rather than impose a custodial sentence.

Duncan felt torn. At least Craig's age freed him from agonising over how much of the story to report. There was no such escape clause, however, when two hours later one of Ken's police contacts tipped him off that detectives returning to the crime scene had discovered Henry's mobile beneath a pile of leaves.

'Do we follow it up or do we back off because he's one of our own?' Ken asked.

'We back off because there's nothing to it,' Duncan replied with more confidence than he felt. 'He's the vicar of the Cliff Top Church. The woods are on his doorstep. He often walks his dog there. I've gone with him myself.'

'At eleven o'clock at night?'

'How do you know he didn't drop it earlier in the day?'

'Because it was the number that was used to call the ambulance.'

'Really?'

'Seems our Henry is one of those naughty vicars you read about in the papers. Though not of course the *Mercury*,' Brian piped up from across the desk. 'Still, you know what they say: "a stiff prick has no conscience".'

'A limp one doesn't have many scruples either,' Duncan replied pointedly and left the room.

He was relieved when at seven o'clock everyone went home and he was able to put the events of the week behind him. The atmosphere in the office, already tense, had been further strained by the arrival of assessors to value the fixtures and fittings. He had kept the staff as fully informed as he could, assuring them that a rescue plan was in place, which he hoped to announce within a fortnight, but they had greeted the news with responses ranging from mild disbelief (Sheila) to out-right derision (Rowena and Brian).

For once he was thankful not to be spending the weekend with Jamie. He had nothing in the diary but dinner with Ellen at her line manager's on Saturday and lunch with her at Ridgemount on Sunday. He went to bed early, waking soaked in sweat from a nightmare in which he was forced to witness the attack on Chris. His horror at his inability to protect the broken body intensified when he caught sight of the hooded face and saw that it had transmuted into Henry's. Lending more credence to his subconscious than usual, he decided to pay Henry a visit and, receiving no answer from the vicarage phone and knowing to expect none from his mobile, he drove to Salter in the hope of catching him in church. As they edged up the slippery road, Rocinante appeared to be as nervous of the encounter as he was. Despite the difficult journey, he was almost relieved that St Edward's was locked, but the respite proved to be short-lived since, crossing the lane to the church hall, he found the door open and Henry laying out chairs. The contrast with his last visit could not have been more marked. The mural had been painted over and the entire room was a sanitised white.

'Paradise has vanished from our walls,' Henry said, 'although if you look closely at the far left, you can still see the shadow of peacock feathers. Or is it a trick of the light?'

'Did the probation service send you a second team?'

'No, they had no one available. But members of the congregation were queuing up to pitch in.'

After helping Henry to prepare the hall for the quarterly strategy meeting, Duncan followed him back to the vicarage.

'Any more news on the takeover?' Henry asked, bringing two steaming mugs of coffee to the kitchen table.

'It's ninety-nine per cent certain we'll go with Newscom. They've made a derisory offer for the shares but a decent one on jobs and pensions. So no one should be dependent on Press Fund handouts.'

'I can't see them keeping on "Notes from the Pulpit".'

'Me neither. It'll be twenty pages of celebrity interviews and gossip with a four-page insert of local news. I can't work out if the community will lose its mouthpiece because the *Mercury*'s failed or the *Mercury*'s failed because there's no longer a community that needs a mouthpiece.'

'Perhaps a bit of both?'

'Still, why should anyone care so long as they can log on to a chat room full of like-minded people? Internet communities – what a contradiction in terms!'

'Be fair, you've never been the web's biggest fan.'

'I've always said it's a useful source of information – '

'And misinformation.'

'That too. But there it ends. People talk about "a virtual world", yet they use it to give their lives authenticity. They look at what's on their screens rather than in front of their eyes. What's that phrase of St Paul's about our imperfect vision?'

'"For now we see through a glass darkly."'

'Right. That's another metaphor that's become a reality. Except that the glass is a screen.'

'I wouldn't repeat that to any of the big shots at Newscom if you're hoping for a place in their integrated media team.'

'It's too late. I've already received my marching orders.'

'Really? That's their loss. I'm very sorry.'

'It was inevitable. There's no way I could have worked for the new management.'

'So have you given much thought to what's next? Will you even stay in Francombe?'

'You won't get rid of me that easily. Can you keep a secret? I'll be moving in with my new wife.'

'You're going to marry Ellen? But that's wonderful!'

'You must promise not to breathe a word. We've not even told family.'

'My lips are sealed. But you can't stop me praying for you. I'm delighted – absolutely delighted – for you both.'

'Thank you. Let's hope everyone else feels the same.'

'Still no rapprochement between Jamie and … I forget the other boy's name?'

'Neil. No, quite the reverse. It's no longer just the fallout from Christmas. They've both been involved – thank God at one remove – in a vicious attack on my mother's carer. He was queer-bashed in the Nature Reserve.'

'I know.'

'You do? How?'

'The chaplain at the Princess Royal is a friend,' Henry replied, giving nothing away.

'I tried to ring you this morning,' Duncan said, seizing the moment. 'But I got no answer from your mobile.'

'I lost it yesterday when Brandy and I were w-a-l-k-ing on the beach.'

'No, you lost it in the woods,' Duncan said sadly. 'The police found it next to the spot where Chris was attacked.'

Henry stood up slowly and moved away from the table. For several moments he gazed out of the window, before turning back to Duncan.

'What must you think of me?' he asked, sweat beading on his brow.

'The same as ever. That you're the best friend I have in this town.'

'Ah yes. They should carve it on my grave. Always a friend, never a lover. Like a cautious investor I prefer to spread the risk.'

'Is it such a risk?'

'You tell me. I'm fifty-six years old. I've never known love, except for God's love of course. I bang on about that on a daily basis. But if it really were infinite, would He have made me gay?'

'You can't mean that?' Duncan said, alarmed by the depth of his self-loathing. 'I thought it was only evangelicals who went in for all the "male and female created He them" twaddle.'

'Yes, like my old Director of Ordinands who claimed to know that homosexuality was a sin because every time he thought about it his genitals came out in a rash. Don't smile! It's the gospel truth. And don't get me wrong. I'm not speaking for anybody but myself. God gave me a vocation and then made it impossible for me to fulfil it. I preach about the need to be whole and at the same time I'm forced to compartmentalise my life. Do you know what it is to long for someone's touch? I don't mean Ellen's or anyone special's. Just A. N. Other's. I can go for weeks when my only human contact – that's physical contact – is the Sign of Peace. Let's hope that my congregation is more at peace than me.'

Duncan walked across the room to hug him but lost his nerve. 'Would you like some more coffee?' he asked, veering towards the kettle.

'I've been told to cut down on caffeine. But thanks.'

'So don't you ever ... touch anyone when you're in the woods,' Duncan asked hesitantly.

'Never,' Henry replied with a sad smile. 'I'm what's politely called a Peeping Tom. It sounds so quaint. Like a character in a children's storybook: Old Peeping Tom ambled down the lane. I can think of more appropriate names for it.'

'Please tell me if it's none of my business,' Duncan said, never more conscious of the barrier that Henry's priesthood posed to intimacy, 'but have you ever had a lover?'

'You mean before I made impotence my saving grace: psychic castration?' He glanced at Brandy, placidly licking his scrotum. 'I suppose it depends on your definition. I've never made love with the same man twice.' Duncan struggled not to betray his shock. 'But there was one unforgettable night in my early twenties with a German language student in Brighton. His skin was so pale – almost translucent – apart from his penis, which was significantly darker, like a steeple that had been added later. We only met once but he's been the stuff of my romantic – no, what the hell, erotic – fantasies for nearly thirty years. I'm sorry. Does that disgust you?'

'Of course not.'

'I was wrong. The problem isn't that God made me gay and a priest, but that He made me gay and a priest and an Anglican. He could at least have made me an RC. Then loneliness would have been my natural state.'

'Perhaps you should leave God out of the equation for a change?'

'Perhaps I should. But of all my desires the deepest, the most overpowering, is to serve a God I'm no longer sure I believe in – or at least that I believe in the way I'm supposed to. Isn't that perverse?'

'No, what's perverse is to shoulder all this guilt.'

'Trust me, this is nothing. Catholics have guilt; Calvinists have guilt; Anglicans just have lassitude.'

'Not from where I'm standing.'

'No doubt you consider me the worst kind of hypocrite?'

'I'm not in the job of judging. But you did endorse our Clean up the Woods campaign after the attack on Dragon.'

'I pray "Lead me not into temptation". Perhaps I should

change it to "Give me strength to resist the temptation I can't avoid"?'

'Aren't you worried about being recognised or even bumping into one of your parishioners?'

'It's already happened. Although men come here from halfway down the coast (especially now it's listed on websites), it's mainly the same old faces, particularly at this time of year. Have you never wondered why Chris is so hostile when I visit your mother?'

'I assumed it was generic. He sees being gay and a vicar as incompatible.'

'No, he sees being voyeuristic and a vicar as incompatible. And he's right. Did I go to his rescue when those lads were laying into him?'

'You rang for the ambulance,' Duncan said, the words sticking to his tongue.

'How do you know that?'

'The police traced the call.'

'Of course! Maybe I should have run back here and pretended I'd heard his cries for help? But even I'm not that much of a coward. So,' he said, digesting the information, 'the cat's out of the bag, eh Brandy?' He smiled at the dog, who wagged his tail. 'They'll summon me to give evidence in court.'

'There may not be a trial. One of the youths has already confessed. Craig, Derek Weedon's son.'

'I'll have to inform the bishop: hand in my resignation.'

'Why?'

'How can I stand in the person of Christ ... how can I celebrate the Eucharist when people know the sort of man I am?'

'What people? The culprits are under eighteen so the case can't be reported.'

'There'll be rumours, gossip.'

'In other words, business as usual. And if anyone does ask, you can say you were taking Brandy for a late-night walk.' The dog sprang to his feet. 'No, sorry, boy, false alarm,' he said, stroking his muzzle. 'And as for the "person of Christ" thing, I'm no theologian but Christ was a man, wasn't He? I've never understood all the dualism stuff: so much ink – and blood – spilt on arcane conjecture. I prefer to think of Him as a good man with a touch of the divine. But even if I were a regular churchgoer, I'd want a vicar with experience of human frailty.'

'Feet of clay?'

'Doesn't the Bible say that's what we're all made of?'

Having declined Henry's invitation to lunch, Duncan heard from him again in the late afternoon with news that he had given a witness statement to the police in which, taking Duncan's advice, he claimed to have been out walking Brandy when he chanced on the attack. He refuted Craig's allegation that Chris had made advances to him while he was urinating, insisting that, on the contrary, Craig had flaunted himself in the thicket, holding out his penis 'like a canapé'. To his immense relief he was not called to testify in court since all three defendants, faced with the incontrovertible evidence on film, pleaded guilty: Craig and Alan to assault occasioning actual bodily harm; Rosalie to aiding and abetting an assault.

Despite all the stories of legal logjams – many of them in the *Mercury* – the hearing, which had been expedited on account of the defendants' youth, was held the following Thursday. The court was closed, with only parents and, by special dispensation, step-parents present, which, given that Craig, Alan and Rosalie were all the children of divorce and only Rosalie's mother had yet to remarry, ensured that the public benches were more than usually full. With Duncan not permitted to attend – let alone report – proceedings, he was dependent on Linda for the facts, which she gave him by phone later in the day during a break from consoling Derek.

The prosecutor had opened the case with an account of the attack, after which the magistrates watched the footage on DVD and studied photographs of Chris's injuries. The prosecutor read out witness statements from Sue, whose attempt to exculpate her friends by detailing how much they had smoked and drunk merely added to the general picture of delinquency, and Henry, whose description of Craig exposing himself ruled out any plea of 'homosexual panic'. She concluded with a victim impact statement from Chris that dwelt more on his emotional than his physical trauma. The defence solicitors offered mitigation, focusing in each instance on their clients' broken homes and lost childhoods (which made painful listening on the public benches). The magistrates retired for barely ten minutes before the chairman announced their verdict. In respect of Rosalie, they ordered a pre-sentence report and instructed her to return to court in two weeks' time. In respect of Craig and Alan, they decreed that the savagery of the attack, compounded by its filming, left them no choice but to impose the maximum sentence: two years in a young offender institution.

The sentence was harsher than Duncan had expected. He asked Linda to convey his sympathies to both Craig and Derek, but her curt 'We'll see' showed that, like her husband, she blamed him for forcing Craig's hand.

'I don't always agree with Derek but in this case he's right. You would have felt differently if it had been Jamie.'

'Of course. But I hope I'd have acted the same.'

'What a comfort it must be to you, Duncan!' Linda said. 'Free of all the doubt and confusion that plague us ordinary mortals.'

Duncan mulled over her gibe as he went down to the boardroom to check that everything was in place for the morning. He had asked his mother and sister to Mercury House to ratify the sale of the company to Newscom. Barring a miracle, it would be the last board meeting ever held there and he felt deeply moved as he gazed up at the array of ancestors, not least his great-grandfather, whose judicious choice of portraitist (a Sotheby's expert had valued the Sargent painting at £280,000) had been a factor in Newscom's decision to buy the company outright, taking on both its assets and liabilities. While paying a token £10,000 each for his, Adele's and Alison's shares, and transferring both the editorial and production operations to its Basingstoke headquarters, they had undertaken to preserve the title, retain the majority of the staff, provide a generous redundancy package for the rest and, crucially, protect the pension fund.

At ten o'clock the next day Alison, who had driven down from London, brought Adele to Mercury House, where Duncan greeted them together with Dudley Williams, the long-serving accountant whom Adele valued as much for his deference as for his expertise. Dudley outlined the terms of the Newscom offer, adding that in his view it was by far the best available. Duncan was both relieved and touched when Alison not only endorsed it but proposed 'a vote of thanks to my brother for all his hard work'. Adele was less magnanimous. With a pronounced sniff, she implied that the sale was the final proof of his mismanagement. Pointing to his father's portrait, she declared that her one consolation was that he had been spared this humiliation, before grimly signing the papers. Then with a sweeping glance around the room as if she were playing herself in *The Mercury Story*, she inclined her head towards Dudley and tottered out. Her children soon followed, returning to Ridgemount where Duncan took the opportunity to underline the change in her circumstances. Although the deal with Newscom protected her share of his father's pension, the loss of the annual dividend would require her to cut her expenditure drastically.

'Why not pack me off to Castlemaine and have done with it?' she asked.

'There are other options, Mother. I had hoped … we had hoped,' Duncan said, determined to involve Alison, 'that you'd be able to stay here for the rest of your life.'

'Forgive me if I've upset your plans.'

'Even if you could pay for the upkeep, this house is far too big for you. Either you'll have to move somewhere smaller or else we must split it up into flats.'

'I agree,' Adele said cheerfully.

'You do?' Duncan asked, turning to Alison, who shrugged.

'We should make a flat for you.'

'What?'

'It's the perfect solution. You'll have to leave Mercury House and you can't afford to rent anywhere else. This way I'll be able to keep an eye on you, make sure you don't brood on what went wrong. And you'll be able to take over some of Chris's jobs – that's if he ever deigns to come back.'

'You mean I'll be an unpaid carer?'

'You're the one who told me to economise.'

'It's very kind of you, Mother,' Duncan said, breathing deeply, 'but I have other plans. I hadn't intended to mention it yet but now's as good a time as any. I'm going to marry Ellen.'

'What? Since when?'

'That's marvellous news, Duncan,' Alison said, springing up to kiss him. 'I'm so pleased for you.'

'Thank you.'

'You haven't met her mother,' Adele said to Alison.

'I'm not her greatest fan either,' Duncan said. 'But it's not her I'll be marrying.'

'Of course not, darling. I'm thrilled for you. I'll cross all my fingers that this time it'll work out. But it needn't stop you living here. There's plenty of room for Ellen.'

'She has her own house in West Francombe. I'll move in there, at least for the time being.'

'Have you set a date?' Alison asked.

'Not yet, but we're looking at March. At our age there's no point in hanging around.'

'"Marry in Lent, live to repent."'

'Mother!' Alison said.

'I'm not the one who wrote it! Anyway, I don't suppose they'll be having a church wedding.'

'That's where you're wrong. I've asked Henry if we can use St Edward's.'

'But you made such a fuss last time,' Adele said.

'Because we were under so much pressure, from Jack and Brenda as well as you. Ellen and I are agreed. We're not worried about making our vows before God but we do want to make them in public, before the wider community. And these days a church congregation may be our best bet.'

'Will you be using the 1662?'

'I doubt there'll be much "obeying" but for the rest, yes. I still squirm at the memory of Stewart and Laura Canning's promise to take on each other's "brokenness". What's more, we thought we might use one of grandfather's anthems, maybe the *Magnificat*?'

'Oh darling, that would be splendid,' Adele said, her face glowing. 'I'd be so proud.'

'I'll say one thing for you, Duncan Neville,' Alison whispered in his ear. 'You certainly know how to get the old girl eating out of your hand.'

Doubtful of his mother's discretion, Duncan alerted Ellen to the need to break the news to their children as soon as possible. All three in their different ways were victims of the woodland attack. Rosalie's friends, ignorant of Sue's attempt to intervene, accused her of betraying her companions to save her own skin. Shunned by her schoolmates, she was now content to spend her evenings at home studying for her GCSEs, with the result that a mere two weeks after the hearing her form teacher had revised her prospective grades from Cs to Bs. Neil, meanwhile, had been targeted not only by Craig's and Alan's friends but even by some of their enemies who set aside past differences to join in condemnation of the 'snitch'.

Jamie was hit hard by Craig's imprisonment. However regrettable the circumstances, Duncan rejoiced at his release from his stepbrother's tutelage. Linda had been convinced that the rupture would occur when Craig went to university, but that might have been too late. Who could say what trouble they would have been caught up in before then? Craig's sentence offered Jamie the chance of a fresh start. Besides, with Craig out of the picture, Duncan dared to hope that Jamie would be more agreeable to Neil. So it was with new confidence that, on the Sunday afternoon he had appointed with Ellen for their disclosures, he took Jamie on to Salter cliffs, stopping beside the ruins of the Martello tower where, with waves lashing the rocks and herring gulls wheeling in the sky, in the very spot that he had previously chosen for his proposal to Ellen, he announced his engagement.

'You mean you're going to live with Neil Nugent?' Jamie asked, with such desperation that Duncan regretted not having stayed at sea level.

'The same way that you live with Derek. I hope we'll become friends,' Duncan said, drawing him away from the edge, 'but I'll only ever have one son and that's you.'

'What will he call you?'

'Duncan, I suppose. Probably "hey you",' he said, failing to raise a smile. 'Remember he calls his grandmother Barbara.'

'He's an arse wipe.'

'May we dispense with the insults? I'm asking you to make an effort. You've been gratuitously cruel to him and I'm not just referring to that text. Suppose it had been the other way round and you were the one who'd moved to a new town.'

'When you and Mum split up, you said you'd always put me first. Now's your chance to prove it.'

'I do put you first but that doesn't mean I have to order my life around your prejudices,' Duncan replied uneasily.

'In other words you're a liar and a hypocrite. Can we go now? Why did you bring me out here? Couldn't you have been normal for once and told me in a room?'

After driving Jamie home, Duncan returned to his flat where he texted Ellen that he had told Jamie, who took it 'much as expected'. She rang him an hour later in a voice so strained as to be barely recognisable.

'It's done,' she said.

'And?' Duncan asked, praying that the strain was due to emotion rather than effort.

'Sue was amazingly positive. She said she was happy for me. *For me*: can you imagine? Just a few weeks ago she treated happiness like a playground where adults were only allowed in if accompanied by a child.'

'And Neil?' Duncan asked hesitantly.

'Well, you can't have everything – or anything when it comes to Neil. He says he hates you and he hates Jamie even more. He wants us to leave Francombe and, when I refused, he accused me of putting my pleasure above his future ... actually, the phrase he used was a good deal more graphic.'

'I can imagine.'

'I told him that running away from your problems was never the solution. So he asked why we'd left Radlett and called me a liar and a hypocrite.'

'What?'

'A liar and a hypocrite.'

'That's exactly the phrase Jamie used about me.'

'Then at least they have something in common,' Ellen said, with what was either a stifled sob or a muffled laugh. 'I told him that we'd be a proper family again and life would be better for all of us. I truly believe that, Duncan.'

'So do I.'

'But is he right? Am I kidding myself? Pursuing my own happiness at the expense of his?'

'Neil has to find his own happiness. At least now you – we – can set him an example.'

'He spat out more of my mother's vitriol.'

'Oh no!'

'I'm sorry, I shouldn't have mentioned it. Doesn't she realise the harm it can do to an impressionable boy?'

'I'll just have to try twice as hard to make up for it.'

'No matter what you say about bridges and bygones, my mind's made up; I won't have that woman at the wedding. Being with you has finally given me the strength to cut her out of my life.'

Nine

Well-loved Editor Retires

by Ned Knobwel, Rodney Arsewibe & Rianna Bong

Thursday, 13 February 2014

Double negatives, split infinitives and dangling participles from Switherton to St Anselm rejoiced this week at the news that Duncan Neville, editor and proprietor of the *Mercury*, was stepping down to spend more time with his lexicon.

Having lost the battle to turn the 'On This Day' column into a four-page weekly insert and had his demand to include at least one classical tag or epigram per feature branded 'dragonian' (sic) by Mother of the Chapel Sheila Lewis, Neville, who has edited the paper since the age of five, declared that it was time for him to move on.

As news of his departure swept through Francombe, total strangers wept in each other's arms. Mrs Ava Larfe, 64, who did not wish to be named, said: 'He was always on the side of the common man – though he was a real gent himself. Who can forget the way he took on the Council over its decision to shut Welch's whelk stall? Or how he marched up and down the Prom chanting "Hands Off Our Molluscs"?'

Tributes to Neville have been pouring in from across the globe, and even further. Fellow newspaper magnate, Rupert Murdoch, declared: 'He's the man! He's the one we all look up to. Whenever I have a problem, it's Dunc I turn to for advice. It's Dunc who showed me a fail-safe way to rig a coffee machine. It's Dunc who taught me the mantra: "Keep 'em poor; keep 'em raw".'

Former *Mirror* group chairman Robert Maxwell, channelled by medium Dotty Flake of the Sunlight Spiritual Centre (dotty@soulsunited.com), recalled an early glimpse of Neville from a stall in the Newspaper Society lavatory: 'I knew at once he was a man of integrity from the way he washed his hands even when he thought there was nobody watching.'

Neville's reputation as Mr Clean extends far beyond personal hygiene. Although the victim of countless bribery attempts, from the honey trap sprung by Councillor Wanda Ringhands during the vanishing ice sculpture scandal, to the Mars bar slipped him by eight-year-old Ben de Rules inside his entry to the Primary School Paint Your Pet Guinea Pig competition, he has remained inviolable.

To the end, he has held

true to the motto, Celery and Vermouth, which has graced the *Mercury*'s masthead ever since the paper was founded by his great-great-great-great-great-great-great-great-great-great-great-great-great-great-great-great-great-great-uncle-once-removed in 1066.

Meanwhile, in Francombe, speculation about his future has reached fever pitch. According to one source, he is to retrain as a tattoo artist and open a parlour on the Front specialising in designs drawn from Aztec and Mayan mythology; according to another, he is to give tango demonstrations in tea dances at the Metropole Hotel. Close associates of controversial con man, Geoffrey Weedon OBE, claim that he has accepted the post of director of the proposed sex museum on the pier.

Whatever he decides, you can be sure it will be reported in your new relocated *Mercury*. Remember, Basingstoke is only an email away.

The stopped clock on the Town Hall tower confirmed the drop in temperature. Three years ago Duncan had written an impassioned leader on the blow to civic pride dealt by a mechanism so susceptible to the cold that every winter, 'as regular as clockwork', a severe icy spell thickened the oil in the lubrication system and clogged the works. The only official response, however, had been a letter from the Director of Finance citing budgetary cuts. As he walked up the slippery steps into the building, he acknowledged with a mixture of relief and regret that in two days' time it would be somebody else's concern.

He entered the lobby, its black lacquer console tables, cream leatherette sofas and angular chrome coat stands (which, as a boy, he had secretly anthropomorphised on visits with his parents) contrasting sharply with the austere neo-classical exterior. He climbed the sweeping white marble staircase to the first floor, his eye as usual drawn to the large mural in which an affluent man sporting a trilby and cane and his elegant wife wearing a cloche hat and wrap-over coat, greeted a heavily mustachioed fisherman who was selling his catch on the Front, while his ruddy-faced, ample-bosomed wife sat placidly mending his nets and their four barefoot children played hopscotch on the sand. Duncan could not restrain a smile at this fantasy of social cohesion painted in 1923, two years after the town had been torn apart and the Town Hall itself burnt down by rioters, many of them ex-servicemen, protesting at rising prices and unemployment. But his smile faded at the thought of how completely the event had faded from the collective memory, with no longer any prospect of an 'On This Day' column to bring it back.

He made his way down a corridor lined with seascapes of tablemat blandness to the Council Chamber, another striking example of art deco design, with a mosaic allegory of the seasons on the ceiling, pressed-metal panelled walls and bronze-and-alabaster sconces. Having attended more

Planning Committee meetings than all but the longest-serving councillors, he knew the form. As an interested party, he took his seat on a cracked leather banquette alongside Glynis Kingswood and Jocelyn Dunning of the High Street Traders Association. Geoffrey Weedon, with his architect and agent, sat two rows in front and Ken Newbold, assiduously covering his last ever story for the *Mercury*, was in the row behind. Lucy Blackstone, the Committee Chair, flanked by a clerk and a legal adviser, presided beneath a large bronze sunburst. To her left were the planning officers presenting the applications; to her right, twelve of the fifteen councillors who made up the committee. The general public was confined to a cramped gallery at the back. Twisting round, Duncan spotted several familiar faces and one unmistakable hairstyle: Lea Brierley's multicoloured fringe.

Knowing the pier application to be the last item on the agenda, he had timed his arrival to avoid the usual batch of garage extensions, loft conversions, tree removals and changes of use, along with the routine disclaimers by councillors that any discussions they had held on the proposals were prejudicial. Even so, he had to sit through applications to build four petrol pumps and two jet car washes outside the Bartholomew Road Tesco; to adapt the main gatehouse at Seacombe Court into a farm shop; and to turn a piece of arable land outside Switherton into open storage. The first two were passed, while a decision on the third was deferred pending a site visit.

Finally, they came to item twelve: Application FS2014/37286 for planning permission and listed building consent for the partial demolition and reconstruction of Francombe Pier, the erection of new pier buildings with alternative leisure use, the extension of the existing footprint and landscaping of the immediate surroundings. 'I'm aware that there's a lot of feeling locally about this application,' the Chair said, as an air of anticipation permeated the room, 'but members of the committee, led by myself, will consider it without fear or favour, just as we have many similar applications in the past.' As two planning officers placed the architect's model in front of the dais, several male councillors craned forward to study it with playground excitement. The designated planning officer, whose dark hair, thick-rimmed spectacles, neatly clipped beard and black turtle-necked sweater gave him the look of a man about to deliver a lecture on structuralism at the Sorbonne rather than to discuss the nuts and bolts of a building project in Francombe, set out the application.

After emphasising that his decision to recommend it was based solely on merit, he outlined the conclusions of the Environmental Impact Assessment that there would be no discernible damage to the air, soil, water, natural landscape or cultural heritage either during construction or after completion. The minimal increase in noise in the immediate vicinity, where the only residential dwellings were DSS hostels, would be offset by a significant reduction in both noise and congestion in the centre of town as traffic shifted away from the existing pubs, clubs and leisure facilities. Moreover, the developers had pledged to extend and improve the Promenade in front of the pier, setting back the entrance pavilions and putting up a new pelican crossing.

Dimming the lights, he showed a series of slides of the proposed buildings, followed by highly idealised artist's impressions of the completed pier, both by day beneath a canopy of leaves, and by night as brightly illuminated as a cruise ship in port. He concluded by reminding the committee that 'this site has a lot of planning history. There's no reason at all why, in fifty, forty or even twenty years' time it shouldn't be transferred to a different usage. But at present, after balancing the protection of the historic and social environment with the need for economic growth and agreeing with the developers an extensive list of Section 106 underpinned controls relating to design, development, implementation and management, I strongly recommend that approval should be granted.'

Having thanked the officer for his concise presentation, the Chair announced that they had received a record 182 objections to the application. Four community representatives had been allotted three minutes each to put these in person, after which the developers would be afforded equal time to reply. She called on Jocelyn Dunning to speak first, failing to mask her surprise at the bass voice that responded. Casting repeated glances at his watch, Jocelyn declared that although the developers had trumpeted the support they had received from hotel owners and the Chamber of Commerce, his own members had grave anxieties about the impact of the scheme on their already ailing businesses. Such a radical reordering of the town's amenities would leave the centre deserted, particularly at night, resulting in increased antisocial behaviour and crime. Jocelyn was followed by Nigel Taylor, the Methodist minister of St Anne's, who argued for the preservation of Francombe as a family resort, even if this entailed demolishing the pier. While in the light of recent events Henry's reluctance to act as clerical spokesman was understandable, Duncan had hoped for a more impressive substitute. For all his sincerity, Taylor's reasoning was naïve and his delivery surprisingly hesitant for someone with chapel training. It came as a relief when, showing little respect for his cloth, Councillor Blackstone carried out her threat to switch off his microphone when he ran out of time.

With Glynis having renounced her right to speak in order that Duncan might present a more sustained argument, he had double the time available to his two associates, a fact to which he drew attention when, constrained by the need both to stay seated and talk into a fixed microphone, he began. 'I have six minutes – a mere 360 seconds – to save this town from the greatest peril it has faced since the threat of invasion in 1940. Then, Salter Pier was blown up to prevent its furnishing a landing stage for the enemy. Now, the enemy has taken over Francombe Pier and is using it to launch a direct attack on the moral and social fabric of the town. Some of you may accuse me of scaremongering, but anyone who's read the *Mercury* over the past few months will be under no illusions about the risk. I trust that I'm as conscious as anyone here of the hardships that Francombe has endured in recent years, but this is no way to set about reversing them. Strange as it sounds, the Recession that has caused us so much pain now hands us a golden opportunity. With more and more families choosing to holiday at home, we should be targeting them, restoring the pier to its glory days as a place of all-round entertainment, not turning it into a replica of a sleazy backstreet in Bangkok.

'Take this drawing.' Duncan pointed to the artist's impression of the pier at night, the final slide, which remained a ghostly presence on the screen in the glare of the overhead lighting. 'It looks so inoffensive, decked out in fairy lights as if the town is finally enjoying the festive display it was denied on the Parade this Christmas. What it doesn't show is the corruption, the crime, the intemperance (by which I mean far more than drunkenness), the exploitation and misery that inevitably accompany such enterprises. It doesn't show the danger to children for whom the illicit amusements will offer both a lure and a challenge. I appeal to the members of the committee not to be deceived by all the talk of profit to the town. This is a project that exists for one reason and one reason only: to line the developers' pockets.

'To which end we, or rather you, the members of the Planning and Regeneration Committee, are being asked to grant an application that will change the nature of our town for ever.' It may have been his reference to 1940 but he heard his cadences becoming Churchillian. 'I entreat you to save us from a development that will be a blight on our lives and a blight on the lives of all those who come after us, a development that is a betrayal not just of the people of Francombe but people the length and breadth of the country – and beyond – who come here to enjoy the innocent pleasures of the seaside.

I speak in fervent opposition to this application, which I ask you to reject.'

Duncan's plea drew loud cheers from the public gallery and a single clap from one of the councillors, cut short by a glare from her neighbour. Glynis Kingswood clasped his hand in support. Councillor Blackstone, who remained impassive, declared that having heard all the objections (prompting a cry from the gallery of 'Not half you bloody haven't!'), she would now call on the applicants. First to speak was the architect, Archana Nayar, wearing a far more sumptuous sari than at the consultation: cream silk with a motif of pink and blue petals. Grinning at the committee as if already thanking it for its endorsement, she defended her designs, explaining that they were inspired – albeit loosely – by several of the previous structures on the site and had received the full support of the Victorian Society, the National Piers Society and the Francombe Civic Society. At the mention of the last, Duncan turned to the gallery where its secretary and leading light, Jamie's former history teacher, David Westbrook, determinedly avoided his gaze.

Archana was followed by Geoffrey himself, reading from a prepared statement. He spoke so haltingly that Duncan wondered whether the shock of Craig's imprisonment had triggered a recurrence of his angina, before realising that it was a skilful ploy to avoid sounding overconfident. He began by professing his gratitude, first to the planning officer for presenting the application so cogently, then to the committee for adjudicating on such a vexed issue, knowing that whichever way they voted ('rightly or wrongly,' he said with a roguish smile), they would alienate some of their constituents, and finally to the public for its enthusiastic response to the consultation process. 'We received over a hundred comments on the plans. After examining them closely, we chose to make several modifications to the original designs, as you can see from the model in front of you.'

Oblivious to the differences, Duncan wished that he had paid more attention to the display in the library.

'The development is ecologically sustainable and carbon neutral. As you've just heard it meets the highest environmental standards. It will create hundreds of jobs both during construction and once it's operational. I stand accused here tonight – and not for the first time – of selling Francombe down the river (or should that be into the Channel?), sacrificing its identity, its prosperity, even its moral fibre to satisfy my own greed. There's only one word I can say to that and I'm sorry if it offends any of you but I speak as I find: Balls! I'll say it again: Balls!' Councillor Blackstone looked to her right as if for a legal ruling, but none was forthcoming. 'I love this town. I've lived here all my life. I hope to die here – although not for a good while yet! I've made my commitment to it clear by funding many community initiatives in the past and I can assure you that my support will continue.' He put down his notes. 'This is a planning committee, not a moral rearmament meeting, but I have to address, if only briefly, the concerns raised by one of the speakers, the editor – or rather former editor – of the *Mercury*. He charges me with destroying the family-friendly atmosphere of the town. So where is it? When I walk along the Front or Jubilee Precinct, I see pensioners; I see drunks and druggies; I see scroungers; I see groups of bored teenagers. But the only families I see – the only mums and dads with their two point two children (though, in this case, it's seven or eight) – are immigrants and asylum seekers.' Duncan looked up at the gallery where there was not a single non-white face in evidence. 'Is this the Francombe Mr Neville is so keen to preserve? I say to him and to all the other opponents of our plans: "Get real! We may look out on to the sand but that's no reason to stick our heads in it."

'Far from undermining families, this development will strengthen them. The work it provides will keep young people – the mothers and fathers of tomorrow – in Francombe. The cash it generates will filter through the community. And as for the danger that our ... what was it?' – he made a play of looking through his notes – '"illicit amusements" constitute to children: well, Mr Neville, Dr Kingswood and their friends may not have explored the darker reaches of the Internet, but take it from me, any ten-year-old with a laptop can – and does – access far more hardcore material in his bedroom than anything we propose to allow.'

'Thirty seconds left, Mr Weedon,' the Chair interposed.

'Granting this application will do far more than simply rescue a much loved local landmark (although of course it'll do that too); it will be the springboard for a groundbreaking leisure concept that will put Francombe back on the holiday map. Tonight you have a unique opportunity to approve a project that will be instrumental – some would say vital – to the survival of the town. I urge you to take it.'

Geoffrey's exhortation was greeted by an unexpected and, to Duncan's mind, encouraging silence. The Chair then turned to her right and invited any of the committee who wished to speak to do so. 'Traditionally, councillors don't have a time limit on their contributions,' she said, 'but in this case I'd ask you to be as succinct as possible and to restrict your comments to planning issues.' This sparked a protracted debate among members as to whether all of them or only ward councillors had the right to take part, which was finally resolved by the legal adviser's ruling that everyone had the right but ward councillors the priority.

Duncan was both angered and depressed by the time wasted on procedural issues, which said more about the committee's self-importance than its civic concern. He was equally frustrated by the inconsequential questions that the members put to the planning officer. One asked whether, since the sex museum was to be built on the site of the Winter Garden, it should be made of glass ('opaque, of course,' he added, laughing at his own witticism). Another wanted to know why a bus stop opposite the pier, for which she had led a ten-year campaign, was not included in the artist's impression. A third queried the appropriateness of the eighteen-foot reliefs of mermaids on the entrance pavilions, only to be told by the increasingly tetchy planning officer that, since the pier was not in a conservation area, the decoration did not fall within his remit. Finally, Jim Dawson, a three-times Mayor, stood up with his hands clasped across what would once have been called his corporation and which remained a fitting term for a man reputed to have the Council in his pocket. 'I've listened to both sides,' he said in his elder statesman's voice now choked by emphysema, 'and find myself more persuaded by the developer. It's clearly a contentious scheme and one not without risks, but in my view they're far outweighed by the benefits. I therefore intend to support it.'

As if Dawson's intervention had been her cue, the Chair proposed that the matter should be put to a vote. After the extensive preliminaries, this was remarkably quick: a show of hands with ten in favour, one abstention (the bus shelter champion), and one against (the man who had cavilled at the mermaids and who remained visibly piqued by the planning officer's putdown). A chorus of boos, peppered with cries of 'Fix' and 'Sell-Out', rang out from the gallery and Glynis Kingswood sank her head in her hands. Duncan, however, felt strangely detached. Defeat was now such a part of his life that he was inured to it. He watched while Geoffrey shook hands with the architect and planning officer before crossing to talk to some of the councillors. The Chair struggled to maintain order as she wound up proceedings, but people were already starting to slip away.

'I'll have twelve hundred words on your desk first thing tomorrow morning, boss,' Ken said to Duncan as he passed him on the way to the door.

'I'll look forward to them.' Ken looked at him quizzically. 'You know what I mean. I think it warrants a final one-word headline. "Shame!"'

As Ken left, Duncan turned back to Glynis.

'Well, nobody can say we didn't give it our best shot.'

'There's always the High Court. We can apply for a judicial review.'

'True,' Duncan replied without conviction. Whatever the flaws in the committee's decision, Geoffrey was far too shrewd an operator to have bungled the application process.

'So Weedon's won?' Glynis said, catching his drift.

'The Weedons of this world always do. The Francombe we held dear is dead and buried. The tunnel of love has been boarded up and replaced by a massage parlour.'

He broke off as Geoffrey Weedon walked up to him, holding out his hand. 'No hard feelings?'

'Excuse me,' Glynis said, heading for the door.

'Is it something my best friends don't tell me?' Geoffrey asked, dropping the hand unshaken.

'Oh, I'm sure they would,' Duncan replied. 'You look pleased with yourself.'

'It takes forty-three muscles to frown and only seventeen to smile, or so I'm reliably informed.'

'How many does it take to smirk?'

'You should know by now that that's not my style.'

'I'll leave you to enjoy your victory. I don't see any sign of Derek.'

'He and Linda had some meeting to do with Rose. Frankly it's no great loss.'

'Or Frances,' Duncan added, refusing to become enmeshed in Weedon politics.

'She's a little down after all the business with Craig,' Geoffrey said, lowering his voice accordingly. 'She and Derek went to visit him in Ashfield on Saturday.'

'How's he coping?'

'Not too well. Apparently he's had a Union Jack tattooed on his wrist.'

'No doubt you're another one who blames me for what happened.'

'On the contrary, I think it was the best thing for all concerned, especially Craig. He was out of control. Ashfield will knock him into shape. He'll be taught discipline and respect.'

'But Frances doesn't see it that way?'

'She's more worried about his GCSEs. As you know, I don't set much store by academic qualifications.'

'No, as you never cease to remind us, your own alma mater was the University of Life, or was it the School of Hard Knocks?'

'I always enjoy our skirmishes, Duncan. And not just because I usually come out on top. You're the one person in this town who's a worthy opponent.'

'Am I supposed to feel flattered?'

'Ever since we were at St Columba's. Do you remember when you won the form prize and I won one for industry?'

'That was forty-odd years ago!'

'You'll never know how much it rankled. I thought it was because of my dad's car repair shop. Your dad owned Mercury House and mine was just a mechanic. Industry, see?'

'You know perfectly well it means application … hard work.'

'It's still sweat, if only on the forehead.'

'I wouldn't complain. Look at you today. Industry pays.'

'What will you do now you've sold the paper?'

'I didn't know you cared!'

'There may be an opening at Weedon's. We'll certainly need some PR work for the pier. I've always admired your way with words.'

'Is this what you mean by not smirking?'

'I'm serious. Never at a loss for a pithy epithet, present company excepted. Have you totted up how often the *Mercury*'s described me as "controversial"? Derek says it's a euphemism for shady, but I tell him my old pal Duncan would never resort to such underhand tricks.'

'Thank you. To answer your question, I won't be looking

for anything else for a while. I need some time to reflect: cultivate my garden.'

'I didn't know you had green fingers.'

'It's a metaphor.'

'From Voltaire, yes, I know. Don't look so astonished. I told you you were a worthy opponent. If only you'd realised the same was true of me.'

With a smile that stretched his seventeen muscles to the full, Geoffrey rejoined his architect and agent, leaving Duncan to commiserate with his allies. He finally escaped and drove back to Mercury House where, surprised to see the lights on in his flat, he assumed that Neil must have stayed late, until he heard a familiar drone from the stairs.

'I wasn't expecting you,' he said to Mary who was vacuuming the sitting room carpet, a pointless exercise given the boxes stacked against the wall, ready for the removal men on Friday.

'I'll be out of your way in two ticks.'

'There's no rush.'

'Only they kept me late at the Metropole and I knew you were at the Town Hall, so I thought I'd do downstairs first.'

'That's fine. It's good to see you. I need a drink. Can I tempt you with anything? Whisky? Brandy? I may still have some sherry.'

'No, I mustn't.'

'How about if I open a bottle of wine?'

'Well, if you twist my arm. Only a small one mind.'

Duncan went into the kitchen, bringing back a bottle of office Shiraz. Dearly hoping that it now belonged to Newscom, he unscrewed the top and poured them both a glass.

'To tell the truth I'm glad of your company.'

'Did the pier thingamajig go through?'

'I'm afraid so.'

'It's wicked. After all your hard work.'

'If only it were just the work. Sit down a minute and enjoy the wine.'

'I can drink and clean at the same time. It's what Janine calls multitasking. Not that she'd know!' As if to demonstrate her dexterity, she clasped her glass in her left hand while vigorously dusting the television stand with her right.

'Was Neil here when you arrived?' Duncan asked.

'No, but he left his mark.'

'The lavatory?'

'I've got two sons so I know accidents happen, but with him it seems to be every time.'

'I'm sorry you've had to deal with it. Neil has problems.'

'It can't be easy for his mum.'

'It's not.'

Duncan was reluctant to admit that he had yet to mention Neil's bathroom mishaps to Ellen. Over the past few weeks Neil had noticeably warmed towards him, seeking his help in the final stages of his history project and using his flat as a bolt-hole after school. Even the unfortunate choice of *David Copperfield* as his English set book had cast only a faint shadow over their rapprochement. Duncan was anxious not to threaten it by betraying him to his mother, who would either know about the problem already and be mortified that it had come to Duncan's attention or else wonder why a boy who was so clean in his habits at home should be so messy at Mercury House.

'And you?' Duncan, asked, eager to change the subject. 'Things can't have been easy since Norman's release.'

'They haven't,' Mary said, putting down her duster. 'We're squashed in together like a tin of sardines. Honest, I sometimes feel like the old woman who lived in the shoe – you know, in the nursery rhyme? The two boys are at each other's throats. Norman won't take Nick's depression seriously. He says it's all in the mind. Still, it's not all bad news. Now he's back, we don't have enough beds. So he has to bunk with his dad while I squeeze in with the girls.'

'Is that a good thing?'

'Oh yes,' she replied, her eyes glistening.

'Let's be devils,' Duncan said, refilling their glasses.

'I've been to see Jordan in Feltham,' Mary said tentatively.

'Really? He must be coming home soon.'

'No, he was due out in March when he's done three months. But he's been in some trouble – he wouldn't say what but his face was a mass of bruises – so they're making him serve his full term.'

'I'm very sorry.'

'He sent me a visiting order. Put me down as his mother.'

'Didn't anyone check?'

'He told them I was his real mother who gave him away when he was born.'

'He's playing the system. It's always easier for family members.'

'No, he's ashamed of me. He used to see things so strange and special. Now he sees them same as everyone else. And what does he see when he looks at me: a fat old bag!' She began to shake violently.

'That's nonsense!'

'Is it? How would you know?' She jerked her glass and splashed wine on the carpet. 'Oh lord, I'll fetch a cloth.'

'It's only a drop; it doesn't matter. Don't forget, I'm moving out on Friday.'

'Of course it matters. I'm the cleaner!' She fell into a strange rhythmic sobbing. 'That's what I am: the cleaner.'

'And I'm the boss. At least for another two days. So please don't worry.'

'You do understand, don't you?' she asked urgently. 'I know what they think of me downstairs: a silly tart with a toy boy. But you know that I really loved him. We were Adam and Eve.' Duncan pictured the whitewashed wall. 'Age didn't count. I remember when the vicar said how it only came into the world with the snake and the apple. I thought that was beautiful. I thought it was paradise. And now I'll never see him again.'

'You mean not till he's released?'

'I mean not till never. He says he won't come back to Francombe. He's through with this place.'

'What about his mother?'

'She's gone into a home. I looked in on her Christmas time. She had carers from the Council. Kurds. She said she only wanted English, so they've sent her over Leversden way. I'd visit but it's three bus rides.'

'If you'd like a lift…'

'What's the point? What's the point of any of it? Tell me! You're a clever man, Mr Neville.'

'No, I'm an educated man. There's a difference.'

'Do you ever wonder what it's all for? Life, I mean.'

'I do indeed. Far too often.'

'My mum never had much of anything, except kids. But she had God. In her eyes everything happened for a reason. It was all part of His plan. And as a kid I believed that too. Because she told me. And the teachers told me. And the Bible told me, in words that sounded like answers even when they weren't. But I can't believe it any more. If God's all-good like they say, then why does He make things so hard for us? If it's a test, why doesn't He give us one we can pass?'

'Have you thought of speaking to Henry … Father Grainger?'

'I tried after Jordan's arrest. But all he said was that God didn't want us to feel too sure of ourselves; He wanted us to ask questions. Why, when it just makes us more unhappy? If there's no hope in this world and there's no hope in the next, what's the point of us being here?'

'I wish I had all the answers – I wish I even had one – but I don't.' After giving up on God, Duncan had told himself that the purpose of life was to make the world a better place for the next generation but, having seen how little respect that generation had for the one before, he was less convinced. He racked his befuddled brain for evidence that all the scientific and technological progress over the centuries had been matched by comparable advances in morality, empathy or behaviour. Nevertheless a vestige of his father's seigneurial code prevented his abandoning Mary to her despair. 'That said, maybe Henry's right and our curiosity is what saves us? Maybe the only way we can change the world is by questioning the universe? In the meantime let's polish off the bottle.'

How ironic that like a disillusioned priest the one consolation he could offer her was wine! He refilled her glass, which she downed in three gulps as if anxious to escape before divulging anything else. Then, staggering to her feet, she proposed to return to work. Gently overruling her, he guided her to the door with the reminder that he would see her at the leaving party on Friday. Feeling unusually energised, he decided to check his email, only to recall that his laptop was being repaired and he would have to go down to the office. While there he would write to Tim Barker (Mr Fixit) who, having promised to sort out the problem over the weekend, had rung on Monday to say that he was having trouble recovering data from the hard drive. Baffled by the workings of a telephone, let alone a computer, he had been reluctant to take issue with him, simply stressing the importance of speed since, from Friday, he would no longer have access to the *Mercury* system and be forced to join the Internet surfers at Chomp 'n' Click Cyber Café.

All thought of email was swept aside when he made his way downstairs and into the reporters' room, stopping to savour the unique stillness of what a few hours ago had been a hive of activity. He cast his mind back to the day when his father had first introduced him to the gang of impassioned, irreverent, serious, funny men and women whose lives were far more thrilling than any he had read about in books. How he had loved to watch them as they went about their work! On special days they gave him the job of cutting up the paper and date-stamping stories for the files (putting his friends' pop-up farms and home-made greeting cards to shame). Stirred by the memory, he walked towards the case room, which had lain empty for years. No sooner had he entered than it was once again filled with the clatter of typesetting machines and the dense heat of molten metal. Brushing against a crate, he instinctively recoiled as though from a trolley that held a forme ready for the press. He vividly recalled his own delight and the compositors' horror when, minutes before deadline, one slid off and smashed into gibberish. Somehow they managed to reset it in time, adding to the romance of a process that could not have been further removed from the cold, clinical world of digital technology.

Despite all his years in the editor's chair, it was his childhood memories that predominated. Giddy with nostalgia, he decided to make a final tour of the building, going first to the boardroom where three of his four predecessors remained to greet him while the fourth had been crated up and sent to auction, ready for a probable relocation to America, where he would be no more than an incidental name on a label. Studiously avoiding the archives, which, holding no interest for Newscom, were to be stored in the Central Library, he walked through the entrance hall to the basement, for sixty years home to the printing presses and the hub of the entire operation. Although it now housed nothing more sinister than a colony of rats, the thunderous room crammed with brawny men reeking of sweat and dust and the waxy barrier cream that they rubbed on their hands had once given the descent to hell a very specific meaning.

Chastened, he went up to his office where he read through his mail. He was both surprised and touched by the messages of support prompted by his departure and impervious to the occasional gibe, such as that from Luca Salvatore who claimed that Francombe in general and the Pizza on the Prom in particular would be a happier place without his meddling. After replying to a batch of well-wishers, diligently finding a distinctive tone for each, he glanced at his watch and, not wanting to call Ellen from his desk, returned to the flat.

'I'm sorry,' he said, ringing her from the sitting room, 'I lost track of the time.'

'Did the meeting go on longer than planned?'

'No, it was over hours ago. Actually it was over months ago.'

'I see,' she said quietly. 'At least you did your best.'

'Trouble is it wasn't good enough. Take no notice,' he said, sensing her disquiet. 'I'm just a bit down.'

'You and me both.'

'More problems with the kids?'

'Not mine for a change. I spent the afternoon at Rose's tribunal.'

'Of course. With so much else going on it slipped my mind. What did they decide?'

'As I expected, they went for Haycock Road.'

'Linda must be devastated. No wonder Derek wasn't at the Town Hall.'

'They did everything they could: hiring a barrister so for once it wouldn't be David and Goliath. But the panel agreed with the LEA that Rose's needs would be best met at a special school.'

'So they didn't listen to you?'

'Oh, they listened. Not that it did Rose much good – or me for that matter. Technically I'm an independent witness but there's still a sense that I was breaking ranks.'

'Can Linda and Derek appeal?'

'Yes, on a point of law; not merely to repeat old arguments.'

'It's the same for us with the pier. We could apply for a judicial review but only if there'd been a fault in the application or consultation process. I'll give Linda a ring tomorrow. Truth is we've barely spoken since the business with Craig.'

'I'm sure she understands. When we were chatting before the hearing, she was anxious to know how you were coping with the move.'

'I trust you told her "well".'

'I know my job. But I hope it's the truth.'

'I think so. I really do. Right now I'm a little demob-happy. Tomorrow I put my final issue to bed and clear my desk. Though the real test will come on Friday afternoon when the bigwigs from Newscom arrive for some gruesome retirement presentation to Sheila and Ken and me.'

'I'm sure you'll sail through it. Unflappable as ever.'

'At least I have Friday evening to look forward to.'

'Me too! Matthew used to pour scorn on Valentine's Day, at any rate once we were married. Strange when you think how much they loathed each other but it wasn't that different from Barbara's contempt for Mother's Day. Stop it, Ellen! Won't you tell me where we're going?'

'It's a surprise.'

'Not even a hint?'

'I've already given you one: backcomb your hair!'

Lulled by the prospect of the dinner dance at the Metropole, Duncan sank into a deep sleep, waking reinvigorated for his last day at work. As he sat in his office waiting for Ken to finish his piece on the planning decision, he read through the page proofs. Despite the entreaties of his staff, he had curbed any valedictory impulse. There would be no spread of highlights from 'my twenty-seven years as editor', let alone 'my family's 144 years as proprietors'. He had confined his contributions to a leader attacking the Council's failure to meet its affordable housing quota and an 'On This Day' column celebrating Francombe's first cinema, the Alhambra, which had opened in February 1914 with *Dr Jekyll and Mr Hyde*. Elsewhere there was the usual assortment of horror stories, such as the cannabis farm at the Exeter Road children's home, the racist attack on the Stafford Cripps estate and, most distressing, the quadriplegic man left to look on helplessly all night after his carer suffered a stroke; interspersed with feel-good stories, such as the motorist who married the student she picked up on the St Anselm bypass

('Hitchhiker Hitched', in the jaunty caption), and the grandfather, father and son who had shaved their heads for Autism Awareness.

Duncan wondered how much of this mixed bag would survive under Newscom and the transition to what Brian, who was being kept on by the new management, had described without a shred of embarrassment as 'churnalism'. But then what else could one expect from a man whose job description was no longer that of 'writer' or 'journalist' but 'linear supplier'? With only Rowena and Jake remaining in Francombe, the scope for local news would be strictly curtailed and the bulk of the paper filled with syndicated pieces on celebrities and lifestyles and, wherever possible, celebrity lifestyles. Mindful of the irony, Duncan pinned his hopes on the emergence of a latter-day version of the *Francombe Citizen*.

'Knock knock!' Sheila called through the half-open door and walked in with a plate of gingerbread.

'But it's not Thursday,' Duncan said, as she handed it to him.

'I didn't think you'd be in tomorrow.'

'Delicious,' he said, breaking off a piece and eating it quickly for fear that she was about to cry. 'I shall miss this.'

'Won't I be able to bring you any at home?'

'I most certainly hope so. But I can't expect it on a weekly basis.'

'Who else do I have to bake for?'

'Yourself,' Duncan said, without thinking.

'My GP tells me I'm borderline diabetic. One of the old ladies at Castlemaine died on Monday.'

'I'm sorry.'

'I hardly knew her. There's some hoo-ha over her funeral. Jean asked if I'd made my own arrangements. She said people like us – she meant her and me – with no one to look out for us couldn't leave it to chance.'

'You're retiring, not dying, Sheila!' Duncan said, stifling

his impatience. You're healthy … independent. The world's your oyster.'

'But I don't like cruises! I'm sorry. I should go and buy the champagne.'

She hurried out, leaving Duncan acutely aware that he had secured her pension but not her future. He made a mental note to take her out to lunch in the next fortnight and discuss the various options open to her from voluntary work to adult education and even – he pondered as he munched a piece of gingerbread – setting up her own baking business. At noon Stewart sent through the proofs of Ken's copy: the concise, dispassionate and vibrant prose demonstrating why he remained at the top of his game after four decades. Two years ago Duncan would have predicted that his retirement would be an even greater wrench than Sheila's, but he had lost his zest along with the libel case in which Megan Riley, high priestess of the Salter Wood coven, alleged that he had irrevocably damaged her professional reputation with his report that she had invoked a curse on the Mayor during a rally to save the Ley Park adventure playground. Besides which he had a project to occupy him in the shape of his long delayed *History of the Fishing Industry in Francombe from the Middle Ages to the Present Day.*

'Catchy title, that,' Brian had said. 'Should fly off the shelves at the Seafood Festival.'

Having signed off the pages, Duncan steeled himself to enter the reporters' room where the entire staff was gathered, including Trevor who, having guaranteed his position with Newscom, greeted his outgoing editor more affably than he had done in years. Overplaying his ineptitude, Duncan opened the first of the champagne bottles that Sheila had bought ('three for two' to the end) and poured everyone a glass.

'I'm not going to make a speech,' he said.

'Hear hear!' Trevor interjected. 'I mean…'

'We'll save that for Friday,' Duncan said, sparing his blushes, 'but I can't let the occasion pass without saying a few words. This is a sad but inevitable moment. In recent years I've often felt like the little Dutch boy with his finger in the dyke.'

'Oh, for God's sake!' Rowena said, as Brian sniggered.

'For me this hasn't been a family business so much as a community one – there, you knew you wouldn't get away without hearing the word one last time. Perhaps I'm being too much of a Jeremiah in fearing that everything will change. After all, the *Mercury* name is being kept on along with several of you: Brian and Trevor in Basingstoke; Rowena, Jake and Stewart here, even if your roles will be redefined.'

'Yes, how many "s"s in Sassenach?' Stewart asked to general bemusement. 'I'll quite likely be subbing the *Aberdeen Advertiser* or the *Hull Gazette*.'

'I'm keeping what I really think about you all till Friday … oh, that came out wrong! For now I just want to thank you for the support you've given me over the years and say that, although I'm leaving the *Mercury*, I'm not leaving Francombe and I look forward to seeing you socially.' He found himself staring at Brian, whose eyes were a blank. 'So I ask you to drink to the future of everyone here and of the *Mercury*. The future!'

'The future!'

Duncan raised his glass as the toast was echoed. Then, feeling a desperate urge to escape, he edged towards the door. 'If you don't mind, I think I'll slip away.'

'Not so fast, boss,' Ken said, stepping forward with a package that Duncan immediately identified. 'Your last paper won't be out till tomorrow but we've got together to give you a sneak preview of the front page.'

Taking a gulp of champagne Duncan unwrapped the *spike* and studied the tribute from his anagrammatic reporters. 'I shan't read it now,' he said, his eyes misting over at the allusion to the well-loved caretaker, who had once provoked such ridicule. 'But I shall do as soon as I'm upstairs. Thank you ... thank you all so much. I'll truly treasure it.'

Thuds and thumps resounded around him as he made for the door and they banged him out in the time-honoured way. He went up to the flat where, suddenly feeling confined, he decided to take himself out for lunch and then to a film matinée, an indulgence that he had not enjoyed for years. But a glimpse of the snowfall outside his window deterred him so, after heating up a tin of soup and wishing that he had drunk another glass of champagne, he sat down to read the *spike*. Laughing out loud at the affectionate raillery, he was startled by a knock at the door.

'Missing me already?' he said, opening it to find Sheila.

'I'm sorry, Duncan, but there are two policemen asking for you downstairs.'

'Can't somebody else deal with it? I'm officially retired.'

'They asked for you by name. One of them's Ted Ravenscroft.'

'Perhaps he hasn't heard about the takeover. Where are my shoes?'

Having slipped them on, he made his way downstairs with Sheila following anxiously. As he passed the reporters' room, he was surprised to find Brian and Jake hovering in the doorway. 'No rest for the wicked,' he said as he headed down to the ground floor.

'Hello, Ted ... Constable,' he said to the two policemen who were waiting warily. 'You're a bit behind the times, Ted. I've edited my last issue. If there's anything you want from now on, you should speak to Rowena Birdseye.'

'Duncan Neville?' Ted asked, his voice even more uneasy than his stance.

'Yes, of course,' Duncan replied perplexed.

'Are you the owner of the Apple MacBook serial number W88134K20P2 left at Mr Fixit, 32 Bartholomew Road, Francombe on Friday, 7 February 2014?'

'I'm the owner of an Apple MacBook, which I took in for repair last week, but I've no idea of the serial number. What's this about? Has it been stolen?'

'I'm arresting you on suspicion of possessing indecent images of children. You don't have to say anything but it may harm your defence if you don't mention when questioned something you later rely on in court.'

Ten

Your *New Mercury*

by Andrew Falkirk, Newscom Media (South East) Divisional MD

Thursday, 13 March 2014

Regular customers will notice many changes in their paper this week. Last month Newscom Media, one of the UK's largest local and regional media groups publishing over 130 weekly titles in print and digital form, bought the long-established *Francombe & Salter Mercury*. To celebrate this new era in the paper's history, we have given it a much-needed makeover, starting with the title.

The *New Mercury*, as it is now known, will continue to provide comprehensive coverage of local news and events but in a fresh, accessible form that's fully in line with today's busy lifestyles. So you'll find shorter, snappier articles, a 50 per cent increase in the use of colour photography, plus a regular four-page cartoon and puzzle supplement.

We shall maintain the paper's honourable tradition of campaigning journalism but, in the belief that the most effective action stems from the grass roots, we'll leave it to you, our customers, to lead these campaigns, offering you a platform to highlight official abuse, waste and sleaze, to protest against cuts to services, and to raise funds for worthy causes.

At Newscom we aim to reflect the concerns and values of our customers and advertisers, giving our customers a fuller understanding of the events and activities taking place in their local areas and providing our advertisers with unrivalled access to local markets.

At the same time we're convinced that in today's world there's more that unites the purchasers of our various titles than divides them. In this global village the local is universal and the universal local. We're all interested in the same fashions, the same trends and the same celebrities. So in the *New Mercury* we aim to share content with our neighbours from Land's End to John o'Groats. We intend to reach outwards rather than look inwards.

For too long the old *Mercury* swam against the tide of technological change. At Newscom we recognise that our customers want choice in the way they consume content. With our unique ability to synergise our print and online operations, we're able to provide our customers and advertisers with up-to-the-minute material across a variety of media.

These are exciting days for Francombe. Work is soon to start on the renovation of the pier, which will put the town back at the forefront of the leisure industry. We at Newscom are drawing up plans to turn Mercury House into the UK's first vertical shopping mall. We hope that you'll support us as we both generate and report on this change.

For someone so reluctant to celebrate her seventy-fifth birthday, Adele had taken a keen interest in the preparations for the party. As Duncan had predicted, her misgivings, prompted by the sale of the paper and his own arrest, dwindled as the day approached, to be replaced by a constant fear that he would bungle the arrangements. He had respected her wish that it be an intimate gathering; not that there was much choice, given her reduced social circle. So along with Alison, Malcolm, their two sons and Jamie, he had invited her three fellow bridge players, two former colleagues from the Townswomen's Guild, the president of the horticultural society and Henry.

On the day itself Chris came to cook, set out and serve the food, while his friend Paul, whose artistic talents were not confined to doll-making, decked the sitting room, dining room and hall with bunches of balloons, garlands of paper flowers, strings of tissue pompoms and, most strikingly, eight full-size photographic cut-outs of Adele aged between ten and sixty (vanity had vetoed any later image). Chris who, much to Duncan's embarrassment, refused any payment for what he described as a birthday gift, had returned to work soon after Duncan moved back to Ridgemount. Having agonised over cutting Chris's hours now that he himself could attend to his mother's basic needs, he discovered that Chris in turn had been worrying how to tell them that, with his grandmother safely installed in Castlemaine and his injured shoulder ruling out lifting, he had decided to go back into catering management. He would, however, be happy to help out with Adele whenever he could.

Duncan pondered the irony that for all the damage Neil had done him, he had unwittingly solved the problem of how to limit Adele's expenditure. It's an ill wind, he thought bitterly as he found himself once again reliving the ordeal of his arrest. He sensed Ted Matthews's discomfiture and his colleague's contempt as they drove him to Falworth Road police station. Once there, he had his watch, wallet, keys, belt and mobile confiscated – although he was permitted to make a call on the station phone to Victor Sheringham, his solicitor – before being escorted down to a cell. Victor, who had planned to leave work early to take his daughters sledging on the South Downs (inducing Duncan's one authentic pang of guilt), headed straight for the station, where he learnt that, when Tim Barker examined Duncan's hard disk, he had uncovered over four hundred indecent images of children.

'What children?' Duncan asked. 'Are they friends or strangers? How old? Girls or boys?'

'I know nothing except that they're underage,' Victor replied wretchedly, 'There are some girls but mainly boys.'

'There you are then!' Duncan said, with a momentary sense of exultation. 'How can they be mine? I haven't felt the slightest stirring in that direction since school.'

Victor who, to Duncan's dismay, seemed more concerned to find a valid reason for his having looked at the images than to accept that the very notion was preposterous, asked whether he might have downloaded them during the course of an investigation into child pornography that had subsequently been dropped.

'You're saying that under the pressure of weekly deadlines I managed to forget that I had four hundred pictures of unspeakable wickedness and degradation on my screen? No!'

Duncan reaffirmed his innocence when shortly afterwards he was taken up to an interview room, which reeked of body odour and air freshener, and questioned. Having explained that the laptop did not have a password and that the only people who had access to his flat were his son, his fiancée, her son and his cleaner, he asked whether it might have been possible for someone with a grievance against him ('the sort of computer whizz-kid who hacks into the Pentagon') to make it look as if he had downloaded the images in order to incriminate him.

'Who would want to do that?' one of the two interviewing officers asked incredulously.

'The Mayor, half the Town Council, assorted hoteliers, property developers, publicans, supermarket chains, bus companies, hospital administrators, not to mention your own chief constable. Anyone whom the *Mercury* has held to account over the past twenty years!'

To his own relief and Victor's surprise, Duncan was not charged but released on police bail pending further investigation. Victor drove him home, where his parting remark that 'At least I don't need to give you my usual spiel about not talking to the press' fell flat. Duncan had not realised how deeply he was in shock until he struggled up the stairs. Every step seemed like ten and by the time he reached the top he was gasping for breath. He stumbled through his front door, poured himself a tumbler of whisky and sank on to the sofa, but the respite was short-lived. Having ignored the flashing *nine* on the message indicator of his answering machine, he was forced to respond to the call that came through a few minutes later. Sounding strained, Alison announced that she was on her way to Francombe, having been rung up by a distraught Adele with news of his arrest. His horror that his mother knew was heightened by the memory of the firebomb attack that had triggered the death of Mrs Ponsonby. Panic-stricken, he proposed to drive straight over to Ridgemount but Alison dissuaded him, insisting that Adele was safe in the hands of Chris and that he himself needed rest.

The mystery of how Adele had found out was solved by his next caller. After pledging his support 'moral, practical and liquid if you just want to get soused', Ken described how, to the fury of the entire office, including Trevor, Brian had written up his arrest on the *Mercury* website. 'No doubt it's a taste of the balanced, informed reporting we can expect from Newscom,' he said, as if the decline in journalistic standards were the true offence. Having promised to ring him if there were anything he needed, Duncan hung up and contemplated this latest blow. If his mother, who had no access to what she dubbed 'the interweb', had heard what had happened, the news must have spread all over town. For now he was concerned solely with Jamie and Ellen. However painful it was to repeat a story that seemed more unreal with every telling, he owed them an explanation – or at least an account. He dialled Jamie's mobile, only to lose heart and instead ring Linda, whose outraged incredulity ('If they can muddle up babies in a maternity unit, they can muddle up hard disks at a computer shop') reduced him to tears. Despite a nagging doubt over her unwillingness to put Jamie on the line if he had indeed 'rubbished' the charge as she claimed, he rang off feeling reassured.

Musing sourly that the one virtue of his arrest was to remove any need for sobriety, he poured himself another tumbler of whisky and rang Ellen.

'Duncan, thank God! I've been so worried. Did you get my message?'

He glanced contritely at the flashing *nine*. 'I'm sorry. I haven't played any of them back yet.'

'I can't believe it.'

'I should hope not!' he said with a rush of anguish.

'I mean I can't believe it's happened to you. Neil showed me the *Mercury* website. Did you know that people can write comments underneath? Whatever you do, don't read them,' she added quickly.

'I can't. I don't have a computer. I could go down to the office but they've probably changed the locks ... or at any rate the password.'

'It's not a joke!'

'I know. Ellen, I'm sorry.'

'Why? You haven't done anything.'

'Of course not,' he replied, unsure if it had been a question or a statement. 'I mean I'm sorry that this has flared up around us. Just when we should be ... when we have been ... when we will be so happy. Oh God, Ellen, I want to see you so much.'

'Me too. But there's no way I can get away right now.'

'I could call a cab and come to you. Unless I'm already on a minicab blacklist throughout Francombe.'

'It's not a joke!'

'I know, but I have to keep my sanity somehow. Shall I come round?'

'No, not this evening. Tomorrow will be better. I've got Neil ... he keeps saying "it could have been me".'

'What could? Nothing could. It's all some terrible nightmare. You do believe me, don't you?'

'Yes. Yes, of course I do. Everything will be easier tomorrow.'

While he had hoped for a more emphatic endorsement, he told himself that an element of caution was inevitable. After all, she had been married to Matthew for nineteen years without realising that he was committing a multimillion-pound fraud. Moreover, she had had to endure her mother's insinuations that his attraction to her cloaked an attraction to her children. Under the circumstances it was remarkable that she had any faith left in him at all.

'Believe me, it'll sort itself out. And whatever else we mustn't let it spoil our Valentine's Day date.'

In the event, Duncan spent the evening with his mother. He had quit Mercury House first thing the previous day, unable to face the questions, suspicions and, most painful of all, the sympathy of the staff, and had driven to Ridgemount where Adele greeted him with moist eyes and the veiled reproach that she had been up all night. Alison, whose cool head had never been more welcome, at once began organising both him and his defence, promising that straight after breakfast she would ring Malcolm and ask him to find the leading London lawyer in his field since they couldn't trust anyone in Francombe, a remark that revived Adele's tears.

Alison's misgivings were confounded when, on Friday morning, Victor rang with the news that the police had provided him with the forensic evidence for which he had been

pressing. Analysis of the hard drive showed that all the offending files had been created in two sessions with none having been
accessed or modified since then. The sessions in question were
between 6 and 9 p.m. on Thursday, 30 January and between 6
and 10 p.m. on Wednesday, 5 February. Duncan's immediate
task was to account for his whereabouts during each, which
turned out to be remarkably straightforward for, although the
police had impounded his pocket diary, along with his entire
collection of DVDs and his battered Penguin edition of *Lolita*,
Sheila kept an office diary into which all his engagements were
transferred. Alison drove straight to Mercury House, returning with proof that on the evening of 30 January he had chaired
a protest meeting at the Morley Road refugee centre attended
by, among others, two police community support officers, and
on the evening of 5 February he had taken Ellen to Brighton to
see a touring production of *Tosca*.

Victor arranged for him to attend the police station that
afternoon with details of both events, along with credit
card receipts from the Brighton theatre car park and Terre
à Terre Restaurant. Duncan's relief was qualified since, as he
revealed first to Ellen and then to the police, Neil had been at
his flat on both occasions, purportedly working on his local
history project. Later that evening, when they were due to be
at the Metropole, twisting and shaking to the retro sounds
of The Crimplenes, Ellen rang with the news that Neil had
been arrested after school and she had accompanied him as
his 'appropriate adult'. Confronted with the evidence, he had
made no attempt to deny his guilt, while steadfastly refusing
to offer any explanation, even after the interviewing officer
warned him that being over the age of ten he risked prosecution. He claimed that he bore Duncan no grudge and when,
as though in a last-ditch attempt to justify their tactics, the
officer asked whether Duncan had ever done anything to him
'like the men in the pictures', he shook his head.

Now it was Neil who was charged with possessing indecent

images, but the CPS lawyer requested that in the first instance he be sent for psychiatric evaluation. After examining the report, the CPS decided that no public interest would be served by putting him on trial and that a prosecution might endanger his already fragile mental and emotional state. It ordered instead that he be referred to the social work and psychiatry team at the North Francombe Child Development Centre (the venue intensifying Ellen's sense of shame). Duncan, severely shaken by Neil's pathological malice, was grateful at least that he was to undergo treatment. Ellen persisted in the belief that Barbara was to blame for having poisoned Neil's mind, but Duncan was less convinced. It was patently clear that Neil had set out to entrap him, feigning a reconciliation to gain access to his computer and then damaging its hard drive so that the images would be exposed.

He tried to be as angry as so many others were on his behalf, but his overriding emotion was grief. How could someone so young be so full of hate? This was far more than the routine resentment of a boy for a man whom he suspected of trying to take his father's place. While loath to pre-empt the experts, Duncan saw it as an attack on men – or at any rate father figures – in general. He had been wondering how he would ever repair a relationship with a person who detested him so much, when Ellen relieved him of the need. In the two weeks since Neil's arrest they had met only twice. Although he had more time than ever at his disposal, she was determined to devote each spare moment to her children, as if somehow the freedom she had allowed herself over the past five months had been the root of all their trouble. She invited him to tea at the Sea Breeze Café, which, despite being on the Promenade, boasted a vast photograph of a tropical beach across its back wall. Extracting his promise to hear her out, she told him that she had decided to leave Francombe in July.

'But you can't!' he said, stirring his glass cup so violently that coffee splashed on to the table.

'You promised,' she said quietly. 'I've discussed it with the team at the Centre and they're happy as long as Neil continues his treatment elsewhere. I shan't do anything until after Sue's GCSEs. Ruining one person's life is enough – '

'That's not true. You've ruined no one's life. What's more, you've transformed mine!'

'You promised! I thought we'd find somewhere near Bedford. The psychiatrist thinks Neil needs to rebuild his relationship with his father.'

'In a prison visiting room?' Duncan asked bitterly.

'At first, yes.'

'What does Matthew think about it?'

'He doesn't know.'

'And Sue?'

'She wants to live with my mother in Dorset,' Ellen said, taking a deep breath. 'She says if I don't let her, she'll leave home and become a … Let's just say that recent events have left us all scarred. And whatever my own feelings about Barbara, I can't deny how well Sue gets on with her. Besides, she's much more mature than I was at her age. She won't let any of her grandmother's nonsense rub off on her. And I don't seem to have any other options.'

'I can think of one.'

'Don't, please!'

'Marrying me and staying here where we can make a home for us all.'

'With a boy who hates you so much he contrived to have you charged with the most abhorrent crime? Be reasonable, Duncan, it's not going to happen.'

'If I can forgive him, surely you can?'

'The only person I can't forgive is myself. I've spent my life claiming that I put my kids first. It's been my credo … my rationale. Then the first chance that comes my way, I blow it.'

'They're not babies. They don't need twenty-four-hour care. In a few years' time they'll leave home and lead their own lives.'

'That's their privilege, not mine. I'm going now. I don't know what else to say.'

'Say nothing. Take some time – as long as you need – to think it over.'

'I already have. I've beaten myself up till I'm black and blue. I do love you, Duncan – not respect, not like, not fancy, though all of those things too – but love. Yet you know that isn't the be-all and end-all. If you love me, you won't make it hard.'

'No, that's not fair. "Give me up, Duncan, because it's the honourable thing to do." But I won't. I've given up too much in my life. I won't do it again now.'

'You don't have a choice. I must go. Will you get the bill or shall I?'

'Fuck the bill! I'm sorry … No, I'm not. Fuck the bill and everything else.'

'I want to make a clean break. This is a small town and we may – we're bound to – bump into each other. I've finished working with Rose so it won't be at Linda's. But if we do meet, I hope it can be as friends.'

'This isn't real. Is this how it feels when the doctor tells you you've got terminal cancer?'

'But you don't. You're going to live and find someone else, not someone who loves you more – I don't think that's possible – but someone who loves you more easily. Do you remember what Charlie Lyndon said when we went round after the show?'

'She said a lot of things,' he replied flatly.

'But one thing in particular: that you had the memory of her youth on your face. It struck me as beautiful.'

'It struck me as rehearsed.'

'I wish I could have said it. I wish I'd known you in my youth, then all of this would have been very different. But you'll always have the memory of my love.'

'So that's all we have left: memories?'

'The most precious ones, at least for me.'

She stood up and walked away, taking a note from her purse and handing it to the manager at the counter. Duncan sat at the table, oblivious to his surroundings, until the waitress asked if there were anything else he wanted and he saw that he was still stirring his coffee. He hurried out and returned to Ridgemount, where he found scant consolation. What was to have been a temporary arrangement until his marriage had now become permanent. As Adele alternately petted and scolded him, welcoming the company and resenting the intrusion, he felt as if his life had turned full circle. With time stretching out before him like a physicist's theorem, planning the party offered a welcome distraction.

Alison and Malcolm arrived on the eve of the big day. With her old room stacked with books and boxes from Mercury House, they were sleeping in what to Duncan's embarrassment Adele insisted on calling the Egyptian room after the papyrus scrolls and basalt busts of Ramesses and Nefertiti. Tim and Graham came down with their parents but preferred to stay at the Metropole, ostensibly to use the power showers and functional razor points, although Duncan suspected that its proximity to the Sugarbaby nightclub was the true draw. Having absented themselves for the day so as not to 'pre-empt the party', Graham went kite-surfing in the squally sea and Tim, ever the asset manager, was taken on a site visit of the pier. They turned up at Ridgemount at six, greeting Duncan with outstretched hands as though to stave off the threat of familial kisses, while addressing him as 'Uncle', as though to account, if only to themselves, for an otherwise implausible intimacy.

Elated at seeing her two elder grandsons, Adele stood up unsteadily, kissing them and stroking their cheeks. 'It's not possible! You both get more handsome every day. You're the spitting image of your grandfather, Graham. Doesn't he remind you of your father, Duncan?' Duncan agreed, eager to dispense with the compliments before the arrival of Jamie, who was a carbon copy of Linda's father, Jack. Indeed, he sometimes wondered if the weakness of Jamie's paternal genes were nature's revenge for his having thwarted it over the KS. At first he was disappointed to see so little of himself in his son, but having borne the burden of parental expectations all his life he had come to welcome the reminder that Jamie was his own man.

Jamie arrived a quarter of an hour after his cousins, face scrubbed, hair combed and liberally doused in aftershave, which Duncan suspected was less in honour of his grandmother than of his girlfriend. Linda had confided that Jamie had begun dating a fellow pupil from Francis Preston who, giving him added kudos, was in the year above. He had made Linda promise to say nothing to Duncan, which she maintained was out of shyness but which he imputed to lingering anger over his arrest. While his exoneration had been reported both in the *Mercury* and on its website (albeit with far less prominence than the original story), the 'no smoke without fire' adage seemed to strike a particular chord with teenagers. Jamie had been vilified and ostracised on account of Duncan's alleged crime and, to make matters worse, the actual culprit was someone whom he had repeatedly warned his father not to trust.

Jamie's new self-confidence was evident as he sauntered over to Graham and Tim and high-fived them. Even more notable was his unsolicited greeting of Chris, especially since he had refused all Duncan's appeals to visit him after the attack. Across the crowded room Duncan was unable to hear what they were saying but, as Chris touched his collarbone and held out his hand, he appeared to be replying to a question about his injuries. The girlfriend might be vain, vulgar, empty-headed, tattooed and even a member of the BNP, nevertheless Duncan owed her a permanent debt of gratitude for so validating Jamie's masculinity that he no longer regarded Chris as a threat.

'Duncan,' Adele called, rousing him from his reverie, 'isn't it time to serve the champagne?'

'Of course, Mother, I'll open it.'

'Not you, darling. Knowing you, you'll have somebody's eye out,' she said, with a genial laugh to mask the emasculation. 'Leave it to Graham and Tim. They know what they're doing.'

'Not Graham,' Alison interjected.

'Don't worry, Ma, I won't have a wobble.'

'What's wrong?' Adele asked. 'Have you hurt your wrist?'

'No, Granny, I'm on my twelve-step programme.'

'Is that something you do for Lent?'

'No, for life. I'm a recovering alcoholic.'

'Don't be ridiculous. You're twenty-three years old.'

'Exactly.'

'You shouldn't say such things.'

'But I'm proud of my sobriety. One hundred and eighty-two days.'

'Young people today, they exaggerate everything,' Adele said to Enid Marshall and Lillian Faulkes, who for years had been fed the myth of the perfect grandsons. 'One bad hangover and, hey presto, they're alcoholics.'

While Graham and Tim served the drinks, Duncan gazed affectionately at Alison who was talking to the two townswomen. Whatever their differences in the past, he was deeply grateful for her support over recent weeks. Catching her eye, he raised his glass before crossing the room to rescue Henry from Catherine Lightwood, who combined the presidency of the Francombe and District Horticultural Society with that of the East Sussex Humanists.

'I owe you for that,' Henry said, as they escaped into a corner. 'She's read a couple of articles about the discovery of the so-called "god particle" at Cern and seems to think that she's penetrated the mysteries of the universe.'

'Other than that, how's the play, Reverend Lincoln?'

'Meeting Chris wasn't as painful as I'd feared. I wouldn't go so far as to call him friendly but he thanked me for my witness statement.'

'What did I tell you?'

'I'm still watching out for ground glass in my food.'

'We'll swap plates.'

'It's the first party I've been to since … for a couple of months. You never know who's heard the rumours.'

'I feel much the same myself.'

'Yes, but you weren't charged.'

'Neither were you except in the court of Henry.'

'Not quite.'

'But the hearing was closed; how did your name leak out?'

'Your pals, the Weedons, I presume, or else the parents of the other children. The general reaction hasn't been too hostile. A few raised eyebrows and lowered glances. A couple of poison pen letters and defamatory posts on my Facebook wall.'

'Are you on Facebook?'

'Not any more. Most of my congregation seem to be either unconcerned or oblivious, although one old dear, totally bewildered by *dogging*, told me that she didn't mind what I got up to myself but I had no right to involve Brandy. On the plus side I've received support from the most unlikely people, including Benjamin Kabumba, pastor of the Switherton Baptists, who quoted a proverb he'd learnt in Uganda: "You don't judge the sweetness of a chicken by the dirt on its feathers." I expect it loses something in translation.'

'So things are looking up?'

'Up to a point. Last night I dreamt I was in hell. I say hell but it bore a distinct resemblance to the Pudsey Road estate, except that the houses were all in flames and the estate agents were devils straight out of a medieval woodcut. One, who was showing me round, said that he was sorry but every property was taken. "Don't worry," I replied, greatly relieved, "I have an appointment to view some in heaven." The next moment we passed a house with a large For Sale sign on the gate. "Look," he said. "This one will suit you perfectly." I turned away to find For Sale had been replaced by Sold and I was being sucked down the path into the flames.'

'What happened then?'

'I woke up in a pool of sweat.'

'Sounds nasty,' Alison said as she joined them. 'Sorry to interrupt, but may I steal my brother?'

'Of course,' Henry said, moving away.

'Are the musicians all set?' Alison asked.

'Should be,' Duncan replied. 'Last time I checked, they were having tea. I'll pop back to the dining room.'

'It's the most generous, inspired present. I only hope Mother appreciates it.'

'Me too. It might go some way towards absolving me for being the world's oldest "boomerang kid".'

'She loves having you here; she told me.'

'In principle, yes, but not when I put the plates back in the wrong place or grill when I should fry (or vice versa) or turn off the radiators in rooms we don't use or leave her to watch TV on her own or … you get the picture. The fact is, of course, that she wants me here but as an obedient little boy, not a middle-aged man with a will – or, at any rate, a mind – of his own.'

'If it's not working out, you don't have to stay.'

'The sad truth is that I do. There's nowhere else I can afford, at least not until I've sorted out my life. And at the rate I'm going … Besides she needs someone with her. She grows dottier by the hour: poring over catalogues; ordering things with the sole intention of sending them back – last week it was a foot massager. The other day I came home to find a fortune teller in the kitchen. What was that all about?'

'There are other possibilities, for her if not for you. Sheltered housing. A private home – I'm not talking Castlemaine. A paid companion. You mustn't throw your life away.'

'You might have thought of that twenty-odd years ago when I still had a chance to do something with it.' Alison looked pained. 'I'm sorry. That was mean.'

'We can't change the past, Duncan. That's why I'm trying to help now. You always wanted to write. What's to stop you?'

'Talent, I suspect. What was once an ambition now feels like a threat. Shut up, Duncan! This is a celebration. People are looking at us and wondering what's wrong.'

'It's bound to take time to get back on your feet. You put your soul into that paper.'

'And gave my heart to Ellen. All in all if you cut me open you wouldn't find much inside.'

'I wish I'd met her. I was hoping to have the chance today.'

'I was hoping to marry her in the spring.'

'You really loved her?'

'Yes. I never expected it would happen to me again. Not just because I'm forty-eight and set in my ways, but I've kept such a tight rein on my emotions that it's hard for a single one to slip out.'

'And there's no chance of you patching things up?'

'None at all. I thought one benefit of growing older was that life stopped being about either/or. Not, apparently, when it comes to "Duncan or Neil?". I miss her so much: I miss her smile and her charm, her integrity and her sparkle and her seriousness and, yes, the sex.'

'To some of us a break from that would be a relief. No more lying back and counting the cracks in the ceiling.'

'You still make love with the light on?' he asked, relishing an intimacy with his sister that he had not known for thirty years.

'It's a turn of phrase, you twit!'

'You sound like Mother. Don't you remember: "The two great delusions of modern life are that men should enjoy work and women should enjoy sex"?'

'Stop it! You'll make me spill my drink.'

Duncan glanced over at Malcolm surreptitiously picking his teeth and wondered if he gave the impression of always having somewhere better to be even when he was in bed. 'There must be parts of it that excite you.'

'The post-coital cigarette.'

'But you don't smoke.'

'And your point is?'

He was framing a reply when Jamie came up to them. 'I've been to the kitchen,' he said.

'Is there a problem?' Duncan asked.

'Since when has Granny been a ballet fan?'

'What? Oh, I see. There was a mix-up at the cake shop. The assistant thought I ordered *Happy Birthday Adele, Seven* instead of *Seventy-Five*. She claims I agreed to a ballet shoes design but she had such a thick accent I didn't like to ask her to repeat anything. Still, no harm done! They were able to add the extra letters, even if it was a squeeze.'

'Can't you ever do anything right?' Jamie asked.

'That's no way to talk to your father, Jamie,' Alison said gently.

'You see him a couple of times a year,' Jamie replied. 'You don't know what it's like growing up with him.'

'You forget I grew up with him in this very house.'

'Yeah, but you were older.'

'I'm sorry if that's how you feel,' Duncan said. 'I don't know what more I can do.'

'Stay away from pond life like Neil Nugent. I told you he was a psycho.'

'You were right and I should have listened. But think about what you've just said. If Neil's sick, then he needs our help.'

'He's the reason people called me "Paedo". I swear I'll kill him if he ever comes back to school.'

'Then we can thank our lucky stars that he won't.'

'Let me tell you a story about your father,' Alison said. 'I haven't always given him the credit he deserves and I'm sorry. But it's far more important that you do.'

'What story?'

'Something that happened to him at school.'

'I must make sure the musicians have everything they need,' Duncan said.

'No, wait! You should hear it too,' Alison said. 'There was a boy in his class who had a collection of birds' eggs – rare ones he'd built up over the years – which three older boys wantonly smashed.'

'Hang about! Didn't you tell me this already?' Jamie asked Duncan.

'Yes.' Duncan turned to Alison. 'So there's no need to bore him again.'

'I'd like to bet he didn't tell you what happened next. Your dad went in to breakfast the following morning with six eggs – ordinary hen's eggs he'd pinched from the kitchens. In front of the entire school he walked up to each of the thugs in turn and cracked them open on their heads.'

'You told me you felt ashamed because you did nothing,' Jamie said to Duncan. 'Why?'

'I didn't want to set you a bad example.'

'What's bad about it?'

'The story didn't end there. I was beaten up by the boys and beaten by the headmaster, who wrote to my parents saying that I was a disgrace to the school and the next time I stepped out of line I'd be thrown out.'

'But why did you do it? Didn't you say you disliked the guy?'

'I disliked bullies even more. Anyway, it was a long time ago. I don't know why your aunt's dug it up now.'

'Because it's the code you've lived by ever since and the way you ran your paper. I don't know if it's the same today, Jamie, but when I was your age we were constantly being told by teachers, vicars, Guide leaders and the like that the key to behaving well was to follow your conscience. Your father is the only person I know who does that without tinkering with it first.'

'*Basta!*' Duncan said. 'This is meant to be Adele's day. Save the tributes till *I'm* seventy-five.'

He hurried into the dining room where the table, gleamingly polished and groaning with food, had been pushed against the end wall, beneath the portraits of his father and grandfather from the *Mercury* boardroom. Fourteen chairs were set out in rows opposite the music stands for the Gardner Quartet, a group of young graduates from Sussex University who had been steadily building up a reputation across the South-East. Until now the only twentieth-century piece in a repertoire founded on Mozart, Haydn, Beethoven, Schubert and Brahms had been Samuel Barber's *Serenade*. Duncan, however, had commissioned them to play Stafford Lyttleton's *String Quartet No. 2, Opus 11* as a birthday offering for his mother.

Having managed to keep their presence secret not just from his mother but from anyone who might have spoilt the surprise, he confirmed with their leader, Celia, that they were ready to start before summoning the guests from the sitting room.

'Goody goody, food!' Enid Marshall said, with an eagerness that betrayed her circumstances.

'Any moment,' Duncan said. 'First, we're going to enjoy some music. Would you all please take a seat. Not you, Tim, or you, Jamie. I'm afraid the three grandsons will have to squat on the floor but there's room for everybody else.'

'What is this, darling?' Adele asked, looking apprehensive.

'It's my birthday present to you, Mother. So you take the place of honour. Pretend you're Marie Antoinette. Yes, that's right, Mrs Lightwood, you sit next to her,' he said, mildly piqued that she had not left the chair free for Alison or himself. 'Is everyone comfortable? Good. Chris!' he yelled into the kitchen. 'Whatever you're doing can wait. You and Paul should come and listen to the music … Now, as most of you know, my mother's father was a brilliant composer. Sadly, we haven't had much opportunity to hear his work in recent years. So I'm thrilled that the wonderful Gardner Quartet are here to play us his *Second String Quartet in E minor*. Please welcome the Gardner Quartet.'

Leading the applause, he drew people's attention to the door, but instead of the musicians Paul and Chris walked in; the former looking sheepish, the latter bobbing a curtsey as they headed for the two empty chairs in the back row. Moments later, the musicians filed in without fuss, took their seats and began to play. Duncan listened intently as a moody viola solo opened the unfamiliar piece before the violins launched into the traditional folk melody of 'The Cherry Tree Carol', which was repeated in a series of increasingly intricate variations. The second movement was lighter, freer and faster, beginning with a duet between the two violins, which was taken up by the cello and woven into a rich contrapuntal pattern. The third movement was more sombre, with the first violin's plaintive theme picked up by the other instruments, interrupted by a flurry of discords and brought to a sudden, disconcerting end. The final movement reprised the 'Cherry Tree' motif, initiated by the cello and echoed by the rest of the instruments, culminating in a lyrical coda.

With Jamie leaning against his legs, Duncan was palpably aware of his gradual surrender to his great-grandfather's music, although he was under no illusions that the head resting on his knees did so for anything other than support. He turned expectantly to his mother but, seeing the tears rolling down her cheeks, wondered whether he would have done better to have saved the performance for a less emotionally charged day. His mind was eased when no sooner had he stood up to congratulate the musicians than she pre-empted him.

'Thank you. Thank you all so much,' she said. 'You don't – you can't – know what it means to me to hear my father's music played again in my house and played so beautifully. You've shown that it will live. Even if it's heard only once in a hundred years it will live.'

'It's been a voyage of discovery for us,' Celia said. 'We're keen to include it in our repertoire. Plus there's a new record label based in Brighton that wants us to bring out a CD of English rarities. All things being equal and if you approve, we'd like to record it.'

'Oh dear,' Adele said, sinking heavily into her seat.

'I'm sorry,' Celia said. 'Have I said the wrong thing?'

'Far from it,' Duncan replied, 'you couldn't have said anything better.'

'Duncan? Where's Duncan?' Adele asked frantically.

'Here, Mother, at the end of the row,' he said, amused that even now she should switch so freely from genuine feeling to play-acting.

'Thank you so much, darling,' she said. 'It's the most beautiful present I've ever been given.'

Duncan glanced at Alison, who beamed at him. 'Right, let's move the chairs out of the way,' he said, 'and tuck into Chris's delicious feast.'

'The musicians first! They're the ones who've been working,' Adele said, smiling at the quartet, who looked grateful for their elevation from performers to guests.

As the musicians stood up to put away their instruments and the audience to put back the chairs, Chris moved forward. 'Not so fast! Before you all smear food on your faces or down your frocks – '

'What does he mean?' Lillian Faulkes asked crossly.

'I've been instructed to take some photos.'

'Oh no,' Adele said. 'I've changed my mind. My eyes are all puffy. I must look a fright.'

'You're gorgeous! Now don't shilly-shally or the lettuce will go limp. If you ladies would sit on the front row, with the birthday girl in the middle. Then if you, Vicar, and you, Mr Neville, and you …' He looked at Alison. 'Silly of me but I don't know your name.'

'Neville-Bruce.'

'Mr and Mrs Neville-Bruce,' Chris said, sounding flustered by the double barrel, 'and Paul – yes, you too – could stand behind them.' Duncan took his allotted place between Alison and Henry. 'Then the three grandsons and the musicians – yes, don't think you're going to escape – can crouch or kneel on the floor in front.' As Tim, Graham and the quartet moved into position, Jamie hung back.

'No offence, guys, but I want to stand next to my dad.'

Stupefied, Duncan watched as Jamie slipped in between Henry and himself.

'Right, everyone, smile,' Chris said. 'This one's for *Crimewatch*.'

The joke had the desired effect and Duncan felt his face light up, only for the glow to suffuse his entire body when moments later, hidden from the camera, Jamie reached for his hand.

Acknowledgements

I am indebted to many people for assistance in my researches, among them Bryan Allan, David Bradbury, Jennie Brindley, Allan Brodie, Robert Burnett-Hughes, Dan Carrier, Helen Cockerill, Rhiannon Edwards, Alice Gallimore, Charles Glenville, David Horbury, Camilla Lake, Duncan Lewis, Louis Mander, Jeffrey Manton, Carole Steyn, Penny Thexton, and the staffs of the *Camden New Journal* and the *Ham & High*.

I am, as ever, deeply grateful to Hilary Sage for her help with the text.